TANK OF SERPE

James Leasor has w
and novels, a number of which have been
filmed. He is married with three sons and lives
in Wiltshire and Portugal.

JAMES LEASOR

Tank of Serpents

FONTANA/Collins

First published by William Collins Sons & Co. Ltd 1986
First issued in Fontana Paperbacks 1987

Copyright © James Leasor 1986

Made and printed in Great Britain by
William Collins Sons & Co. Ltd, Glasgow

Conditions of Sale
This book is sold subject to the condition
that it shall not, by way of trade or otherwise,
be lent, re-sold, hired out or otherwise circulated
without the publisher's prior consent in any form of
binding or cover other than that in which it is
published and without a similar condition
including this condition being imposed
on the subsequent purchaser

TO BILL CATTO,
in memory of his questing spirit.

Chance is powerful everywhere: let your hook
be always hanging ready. In waters where
you least think it, there will be a fish.

Ovid

1

I entered the cemetery by a little-used side gate, and paused for a moment, surveying the silent city of suburban dead. A wide asphalt path, marked on either side by metal litter bins, stretched before me up an incline, between granite tombstones, alabaster urns, sad-faced angels and columns broken to symbolize a life ended before its time.

To keep my mind away from the distasteful task that faced me, I forced myself to read inscriptions on the graves as though I was simply another visitor in a strange place, looking for one particular name. It is a curious fact that often the leaving of life can bring virtual canonization from those who stay behind. Under the careful chisel of the monumental mason the hated husband and the adulterous wife are transformed into the epitome of perfect love. Death pays all debts, but, in my experience, no dividends. Would my visit here change this rule?

Of all the men I have met, the man whose funeral had drawn me here probably meant most to me. Although we came from totally different backgrounds, we had shared so much – and lost so much. I felt I had failed disastrously on every level to communicate to him my trust, my hopes, my regard, at that terrible time when he had no friends at all.

I reached the brow of the little hill and paused to marshal my thoughts and regain my breath. The slope was not steep; gradients never are in cemeteries. Local council architects realize that most visitors will be elderly, but I am little given to walking, and the nature of the prospect ahead did not make me wish to hurry.

I walked on towards the crematorium chapel. Three black Rolls-Royces, each with the quaint and deliberately outdated coachwork favoured by expensive undertakers, waited in line. Their chauffeurs were listening to a radio in the leading car. I could hear the high excited voice of a commentator describing a horse race; the favourite was winning. A man wearing a swallow-tailed coat and the sallow face of professional grief detached himself from the crematorium doorway.

'You with this party, sir?' he asked me with the strange mixture of obsequiousness and hidden insolence the British adopt so easily when unsure of the social status of a stranger. 'Name of Blake?'

'Yes,' I replied.

'You're late, sir,' he said accusingly.

'I know,' I said. 'I did not want to come to the service.'

'It takes some people like that,' he replied and nodded as though he entirely understood my reasons. Death might take everyone in a different way; it still took everyone in the end.

Through the crematorium's closed wooden doors with their mock-Tudor plastic hinges and bolt-heads, I could hear the faint sound of piped music. I had not wished to face this neutered version of a burial service, carefully adapted to suit the needs of every denomination, and of none. Whatever was said or sung must conveniently soothe every religious susceptibility, and arouse neither doubt nor discord in the minds of the mourners.

Nor had I any wish to hear rollers squeak as the coffin began to move forward slowly and curtains parted to close sharply behind it. For the mourners, there would follow a brief moment for silent contemplation or prayer, or thoughts about the stock market, or their chances of catching the fast train back to London. They would then file out and make the expected examination of what the local paper would later refer to as floral tributes, to check that their particular wreath was prominently displayed. This charade was not for me.

Then the coffin, which frequently cost more than many could afford, would be speedily dismantled and removed in its component parts, probably in one of these glossy limousines, to be sold to another customer, and then used again, charged to the next of kin as new on each occasion. Any flowers still fresh enough could be sold a second time for another funeral, and even the most wilted wreath must possess enough blooms to sell as buttonholes or as part of a smaller bouquet. These sad, shabby fiddles might have amused the man to whom we had all come to say farewell, as would the thought of the favourite winning. How different his life would have been, had more favourites won!

The wooden doors opened suddenly and unexpectedly. One

driver instantly switched off the radio. The others hurried to their cars, and stood by the rear doors, impassive as the stone statues around them. I walked along one side of the chapel where several cars were parked in order of precedence. At one end stood a green Bentley, with a chauffeur in matching green uniform; then a Jensen, a couple of Jaguars, a Rover, an Austin Sheerline, for in the early nineteen fifties few motorists in Britain drove cars of foreign make.

From where I stood, I could see the mourners but they could not see me. I knew this, because I had checked all possible positions on the previous day. Their pace quickened as they approached their cars, as though instinctively they wished to distance themselves as swiftly as possible from all unpleasant reminders of their own mortality. As Blake used to say, man alone of all living creatures knows that eventually he must die, but if he ever admits this to himself he always tries to mask the knowledge.

They were in their cars and away within seconds, until only the Bentley remained. There was no gathering in any house or hotel to share drinks and smoked salmon sandwiches and reminiscences of the past. Could that be because they already knew – or suspected – too much about the past of the man they had come to mourn?

The chauffeur in green livery began to walk smartly from the Bentley towards the chapel. His master had been delayed for some reason, but now he appeared, and handed a briefcase to the chauffeur, as though in his condition of grief it was altogether too heavy for him to carry. Then he turned and looked back at the crematorium as if wondering what it would cost to build now, or how many cheap semi-detached houses he could squeeze into the area if ever it should be deconsecrated. He was that sort of man; the only god he knew was Mammon and at his shrine he was a devout worshipper.

I did not move. Any movement might draw attention to me, and this was the last thing I could afford at that moment. I saw his face clearly; soft and pale with that smooth patina of success that comes with years of savouring the finest brandies, the best coronas. As a young man, David Glover had appeared unsuccessful, even unsure of himself, according to Blake. Now, Glover had no such illusions of modesty, for his name appeared in newspaper diaries as often as it did in the City pages. He was the

11

success of the age, a North London lawyer who, through astute buying of streets of houses and wartime bombed sites, was now one of the richest men in the country, possibly in the world.

But while almost everyone had heard of David Glover's phenomenal success, only a handful had any idea how he had really made his first money, and even fewer had ever heard of the Tank of Serpents. I was one of the few. Blake had been another. Why should I be content to mourn one man's death when the person who had caused his downfall, and then received such universal respect and acclaim, could still live and prosper? I had considered all aspects of the problem, but could find no answer, except the one I intended to deliver personally to David Glover, in full and final payment of all debts.

He was the man I had come to kill.

When Glover arrived as a freshman at Oxford, nearly seventeen years previously, no-one wanted to kill him. Very few even wanted to know him, and afterwards, fewer still remembered him.

Glover was slightly built then, and always eager to please. He had, as one of his friends remarked, the air of someone born to be a butler. I don't think that Glover heard this, but if he did he might have taken it as a compliment, for he seemed destined – and content – to fetch and carry for contemporaries whose charm or wealth or both were then so much greater than his.

His father was a solicitor in Willesden or Neasden; somewhere unfashionable. David wanted to start his own firm somewhere near, perhaps in Maida Vale; a curiously modest ambition for someone who was obviously extremely clever: he had won one scholarship to his local grammar school and another to Oxford. I didn't know then what he really intended to do with his life. Perhaps he hadn't decided, either; or if, as I suspect, he had, he was too astute to tell anyone of his plans.

His rooms looked out over a narrow lane behind the college. On the bedroom floor lay a coiled rope, tied at one end to a hook in the ceiling. In time of fire, the occupant was expected to throw this rope out of the window and then climb down to safety.

'Alternatively,' said Glover, 'I could use it to escape from creditors. Do an Errol Flynn, a Tarzan.'

'I wouldn't think you'd ever need to – as a lawyer,' said Blake.

'The way my creditors are creating, that sort of exercise is more my line of country.'

'With your money,' said Glover, not enviously, but with a certain reverence in his voice as he mentioned the word 'money', 'you'll never need to.'

'I'm not rich,' Blake protested, 'I just spend money as if I were.'

'My father says it's the appearance that really counts. So long as people believe you're wealthy, they're happy for you to run up debts. They think that somehow your success may also enrich theirs. A fallacy, of course.'

'Of course,' agreed Blake, smiling, 'but it's how I seem to live.'

There were three sets of rooms on that staircase. Blake was in his rightful place, on the top landing. He was a born leader; handsome, with fair hair that turned blond with the sun, six foot four inches tall and possessing the confidence that stems from never having had to worry much about anything. He was clever enough to pass every examination at school, and then university, possibly without distinction, but also without the need for any applied effort. Nor had he ever been forced to save money; to walk, not because he could not afford a taxi, but because he did not have the bus fare. He liked to say that coins were made round because money was meant to go round, and with him it did so with all the speed of a catherine wheel. He was quite open about his debts: to his tailors, his shirt-maker – fancy, a shirt-maker at nineteen! – his bootmaker, his bookmakers. Especially his bookmakers.

Some people said later that Blake had always been spoiled, another case of too much, too soon, too easily. But this was after the events involving the Tank of Serpents, not before. When Blake talked to anyone, he had the ability to make them feel that they were the only person about whom he was concerned, and their views the only opinions that mattered to him. I think he genuinely cared.

Blake excelled at games. He was a member of the Jujitsu Club and the University Boxing Club. He could have got his Blue easily enough, but the training irked him. He rowed for the college second eight when they went head of the river – and he could have made the first eight, but that would have required cutting down on parties; not a sacrifice he was prepared to pay.

Blake was very good with anything mechanical. An elderly

13

maiden aunt left him a hundred pounds in her will and he bought a second-hand MG J2 two-seater, smartened it up with red paint and sold it at a profit. He invested this money in another car, did the same again, and then with several others. He made a profit on each, and by his third year, in his last term, he was driving a scarlet SS 100, with a big exhaust pipe, that made a rumbling roar like a cage of angry lions. He liked red cars; the colour smacked of virility – and danger.

The sight and sound of this car turned girls' heads, of course, as he drove past, windscreen folded flat across the bonnet, his spotted silk foulard cravat trailing like a pennant in the wind.

Blake was reading philosophy, which should have alerted him to the whims of chance, but he could never resist a bet, a wager or a dare. For example, he claimed the fastest time from the High to the Trout Inn at Godstow, and two minutes off the standing record to the Bear at Woodstock.

Someone at BNC said he could beat him in his Alfa. Blake accepted the challenge at once – although it was probably never intended as a serious challenge, only an idle remark. The other driver could not back down, and agreed to put the matter to the test at seven o'clock one Sunday morning, when the roads would be empty; loser to buy the winner a magnum of champagne.

Blake drove as he liked to live, on the limit. The Alfa was quicker on the corners, but Blake caught up with him on the straight, and took him on a roundabout at the by-pass. When the other man cautiously backed off, Blake went past, foot flat on the floor, and cruised in the winner, to claim the prize.

A crowd of undergraduates had gathered in Woodstock, expecting him to open the bottle and pour them all a drink, but he did no such thing. He didn't even offer his challenger a glass. Instead, he came back to the college and gave the magnum to his scout.

'But he doesn't drink champagne,' Jerrold pointed out.

'Only because he's never had the chance,' Blake retorted. 'Now he can make up his own mind whether he likes it.'

Whereas Blake was a complex character who lived far above his means, who extended his extravagance to entertaining friends and to tipping humbler folk much more than they ever expected, Rex Jerrold was a watcher, a looker-on – and a looker-in. He had a gift – if I could dignify this ability with such a description

– of knowing what was happening but usually without taking part himself in any of these happenings. He would discover all manner of unlikely facts: that a don had been found drunk in the street; that the Stroke was being dropped from the college first eight; that someone else had just inherited a fortune. With this ability I suppose it was inevitable he should gravitate to journalism, and he was proud of the fact that he made several pounds a week by telephoning little snippets of such information to London newspapers. The editor of one, the *Globe*, actually offered him a job when he took his degree.

Jerrold's rooms were below Blake's, and as featureless and unindividualistic as his character. The walls of Blake's rooms were covered with amusing eighteenth-century prints, posters of car races in the early years of the century and, of course, he had a table of drinks. He was wearing white tie and tails and pouring himself a brandy when Jerrold came in to see him.

'Join me?' he asked. Jerrold shook his head.

'I'll fall asleep if I do, and I'm trying to put a whole year's work into one night. How's your revision?'

'I admitted the immensity of my ignorance at the beginning of term,' Blake explained. 'It is useless now trying to rectify the impossible. I shall rely on bluff.'

'You can't answer six papers on bluff.'

'Others have, and survived. Remember what Seneca said about too much study? "We learn our lessons not for life, but for the lecture-room." '

'Unfortunately, Seneca isn't marking our papers. I didn't come to discuss that anyhow. I just called to tell you that your father dropped in to see you earlier and was sorry he'd missed you. He asked me to tell you.'

'What did he want, exactly?'

'He didn't say. He seemed rather down, I thought. Not his usual self.'

'Probably his time of life. Nothing to worry about. Sure about that brandy? It's a Martell, three star, you know.'

'Even so, I won't. But where are you off to in this gear, with Schools next week?'

'A ball. Sounds of revelry by night. In a country house near Witney.'

'You're mad. Everyone else is working like beavers.'

'Which surely shows how mad they are, how sane I am.'

Blake finished the brandy, adjusted his white tie, went out of the room, and down the wide oak staircase into the central quad. A bell was chiming eight o'clock, and some undergraduates were already walking into hall for dinner. He nodded to those he knew, as he walked past them into the street. The one-armed parking attendant, who always reserved a place for his car opposite the college gates, saluted respectfully. Two half-crowns changed hands. Blake was a generous tipper; for him, tips were insurance premiums against not having the best table, the quickest porter, the most convenient parking place.

The traffic was heavier than he had expected for that time of evening, and he was some miles along the Witney road before he checked the dials on the dashboard, which he usually did instinctively when the engine fired. Damn. He was almost out of petrol. He had meant to fill up earlier that day, and had somehow forgotten all about it.

He turned off into the first garage on his side of the road, a small, two-pump, Redline affair; a galvanized iron shed plastered with chipped enamel advertisements for Palmer Cord Tyres and Essolube Motor Oil. He blew his air horns. Nothing. He climbed out of the car, walked towards the shed. The main doors were padlocked. A cardboard notice hung in a cobwebbed window: CLOSED.

Damn again. And there wasn't another garage for five miles. He might not make the distance. Cars swept past him on the road, and a rusty sign creaked in the wind above his head. As he walked back to his own car, a green and black Wolseley pulled in behind him. The driver climbed out.

'Out of juice?' he asked sympathetically.

'Nearly.'

'Same thing happened to me last week. I've a couple of gallons in a can in the boot, if that's any use.'

'Thank you very much.'

The driver walked to the back of his car, opened the boot, took out a can and a funnel, poured the petrol into the tank of Blake's SS.

Blake felt in his back pocket for some money, but he had given his last two coins to the parking attendant. He hated coins; they spoiled the fit of his trousers.

'I've only a note,' he said apologetically.

'I've change,' replied the driver cheerfully. Blake walked back to the Wolseley with him. A front-seat passenger was out of the car now, stretching his legs.

'You Richard Blake?' he asked him.

'Yes, why?'

'Thought I recognized the car.'

Blake put his hand into his trouser pocket to take out a ten-shilling note and the man suddenly seized his arm and twisted it behind his back and then swung him against the side of the car so roughly that he hit his head on the roof. Blake reeled, dazed by the unexpected attack and the pain.

'What the hell's that for?'

'For you, buster. We act for bookmakers. You owe them four grand.'

'Impossible,' said Blake.

'You think?'

The driver took a sheet of paper from his pocket.

'At Newbury, a thousand pounds to Angus McBeth. Salisbury, eight hundred and fifty pounds to Honest Joe Jackson. Epsom, five hundred pounds to Jack Jones. Ascot, four hundred pounds to Bill McMurty. Want me to go on?'

'I'd no idea it could be so much.'

'More money than most of us make in a bloody lifetime,' said the other man bitterly. 'And you spend it in a few afternoons – and then don't pay it back. No idea, eh, you bastard?'

'And you act for all of them?'

'For the man who controls them all. Hamish McMoffatt.'

'Never heard of him.'

'You have now.'

'Apparently. But you – and he – must know I don't carry that sort of money on me.'

'We don't expect you to. But all toffs carry a chequebook, don't they, now?'

The driver expertly inserted a hand inside Blake's jacket pocket and removed his chequebook.

'There. Like I said. Write us a cheque now for four grand, and we'll say no more about it.'

'It wouldn't be honoured if I did. I've nothing like that in the bank.'

'Then you'd be done for passing a dud cheque. Kicked out of Oxford. Sent down, as you lot say.'

'And if I don't pay? You can't sue for a gambling debt.'

'We know that, matey. But there are many different ways to kill a cat. Some more painful than others. And if you won't pay, you'll discover one or two. So write us that cheque. Now.'

'I can't.'

The passenger brought up his boot smartly, kicked Blake hard on his left kneecap. He cried out with the pain and would have fallen if the driver had not held him upright, banging his head again on the car roof.

'See what I mean?'

'All right,' agreed Blake. 'I'll sign. But I need my right hand.'

They released him, stepped back a couple of paces, still watching him. Blake flexed his shoulder as though to ease the pain in the muscles. Then he opened his chequebook on the flat top of the Wolseley's bonnet, removed the cap from his fountain pen and turned to the two men.

'Who will I make it out to?' he asked them, looking from one to the other enquiringly.

For a fraction of a second, in a reflex action, they also looked at each other, following his eyes. In that moment, Blake hit a straight left to the driver's jaw. As the passenger swung at him, Blake dropped his pen, seized the man's left arm, and with a jujitsu movement, threw him over his shoulder. He fell heavily on the concrete drive-in. The driver clawed his way round the car, opened his front door and reached in for the crank handle he kept under the seat. Blake slammed the door on his wrist. The man screamed as pain swamped him. Blake picked up his pen and his chequebook, put them back in his pocket.

'Another way to kill a cat,' he said. Then he bent down, removed the valve cap on a front wheel, turned it upside down, unscrewed the valve. Air hissed from the tube as the wheel came down on its rim.

Half a mile along the road in his SS, Blake stopped and rolled up his left trouser leg. His knee was bleeding, and he felt slightly sick; not so much from reaction or pain, but from the certain knowledge that this was only the first skirmish in what could be a long and painful battle. He always ignored demands from bookmakers, along with Final Demands delivered by sturdy bowler-hatted men wearing highly polished toe-capped boots and shiny blue suits. He didn't have the money to pay any of them. He had spent it at the races or in private gaming parties, or in absurd private bets, hoping that one day – as with the race against the Alfa – his luck must turn and then in one tremendous win he could settle all arrears.

I know that Blake did not realize how, in believing this, he was simply following what bookmakers call the Monte Carlo Fallacy. When a gambler experiences a long run of failures, he becomes convinced that he must win next time, or the time after that. When he is losing, he is certain that what he calls his luck, must – like the wheel of fortune – turn in his favour. Yet when he is winning, he quite absurdly assumes that what he calls his lucky streak will continue. I could have told Blake that this is obviously ridiculous, and he might have believed me. But I didn't know him then, and by the time I did, it was all too late.

There were so many other debts: his champagne, his car, his clothes. He dared not ask his father for any more money. In any case, what use would a few hundred pounds be against his probable total debts of several thousand pounds – a fortune in 1938?

Blake had heard so often from his father that the average adult weekly wage in Britain was thirty shillings, and he would spend that amount on a bottle of vintage champagne probably several times a week. He could expect no more help there. Nor could he ask for any; he had taken enough, and he had been a bloody fool. But, like a man who has foolishly jumped into a mill race or a whirlpool for a swim, he was powerless to escape; he felt numbed, almost mesmerized by the hopelessness of his predicament.

Blake drove on slowly, glancing every now and then in his rear-view mirror, in case he saw the green and black Wolseley behind him, following him.

He didn't, but he knew that one day he would, and soon.

Next time, he might not escape so easily.

Mr Arnold Marsh leaned back in his swivel chair, crossed his legs and pressed his fingers together. He was the manager of one of the smaller banks in Oxford, and his was not that bank's most important branch, but he was never in any doubt about his own financial abilities. After all, he was still on the right side of fifty, and how many millionaires had not achieved real success until their middle or even their later years? He would be among them one day. All he needed was the opportunity – and the ability to recognize it, however much it might be disguised.

At that moment, Mr Marsh's middle-aged secretary, Miss Grout, poked her head round his door.

'Mr Blake to see you,' she announced.

The manager wished she had added 'sir', but one couldn't be too pedantic about these things. Equally, one should not condone familiarity among the staff, for that could undermine his position. So where exactly did one take a stand? He faced the eternal dilemma of the weak man: the inability to make decisions.

'Do have a seat,' he told Blake, nodding a frowning dismissal to Miss Grout.

Facing the bank manager's desk were two chairs; one an armchair of button-backed brown leather. The other was wooden, upright and uncomfortable. Instinctively, Blake sat down in the club armchair; only a fool would show lack of confidence by sitting in a chair hard and uninviting as a penitent stool.

'A long time since we had the pleasure of meeting,' said Marsh. 'As a matter of fact, I was on the point of writing to you.' He cleared his throat and leaned forward, elbows resting on the desk, in the position of a generous father about to admonish an erring but still well-regarded son.

'Regarding the matter of your account, Mr Blake. You have received your statement?'

'Of course. But I never open bank letters.'

'But these are serious documents, evidence of your finances.'

'My finances *here*,' Blake corrected him.

'You have other accounts elsewhere?' Marsh asked sharply.

Blake shrugged.

'There are trusts,' he said casually, wishing to avoid the lie direct. 'Bequests. That sort of thing.'

'Ah, yes, of course. Well, Mr Blake, perhaps you would care to transfer funds from one of these trusts? A sum of' – he glanced down at the pencilled figures on his blotting pad – 'nineteen hundred and seventy-five pounds, three shillings and threepence. We could, in point of fact, let you off the threepence.'

'That is kind of you, Mr Marsh, but not how the great fortunes were made – letting people off thruppences. I will pay the full amount.'

'Of course. That was only my little joke. I know your account is supported by your father, and he has always been most understanding, but I would hesitate to acquaint him with this. Your

20

overdraft limit is one thousand five hundred pounds. And it has climbed up these last few weeks, while I was awaiting your reply to my letters.'

'Please don't bother my father. He would only worry. Of course I'll settle it, have no fear. But I didn't come here today just to discuss day-to-day balancing of the books.'

'No? I naturally assumed you were going to tell me how you proposed to put your account into a more healthy position of credit.'

'In a sense you are right,' agreed Blake slowly. He was still making up his mind whether to go ahead with the plan he had worked out on the way to the bank. Now, he decided, he really had no option.

'You know my interest in cars, Mr Marsh?'

'I certainly know that SS of yours. Makes me wish I were young again, and, of course, with your money and your style. You don't intend to buy another one, surely?'

'Not only one,' said Blake. 'With luck, dozens. To sell, of course.'

'You are going into the motor trade?'

'I have been offered, by the father of a friend of mine up here, the chance to buy a freehold garage business on the Great West Road outside London. It is not yet on the market. He wants a quick sale because he is retiring to the South of France on medical advice. He has offered it to me – knowing my interest in cars – for fifty thousand pounds.'

'An enormous sum, Mr Blake,' said Marsh cautiously, pencilling the figure on his blotting pad.

'They deal mostly in second-hand cars. The mark-up is sometimes as much as fifty per cent.'

'Very large, surely?'

'Not in the car trade. A lot of business is in cash, of course.'

'I understand. And how can I help you?'

'I wish to pay a deposit, subject, naturally, to contract and survey and the fullest examination by the bank's accountants – if you so wish – of the last few years' trading acounts.'

'What figure are you thinking of, Mr Blake?'

'Five thousand pounds. Ten per cent.'

'On what security?'

'I will make over to the bank the deeds of the property so long as any part of the debt is outstanding. Fifty thousand for five.

21

The remainder of the money will come from private sources.'

'And when would the bank receive the deeds?'

'As soon as the deal goes through. I would give you a letter of intent to that effect immediately.'

'I don't think that would really satisfy my directors, Mr Blake. It is a large amount, and you have not been, shall I say, provident with much smaller sums.'

'If all the customers of your bank were provident,' replied Blake shortly, 'you'd be out of business. However you dress it up, a bank only exists to lend money. As little as possible, for as much as possible, for as long as possible.'

'We like to think there's more to it than that.'

'There is. There's security,' said Blake. 'You only lend on security. I'm offering you security – ten times over – once I have a deal. Say, a matter of one or two weeks.'

'When would you wish a decision?'

'Today.'

'That would be quite impossible, Mr Blake. I would have to consult, ah, other colleagues. My regional director has unfortunately had a heart attack and his deputy is on holiday. There's a limit to what I can lend without consultation.'

'How much is your limit?'

'That's confidential.'

'So is this, and the offer cannot remain open to me indefinitely. I'm meeting my friend this afternoon, and then I have to tell him, yes or no. I would, naturally, bring the business account for the garage to your bank here.'

The manager leaned forward, pondering the problem. Could this possibly be the chance for which he had been waiting for so long?

Blake watched his face closely, guessed at his thoughts and added, almost casually, as a throwaway remark: 'I would like someone to advise me on general financial strategy. Not a full-time job. The sort of thing someone with your experience and knowledge of business procedure could do easily in his spare time. For a fee, and a share of the profits, obviously.'

Mr Marsh nodded. His mouth suddenly felt dry. He could feel his heart beat heavily as though he had been running uphill a long way.

'It is unorthodox, of course, to advance such a large sum on what is only a verbal assurance,' he said, hardly believing he

22

could be so foolhardy. 'But then we cannot always go by the rule book, can we? You have banked here since you arrived in Oxford, straight from school, nearly three years ago. I think I am a reasonable judge of character – and of business. I will, in fact, advance you five thousand pounds for one week on your written assurance that the deeds of the buildings will be deposited at this branch as soon as the deal goes through within that time.'

'Agreed,' said Blake quickly, almost too quickly. 'Call in Miss Grout and I'll dictate the letter now.'

'Perhaps I should have a word with the area manager,' said the manager, suddenly nervous. He was talking about a sum that represented nearly eight years' salary.

'Discuss it with anyone you like,' said Blake patiently. 'But let me have a cheque, otherwise we will all lose. I would be most reluctant to move my account but I am determined to buy this property. There will, of course, be the certainty of very large amounts coming into the account from sales and so on. Regularly.'

Mr Marsh nodded and swallowed. He pressed a bell on his desk for Miss Grout.

'I will dictate the letter,' he told Blake. 'You will sign it. In point of fact, this is irregular, you know. Highly irregular. I am trusting you, Mr Blake.'

'I appreciate the compliment. You know what Democritus said on the subject? "Do not trust all men, but trust men of worth. The former course is silly, the latter a mark of prudence." '

'Very true, in my experience, and most apt in my profession,' replied the manager, scribbling the quotation on his blotter. 'Democritus, you say? I am not acquainted with his work. What it is to have had a classical education, Mr Blake!'

Half an hour later, Blake was drinking a large whisky and soda in the back bar of The Mitre. On the way, he had gone into the Westminster Bank opposite the hotel to open an account and pay in the cheque. He waited while it was cleared and collected a banker's draft for £4,000.

Mr Marsh was meanwhile still at his desk, awaiting two telephone calls. He had immediately telephoned his bank's Hounslow branch and a sub-branch in Uxbridge, and given them both details of the garage, asking for quick opinions on its value. One reply came within half an hour, the second shortly afterwards. The garage certainly seemed large and prosperous, and as such

23

must be worth at least £50,000; very probably a lot more. Mr Marsh thanked them both. He suddenly felt tired, almost exhausted.

Had he been wise – or had he been an idiot? He reached into the bottom drawer of his desk where he kept a bottle of sherry and three glasses for entertaining important clients. Then he hesitated. It would not do to use only one glass; Miss Grout would think he had been drinking alone, which was always very suspicious, and it was beneath his dignity to wash the glass himself. He paused for a moment and then unscrewed the top of the bottle and raised it to his lips and drank greedily and thankfully.

As the cheap, sugary, metallic-tasting liquid went down his throat, he felt more cheerful. No doubt about it; he must be on his way to wealth.

Blake was back in college by half past one, elated at the thought of having achieved a deal so easily and quickly. The fact that he had no intention of buying anything at all did not at first concern him. Credit and profit and loss were moves in a kind of game. Surely Omar Khayyam had said the last words on that subject? 'Take the cash, and let the credit go.' At breakfast that morning he had read a displayed advertisement in *The Autocar* offering second-hand cars at the garage he had mentioned to Mr Marsh. The bank manager would doubtless discover that the garage was not for sale, or if he didn't, Blake would tell him, explaining that his friend's father had suddenly changed his plans. But Mr Marsh would receive his money – along with Blake's bookmaker, his tailor, his shirt-maker; everyone to whom he owed anything.

Blake felt confident he could do this because a friend's elder brother worked for one of Newmarket's most successful trainers, who had a horse, Sindbad the Second, running at Chepstow on the following day. A dark horse indeed, his friend had told him in the utmost confidence, carrying a hell of a lot of money on his back. The odds were sixteen to one – down from twenty-five last week – and if Blake wanted to cash in, he should follow the big boys and put all he could on Sindbad's neck. But only for a win. No point in diluting his winnings by also betting on a place.

But before Blake could bet anything, he had to have money, and where better to borrow money than from a bank, whose whole business was lending it? The irony was that if he had asked for a loan of £5,000 to bet on a certainty, it would almost certainly have been refused, but because he asked for money for a totally fictitious project, that at least sounded feasible, it was immediately forthcoming. Now, within twenty-four hours, all would be resolved in his favour.

As he crossed the quadrangle, he met Jerrold and hailed him enthusiastically. He was not particularly pleased to see him; he simply wanted someone to share his optimism.

'Hello there,' he said jovially. 'What about a trip on the river? I'll get my scout to make some sandwiches and put half a dozen bottles of champagne on ice. Just the day for it.'

'Not for me, it isn't,' Jerrold replied shortly. 'Schools next week, as I keep telling you. I'll come after that.'

'You may be dead after that. Let's enjoy ourselves now. While we can. That's my motto. Well, if you won't come, who else will?'

'Lots. Glover, for one. I saw him going up to his room with a girl.'

'Glover? With a girl?'

'He's human, you know.'

'Only just.'

Rather irritated that Jerrold had declined his invitation, Blake went into the college telephone box, and rang three numbers in order of interest. The first was the porter's lodge of a women's college. The porter was sorry, sir, but Miss Browne was out. The next was a landlady. No, Miss Jones was not in her room, and she had no idea where she was or when she would be back, and was there any message? The third number did not answer.

Hell. He wanted to take some girl out on the river for the afternoon, for he felt he had something to celebrate. There must be dozens of girls dying to come out with him, if only he could contact them. Well, what about the girl in Glover's room?

He knocked on Glover's door, and went in without waiting for an answer. Glover was standing by a table with a girl. He had just poured out two small glasses of British sherry.

'Join us,' he said without much enthusiasm. 'You know Corinne Gieves?'

'I do now,' Blake replied, shaking hands.

'St Anne's. Second year. Reading English.'

'You make me feel very old,' Blake told her untruthfully. 'I'm going down next week, after Schools. Just popped in to see if you'd both like to come out on the river with me?' Again, not strictly true, but what the devil?

'Oh, I'd love to,' Corinne replied quickly. She was small and dumpy and wore a thin dress of some clinging shiny material that amplified the outlines of suspender clips and shoulder straps in an unattractive way.

'I'm not much good in a punt,' said Glover, grimacing.

'You don't have to be. My scout will rustle up some food and strawberries and cream. You organize a car to take us to the boathouse.'

'Oh, what fun!' cried Corinne excitedly, now looking at Blake in total admiration. She kept pushing wispy, mousey hair out of her eyes, so that she could see him more clearly. She was short-sighted but hated to wear spectacles. Blake saw the effect he was having and was not surprised. Corinne was neither pretty nor witty, but she was an audience and she was female. For the moment, these attributes were sufficient.

'Well, that's settled then,' he said easily.

'But how do I organize a car, as you say?' asked Glover. This sort of thing was outside his experience.

'There's a fellow near the station who hires out an old white Rolls-Royce for weddings. That would do.'

'Expensive,' warned Glover gloomily.

'My dear fellow, what is money but dross by which inferiors can measure the enjoyment of their superiors? Remember Oscar Wilde's last words as he lay dying in Paris? "I am dying beyond my means." That's the spirit – so long as you've lived beyond them first. See you outside in five minutes.'

'Well . . .' said Corinne, when she and Glover were alone. She had often seen Blake, usually in his car, but never to speak to, never in the same room, and he had impressed her, as Glover noted sourly. As she put down her empty glass, Glover saw for the first time that the platinum watch on her wrist was encrusted with glittering stones. Were they real or fake? He did not know that Blake had already noted their brilliance and decided they were real – an opinion that was to influence all their lives from that time forward.

Blake was waiting by his car outside the college, windscreen folded flat across its long louvred bonnet.

'Where's the Rolls?' he asked Glover, frowning.

'Couldn't get it. Man says it's out. A wedding.'

'Hadn't he anything else?'

'I didn't really ask him. You suggested the Rolls.'

'Oh well, too bad. We'll have to go in this.'

Blake opened the passenger door for Corinne.

'Two seats only, I'm afraid,' he told Glover. 'See you at the boathouse.'

Glover looked at him for a moment as though he was going to argue, then shrugged philosophically, took his bicycle out of the rack and began to pedal down the High. He did not respond to Blake's wave as the SS swept past him.

All the best punts had already been hired, but Blake was a good customer, and a folded ten-shilling note in the boatman's hand produced a splendid new punt, sparkling in fresh varnish with a newly painted gold line along her whole length and the name *Lotus* spelled out on a scroll on both sides of her bow.

Blake handed Corinne carefully into the stern. She sat down cautiously on the red canvas cushions, knees modestly together.

'You smoke?' he asked her.

'Well, yes. A little. But I haven't brought any with me.'

'I have. They're specially made.'

He opened a silver case.

'Turkish.'

He lit two expertly, handed one to her, snapped shut the case as Glover arrived.

'We'll have to wait a moment for the food,' Blake explained.

'I thought you were bringing it?'

'Heavens, no. My scout's dealing with that. He's gone to get some ice. We don't want to drink warm champagne, do we?'

'Any champagne is better than none,' said Glover.

Blake shook his head. 'I can't agree,' he replied. 'Never lower your standards.'

'Aren't you worried about Schools?' Corinne asked him, much impressed.

'Not at all. You're not, are you?'

'Well, not yet,' Corinne agreed. 'But I don't take them until next year.'

'She's like you. Doesn't need to worry,' Glover explained tartly. 'Her father owns Gieves Industries.'

'Really?'

27

Blake looked at Corinne now with more interest. He had never heard of Gieves Industries, but this was not the moment to say so.

A motorcycle and sidecar chugged along the towpath and stopped. Blake's scout climbed off the machine and carried a wicker hamper and bottles of champagne packed in ice aboard the punt. Blake jumped in expertly. The punt dipped slightly under his weight. He took off his jacket, handed it to Corinne.

'Now,' he told Glover. 'Let's see how you do it up in Willesden or wherever.'

'I told you, I'm not very good,' said Glover uneasily.

'This will give you the opportunity to improve.'

Blake cast off.

'I'd take off your shoes, if I were you,' he advised Glover. 'You're less likely to fall in with bare feet. And don't push at an angle, or you'll be left hanging on. Like this.'

Blake drove the pole down almost vertically, let his hands slip effortlessly up to the top, twisted the pole, pulled it out. A stream of droplets sprayed into the air like a broken diamond necklace. They reminded him of the jewels around Corinne's watch. Gieves Industries. He must find out exactly who and what they were.

He handed the pole to Glover, and as he struggled with it in the stern, trying to appear more expert than he would ever be, Blake wound up the gramophone. The strains of Ambrose and his orchestra playing "Change Partners" wafted across the river. Half a dozen records later, Glover's perspiring face drew the comment from Corinne to Blake: 'Why don't you have a go?'

'Horses for courses. David's getting good at it.'

'And what are you good at?'

'Perhaps you will discover one day,' he said, smiling. 'But you have a point. Let's pull in for a drink. Nothing's too good for the workers.'

'You're not doing much work,' retorted Glover, ducking his head as he guided the punt inexpertly beneath the overhanging branches of a willow.

'I organized the whole thing,' replied Blake, pretending to be aggrieved. 'If it hadn't been for me, you would still be drinking British sherry in your rooms. Now you are going to enjoy French champagne as my guests on the river.'

He opened a bottle, poured out three glasses. Glover climbed

28

out of the punt and sat down thankfully on the bank. He felt safer on earth than on the trembling slippery deck.

They finished one bottle of champagne quickly enough, opened a second. Blake's scout had packed slices of smoked salmon with thinly cut brown bread and butter, and plovers' eggs with green salad, and strawberries soaked in kirsch, and a carton of cream.

By the time they had finished, the afternoon was dying. Shadows grew long, and the sun slid down behind the tops of the tallest trees. Midges and mayflies danced away the evening of their one-day lives above the placid water, broken now and then into gentle ripples by a rising trout. Other punts, with girls in summer dresses lolling in the stern under wide-brimmed hats, and barefooted escorts in shirt sleeves, trousers rolled up above their knees, moved gracefully downstream to dance music from gramophones. Blake glanced at his watch.

'Quarter to seven,' he said briskly. 'Time to cast off and rejoin the human race.'

Blake's scout was patiently waiting for them as they drew alongside the mooring platform. The boatman came out of his hut to check their return.

'That will be two pounds, sir,' he said to Blake.

'Can you manage a couple of quid?' Blake asked Glover. 'I've only got ten bob on me.'

He gave the note to the boatman, who saluted smartly. Mr Blake was a gent. He knew how to behave.

Glover said uneasily, 'It'll leave me a bit short. Can't we owe it?'

'Not done, old man,' said Blake, shaking his head disapprovingly.

'You're a bit cool, aren't you?' asked Corinne as she climbed into the car. 'Poor David poled us all the way there and back, and now you ask him to pay.'

'Purely a temporary loan. Division of the spoils. Now, where can I drop you?'

'St Anne's. Know where it is?'

She bit her lip, wishing she hadn't asked such a ridiculous question. He must know where all the women's colleges were, for he must have collected or delivered so many other girls. Blake stopped outside the gates, and leaned across her so that the back of his sleeve lightly brushed her thighs as he opened the door.

Corinne climbed out and stood for a moment, reluctant to leave. It was the first time she had been in a sports car.

For her, the afternoon seemed symbolized by the mayflies she had watched dance above the river, an enjoyment over too soon. Now she was back to the routine of tutorials, cycling to lectures, drinking cups of coffee in the Tackley with other plain, earnest girls in artificial silk stockings and flat-heeled shoes, all pretending they knew exciting people with whom they spent romantic evenings, when reality was a mug of cocoa and an early night alone. Sadly, Corinne watched Blake's crimson car drive away.

Blake parked the car outside the college. Glover's bicycle was in the first quad, upside down, resting on its saddle and handlebars. He was removing the rear tyre. 'A puncture,' he explained shortly.

'I've a better set of spanners if they're any use,' Blake told him. He felt rather mean about the way he had treated Glover, and yet there was something about the man that irked him, and not only him, but so many others. Somehow his chemistry was wrong.

Glover shook his head.

'Got my own,' he replied.

'Oh, well. I'll pay you back that two quid tomorrow.'

'Any time,' said Glover, surprised that Blake had even mentioned it. According to his reckoning, Blake already owed him nearly £50.

'Hope you didn't work too hard,' Blake went on, to assuage a tiny lingering twinge of conscience.

'I learned about punting. And human relationships.'

'Then I should charge you,' Blake told him in mock seriousness.

'You already have. Two pounds.'

Blake laughed as though the debt had now been discharged.

'Nice girl, Corinne,' he said.

'There's more to her than you think.'

'How much more?'

'A lot. Her father's the fifth richest man in this country, for a start.'

'I had no idea.'

'You have now. My old man does some conveyancing for the Gieves property side. When her father heard I was here, he asked me to keep an eye on her. We have tea in my rooms from time to time.'

'Any brothers?'

'None. Father dotes on her.'

'Surprised I haven't seen her around before.'

'She doesn't want to be taken out just because she's rich. And, well, she's a bit shy.'

'So I noticed.'

Blake walked thoughtfully across the quad, up the wide stair-case, into his room. He felt unexpectedly tired; flat would perhaps be a better word. Needling Glover was a pointless way to spend an afternoon, as was drinking champagne he couldn't afford, with people who didn't really attract him. So why did he do it? To prove something? If so, what?

Because of Blake's looks and the aura of wealth that hung around him like a halo, people deferred to him and his opinions. He had never thought much about this before, because there had been no occasion to do so, but lolling back in the punt, watching Glover sweat inelegantly with the pole, he suddenly realized belatedly that life did not treat others less well favoured so generously.

I have taken so much for granted, he thought, as he walked up the wooden stairs to his room. I wanted to do this or that and, somehow, it always seemed possible. Was this just because of his strength of will, or because the combination of appearance and his apparent affluence encouraged all opposition to melt?

His mind was miles away, so that he was inside his room with the door closed behind him before he saw the two men waiting by the fireplace. The taller was standing to one side against the wall, a thorn walking stick in his hand. Blake had last seen him lying on the ground beside the Wolseley car in the garage on the Witney Road. The other man was smaller, fatter, with close-cropped hair, a dark-bluish chin. His suit fitted so well he appeared to have been poured into it like a plaster mould. He had been sitting out of sight of the doorway and stood up as Blake came into the room.

'That's him,' announced the man with the stick. 'Blake.'

'You're trespassing,' Blake told them both. 'Please leave.'

He made to open the door, but the bigger man had already turned the lock behind him, and pocketed the key. Blake glanced around for a weapon. He could see nothing within reach.

'My friend and I have come to collect a debt,' the smaller fat man explained.

'Who are you?'

'Hamish McMoffatt.'

'The man himself,' said Blake. 'From what clan?'

'Shall I teach the bastard a lesson?' asked the man with the stick.

'Not just yet,' said McMoffatt. 'Clan of Bethnal Green, if you must know. And you are one of the Dorset Blakes, I understand? Now, with all that out of the way, to business. You owe my firm four thousand pounds. Most of it outstanding for far too long.'

'I didn't think that Hamish McMoffatt would come here in person to collect what must be a small and insignificant debt.'

'I wouldn't usually, but Oxford is on the way to Chepstow. The races. Thought I'd call in and see how the rich and educated live.'

'How do you want the money?' Blake asked him, to give himself time to think, to devise any means of escape.

'In cash or kind. I would prefer cash, but I don't care too much if it's kind. My friend here would actually prefer that.'

'Shylock syndrome?' asked Blake.

'Except, this time, he could spill blood,' McMoffatt assured him.

'It's two to one,' said Blake easily, crossing the room. 'And since I'm totally unarmed and it's been a very tiring day, you leave me with but one course of action.'

He paused, opened the lid of his desk, took out the banker's draft he had collected from the bank that morning.

'To whom shall I make it out?'

'Me,' said McMoffatt. 'Personally.'

Blake pushed the draft across the desk, then gave it a slight flick so that the paper fluttered to the ground. McMoffatt did not move, but nodded his head slightly, almost imperceptibly, to the man with the stick. As he bent to pick up the paper, Blake brought the edge of his right hand down on the man's neck with a karate blow. His face struck the top of the desk with the force of a hammer hitting a nail. Blake twisted the stick out of the man's hand as he staggered, fell sideways, and collapsed on the carpet.

'That should teach you some manners,' Blake told him, and turned towards McMoffatt, secretly surprised and impressed that he had not moved. For all the concern McMoffatt displayed, he might have been watching a moving picture; the violence had not affected him in any way.

'Take the money,' Blake said. 'It's yours. But next time you come to collect a debt, please come alone. I don't like the company you keep.'

'So it appears. Nevertheless, I admire your style, Mr Blake. And, of course, as a long-standing client, your credit is now automatically extended to the amount of this cheque. Another four thousand pounds.'

'No way,' Blake replied firmly. 'In future, I'm going to make money, not help you make more.'

McMoffatt smiled.

'Then here's a chance to do just that. The three-thirty tomorrow at Chepstow. Rainbow Trout. You can get ten to one. Not with me, of course, but through someone who owes me a big, big favour. With four thousand, you could pick up forty. Plus your bet.'

'I could also lose it all.'

'I'm giving you a tip.'

'I appreciate it. But still, no way.'

'Rainbow Trout. Remember the name. Rainbow Trout to win.'

'Why are you telling me this?' asked Blake.

'Because, as I said, I like your style. Maybe we could do business together one day. On the same side of the street.'

'I think not, but thanks for the offer.'

Blake paused.

'One thing puzzles me, Mr McMoffatt,' he said. 'You don't look as though you could put up too much opposition – just like your friend here. But, equally, you don't seem one little bit afraid.'

'I've no need to be. The reason's right behind you.'

Blake turned. Another man, broad as a bear, with hands that hung ape-like at his sides, almost to his knees, stood on the far side of the door. He must have been crouched down behind the settee out of Blake's line of sight.

'Don't worry,' McMoffatt told Blake reassuringly, smiling at his surprise. 'But think about what I said. The same side of the street. And remember: Rainbow Trout.'

The man on the ground stood up slowly, leaned wearily against the wall. McMoffatt nodded briefly towards his companion, who led him out of the room, down the staircase.

Blake closed the door behind them all, poured himself a brandy and sat down to drink it. He felt weak and weary. He had smugly congratulated himself on his own cleverness – and totally underestimated the strength of the opposition. He had acted like an idiot. Should he bet on Sindbad the Second – or on Rainbow Trout? McMoffatt's tip might be good, but after the dust-up on the Witney Road, this seemed at best doubtful – not something he would care to bet on.

Unable to reach a decision, he picked up the morning paper, glanced through the advertisements for houses and cars, wanting neither, but hoping he might find a sign he could follow, one course or the other. He could buy a 1500-acre estate with a manor house, a farm and three cottages for £2000. A year-old Rolls-Royce would cost him £600, a suit made to measure in Savile Row, £5. He could invest £5000 and have sufficient income to live on modestly for the rest of his life. Invest the money. That was what he was doing, of course, for a huge return.

Blake finished the brandy and made his decision. He'd bet his thousand, and with the four thousand credit with McMoffatt, he'd put on five – to win a fortune. He telephoned his contact at the racing stables in Newbury. The man laughed at the thought of Rainbow Trout. A horse with a name like that would be more at home in water than on land, whereas Sindbad the Second was an absolute cert. Blake accepted this; the man knew. He telephoned his bet to McMoffatt's office: Sindbad to win.

All the next morning Blake sat in his room, now and then picking up a book, glancing at it, putting it down again, unable to settle or concentrate, while the hands of the clock on the mantelpiece crept slowly around the dial.

Just before noon, the under-porter knocked respectfully on his door. There was an urgent telephone message, he said. From a Mr Marsh. Would Mr Blake please telephone or call at his office immediately? It was a very important matter.

Blake nodded. It was probably more important to Mr Marsh than to him. He would be there on the following morning as soon as the bank opened to pay in his winnings and clear his debt.

He had no lunch. He did not feel hungry, only nervous inside, willing the hours away until the race was over.

When he heard newsboys on the street outside calling: 'Results! All the results!' he went out, and bought an *Evening Standard*.

He turned immediately to the racing pages, and skimmed

through reports from Kempton Park, Epsom, Brighton, until he found Chepstow. Then his heart contracted like a vice, squeezing blood from his body and his brain. He stood for a moment, not hearing the rush of traffic in the High, and the hoarse calls of the newsboys: '*Star! News! Standard!*' Horror and disbelief swelled in his stomach like stones.

As McMoffatt had forecast, Rainbow Trout had won. The odds had actually lengthened to twelve to one. He would have collected £60,000 – and he had not put on a single penny.

Sindbad had lived up to his name and come in second. And Blake had not betted on a place. So, he had lost his £4000 credit, plus the £1000 remaining from his bank advance, and was £5000 worse off than he had been twenty-four hours earlier.

Like a man in a trance, Blake found his way back to his rooms and threw himself on his bed, fully clothed. He lay as one in a coma, unable to concentrate his mind on the full horror of his predicament. Slowly, dusk darkened the little window, and some time between darkness and dawn, Blake fell into uneasy slumber.

Jerrold's tutor rose as Jerrold came into the room. He was a round, tubby bachelor with ginger hair and half-glasses. He had inherited a glue factory in the West of England which enabled him to subsidize his modest stipend as a don.

'How kind of you to come in the middle of your revision,' he said with all the sincerity of the insincere. 'A sherry?'

'Thank you,' said Jerrold, glancing enquiringly from the tutor to the other man in the room. He stood with his back to him, glass in hand, looking out of the mullioned window. The afternoon sun caught the faded calf bindings on rows of old books; dust motes danced in its golden light. Jerrold felt like an actor: Act Two, Scene Three – Rooms of a bachelor don in Oxford.

'Mr Dermott,' the tutor said apologetically. 'You haven't met, I think!'

The man at the window turned, held out his hand. The grip was strong and the flesh dry and rough; he could have been a labourer but he was not. His eyes were cold and blue, like an ice-floe. His nostrils flared like the ends of shotgun barrels. There was something totally unpleasant about him, Jerrold thought. He might have been a creature from a Greek myth: part man, mostly beast.

'I have been hearing good things about you,' Dermott said.

35

His voice was curiously high-pitched, as if transplanted from a boy.

'Your tutor and I are old friends. He tells me you would like to get into Fleet Street. He suggested we meet for I have some contacts in that world.'

Dermott paused. The tutor looked at his watch.

'Dear me,' he said. 'I'm late. I promised to see Semaj Rosael at Balliol for lunch. Please excuse me. I think you and Dermott will get on well together. He can help you a lot.'

Dermott waited until he was alone with Jerrold, and motioned him to a seat.

'Have you applied for a job anywhere yet?'

'Not yet. But the editor of the *Globe* offered me one, actually. On trial, of course.'

'I have a good contact at the *Globe*,' said Dermott thoughtfully. 'The foreign editor. You would have to do a spell, of course, as a junior reporter, but you can pick up the rudiments fairly quickly, I'm sure.'

He helped himself to another glass of the tutor's sherry, offered the bottle to Jerrold, who shook his head.

'I'm not actually in Fleet Street,' Dermott went on. 'I'm attached to the Foreign Office, but we like to liaise with foreign correspondents when we can. Sometimes they can find out things we would like to know, which isn't always easy when the Treasury holds the purse strings. Know what I mean?'

'I think so.'

'Simply a matter of keeping your eyes and ears open. We can also help you meet people who might not otherwise want to meet the press. A nod here and a wink there. You follow me?'

'Partly,' said Jerrold.

'Of course, there won't be much money in it. But we could pay a retainer of a few hundred a year, depending on the sort of information you turn up. What do you think?'

'It's all rather sudden,' said Jerrold. 'I haven't taken my degree yet.'

'Don't worry about that, dear boy. This is the university of life.'

'If I agree to help you, could you put in a word for me at the *Globe*?'

'Many words, dear boy,' Dermott answered him.

'How can I get hold of you?' Jerrold asked him.

'You can't, really. I move about. But I will be in touch, and soon. I think we could help each other a lot.'

They shook hands. As Jerrold went out of the room, Mr Dermott, his back to him, was already pouring himself another sherry.

From across the quad, Glover watched Jerrold come out of the tutor's rooms. He had seen Dermott ushered in by the head porter and decided he would find out who he was, why he was there. He didn't particularly like Jerrold, but he sensed that Jerrold could be useful to him if he ever worked in Fleet Street. Glover had seen from his father's experience how good publicity could help a deal along, and how a bad press could ruin it. His feelings towards Jerrold were benevolent compared with his feelings towards Blake. Yet he envied Blake while he did not envy Jerrold. One had the assurance and poise of inherited wealth; the other was only a step up from his own position. He had been a fool to introduce Blake to Corinne, and yet, in the circumstances, he had been forced to do so.

Blake was so damned good-looking, so confident, so urbane, she was bound to be attracted to him. All girls were. And to increase his own importance, as a friend of the wealthy, he had foolishly blurted out that Corinne was rich, which must surely only increase Blake's interest in her. Glover caught sight of himself in the cheap gilt-framed mirror he had bought from a market stall, thinking it would add tone and taste to his room. The edges might be scratched and yellow and stained, but the mirror image still showed his face contorted with bitterness and hate, consumed by ambition for revenge against the slights – some real, some magnified by envy – that he felt Blake had deliberately inflicted upon him.

2

As the lights went out one by one in college windows, and church bells pealed midnight across an empty Oxford, dawn was about to break 7000 miles away in the foothills of Mount Everest.

A crescent moon hung in a white milky mist that gradually grew pink as the sun came up behind the jagged rim of peaks. The sun glowed orange at first, then slowly turned into a blazing white ball tinged with green as the mist drifted. From where the Scottish doctor stood, the Himalayas seemed only ten minutes away; in fact, he knew they were nearly fifty miles beyond the valley.

Fifty elephants in line, their tusks tipped with polished silver, turned away from the approaching day. Several stamped huge feet nervously, and clouds of dust billowed about them. Each elephant supported a richly caparisoned howdah on its back, with gilded sides and red plush seats. In front of the howdah on the beast's skull sat a *mahout*, feet tucked up behind the animal's flapping ears. In his hand, he carried a gold-tipped crook to implement his commands: forward; stop; kneel; break an overhead branch. Behind the howdah, barefoot, toes spatulate to grip the animal's enormous flanks, perched a *pachwa*. While the *mahout* steered the elephant, the *pachwa* held a spear in his right hand to prod the animal's grey, wrinkled skin to urge it on should it flag or show any signs of sloth.

As the sun burned away the last of the mist, Everest glowed white, majestic, mysterious. Smoke rose slowly from half a dozen fires in the camp where the elephants had been tethered by chains overnight, and three open American Chevrolets bumped over the rough track towards them. Beside each driver sat a liveried Nepalese servant, who leaped out to open the rear doors as the cars stopped. The hunters who climbed out in a leisurely way were dark-skinned and stocky. They wore polished riding boots and silk khaki shirts. The elephants trumpeted and stamped their feet at their approach. None of the new arrivals glanced at the doctor, who stood to one side, watching the scene with interest.

Dr Jamie Drummond was a bachelor in his fifties. In years of general practice in Perthshire, he had never encountered anything so strange as the situation that had confronted him on his arrival in Nepal. He was now ready to believe Kipling's words: 'The wildest dreams of Kew are everyday things in Kathmandu.'

Drummond had been staying with his brother, a tea-planter, in Darjeeling, and someone asked him casually over drinks in the club one Sunday lunchtime whether he would travel to Nepal to treat a rich patient. Drummond was not sure of the name or even the nationality of the man who had issued the invitation, but his brother thought he had business interests in Nepal. Drummond had become rather bored with life in a hill station, and felt flattered by the offer. His brother's wife made no secret of the fact that she thought him boring and too set in his ways; also, she did not like his pipe, and said so frequently. The chance of a brief trip away was therefore most welcome, for Nepal was a closed country. Apparently, the only foreign presence allowed was that of the British Resident.

Drummond's brother drove him up over mountain tracks to the frontier where another car awaited them, an open Ford V-8, with a driver and a young dark-skinned man in European clothes. He introduced himself as Chet Bahadur Rana.

'You are the patient I have come to see?'

'No. But I will take you to him.'

As the car climbed, the air grew steadily cooler. Grass on either side of the road was studded with hibiscus and white daisies. There were very few houses and these little more than huts, but Drummond noticed that all doors were carefully pad-locked. This was a rough country and possessions, however sparse, must be precious to their owners. Chickens pecked in the dust, but otherwise he could see no sign of life. The hillside had been shaped into neat terraces, bright with yellow mustard flowers.

'Your first visit to India?' Chet Bahadur asked him.

'Yes. And to Nepal, of course.'

'Of course. So let me tell you a little about Kathmandu. Its name comes from the word Kasthamandap, meaning a wooden house, built in mediaeval times at the crossroads of the great trade routes, east and west, north and south. The wood is said to have come from a celestial tree, given by a god who travelled the road in disguise. Despite this, local priests recognized him, and fearing he was angry with them, put him under another god's spell until he promised them a favour. He gave them the tree on which the city is founded.'

'This is a religious country?'

'God-fearing might be a better description, doctor. Literally, fearing gods – many gods – and what they can do.'

They drove past a temple where two stone wrestlers with hand locks on each other guarded the bottom step of a stairway. Above them, stood two carved elephants, and above them two lions, then two griffins, and finally, two goddesses peered down from the top step.

'This is symbolic of relative power, doctor,' Chet explained. 'The wrestlers are strong, but then the elephants are ten times stronger. Now the lions are ten times stronger than the elephants, and the griffins ten times as strong again. Finally, the goddesses are stronger than all of them put together. And inside the temple lies the real source of all strength – the spirit.'

Was Chet Bahadur trying to tell him something by parable? Drummond wondered, with many years' experience of patients who, he realized, desperately wished to confide in him and yet, through shame or embarrassment, could not bring themselves to do so.

They passed a man pushing a bicycle laden with clumps of green bananas; another squatted at the roadside selling fans of peacock feathers. The car turned in between stone gateposts with heraldic lions. A house the size of a palace faced them; rows of windows heliographed messages from the morning sun. The car stopped.

'Follow me, doctor,' Chet told him and led the way up a carved marble staircase, past marble tables inlaid with jewels cut to the shape of flower petals, along a corridor lined with stone figures of men wearing a curious mixture of Roman togas and European court dress. Outside each door a guard sprang to attention as they approached. They entered a bedroom with a view across terraced fields to the distant hills. Under the eaves hung tiny leaf-shaped metal bells, tinkling soothingly in the wind.

'They are to attract the attention of the gods,' Chet explained.

'I am glad to hear it, but what about the patient I have come to see?'

'In good time, doctor. This is the east, remember. Speed is not so important here as in the west. By running, we may reach an unimportant destination a little earlier. We cannot reach the ultimate one second in advance.'

Drummond was intrigued by the logic. And since, as Chet Bahadur said, there was no need for haste, he decided to relax and enjoy his visit; he would never see this land again.

'This is your house?' he asked Chet Bahadur at breakfast next morning.

'Our family palace. It contains a thousand rooms.'

'Is my patient in one of them?'

Chet Bahadur did not reply, and the doctor wished he had not asked the question. There was no way to hurry the east, as Kipling had also discovered.

After breakfast, grooms brought two horses to the palace gates and Drummond and Chet rode out through Kathmandu, past temples where gods held out half a dozen hands, where Hanuman, the god of good fortune in battle, had his monkey face covered by a scarlet cloth in case erotic carvings on the walls of another temple should offend him.

'Why have such carvings at all, then?' Drummond asked in his direct, Scottish way, as Chet explained the reason for the blindfold.

'Because the goddess of lightning is a virgin and she would not consider striking a temple adorned with such scenes.'

Huge drums rested on their sides, ready to be beaten before worship; outside open-fronted shops men crouched cooking in wide copper pans. A blind man playing a flute offered them a bamboo pole with more flutes stuck into holes so that they spread out like musical branches. Soon, the city fell behind them and they were up on a rough track leading into the hills.

'So that is the Forbidden City?' said Drummond with interest, looking back at the red roofs, the cluster of white walls.

'It has been since 1816, doctor, a hundred and twenty-two years, for this is a forbidden country. No-one must realize you are here in your professional capacity,' Chet continued. 'That is of the utmost importance – to both of us.'

'But anyone can discover that I'm a doctor. It's on my passport.'

'Of course. But I have been accepted by St Andrew's University in Scotland to read medicine in the coming term. You are Scottish

41

and trained there, so who better to advise me as to the books I would need, and the equipment? You follow me?'

'Of course. But it is difficult to examine a patient thoroughly if they don't know you are going to examine them.'

'Life is full of difficulties. As the Lord Buddha said, "The greater the difficulty overcome, the greater the glory." Every difficulty presents its own challenge.'

'Which I accept,' agreed Drummond, 'but only because I have to. Now, who is this patient?'

'My father. He is about your age, doctor, and has always been vigorous, outgoing, a great sportsman. Yet, during the last few months, his whole attitude to life has changed. Everything has become an effort to him. He is morose, he lacks energy and appetite.'

'What do you believe is the reason for this?'

'I brought you out riding, doctor, so that we could be alone, to minimize the chance of anyone overhearing us. It is my impression that my father is being slowly and deliberately poisoned.'

'But by whom? That is a very serious allegation to make.'

'I do not make it lightly. I will arrange for you to see him tomorrow morning, but first, I will place in your room a brief history of our country. You will then be able to see for yourself exactly who could do this, and why . . .'

Until Dr Drummond read the typed pages, all he knew about Nepal was that it was the home of the Gurkhas. He had no idea who ruled the country, and what he read astonished and disturbed him.

From the eighteenth century, its history had been one of violence and political murder, by sword, poison, and the gun.

Previously, Nepal had been divided into small principalities on the lines of English and Scottish counties. Then Prithri Narayan Shah, the ruler of Gorkha, one of these states, became alarmed by the spread of British influence and power throughout India, and determined that this control must not extend north to Nepal. He believed the only way to remain independent of Britain or France, as the two paramount colonial powers, was to unify the country. Therefore he seized control of Kathmandu and declared himself King of Nepal.

On his death, his eldest son succeeded him, then died suddenly from smallpox, leaving as his successor a two-year-old son. Meanwhile, the British in India were becoming increasingly concerned at the growth of the new kingdom of Nepal. This extended from Kashmir to Sikkim and so could conceivably offer a threat to British India, with Chinese or Russian help. A border dispute between Britain and Nepal led to a two-year war, in which Britain was victorious. As a result of the peace treaty, Nepal was forced to accept a British Resident in Kathmandu. The Nepalese hated this imposition and the only plot of land they would give him for his bungalow was said to be inhabited by evil spirits. Even so, the Resident survived, and from that year the British were the only aliens allowed into Nepal. Gurkha soldiers had so impressed British officers during the war that they now inducted them into the army in India.

In 1846, a Nepalese general, Jung Bahadur Rana, one of the Queen's lovers, made a bid for power, claiming that the King had gone mad. Blood flooded the gutters of Kathmandu, and vultures gathered over the city, to feed on the bodies of the victims of his coup. Once in command, Rana jailed or outlawed any who could conceivably offer any threat to him. Others he imprisoned for life. Every male member of his family, his relations, and all their sons immediately became generals. He seized the lands of any unwise enough to disagree with his policies, and kept the King imprisoned in his palace. But so that it could never be said that Rana had actually overthrown the King, he allowed the monarch out once a year to prove that he had not been harmed.

Jung Bahadur Rana travelled to England to learn at first hand how the world's most powerful monarchy worked. With fourteen officers and twenty-five servants, he sailed from Bombay in a chartered steamer, and in London he and his entourage were housed in a specially decorated guest house in Richmond Terrace, off Whitehall. Queen Victoria received him at the Palace, and personally invited him to the christening of her son. The directors of the East India Company prudently gave a banquet in his honour.

This visit taught him the importance of the crown as a means of uniting a country of different races and religious creeds. He had every intention of being Nepal's ruler, in fact, if not in name, and to consolidate this position, he married his eight-year-old son to the King's six-year-old daughter – raising taxes to provide a dowry for the boy's bride. As a further safeguard, he married his three daughters to princes of the ruling house.

Rana envied the style of maharajahs in Indian native states, but fully realized the attachment of many Nepalese to their King, however weak Rana might personally consider him. He therefore organized a ceremony in which he ordered his ministers to request him officially to become King so that he could publicly reject this proposal and in return the King, now virtually a prisoner, conferred on him the title of maharajah. The King was also persuaded to declare that the office of prime minister was henceforth to be hereditary, and would be held by Jung Bahadur Rana and then by members of his family forever.

Jung Bahadur Rana now possessed every real royal prerogative, apart from the actual title of King. He could appoint or dismiss his government, declare war, make peace, change any law he disliked, and control the lives of everyone in Nepal. To ensure his succession and popularity with his family he gave to his sons, nephews, cousins, and even distant members of his family by marriage or birth, huge tracts of land. He built a palace containing 1700 rooms, the biggest private dwelling in Asia, importing marble from Italy, mirrors from Belgium, crystal chandeliers and hand-made furniture from Paris and London. His gigantic hall, the *sasaibathak*, was 137 feet long and 38 feet wide. The largest hand-made Persian carpet ever made covered its floor.

Jung Bahadur Rana was intrigued by the clothes of western women. He therefore decreed that ladies of his house wore crinolines. Then he had another notion; ladies of rank should wear enormous padded trousers under saris thirty feet long. These were so cumbersome that they could not walk upright without the help of a maid on either side, and some of the costumes were so grotesque that their wearers had to be carried on the backs of sturdy women servants in specially made leather saddles. Every night, Jung Bahadur Rana would visit a different bed, but none of the women in his harem knew who would next be favoured. If one pleased him, he might make her a maharani. If he found another unsatisfactory, she could be turned out to beg on the streets. He covered his self-designed ceremonial uniforms with jewels, and imported bird-of-paradise feathers from South America to provide the plumes for his hats.

This fantasy life of ostentation and instability was enjoyed by each succeeding Rana prime minister. As Hindus, they were not supposed to drink alcohol, but they drank cognac and Portuguese red wine in huge quantities. Frequently, they would finish several bottles each at a sitting, and stay stupefied for days. Their behaviour became totally erratic and unpredictable.

One prime minister found his son drunk and beat him to death with a club. Other young men desperately swallowed bottles of French perfume to conceal brandy fumes on their breath. Several members of the Rana family died from alcohol or perfume poisoning. But to maintain the myth of their adherence to Hindu principles, they only ate food cooked by Brahmins served on gold plates, in a room where the floor had been ritually purified by cow dung and red soil. One member of the family who spoke out against these dual moral standards was immediately arrested and forced to drink pints of hot urine provided by his guards until he admitted the enormity of his error.

The Ranas could do no wrong, and with each succeeding generation, they had acquired more power, more privileges, more property. They gambled on a huge scale; for houses, land, women. While their titles were hereditary, any one of the family could become prime minister; but never anyone outside the family. And all the time, year after year, they had maintained their extraordinary stranglehold on the politics, economics and life of the country without a break or any weakening of their influence.

Dr Drummond felt that he had been transported into a world that rivalled the Arabian nights. But this was happening here and now – and he had to discover whether one member of this unique family was being deliberately poisoned by another.

He walked around the room, hands in his pockets, pondering what he had read. As he walked, he had the feeling of being watched. The wall facing him was decorated with elaborate dark wood carvings. Ganesh, the god of good luck, with the head of an elephant and the eyes of a sophisticated cynic – green, cold, appraising – stared back at him. Suddenly, Drummond realized that human eyes were actually observing him from the idol's carved eye sockets. In that instant of realization a piece of wood slid silently behind the holes. He was staring at carved and

45

sightless sockets. Who could have been watching him – and why?

He went to bed, but it was a long time before he slept.

Next morning, Chet Bahadur came in to see him, held a finger to his lips to warn Drummond to be careful what he said, lest he could be overheard.

'I would like you to meet my father,' he said. 'He has some doubts about my going to Scotland.'

'I will set his mind at rest,' Drummond answered him. 'I have the happiest memories of my time there as a medical student.'

They drove through the centre of the city, surprisingly clean after the clutter and filth of Indian roads. Pigeons cooed on gold rooftops; serene and secretive plump-bellied Buddhas smiled down from flights of steps. A black god with blood-red hands wore a crown of skulls, a garland of human heads.

'The god of destruction,' Chet explained dryly.

Beneath a pagoda-shaped cover hung a giant bronze bell.

'For the curfew,' Chet went on. 'No-one is allowed out in the streets after dark. It is a rule of the Ranas.'

'But that is your name, too.'

'The family is large. Only a few in it have influence – or want it.'

'I read about the dynasty last night.'

'All is not written. That would be too dangerous to the writer – and the reader.'

'Too dangerous?'

Drummond felt his previous unease returning, a kind of indigestion of the spirit.

'Let me give you an example. Years ago, during our troubles with Tibet, a government agent reported that the Tibetans were said to be planning to advance on Kathmandu. The Rana prime minister of the day did not believe him.

' "If that is so," he told him, "you can be the first to meet them." So he strung the agent up in a cage in a tree by the side of the road, outside the city. The Tibetans did not reach Kathmandu, and the man starved to death, hanging in the air in his cage, waiting for them.'

'Why do people stand for this dictatorship?'

'Because they have no option. The prime minister has spies

everywhere. In the army, in every palace, in the bazaars, on the streets.'

'What about your driver here, then?'

'He is stone deaf. He lip-reads, but not in English. And we speak of the past, not the present.'

'And your father?'

'He is of a different branch. He should be our next prime minister.'

'So he could change all this?'

'If he becomes premier, yes. For this reason, some do not wish him to accede.'

The car drove into a courtyard and stopped. Polished brass lions guarded a staircase that led up to double doors covered with gold plate. A man came out and paused, looking down at them. He was Nepalese and wore a lightweight European suit. A silk foulard handkerchief flowed from his breast pocket, and the morning sun glittered on gold-rimmed dark glasses. His hair was thick and black like the folded wings of a giant raven. Chet paused, suddenly uneasy, almost embarrassed, like a small boy found out in his mother's pantry.

'My uncle, Davichand Bahadur Rana,' he said.

'Good morning, Dr Drummond,' said Rana. So he has checked my passport, Drummond thought. But why should such an important man be concerned at the arrival of a country doctor? Rana removed his glasses, put them carefully in a crocodile-skin case and turned away, but not before Drummond caught a brief glimpse of his eyes. He felt a stab of alarm, like the thrust of a dagger blade. These were the eyes he had seen peering at him from behind the carving of Ganesh.

An open Phantom II Rolls pulled out from one side of the palace. The driver climbed out; a servant held open the door. Rana sat down at the wheel. Guards saluted smartly as he swung the Rolls out of the courtyard.

'He is the most likely choice for our next prime minister,' said Chet, and led the way into the palace.

The hall was tiled like a giant chessboard. Drummond recalled a similar design, the size of a tennis court, in India at Fatehpur Sikri, where the Emperor Akbar had built a palace on top of a promontory. On this vast chessboard, he would set out representatives from the latest army he had defeated. A general might be king; a colonel, queen; lesser ranks, bishops, rooks and pawns.

He would pit these human chessmen against a team drawn from his own army. When a man was 'captured', slaves would instantly remove him, carry him screaming to the battlements, and fling him out on to the rocks beneath.

To drive the memory from his mind Drummond turned his attention to other furnishings in the hall. Above a marble table stood seven vertical drums pivoted on axles at each end. All were heavily carved with script. One was already turning, very slowly and in silence. As Chet walked past the others, he drew his fingers across them to set them spinning.

'Prayer wheels,' he explained. 'We believe that what you in the west call centrifugal force releases the prayers that then go up to heaven . . . The Tibetans say they invented the wheel. If so, that's what they did with it.'

'What are you praying for?' the doctor asked him. 'Or whom?'

Chet turned and looked at him. Drummond saw pain and an infinite sadness in his eyes.

'For a renewal of health in the patient you are about to see. And for the future of the country I love.'

A servant bowed and opened the door into an inner room. The floor was covered with several layers of carpet, and the furniture was dark, heavy and highly polished. A strong sweet scent of sandalwood hung in the air, like incense. From a settee at the far end of the room a man stood up and came towards them, smiling a welcome. He was of medium height, grey-haired, with a pleasant face.

'My father, Sen Bahadur Rana,' said Chet.

'It is my pleasure to meet you,' said the older man. 'You will take tea?'

He clapped his hands; a servant appeared. Within seconds, it seemed, another servant was carrying in a carved silver tray with delicate cups and saucers, a silver teapot. They sat down.

'My son tells me that you studied medicine at a university in Scotland, which he hopes to join this autumn.'

'I did,' said Drummond. 'I know some of the professors at the medical school. They were students with me. I think he will be very happy there.'

'And you live nearby?'

'Within thirty miles or so. A long way in a small country.'

'Ours is also a small country,' said Chet's father, smiling. 'But perhaps your roads are better.'

He coughed, wiped his lips with a silk handkerchief.

'You do not drink tea?' asked Drummond.

'No, thank you. I suffer, I fear, from poor digestion. It is one of the disabilities of age. Yet in my youth, or even in middle age, I was – as you say – strong as an ox.'

'Are you receiving any treatment for this?'

'I am in the hands of our practitioners.'

'Perhaps the irritation is caused by the water here? I read in a medical journal that it contains particles of dust so small that they can pass through the finest filters and then they settle on the stomach lining, like sandpaper.'

'I only drink distilled water,' the older man replied and coughed again. 'Even that does not seem to help me.'

'I would not wish to interfere with another physician's treatment, however unorthodox it might appear to me, but what other symptoms do you have, sir? Pain? Vomiting?'

'Both,' said Chet, before his father could reply. 'Intermittent diarrhoea and a growing weakness. A general lethargy.'

'I must bear these infirmities with fortitude. They are the marks of age, as scars mark the warrior,' said his father philosophically. 'I am lucky to have lived so long. Now, doctor, this is your first visit to Nepal. Tell me, how does it strike you?'

'From what little I have seen, as a country of great beauty, sir,' Drummond replied cautiously.

There was great beauty, of course, in the terraced slopes stretching to the foothills, marked by humps of hay that stood like beehives. Everything seemed green and fresh, and the air was clear and cool, like iced wine. But beneath this lay something infinitely sinister. A harsh climate and fierce extremes of heat and cold against a hard landscape bred a cruelty not readily found elsewhere.

He read the message in Sen Rana's eyes that he had seen in the eyes of countless other patients: the man was dying and he knew it. Death by poisoning would be simple to conceal here, because it was the custom for bodies to be burned; traces of poison would not survive in any ashes.

Conversation obviously tired Sen Rana, so Chet soon made his excuses and they left without mentioning St Andrews again. On the way back to Chet's palace, Drummond asked him who prepared his father's food.

'His personal cook.'

'How long has he been working for your father?'

'About six months. The other one had been with him for years, but he had family troubles in the north. He asked to leave.'

'And your father became unwell shortly after his successor arrived?'

'At least that is when I first noticed it.'

'Who is his present cook?'

'He was head cook for my uncle.'

'You are positive that this driver can't understand what we are saying?'

'I know.'

'I'm glad,' said Drummond, 'because your father is being systematically poisoned.'

'You are certain, doctor?'

'As certain as I can be without a thorough examination of the patient.'

'That would be very difficult. His own physicians would regard it as a deliberate insult.'

'That's as maybe,' said Drummond dourly. 'But if some investigation isn't made, he will die. I am not being alarmist, just stating a fact. Many men would already be dead, long before they exhibited all his symptoms. He must have an extremely strong constitution.'

'In that case,' said Chet, 'we will have to take some action.'

'And sooner rather than later. Poison has a cumulative effect, like a dripping tap that can wear away stone. At any moment, the poison content in his body may reach lethal proportions.'

They were passing under the high side of a cliff that cast a deep shadow across the road. Above it, terraces glowed yellow with mustard flowers. Drummond sensed rather than saw something move farther up the hill. A bird flew out nervously and glided on outstretched wings down the valley.

'Stop the car,' he said. 'There's someone up there. I saw a movement.'

'Probably only a goat,' replied Chet reassuringly. 'Now tell me what you advise, doctor . . .'

Up on the hillside, two men lay on their bellies in the tufted grass. One lowered a pair of powerful binoculars.

'You understood what they said?' Davichand Rana asked the Indian lip-reader.

The man repeated Drummond's conversation with Chet in English as though he had learned it by rote.

'You will be rewarded,' Davichand promised him. 'Your glasses, for a moment.'

The lip-reader handed them over to him, pleased he had achieved his mission, but surprised at what had been said. He made a good living from his gift, mostly in India, and had arrived in Kathmandu on the previous evening. He was due to leave in the morning, travelling as requested under an assumed name. The infidelities and curiosity of the rich were always of value to one with his ability.

He began to walk down the hill now, towards the road. When he was twenty or thirty feet from the edge of the cliff, Davichand called to him.

'One moment! You have dropped something.'

The man turned and looked back at him enquiringly, patting his jacket pockets in case his wallet or diary had fallen on to the ground. Davichand fired a single round from an automatic pistol a foot above his head. The lip-reader ducked instinctively, looked at Davichand in amazement, lost his balance and fell backwards three hundred feet on to the road. By the time Davichand reached him, he was dead. His relatives would not even know he was in Nepal, and if they should ever discover the fact, what use would the knowledge be to them? By then, the lip-reader's body would be reduced to ashes, scattered on some swift-running river.

Davichand climbed behind the wheel of his Phantom II, and, by driving fast, using a loopway across rough country, he reached Chet's palace just as Drummond was climbing out of Chet's car.

'I must explain my haste when we met earlier today, doctor,' said Davichand. 'I was concerned with other matters and so feel that, quite unintentionally, I was discourteous to you. Please forgive me.'

'There is nothing to forgive, I assure you.'

'You are very understanding, doctor, but I still feel my conduct was lacking in civility to a visitor. It is not as though we have many. So I wish to invite you – and my nephew Chet, of course – to be my guests at an elephant hunt tomorrow morning. The tame ones to catch the wild. A very interesting and unusual spectacle, doctor, and not one I think you will see very often in Scotland.'

*

51

As a result of this totally unexpected but very welcome invitation, Drummond now stood watching the elephants march steadily with heavy tread across the scrubby grass. He had been as surprised at Davichand's patience, when he explained exactly how the wild elephants would be caught, as he had been by the invitation in the first place. Perhaps Chet had misunderstood the man, or maybe he had been too ready to believe what Chet had told him? Surely a man of such friendliness could not deliberately be poisoning his own brother?

There was another matter he wanted to discuss with Chet, who had come to see him late on the previous evening and showed him a message he had scribbled on a sheet of paper: 'Stranger found dead on road below cliff after we passed this morning. Body already cremated. Do not mention to anyone.'

But why not? Drummond had wanted to ask whether this was where he had thought he saw movement higher up the hill, but Chet held a finger to his lips and shook his head warningly.

'Later, we will talk,' he promised, but he had not returned and now, surprisingly, although invited, he was not here to watch the hunt. Where was he?

High-pitched cries of the *mahouts* cut into his thoughts as the elephants were divided into two groups: the older ones with their heavier tusks, and the younger ones, the *kunki*.

Somewhere, a bugle brayed, and at once the *mahouts* began to shout and the *pachwas* spurred on the beasts with their spears. The elephants turned in a wide circle, and Drummond saw their quarry, a wild elephant, trumpeting, trunk up in the air, fearful yet defiant. When the elephant saw the number against him, fear triumphed, and as it started to run away, clumsily at first and squealing with alarm, the tame elephants followed him. Dust billowed in clouds. Gradually, one elephant drew alongside. Then its *mahout* expertly headed off the wild elephant. As it tried to turn away, now frantic with terror, the *pachwa* on the back of the second tame elephant swung a lassoo. The loop landed loosely and accurately on top of the wild elephant's head. Immediately, it curled up the tip of its trunk to discover what this strange thing could be.

On this instinctive animal reaction, the whole success of the hunt depended. As the tender tip of the wild elephant's trunk probed beneath the loop, the *pachwa* gently pulled the rope. The lassoo slipped down over the elephant's neck. Immediately, the *pachwa* leaped from his own elephant and, paying out the rope skilfully, wound it half a dozen times around the nearest strong tree. The branches trembled as the elephant reared up, choking and trumpeting with rage. The rope held firm, the wild elephant was a captive, never again to be free. The whole skilful operation had only taken minutes, and while the hunters went off in search of other elephants, the slow business of training the newly caught animals was already beginning.

The *pachwa* in charge would keep the elephant for as long as two days and nights without food or water. During this time, he and his colleagues would secure its legs with ropes so that it could not move more than a few yards in any direction. Finally, when the animal was hungry, thirsty, and very weary, the strongest and most loyal of the tame elephants would escort it to a river to drink.

On the third night, the *pachwa* would light fires around it, to accustom it to flame, which wild elephants fear. The animal would then be tickled for hours on end by men holding thin bamboo slivers, for an elephant's skin is tender, and in the wild state, unable to bear the irritation of a heavy howdah.

Finally, the dispirited animal would come to accept that from now on, it had exchanged freedom for servitude. There only remained an ancient Nepalese custom. In exchange for every wild thing taken alive in the forest, two other creatures must be returned. The price of a wild elephant made tame was by tradition set at two tame chickens to be set free.

Drummond could not help feeling sympathy for the huge, frightened, animal but suddenly he heard a thunder of other elephants' feet on the hard ground. The air grew sharp with the smell of their fresh dung. Something, or someone, must have frightened or angered the tame elephants – or maybe they had sighted a quarry he had not seen.

They had started to swing towards him in a long straight line, trumpeting. He saw their mouths open like huge pink caverns, their small eyes glow hot as live coals.

The doctor felt fear grip his throat, for they were racing straight towards him. Far away, he heard a car horn bray faintly, like a warning trumpet, and someone called his name frantically: 'Dr Drummond! Dr Drummond!'

Chet was running from his car, waving his arms to attract his attention.

'Get back!' he cried in horror. *'Get back!'*

Drummond stared at him, bewildered. What did he mean? Get back where? And then the earth was trembling beneath his feet under the thunder of fifty charging elephants. He shouted, but no sound came from his throat. As he started to run, one elephant raced past so closely he could smell the hot, oiled leather straps on its howdah and hear them creak and see brass buckles glitter like gold through the hot dust. Then he saw a second elephant, and a third, and suddenly, he was down.

Drummond had a brief glimpse of a howdah's crossed straps biting into an elephant's underbelly, and cried out in agony as the herd passed over him. Then he was falling softly, mercifully without feeling or pain, into an eternity of silence and darkness.

Dust blew across the dry earth, and they were gone, trumpeting away towards the foothills.

Chet ran forward towards Drummond's crumpled body, knelt by his side, felt his pulse. He looked up as Davichand jumped down from his howdah.

'You've killed him!' cried Chet. 'The elephants chased him deliberately!'

'Don't be a bloody fool! You couldn't see a thing with all this dust. Nor could the *mahouts*. And no elephant likes to harm a human. I don't have to tell you that. What the hell was he doing standing here, anyway, right in their path? I told him exactly where to stand to be safe.'

'You knew he was here,' retorted Chet angrily. 'He didn't know the danger. He's never been on an elephant hunt before.'

'Then he should have taken elementary precautions – as I advised him. If someone gets in the way of a charging elephant there's only one result. An elephant weighs as much as a car – and hasn't any brakes. He can't stop. What a terrible, terrible tragedy.'

Chet turned away; he felt physically ill. He had just seen a man murdered and he had done nothing. Worse, he would do nothing, for he knew there was nothing whatever he could do. What was the word of one witness against so many?

Davichand signalled to the drivers, who had left their cars, and stood at a respectful distance, watching them. They picked up Drummond's body and carried him back towards Chet's car. Chet followed them. Davichand gripped his arm.

'No-one told me a foreigner was coming to Kathmandu,' he

said coldly. 'I wanted to ask him why he was here, and who arranged the visit.'

'I invited him, through a friend. As you know, I am going to a university in Scotland this autumn to read medicine. It seemed a good chance to find out exactly what I could expect there.'

'And did you?'

'I did not have the opportunity for any serious discussion. We were going to talk about it later today.'

'Since regrettably you will never now have that opportunity, I can tell you that your conversation would in any case have been pointless. You are not going to any western university. I have been discussing this with your father. He agrees. With every possibility of a major European war within months, and one that could easily spread to the east, your place is here, in your own country, with your own people, your own family, the Ranas.'

'But I have accepted a place there. All arrangements have been made.'

'I have cancelled them,' replied Rana coldly.

A servant approached with a polished metal stepladder. He held it against the side of Rana's elephant. Davichand nodded a dismissal to Chet, put on his dark glasses, and began to climb up into the howdah.

The sun was not yet strong, for the morning was still young, but he wished to conceal from Chet the glint of triumph in his eyes.

Blake drove his car into the garage forecourt at Oxford, switched off the engine, climbed out. An overweight middle-aged salesman trying to look slimmer in a too tight double-breasted suit, came out of the showroom, washing his hands without water and smiling a welcome.

'Can I help you, sir?'

'I hope so. I'm thinking of selling this car.'

The salesman tapped the nearside front tyre reflectively with the point of his brown and white shoe.

'Difficult model to move. Wrong time of year.'

'But it's only June.'

'Exactly, sir. Quarter ends this month. People don't like to buy another licence when they buy another car.'

'But it has a year's licence.'

The salesman peered disbelievingly at the tax disc on the windscreen.

'So it has, sir. I didn't see that. But you know how it is. School holidays coming up. People facing extra expenses. Things you wouldn't ever imagine have an adverse effect when you're disposing of a car like this.'

'Strange thing,' said Blake reflectively. 'When you are selling something, it's always the wrong model or the wrong year, the wrong time.'

'That's just what my Daddy says. It's the difference between buying and selling.'

Blake turned. Corinne was standing behind him, leaning on the handlebars of her bicycle. The black ribbons of her commoner's gown fluttered like pennants in the breeze from a passing bus.

'I recognized the car. Only one like it in Oxford. You're not really selling it, are you?'

'Trying to, but maybe I should take this expert's advice and sell it privately.'

'My card, sir. If you have second thoughts.'

Blake put the card in his pocket, turned to Corinne.

'Pity you're cycling or I'd give you a lift.'

'But you can. I'm leaving the bike here. Got trouble with the chain. They've a mechanic here who's very good with bikes. I won't be a minute.'

She pushed her cycle into a workshop behind the showroom, came running out breathlessly, jumped into the car with Blake.

The rev counter needle fled round the dial as the SS took wing.

'This isn't the way to St Anne's,' Corinne cried suddenly.

'You're coming home with me first. To Dorset.'

'Dorset? Dorset's miles away.'

'Not in this car. It's an SS. For space shortener. We can do it in an hour and a half, have tea, and be back here in time for supper. Well, almost.'

What an extraordinary man, and so handsome, Corinne thought. And how refreshingly different from David Glover, or those other diffident pimply youths at the university Socialist Club to which she belonged in the vain hope that membership would somehow make her feel less guilty about being born rich. The countryside rushed by in a haze of dusty hedges and grass verges yellowed by weeks of sunshine. The impression was of seemingly constant, surging acceleration. Revelling in the un-accustomed sensation of speed and the fresh wind in her hair, Corinne closed her eyes.

When she awoke, the car was slowing to turn between two stone gateposts, where grave griffins held up stone crests for her inspection. She caught a glimpse of a lodge, a man opening a black, wrought-iron gate, its metal bars tipped with gold.

'A long way to walk to post a letter,' she said, for something to say.

'Well, we have an odd-job man who does that sort of thing for us. You probably do in the north, too, don't you?'

She did not reply, astonished by the beauty of the house that stood revealed by a bend in the drive. Afternoon sun had transmuted its mellow stone to gold. From giant urns carved with mythical heraldic beasts, fountains of flowers cascaded. Between the car and the house stretched a wide gravel courtyard, the size of two tennis courts.

'How wonderful,' she said in genuine amazement, mentally comparing it with her own home outside Oldham; sooty red brick, dank grass in black sodden soil, rhododendrons and laurels with dusty leaves, and in the distance, the constant hum from unseen mills. Where there's muck there's money, her father liked to tell her. There was money here, too, but the money this represented must surely be divorced by at least one generation, possibly two, and filtered over many gracious years from whatever muck had originally made it.

'Who the hell is that?' asked Blake, surprised.

He had just noticed a small black van parked almost apologeti-cally by one corner of the main balustrade.

Blake stopped the car, came round to the passenger side, opened Corinne's door.

He led the way towards the house, surprised that a maid had not already opened the front door. He pushed it open himself, and breathed the familiar smell of beeswax polish. Two suits of armour stood sentinel at the bottom of the stairs. From the minstrels' gallery hung faded regimental flags shredded with age to the thickness of veins in a leaf. Roses overflowed from polished silver bowls on oak chests and their scent hung sweet as warm honey in the afternoon air.

A leather-padded door opened and closed silently on its pneumatic spring. A middle-aged woman wearing a plain black dress came into the hall.

'Why, Mr Richard,' she said, 'I didn't see your car.'

So that's why you didn't open the door, he wanted to say, to reassure himself, but he did not do so.

'Corinne Gieves,' he said. 'Mrs Taylor. She looks after everything here. I wonder if you would show Miss Gieves the guest bathroom, and then we will have tea on the terrace? And my father? Is he around?'

'In his study, Mr Richard.'

'And whose is that van outside? Why isn't it round the back?'

'Two gentlemen have come to see him.'

'In a van?'

Mrs Taylor said nothing. But he saw concern – could it even be fear? – on her face. The sense of uneasiness he had first noticed only a second before returned more strongly. Or had it ever left him?

'If you will come this way, Miss Gieves,' said Mrs Taylor.

Blake watched them out of sight and then walked down the long hall to his father's study. He had never discovered exactly what his father studied – any more than he had ever found why his mother left home so shortly after they had moved to this house. She remained in his mind as a misty figure, vague around the edges, like an image with a halo. She had spent so little time at home, and he was away at prep school from his eighth birthday, so that everything about her was only half recalled.

The mothers of school friends lived at home all the time and made iced cakes for birthdays and wrote letters each week during every term. That was the way they did things; his mother was different. Was that to say her way of doing things was wrong? He had fought several boys who said it was, but as he grew older, he wondered.

Sometimes, in a dream, he would relive that moment when his father came into his bedroom one morning, very early, and sat down on the edge of his bed.

'I have something to tell you, Richard,' his father began haltingly, and Blake knew at once from the tone of his voice that it was something, without knowing what or why, he dreaded having to be told.

'It's about your mother. I don't quite know how to explain

this, but I believe that the best way to face any trouble, any bad news, is head on. And this bad news is that your mother has left home.'

'Left home? What do you mean?'

'She has found someone she wants to live with more than me.'

Blake wanted to ask him, 'And more than me, too? Why has she left *me*?' But his father's face had suddenly tightened as though he was being strangled by invisible hands, and he could not speak the words.

'She's been away a lot, dad,' he said as though this helped things. His father nodded.

'This time it's different. She is not coming back.'

'Not coming back. Ever?'

'Never.'

In the years between, whenever Blake tried to bring up the subject, to ask his father whether he ever heard from his mother, or had any idea where she was, or with whom, the words would simply not form in his throat.

Now Blake paused for a moment outside the study door to bring his thoughts back to the present: the money he owed to McMoffatt and to the bank. Much as he hated the prospect, he would have to explain these debts to his father; he had no other hope of repaying them.

His father was sitting in his buttoned red leather swivel chair behind his desk. Two men sat on the edge of armchairs. They wore dark double-breasted suits with stiff white collars; the knots on their drab ties were the size of small thimbles. They looked up sharply, as Richard came into the room, as though they had been caught somewhere they had no right to be, doing something they had no right to do.

Colonel Blake said: 'My son, Richard. Mr Crowther, Mr Pinwright.'

Both men stood up and bowed. They did not shake hands.

'We were just leaving,' said Mr Pinwright. 'I think you understand our situation, Colonel?'

'Perfectly,' replied Blake's father. 'No room for any possible doubt. Unfortunately.'

'So, unless suitable and satisfactory arrangements can be made by tomorrow's close of business, under the terms of our agreement, we will go ahead.'

Blake's father nodded, as though it was of little consequence

59

to him. He drummed his fingers on the leather top of his desk. The two men moved towards the door. Blake went to follow them.

'Let them find their own way out,' said his father with unaccustomed sharpness. Blake closed the door behind them.

'Who the devil are those odd coves?' he asked.

'Representatives of the Midland Widows Mortgage Company.'

'What's that, when it's at home?'

'Sit down, and I'll tell you. Feel like a drink?'

'Thank you, no. A bit early for me and I've brought a girl-friend down from Oxford. Mrs Taylor's giving us tea on the terrace.'

'Well, early or not, I'll have a whisky.'

'Those bloody men looked like undertakers,' said Blake.

'In a way they are. They've come to bury our future. Mine, at least. They own this house, and just about everything in it. They're foreclosing. Tomorrow. To use their words, at the close of business. For us, the close of play.'

'You're joking.'

'I wish to God I were.'

'How can they own it? You own it. We do.'

His father smiled, a sad twisted smile. 'That's what everyone thinks,' he agreed. 'But it's just not so.'

'But why? What happened?'

'I married your mother,' said his father, 'just after the Great War. She was a VAD in an army hospital, and I had been wounded at Verdun. She was young and pretty, and rather shaken by some of the sights she saw, people without legs, blinded, whole faces blown away. I suppose, to her, I appeared about the healthiest patient in the place. Only when I had proposed and she had accepted me did I discover how rich she was. I had nothing but my army pay, and after the war, army pay was slashed. With her money, this didn't matter at all.

'She bought this house and paid most of the outgoings. We could have been very happy, but I found it difficult to adjust to a situation where she owned everything. On duty, I might be in command. After duty, well, I wasn't. Then this other fellow came along.'

He paused.

'So she ran off with him?' Blake asked gently.

'Yes. We were divorced, and she married him. They both died

in a car crash on the way to Monte Carlo. She was a bit of a gambler, your mother, you know.'

So maybe I inherited this from her, Blake thought suddenly, but all he said was: 'I didn't see it in the papers.'

'You don't even know his name, and there's no point now in telling you. She left me this house, which was very useful when I came out of the army. The usual reasons – cutting down the forces, one in three officers above certain rank being axed, and so on. I determined, Richard, that you would never make the same mistake as I had done, giving my whole life to an ideal, King and an Empire – and then at forty odd being virtually chucked out. But then men who'd been to Oxford or Cambridge, who knew the right people, belonged to the right clubs – somehow they never felt the pinch. I wanted my only son to enjoy these advantages. I borrowed every penny I could. When a first mortgage wasn't enough, I took a second, a third, and then the most diabolical of all: one that apparently entitles the mortgagee to everything in the house, virtually whether it's mine or not.'

'So you've put everything on the line, just to help me?'

'But willingly, Richard. You didn't ask me to do it, nor did anyone else. It was my wish.'

'I feel very mean,' said Richard slowly. 'I had no idea of any of this.'

'I damn well hope you hadn't. I'd have failed totally if you had.'

'I wish to hell I had known. I wouldn't have spent money like I spent it, if I had.'

'Then you would have spoiled the whole thing, my boy.'

The colonel poured himself more whisky.

'When you say they have a lien on everything in the house, you mean the furniture, silver, glass, everything?' Blake asked him.

His father nodded.

'It's all listed?'

'No. Just as contents.'

'So if we shifted out half of it, they wouldn't know? The silver safe's full of stuff. The paintings. Damn it, they must be worth something. We could do this together.'

His father shook his head.

'Thanks for the suggestion, but that's not for me. I've had enough.'

'You can't be defeated now.'

'I'm not defeated, my boy. I'll never be defeated, because *you* are going to do all the things I have always wanted you to do. The things I wish I'd had the chance to do myself – or the sense.'

'You're not going to do anything silly?' Blake asked him anxiously.

His father smiled reassuringly.

'Certainly not. Whatever I do will be well thought out. Parents, you know, tend to live at second-hand through their children – especially if they haven't made too much of their own lives.'

'So I can take what I want out of the house?'

'Anything, my boy, because this is the last chance you'll have.'

A knock on the door scattered their thoughts.

Mrs Taylor put her head around the door.

'Miss Gieves is waiting for you, Mr Richard,' she said. 'On the terrace.'

'Give her my regards,' Colonel Blake told his son. 'And my excuses. This once.'

'Of course.'

'And take what you want to take now.'

He paused.

'But why come here in term-time? You're not in any trouble, I hope?'

'Trouble? Me? No. A few minor debts, as always, but nothing serious.'

Blake could not possibly explain the gravity of his own situation. He must think of a way out himself. His own way. On his own terms. He shook hands with his father, walked out thoughtfully to the terrace. The table was laid with home-made cakes and scones, a silver teapot and cream jug and sugar bowl.

Corinne was waiting for him.

'What a lovely place,' she said, looking up at the house.

'We rather like it,' Blake agreed. He barely recognized his own voice: he might be mouthing words and listening to someone else speak them. How could this rich girl possibly understand the anguish of his father only a few yards away? This house, which appeared to represent stability, peace and continuity, was in fact, as shallow as a painted stage set about to be struck. Soon, other actors would be playing their parts.

'You look pale,' said Corinne. 'Are you all right? Let me pour some tea.'

'I'm fine,' he assured her. 'It's just my father has had some rather bad news. A family affair.'

'I am sorry.'

He was thinking, I'll get two suitcases from my bedroom, pack all the silver in them.

He said: 'My father wants me to take some silver back to Oxford. I've got to go and pack it up.'

By half past six, they had filled the suitcases with silver. He would have taken more but was limited by the amount of luggage space in the car. He took down several pictures from the wall, tapped them out of their frames, peeled the canvases from the stretchers and rolled them up.

Every now and then on the drive back, Corinne glanced at Blake, wondering why he was suddenly so quiet, so serious, but not wanting to ask. Something terrible must have happened, she decided. What could the words 'a family affair' mean? Death? Serious illness?

It never once struck her that the man at the wheel, who appeared so rich, so confident, might, in fact, be neither.

The jeweller in the small street near the Oxford Playhouse had a face like an ageing monkey, wrinkled, with shrunken cheeks. He screwed an eyeglass into his right eye and examined the silver Blake showed him. Then he removed his eyeglass and shook his head.

'Not really the sort of thing we buy,' he said curtly. 'Sorry, but it's just not our meat.'

Blake went out into the street, not sure of his next move. His only hope of raising money to pay off the bank was by selling this silver and the paintings somewhere – but where? The bank had not been in touch with him again, after the message from Mr Marsh, which he had not answered, but it could only be a matter of days before they were. And if he could not pay off his debt, they would nail him to the wall. False pretences would be the least of the charges. Only that morning he had read in the paper the case of a young man who had been sentenced to two years' hard labour for a confidence trick that had only brought him a thousand pounds. What sentence would he get for five – and an additional debt for four?

The college entrance courtyard was packed with trunks, suitcases and bicycles, all bearing luggage labels. Two under-porters were loading a Carter Paterson lorry. Blake went into the lodge.

'You must be the last one here, sir,' the head porter told him. 'All the young gentlemen have gone.'

'Any address for Mr Glover?'

'I think I can find one, sir.'

The porter rummaged through an address book, wrote the address on a piece of paper, handed it to Blake. A pound note changed hands.

'Thank you very much, sir. Wish all the young gentlemen were as generous. The very best of luck in the future, sir.'

Two hours later, Blake was parking his car outside a small house on an Edwardian estate in North London. A wicket gate led into a narrow garden down a path of imitation crazy paving. Glover answered the front doorbell. He was in shirt sleeves, smoking a cigarette.

'Hello,' he said with surprise, and could it also be embarrassment that Blake had tracked him to such an unfashionable address? 'What brings you here? Have I left something behind?'

'Not really,' said Blake. 'I just want your advice.'

'*My* advice?'

'Well, you're going to be a solicitor. You must have good contacts. I want you to advise me where I can sell some silver. For cash.'

Blake took him out to the car, lifted one suitcase out of the space behind the seat, opened it, unwrapped a spoon, a goblet, two mustard pots with blue glass inserts.

Glover said slowly, 'This is worth a hell of a lot.'

'That's what I thought. But I tried a jeweller in Oxford. He didn't want to know.'

'I may be able to help you. Do you a good turn. Though you didn't do me so many, did you, with Corinne, eh? To come down to basics, if I introduce you to a buyer, what's in it for me?'

'What do you want in it – or out of it?'

'Ten per cent. In notes. Introductory fee. Right?'

'If you say so.'

'I know someone who could be interested. Hatton Garden way. Don't ask his name and he won't ask yours. He'll offer you a price, maybe by the piece, maybe by weight. Not stolen or anything, is it?'

'Of course not.'

'All right. No offence. Just asked.'

They drove south in silence through afternoon traffic, turned off Gray's Inn Road into the back streets behind Hatton Garden, stopped outside a brick building with bars across the ground floor windows. A blue Lammas-Graham was parked outside it.

'Here we are,' Glover told him. 'You take one case, I'll take the other.'

Glover pressed a bell several times; two long, three short touches. The front door opened silently on an electric lock. They went up a flight of uncarpeted stairs. A dark-skinned man in a sharkskin suit came out of a room on the second landing to meet them. He did not shake hands or introduce himself, but motioned them into the room, and locked the door behind them.

The room was empty except for a table, four wooden chairs and a big safe.

'A friend,' said Glover, indicating Blake without mentioning his name. The man nodded as though the matter was unimportant.

'Let's look at the stuff,' he said. Blake lifted one suitcase onto the table, opened it. The dark-skinned man took a pair of wash-leather gloves from his jacket pocket before he handled the silver. When the suitcase was empty except for twists of tissue paper, he walked around the table twice, looking at the silver from different angles.

'Three hundred,' he said.

'It must be worth more,' said Blake. 'I mean, that rose-bowl. It's been in the family for at least a hundred years.'

'Whose family?'

'Mine, of course.'

'There's a crest on it,' said the man. 'Would spoil it, taking it off.'

'It doesn't have to come off. It's the family crest.'

'Your family's not buying the stuff,' the man pointed out. 'Three thirty. Last price. What's in the other case? Save undoing it.'

Blake told him.

'Probably a touch more. Seven hundred for both. Cash now.'

'Too little,' said Blake shortly. He began to wrap up the items and put them back in the suitcase.

'Price only lasts until six o'clock today, son. I can't hold till tomorrow.'

'I'll remember that,' said Blake.

Glover followed him down the stairs in silence. A buzzer sounded behind them, the door opened and closed on its lock.

'Who's he? A fence?' asked Blake, as he lifted the suitcases back into the car.

'Just cautious,' said Glover defensively. 'It's a rough business, dealing in silver.'

'Where does he live?'

'Mill Hill way.'

He gave him the address.

'But I wouldn't contact him there. Reach him through me. He's touchy about callers.'

'Sorry to waste your time,' said Blake. 'That's a ridiculous price, but thanks for trying to help me. Can I drop you home?'

'Thank you, no. I'm going up west myself,' Glover replied.

Blake buttoned down the tonneau cover over the suitcases, climbed into the car, drove slowly south into Holborn. The offer was absurd. The stuff must be worth several times as much, and yet how could he realize it? He hadn't time to put it up for auction, and his experience with the jeweller in Oxford did not augur well for London. Then he reached a decision.

Outside the Holborn Empire he saw a telephone box, stopped the car, climbed out, looked up Hamish McMoffatt in the telephone directory.

Ten minutes later, he was sitting in a room above a tailor's shop in Savile Row. On the panelled walls hung coloured prints of Diomed winning the first Derby in 1780; King Edward VII's Minoru in 1909, the Aga Khan's horse Mahmoud in 1936.

'What do you want to see me about so urgently, son?' asked McMoffatt. 'To thank me for making you a fortune the other day?'

He was sitting behind a vast desk, its leather top green as Epsom turf, and as bare, except for a telephone, the bronze carving of a race horse, and a paperweight made from a golden stirrup. The smell of cigar smoke hung expensively in the air.

'I wish I were,' said Blake. 'But I have to tell you, Mr McMoffatt, I was an idiot. I didn't put a single penny on. I backed someone else's choice to win. Sindbad the Second. I lost the lot.'

McMoffatt shook his head in disbelief.

'You should have taken my tip, son,' he said. 'You'll never get another like it. So what do you want to see me about now? My boys not bothering you again, are they?'

'No, nothing like that. I need a job, Mr McMoffatt. You mentioned when we last met that maybe we could do business together.'

'Ah, that was then. This is now. And doing what? You're a gambler, son. We don't gamble here. This is strictly business. Gamblers are people we take money from. What do you fancy doing, anyway? On the course?'

'I don't know. I don't care. I just need money. Quickly. I borrowed from the bank to pay you. After that race I can't pay it back.'

'How much?'

'Four thousand to you. Five to them.'

McMoffatt raised his eyebrows.

'A lot of money, son. What security did you give?'

Blake paused. He had not meant to tell McMoffatt the extent of his need, but there was something not unfriendly about the man. He had told him so much, why not admit everything?

'I said I was going to buy a garage. Cars are my hobby.'

'And they let you have that amount of money without sight of deeds or anything? You must have great powers of persuasion – or you're a wonderful con man.'

'Not very successful, if I am.'

McMoffatt stood up, turned his back on Blake, thrust his hands in his pockets, stood looking at the traffic in the street below.

'No, you're not,' he said. 'You're a bloody fool. You've had far too much far too easily. You look the part of a gent, but that doesn't mean you are one. Any more than an actor who looks like an ambassador or brain surgeon when he's made up in a play, is one. Someone's given you so much rope you've damned near hanged yourself. But why come to me? Why not go back to your old man or doting aunt, or whoever it is who's paid your bills up to now?'

'I can't. My father's virtually bankrupt.'

'Seems to run in the family then. Now why should I employ

someone with such poor financial judgment? My business is about money. But not spending it or losing it. Making it.'

'You said you liked my style,' said Blake. 'I rather like yours.'

'Thanks for the compliment. But if you work for me it's on a low wage and commission. I'm not a moneylender.'

'I have family silver in the back of my car that must be worth several thousands. It's all I could salvage. Plus some paintings. A Goya, two Turners, and so on. If you don't lend, do you buy?'

McMoffatt shook his head.

'You're honest,' he said slowly. 'But, as I said, you're a fool. Too handsome, too easy a time. You can't help that – it's the sort of life I'm giving my own kids, though I know it's damn silly. However, that's not your affair. You've just been at the wrong end, the receiving end. I won't lend you any money because, as I say, I'm not in that business. I don't buy silver, either, but I'll do something I've not done in a long while. I'll trust you. I'll give you a job and I'll lend you nine thousand quid. When you can, you pay me back. I have some loose cash that the Income Tax people don't know about. It might as well help you as do nothing. But I'm not an idiot, Blake. I'll keep the silver and paintings as security. When can you start work?'

'Now!'

'Give me a couple of days. Then ring me. You'll begin at eight o'clock, sharp, each day.'

'In the morning!'

'No. Evening. I have a house in Grosvenor Square. We hold gambling parties there every night, usually all night. That's where you'll work.'

'I just don't know how to thank you, Mr McMoffatt,' Blake began, astonished at this offer from a virtual stranger.

'Bring your rich friends. That's how. Spread the word. Oh, and by the way, your pay will be ten pounds per week and ten per cent commission on our profit. After all expenses.'

'How do you know there will be a profit? Is it rigged?'

'Never. We don't have a magnet or a brake to slow the wheel. We just work out the odds scientifically. The bias is always on the wheel's side – our side. There must be some wins, of course, or the punters won't turn up next time. But we are the real winners, otherwise we don't stay in business.'

'Why private parties for the rich when you control so many bookmakers under other names?'

'Because, like you, I have a debt to pay – under my own name. I don't like rich people.'

'But you're rich yourself?'

'Relatively. Not really rich – yet. And there's a difference. I made it myself. They inherited it from someone else who did all the hard graft. I take them for everything I can. Every day, every night, every week. I may take their insults and their condescension. But above all, son, I take their money. And now, you will help me.'

McMoffatt smiled, pressed a button on his desk, spoke to his secretary.

'Give this gentleman a bearer cheque for five thousand pounds. Special account,' McMoffatt told her, and lit another cigar.

Blake walked down the stairs with the cheque and the number of the house in Grosvenor Square in his pocket. As he climbed into his car, his mind still in a whirl of relief and amazement, he touched the canvas tonneau cover that covered the luggage space behind the seat. It felt slack, like the side of a tent with a loose guy rope – and it should have been stretched taut as a drumskin above the two suitcases. He ripped the cover from its press-studs. The luggage space beneath it was empty.

In horror, Blake jumped out of the car, looked around it, even underneath, in case by some inconceivable chance, he might for some unknown reason have lifted them out and forgotten he had done so. He hadn't.

A small man sidled up to him, rolling a cigarette, running his tongue along the edge of the cigarette paper.

'Lost something, mister?' he asked Blake, not looking into his eyes.

'Yes,' said Blake. 'Why?'

'I might be able to help you. A quid first. For the info.'

Blake gave him a pound note.

'Right,' said the man. 'I'm a runner for Mr McMoffatt's firms. You looked like a toff who might be going to see the boss, so I watched you. Might be a quid in it for me – as there has been. Bloody great blue car came up behind you. Man got out, walked up to your motor here, lifted out two suitcases, climbed back into his car, and pissed off.'

'What make of car was it?'

'Odd name. Lammas-Graham.'

'The driver on his own?'

'Nope. One bloke sat in the front, looking rather nervous. The driver was very dark. Maltese, maybe. You know 'em?'

'I know 'em. How long ago?'

'Minutes.'

'Thanks.'

Blake climbed into his SS, drove to Mill Hill.

The house was smaller than he had imagined; red brick with a green and white striped canvas cover over the front door to protect the paintwork from the weak North London sun. The Lammas-Graham was parked outside on a short, pink-tinted concrete drive-in. Fifty yards up the road, a boy was sitting on a push-bike, pedal down against the edge of the kerb, carefully writing down in a notebook the numbers of cars that went by.

'Get that blue Lammas-Graham back there?' Blake asked him.

The boy consulted his book.

'Yes,' he said. 'Why?'

'I've a bet with a friend,' replied Blake. 'That's why. Want to earn half a crown?'

'Doing what?'

'By going back to where that car is and ringing the front doorbell. See what the man says when you ask if you can have a look at the engine.'

'I don't like the look of him. I think he'll say, No.'

'That's exactly what the bet is about. Will he agree or not?'

'Funny sort of bet.'

'Funny sort of world. You can have the half-crown now, if you'll do it.'

The boy turned his bicycle, held out his hand. Small fingers closed around the coin.

'You go ahead,' said Blake, when they were still twenty yards away.

'Where are you going, then?'

'The back garden. To see my friend.'

He walked quickly up the path between a wattle fence and the house. Two milk bottles on a concrete step at the back door wore porous terra-cotta covers. He went behind the house, beneath a clothes line. French doors opened onto a small lawn, with two deck chairs and a table. He walked through them into an over-furnished drawing room. Armchairs wore velvet covers, piled with plushy velvet cushions. Pictures in gilt frames showed little girls holding baskets of flowers.

He heard a doorbell ring and the boy ask politely: 'Please, mister, can I look at your car's engine?'

'No, you damn well can't. Cheeky devil. Get out of it.'

Blake recognized the dark-skinned man's voice. He opened a door carefully into the hall, crossed it on tiptoe. In the kitchen, his two suitcases lay open on a table. The silver had already been removed, and was stacked neatly on the draining board. Glover was plugging in an electric kettle. He turned.

'My God!' he said hoarsely.

'What's happened?' called the other man from the front of the house, as he hurried through the hall. As he came into the kitchen, Blake banged the door in his face. He staggered back, still not aware of Blake's presence.

'What the hell?' he asked angrily.

Glover could say nothing. He simply stood trembling, one hand still holding a packet of Typhoo tea. The kettle began to whistle. Mechanically, eyes still on Blake, he reached out and switched it off. The dark-skinned man came into the kitchen, saw Blake – and kicked him hard in the crotch.

The blow could have killed if it had connected, but Blake dodged to one side, seized the man's shoe with one hand, his ankle with the other, and twisted sharply right and left. Then he pulled and suddenly pushed with all his strength. The dark-skinned man collapsed. As he went down, Blake brought up his left knee into his face.

He dropped on the kitchen floor and did not move. Blake pulled a tea towel from a rack above the sink, ripped it in two, knotted the pieces, then bent down and rolled the man over on his face. Blake pulled his arms up behind him and tied his wrists with the towel. Then he turned to Glover.

'What's your part in this?' he asked him.

'I had to do it. My old man owed him a favour.'

'So why are you here? Tea for two? A chat about how it's turned out nice again? I agreed to pay you ten per cent, Glover, the figure you asked for. We've known each other for three years living on the same staircase in the same college. And now – this. Pack the stuff back in the cases and put them in the car.'

Glover began to wrap the silver in tissue paper, glancing nervously every now and again at the man on the floor, who began to groan. Blake prodded him sharply in the stomach with his shoe. The groaning stopped.

Glover carried the cases out of the house, put them behind the seat of the SS, buttoned down the tonneau.

'You won't get away with this,' he said with unexpected bravado.

'What the hell do you mean? He's damn lucky to get away with a few bruises – and you're even luckier with nothing at all. You could both do time for this. Wouldn't help your prospects as a future Solicitor General.'

'Sarcastic bastard, aren't you?' shouted Glover, his face suddenly puce with futile rage. 'I'm fed up with your money and your whole condescending bloody attitude. Sure, we were on the same staircase for three years – and what about it? Did you ever ask me to any of your parties, except to get me to pass round the drinks, or even pay for the bloody drinks? You ask me out on the river – just to make a fool of me. And I even paid for the punt.'

Blake stared at him in surprise. He had no idea that Glover could feel so strongly about his attitude; he had never imagined that Glover might be seriously offended. He had somehow assumed that he would accept his position as someone favoured to be included in Blake's circle of associates. Blake realized now he had been an idiot, unthinking and unfeeling, simply because his own good looks and good fortune had never made him consider other people's feelings. Now he would. But this was no moment for apologies or explanations. He drove away thoughtfully and did not look back.

His first essential need now was to find rooms in London, somewhere central. At a crossroads, with the traffic lights against him, he bought an evening newspaper from a man walking from car to car, and pulled in to the side of the road to look through the classified advertisements for flats to rent. The best bargain seemed to be 'gentlemen's furnished chambers' in Jermyn Street for £3 a week, including maid service.

An hour later, he had taken a two-room flatlet for a month, payable weekly in advance. He placed his suitcases in the wardrobe, locked it, put the key in his pocket. The rooms looked faded, but clean enough, a relic of Edwardian London; a Turkish carpet, heavy brocade curtains, antimacassars on two easy chairs with sagging springs.

He picked up the telephone and asked the operator to connect him to the bank in Oxford. It was after hours, but there was a chance someone might still be there. Mr Marsh answered. Blake recognized his voice.

'The bank is actually closed,' Marsh explained. 'Perhaps you could kindly telephone tomorrow?'

'I think you would rather hear what I have to say today,' Blake told him and gave his name.

'My God,' said Marsh, his voice trembling with relief. 'Mr Blake. Thank goodness you 'phoned. I have been trying to reach you for days without success. There seems to have been some terrible misunderstanding. That garage is not for sale, I discover. What about my money?'

'Not yours, actually; the bank's,' Blake corrected him. 'That's why I'm telephoning. As I explained, it was a secret deal, and now, as you say, it's off. I'm posting you a cheque tonight to cover the whole thing.'

'Thank you,' said Marsh. 'Thank you very much indeed.'

He replaced the receiver and thought longingly of the bottle of sherry in his desk drawer. But, no, that was habit forming. Yet his whole life was ruled by habit: home at six to the little house in Botley, supper with his wife, an hour listening to the radio, then a cup of cocoa and an early night. Perhaps, after all, there was something to be said for living an ordered, routine life, with the reassurance of habit. More than something, he admitted. There was everything.

On an impulse, Mr Marsh changed his mind, unlocked his desk and took out the bottle of sherry.

Blake went out into Jermyn Street, walked up the road to the nearest bar, ordered a whisky and soda, drank it thoughtfully, ordered another. He felt more tired than he realized. The incident with Glover had shocked him, coming on top of the news about his father's affairs. Now that he had a job promised, he must do all he could to help his father. He would have a bath, a meal, and set off right away for Dorset. If he hurried, there might still be a few more things he could save from the broker's men.

A young couple came into the bar, holding hands, and sat down at a corner table. Blake opened his newspaper. Rioting engulfed Vienna; Hitler's patience was exhausted; the world seemed thick with threats and portents of war. He turned the page.

A Scottish doctor had been killed in Kathmandu. Dr Jamie Drummond, of Coupar Angus, Perthshire, had somehow got in the way of a charging elephant and had died instantly.

Blake turned over that page, passing time, and a headline in the STOP PRESS hit him with the force of a body blow. He lowered the page, feeling physically ill. The couple in the corner looked at him and the girl whispered to the young man and giggled. Blake picked up the paper again and read the report for a second time.

COLONEL FOUND SHOT

'Colonel Patrick Blake, DSO, MC, aged 60, who served in France and Mesopotamia during the war, has been found dead in his country home in Dorset. A service revolver was by his side. Police have taken possession of a note. Foul play is not suspected.'

3

Jerrold sat in the back bar of a public house off Greenwich High Street. He used this bar when he wanted to meet contacts who had a story to sell or who required a few pounds down for an introduction to some elusive third party. The bar's main merit was that it was not near Fleet Street, so reporters from rival newspapers were unlikely to see him.

The only other customer, a small man in a shabby suit, sat opposite him, on the far side of a disconnected electric fire. His shirt had no collar, and he had not shaved for the past two days. He possessed the face and physique of a rat, incongruously dressed like a man. He had recently been released from prison, and the *Globe* had serialized his story. The news editor had sent Jerrold to discover whether there was a possibility of extracting another series, even a further single article out of him.

'There must be something,' said Jerrold persuasively. 'What about Mr Big – the mastermind of crime? That sort of stuff.'

The man shook his head.

'Your paper has been fair with me,' he said. 'I could tell you things, but they'd be too risky. I've grown fond of my kneecaps and elbow joints.'

He grinned in a yellow-toothed, horrible way.

'Ever thought of making some money for yourself instead of paying people like me?'

'Often. But how?'

'In a way that a toff like you can do easily. I met a bloke in the Scrubs who'd worked this racket several times. In for drunken driving.'

'Tell me,' said Jerrold, not really interested, but thinking that this might just contain the germ of an article, which in turn would allow him to claim inflated expenses for an otherwise wasted evening.

'Right. You find a young girl whose old man's got a lot of

money. An only child – no brothers or sisters. All the money goes to her when the old man kicks the bucket. He only wants the best for his little girl. With me?'

Jerrold nodded.

'You put up someone who's no good. Old school tie, la-di-dah, nice car – you can hire one for a week. He takes the girl out, maybe even gets across her. You go and see her old man. Wear his old school tie, if he's got one. Find out a bit about him if he hasn't, so that he'll trust you. You tell him you come as a friend, to warn him about a terrible mess the apple of his eye is going to get into. You can stop this, before it's too late – before she's in the club – for a thousand quid, say, maybe two. Not for you, of course. But to buy off this cad before he elopes with her.'

'Would he pay?'

'They always pay, so this bloke said. It's a sort of insurance premium, if you like, for them. And better than working, for you.'

'Ingenious,' allowed Jerrold, 'but I don't think I can make an article of it.'

'Stuff the article,' said the man. 'A thousand – or two or three – nicker up your own shirt would be much better. Get me?'

'Yes,' agreed Jerrold slowly. 'I really think I do.'

The family solicitor was on holiday in Scotland. Blake shook hands with a partner he had not met before, a small man wearing a black suit and a black tie. He looked uncomfortably like the undertaker Blake had already visited about his father's funeral.

'The will is quite straightforward,' the solicitor assured him. 'Everything is left to you. But it appears your late father suffered, shall I say, considerable pecuniary embarrassment.'

'He was very good to me,' said Blake.

'Quite so. You are, after all, an only son, and he was extremely proud of your achievements at the university. You had the sort of life there he would have liked. No doubt you now have a career in mind?'

'Yes,' said Blake. 'You could say that.'

'I'm very glad to hear it. Not all young men today have the sense to keep their feet firmly on the ground. Of course, the times we live in are very unsettling. All this talk of war. I thought that after Munich last year that was finished. But no, it's starting again. Now, to business, unpleasant as it is. We have these very unfortunate documents. The first mortgage here. A second one. A third, and one of the most punitive nature.

'He insured himself heavily, to raise money for you to pay them off. Unfortunately, Mr Blake, there is a clause in the small print in a sub-paragraph at the bottom of the back page of the policy. "Notwithstanding anything that has been agreed in any of the foregoing, a verdict of suicide whether of unsound mind or not would instantly render null and void all the aforesaid benefits of this policy as above described."

'So I'm afraid you won't even get back the premiums he paid. There's also a penalty clause.'

'He couldn't win if he lived, and he loses if he dies. Is anything left at all?'

'I fear not. The mortgagees have already exercised their prerogative. Indeed, they claim that some silver and paintings, which apparently one of their employees had seen and was about to enter in the inventory, have disappeared. Would you know anything about that, Mr Blake?'

'I really know nothing about my father's affairs,' Blake said, thinking of the suitcases now in McMoffatt's office. 'I would like to see the house, even so.'

'By all means,' the solicitor replied.

As Blake drove through the gates of the Grange, he had to pull to one side to let a truck come out.

'A plain van, I see,' said the solicitor approvingly. 'They usually use one in these circumstances. More discreet.'

The house was empty of all furniture. Carpets had disappeared, leaving unpainted floorboards, pale and forlorn, with borders of dark wood stain around the skirting. Lighter patches on walls showed where pictures had hung. All that was left in the hall was a suit of armour, that had apparently been too heavy to move. A sticker was pasted on it: 'Do not remove under penalty of prosecution. Property of the Midland Widows Mortgage Company.'

Mrs Taylor came out of the kitchen.

'I saw you arrive, Mr Richard,' she said. 'I've made some tea for you and your guest. Two things they haven't taken yet, the caddy and the teapot. I hid them.'

Mrs Taylor's tea was sweet, yet it tasted sour on Blake's tongue. If only I had been closer to my father, he thought, perhaps I could have prevented the final tragedy. Death seemed unnecessarily finite. While life remained, there was always the chance you could reverse a situation, however sombre it might appear.

'Have you been paid?' Blake asked Mrs Taylor.

'Only up to the date of your father's death.'

'Is there any money for the staff?' he asked the solicitor.

'I'm afraid not, Mr Blake. There is simply no money at all.'

'And there's nothing we can sell here to raise any? Mrs Taylor has been here for as long as I can remember. So has the head gardener.'

The solicitor shrugged his shoulders and blew on his cup of tea.

'I would like to give each of them at least a month's money,' Blake told him. 'It's not much, I know. But it's all I can afford – at the moment.'

He could not let down these loyal people who had given years of their lives to serving his family.

'I'll give you a blank cheque,' said Blake. 'Pay them and fill in whatever the total is.'

He turned to Mrs Taylor.

'Do let me know when you're settled,' he told her. 'Perhaps one day I can again employ you all.'

Blake drove back to the solicitor's office.

'If there *is* anything . . .' the solicitor began awkwardly, as he climbed out of the car.

'There is,' said Blake. 'Can I use your telephone?'

'Of course.'

He rang McMoffatt.

'Just to let you know I'm ready to start.'

'Good,' said McMoffatt. 'Eight tonight, then. Dinner jacket. Grosvenor Square.'

'I'll be there,' said Blake and replaced the receiver.

'I couldn't help overhearing the conversation,' the solicitor told him in a shocked voice. 'Going to a party this evening, after your father's suicide, and selling up the family home?'

'Hardly a party,' Blake explained. 'It's my first night in my new job.'

A gong boomed plaintively from the hall. Corinne went out of her room, carefully switched off the light – her father hated unnecessary extravagance – walked downstairs to the dining room. Heavy wallpaper, stained wood doors, and a dark table under one heavily shrouded lamp that cast a circle of pale light on the three places laid for dinner; beyond this rim of light the room seemed dark as the hills beyond the town.

'The soup,' her father said shortly. 'It's getting cold. Didn't you hear the gong?'

'I came at once,' Corinne replied.

'Aye well, sit down and tuck in. It's Betty's evening off, you know.'

Her father pushed across a plate of cut slices of bread. She shook her head. She didn't feel like bread. Neither did she feel like this brown Windsor soup, thickened by flour, tasteless, except for salt. She sipped a glass of water.

'Tell me about Oxford,' said her father. 'What are you learning there?'

'Oh, lots of things.'

'You know it's books, Thomas,' interrupted her mother sharply. 'That's all there is at university. She's not learning anything to do with your mills.'

'There are five damned good mills to inherit, and every one now on double shifts. I've been taking on people quicker these last few months than I've done since the war, twenty years ago. We are making a damned good profit, I tell you that.'

'We really need this house redecorating,' said Corinne's mother, glancing around the drab room.

'It's one thing to make money, another to spend it,' replied her father. 'Ever thought about what you're going to do when you finish at Oxford, child? Come down, as I think you call it?'

'I don't know really,' Corinne admitted.

'Well, start thinking. There's no reason why a woman can't sit on my board. After all, you are a Gieves.'

'Perhaps she'd like to be a teacher,' suggested her mother.

'A teacher? In a classroom, breathing chalk dust all day with a lot of snotty-nosed kids? My lass has more sense than that.'

The meal dragged on. The roast lamb was as tasteless as the Windsor soup, and all flavour had been boiled out of the potatoes and cabbage, but Corinne scarcely noticed. She was deep in her own secret private world, driving down to Dorset with Richard Blake, the most handsome man in Oxford, perhaps in all England, who didn't need to pretend she was attractive simply just because she was rich, because he was also rich. She must have made a hit with him. Perhaps she really was attractive – not in the accepted sense of being pretty, but maybe in a deeper, more abiding way?

They were half way through the trifle and custard when a maid came into the room.

'You are wanted on the telephone, Miss Corinne,' she said.

'On the telephone? At this hour?' asked her father in amazement. 'Who's calling? Someone you have met at Oxford, eh?'

He looked at her archly. Corinne smiled. He meant well; he was kind enough, under all that archetypal roughness. Perhaps he would have been even gentle if he had a wife who understood gentleness; if he'd ever had anyone to tell him there were other values than those evidenced by a twenty per cent net return on his cotton mills, and writing down the cost of all new equipment. But then, if he had known other values, they might not be living in this big house with two maids, a cook, a gardener and chauffeur, and she might not be at Oxford. More important, in that situation, she might never have met Richard Blake.

She followed the maid out of the dining room, picked up the receiver.

'Hello,' she said brightly. 'Corinne here.'

Over the miles of wire, faint and metallic, she heard Richard Blake's voice, and she stood there, transfixed with joy and surprise. The maid eavesdropped from behind the kitchen door, but she could only hear Corinne's replies, not what the caller was saying.

'Are you sure?' Corinne asked at last.

Then: 'All right. It's not a joke? No, of course not. Don't be angry, I just asked. I'll be there, as you say. Goodbye.'

She replaced the telephone. The maid banged the kitchen door to make it appear she had just come out of the kitchen and was not going in, but Corinne did not even hear her. She paused for a moment outside the dining-room door, listening to her father's voice. He was talking about Hitler and Czechoslovakia, and what would happen if Hitler marched on Poland. It all meant nothing to her. Nothing meant anything to her except Richard's voice, still echoing like music in her ears.

She came back into the dining room, sat down at the table.

'That was quick,' said her father.

'Yes.'

'Not bad news?' her mother asked anxiously. She belonged to

a generation when unexpected telephone calls or telegrams must mean crisis: news of an unsuccessful operation, a relative's death.

'No, nothing like that,' Corinne answered her, smiling at her parents.

How could she tell them that Richard Blake had just asked her to elope with him? And that she had agreed?

On the evening before Blake telephoned, McMoffatt had called him into his office.

'I have been looking at the returns on Grosvenor Square,' he told him. 'They're dropping.'

'The punters just aren't betting as much as they used to. It's all this talk of war. They're more cautious.'

'It's not entirely that,' said McMoffatt. 'We're just not drawing in enough new people. We need to get in the news, and to become talked about. You want to get yourself in the papers as someone who will bet on anything. Then others will tag along, for you'll be the hook to pull them in.'

'I've a friend on the *Globe*,' Blake explained. 'Rex Jerrold. But unless a gambler's been found shot dead because he can't pay his debts, he says it's not news.'

'Well, make it news. Think up some stunt with your friend. Run away with an heiress. After all, this is the silly season. They'll jump at a story like that.'

Jerrold didn't actually jump, but he did express a cautious interest in McMoffatt's suggestion about the heiress. Why not be chased by her angry father, then have a Gretna Green wedding? He could bring in something about gambling, of course, in the article. Marriage: was it the biggest gamble of all? That sort of thing.

'I'm not marrying anyone,' replied Blake firmly.

'You don't have to. Just race around England and Scotland, and back down over the border to Gretna Green. Her father reaches there just in time to stop the wedding. He could horse-whip you, and you let the girl go. Virtue rewarded.'

'What's in it for me?' Blake asked.

'Publicity. What you want.'

'I don't know any heiress,' said Blake, and then he remembered little Corinne Gieves. He mentioned her name to Jerrold.

'I've heard she's around,' said Jerrold vaguely. 'And she's damned rich, isn't she?'

'She will be. When she's twenty-one. But she's not a socialite. Anyhow, she might not come away with me.'

'With your looks? I don't think she'll say no. Let's work out a basic deal, all expenses paid. We could travel in my car, which means we can charge the *Globe* for three cars – one for you, one for Corinne, and one for me to follow you in – and you collect a fee. Say, a thousand pounds.'

'What's the least I have to do for that?'

'Run off with her. We chase through places where the *Globe*'s circulation is poorest. The West of England. Then up North to Scotland. Then maybe we could hire a plane for the hop south to Gretna. I'll have someone tip off the father so that he is there for a wonderful climax. You back out. "The Gambler who lost the Girl." Bloody good headline.'

'I don't like much else about it. Is Corinne to be in on all this? Or will she think I really care?'

'That would be best, of course.'

'But she'll think me a hell of a heel when she finds out.'

'Doubtless. But, then, that's life. You want publicity and that is the price you pay. You could split the money with her, if you like. It'll only be paid, of course, on publication. But it might sweeten her up a bit. Money can't buy love, but it can lessen a degree of hatred.'

'How long will this rubbish take?' asked Blake in a resigned voice.

'As long as we can hold the public interest. Not a moment longer, I assure you. Corinne is a bit dull and frumpish but she will be bloody rich. She might even think it fun. She'll be wildly flattered if you ask her to elope.'

'She might take the offer seriously?'

'So she ought. And if she does and then discovers it's all a stunt, she'll never let on. Pride. She'd look a fool. A pretty girl can stand that. A plain one daren't take the risk.'

'I feel a total shit.'

'And so you should, Blake. But that's a feeling you'll soon become used to.'

Jerrold nearly added: 'If you haven't already', but stopped himself in time. Blake was the bigger, stronger man and there was no point in antagonizing him unnecessarily.

Corinne paid off her taxi, stood for a moment outside the Ritz, savouring the excitement: Piccadilly in bright sunshine, packed with shining, chauffeured cars, red buses cruising like splendid galleons against the fresh green background of the Park. Blake should be here, but he wasn't.

Had he been joking, making a fool of her? Was it all a kind of April Fool's Day prank that she didn't understand? She fought back such thoughts and walked up the steps. A commissionaire bowed, swung open the door, and she gave a great sigh of relief, for Blake was sitting under one of the palms in the lounge.

In the background, a string orchestra was playing "The Voices of Spring", and Corinne's heart soared with the music. Blake stood up, came towards her. He was smiling, and he embraced her. He did not attempt to kiss her because he guessed that she would be embarrassed. Also, he felt it would be a Judas kiss. He was not in love with her, not even slightly attracted to her. He was simply using her as a means of pleasing his bookmaker employer, and making a thousand pounds for himself from the *Globe*. What would she think of him if she discovered the real reason for his telephone call? For 'if', read 'when', he thought without pleasure. He had no wish whatever to hurt her, but it would be difficult not to, he realized, as he looked down at her eager, trusting, innocent face. Could he somehow manage not to do so, let her walk away from him, instead of the other way round?

'I thought we would start as we mean to go on,' he said with all the enthusiasm he could muster. 'Champagne cocktails.'

'The only time I've ever drunk champagne was on the river.'

'That was the start,' he said. 'Let's take things from there.'

As Blake started to walk towards the foyer, Corinne pulled him back.

'You are serious?' she asked him earnestly. 'It's not just a joke or something, running away with me?'

'A joke?' Blake repeated, trying not to meet her eyes. 'Whatever gave you that idea? Would I ask you to come here – and off with me – as a joke?'

'I hoped not. But it all seemed so sudden. I mean, we'd only been on the river once together and then I came down to your home in Dorset. It's an awfully short acquaintanceship, don't you think?'

'I do think. And I do agree. But with some things – and some people – you know right away.'

'And this is one of those times?'

Blake swallowed and looked away; this was going to be more difficult than he had realized. He could not bring himself to say the words. Corinne squeezed his hand. Her eyes were bright with excitement – or could it be tears?

'And I'm so surprised,' she said softly. 'I mean, we hardly know each other. I wouldn't have thought I was your sort. But I'm so pleased I am.'

Blake ordered three champagne cocktails. Bubbles soared in their glasses as swiftly as Corinne's spirits. Then Jerrold came into the foyer as they sat down.

'I didn't know you'd be here,' she said.

'You know each other?' asked Blake, surprised.

'We have met. Through David Glover.'

'He's coming with us,' said Blake.

'Who? David?'

'No. Rex here. We thought it would be rather fun if he came along for part of the way to write some articles for his paper.'

'About us?'

Corinne looked from one man to the other in amazement.

'Well, yes, but only in the nicest way. Runaway lovers. I thought it would be rather nice for us to keep later on. A sort of memento of the time when we were like Romeo and Juliet.'

'Juliet died,' Corinne said flatly.

'Not a very good example, perhaps, but you know what I mean. You are only young once.'

'Where exactly are we going to, then, the three of us?'

'Why not down to Devon, to some fisherman's cottage by the sea?'

'And are you staying with us?'

'Good Lord, no. Not all the time, at least,' Jerrold replied hurriedly. 'But my car's a bit more comfortable than Richard's and more room for luggage, too.'

'Another drink,' said Blake.

'But I haven't finished this.'

'Well, you had better start as we mean to go on.'

Blake clicked his fingers at a passing waiter, who hurried across to them; Blake had that effect on waiters.

Several cocktails later, they all piled into Jerrold's car, a black Railton saloon.

'You drive,' Jerrold told Blake. 'With Corinne in the front. I'll write my story in the back as we go.'

Corinne giggled. The cocktails had been stronger than she realized; she felt a little dizzy, almost sick, but all this was such fun. She had left her parents a note, saying what she was doing, and promising to telephone them. One day, she would explain everything: she was sure her father would understand, even if her mother didn't.

Blake drove out of London along the Bayswater Road, then around the White City. Slowly, the suburbs fell away and they were on the open road. The car felt old and flabby.

'The brakes are like sponges,' Blake complained. 'And the engine wouldn't pull the skin off a cold rice pudding.'

'You're too critical,' retorted Jerrold. 'Far better than being blown all over the place in your open car.'

'Have you still got that?' Corinne asked him.

Blake turned slightly, smiling at her.

'Until I can find a buyer, yes,' he said.

In that instant of turning his head, he missed the flickering dim glimmer of a mud-caked stop light on the back of a Bedford van twenty yards ahead. Too late, he heard Corinne scream a warning, saw the high tailgate race towards him in a sudden blur of unrelated words: Service and Civility our Motto.

The Railton's brakes squealed in protest as he flung the car sideways. For a split second he smelled scorched rubber and then the world turned white. Their windscreen had frosted with the force of the impact. He became aware of a great pain boring into his head like a drill. Pain grew like a tree within him. He could not see anything clearly, only vague shapes.

He tried to open the car door, but the lock had jammed. People were outside now, with crowbars, levering back the sunroof, shouting down at him.

Then, mercifully, the darkness which had been waiting on the other side of Blake's mind suddenly engulfed him like a tide and he fainted.

The casualty ward in the cottage hospital was small; only three beds. Jerrold was in one of them, still unconscious, a bandage around his head. Blake stood by him, with a doctor.

'Will he be all right?' he asked.

The doctor was middle-aged and tired of sorting out the debris of other men's motor accidents and the results of unthinkingly mixing speed and alcohol, too much money, with too little sense.

'Should be,' he said shortly.

'What about the girl?'

'In a bad way. She's in the infirmary. We couldn't cope with her injuries here. The police will want a statement, as you were driving. Been drinking, had you?'

Blake was about to say, only champagne, but saw the doctor's cold, contemptuous face.

'Only a little,' he admitted.

'A little's too much.'

'We were going away,' Blake said slowly, not sure whether he was trying to seek sympathy or to explain his actions. 'We were going to be married.'

The doctor's face softened slightly.

'I'm sorry,' he said gruffly. 'I feel I should tell you, she'll never walk again, you know.'

Blake came into the room, low-ceilinged, its walls decorated with framed posed photographs of civic luncheons, where plump men shook each other's hands solemnly and mayors wore gold chains around their necks. Gieves was waiting for him.

'You wanted to see me,' Gieves said, making the statement sound like a question.

Blake might have been visiting with a business proposition: a failing mill for sale, the rights of a new dyeing process to be picked up at a knock-down price.

'I felt I should, sir,' Blake began diffidently.

'You were driving, so they said. Been drinking, I understand.'

'We had a champagne each.'

'Unlike my lass, to have champagne.'

'She said it was only the second time in her life, sir,' replied Blake. 'The first was at Oxford.'

'I knew no good would come of that place. My old father said, go to any university and learn how to make a thousand a year. Go to Oxford or Cambridge and learn how to spend it. Well, what do you want to see me about, lad? This has hurt her mother and me very much. She is our only child, you know. We had the greatest hopes for her. But these things happen. No-one's to blame.'

'I am to blame,' replied Blake. 'Corinne had just said something that made me laugh, and I took my eyes off the road for a second, and that was it.'

'She liked you, then? And I didn't know about you until the police told me.'

'Mr Gieves,' said Blake. 'You may hate me for this, but I was running away with your daughter.'

'Running away with Corinne? I don't believe it.'

'It's true. She told me she'd left a note.'

'I didn't know. Her mother never told me. But that's women all over. Endless chatter about unimportant things and over something like this, not a word. What were you going to do, then? Have a dirty weekend?'

Gieves's voice sounded menacing.

'Nothing like that. She wasn't that sort of girl.'

'You're damn right, she wasn't. She was well brought up. She wanted to keep herself for the right man. But now . . . I don't know.'

Blake said nothing, remembering the doctor in the casualty ward. It was as though Corinne was already dead: they were speaking of her in the past tense.

'What was the other fellow doing in the back? The newspaper man?'

'Rex Jerrold was a friend from Oxford,' Blake explained. 'The less said about him, the better for everyone.'

'What about the other thing?'

'What other thing?' asked Blake cautiously.

'You know the bloody other thing,' said Gieves. 'With that newspaper fellow in the car with you. Name of Jerrold, you say.'

'I don't quite understand.'

'Then I'll help you to understand,' said Gieves shortly. 'This so-called friend of yours came to see me a couple of days before the accident. Told me a crook was hanging around my daughter. I could get rid of him for three thousand quid. So I paid him, for otherwise this scoundrel would marry Corinne just to get the money she'd inherit at twenty-one. Was that the arrangement between you and your – ah – friend? That you'd split her money?'

'This is the first I've heard of it,' replied Blake in amazement.

Gieves put his face close to his and stared at him for a moment, eye to eye.

'I didn't make my pile by being taken for a fool,' he said slowly at last. 'I'm a bit like a policeman or an egg-sexer. I can tell a bad 'un a mile off. And you seem honest enough to me. Bit of a waster, but with your background that's to be expected. But not a crook. You give me your word you know nothing about this?'

'Nothing at all.'

'I believe you, lad. I believe you. I'll probably never see you again, and I won't tell my lady wife you called. It would only hurt her. But I'm glad you came, and I'll think about you. And about . . .'

Gieves's voice trembled and broke; he could not bring himself to speak his daughter's name. Gieves turned away and busied himself with a pocket watch so that Blake would not see the tears in his eyes.

August–September, 1939

At half past three on a Wednesday morning early in August, Blake handed over to his deputy, and smiled farewell to the gamblers still around his table. Beneath the green shaded lights, their faces looked as grey and lifeless as the flesh of drowned cadavers. Above and beyond them, chandeliers blazed like frozen waterfalls of stars. Waiters wearing white breeches and red cutaway coats with gold epaulettes eased tight wigs half an inch forward over tired foreheads and yawned behind white-gloved hands. Night after night, the sight of so much money being squandered by such greedy, unattractive people, the proximity of so many rat-trap mouths and hog eyes, flushed with wine and avarice, soon became wearisome when you were only earning three pounds a week plus tips.

Blake stepped out of the huge room into a corridor with an open window, and paused for a moment to breathe the clean early-morning air uncloyed by scent and sweat and stale cigar smoke. In the white-tiled coolness of the men's cloakroom, the figure of a gambler in top hat, white tie and tails was etched briefly on the frosted glass of the door which swung silently shut behind him. A middle-aged punter, lapels stained with wine, wearing a faded rose in his tail-coat buttonhole, was standing behind the door.

'Going home?' he asked Blake.

Blake nodded cautiously. Was the man about to proposition him?

The punter walked quickly in patent leather shoes across the chequered tiles to make sure that all the cubicles were empty. Then he approached Blake.

'I've been watching you for the last few nights,' he announced. 'You can make the wheel stop on any number you like, can't you?'

'No. Let's say it could be done – theoretically.'

'Would a thousand quid convert theory into practice?'

'In what way?'

'To win. I need to make a killing. Badly.'

'Don't we all?' asked Blake. 'But even if you made it, you still wouldn't leave. Not if you are compulsive. I know, because I've suffered from gambling fever myself. In a milder way.'

'And McMoffatt employs you? He must be mad.'

'Or a very good guy. Which is how I regard him.'

'You stop the wheel on, say, my lucky number. What do you say?'

'I say, no.'

'Fifty-fifty each, then.'

'No. I can't do it.'

'What do you mean? Can't or won't?'

'Both. Good night.'

At eight o'clock the following evening, when he arrived at the house in Grosvenor Square, McMoffatt was in the hall, lighting a cigar.

'A moment before we start,' he said brusquely. 'In my room.'

He held open the door, closed it behind Blake, opened a cocktail cabinet.

'Drink?' he enquired.

Blake shook his head. Long hours in the vitiated atmosphere of cigar and cigarette smoke were tiring enough without adding any unnecessary alcoholic hostage to wakefulness. McMoffatt poured himself four fingers of Hine, held up the glass to the light.

'I understand a punter offered you fifty per cent of the winnings – if you cheated,' he announced casually.

'You are well informed.'

'Of course. So why did you turn down his offer?'

'Because I work for you, not for him. Or even for myself – unfortunately.'

'You could have made a fortune – like he said – if you'd played along with him.'

'Or I could have made nothing,' said Blake. 'Either way, I would have been swindling you. And you helped me when I needed help. An odd way to repay your kindness.'

McMoffatt sipped his brandy thoughtfully.

'Life has taught me that if you help a lame dog over a stile, you must expect to be bitten. You're unusually lucky if the bite doesn't poison you. And, brother, you were a very lame dog.'

Blake said nothing.

McMoffatt went on: 'I think I can trust you. I wasn't entirely sure before, but now, yes. So I'll tell you, I deliberately set you up with that guy. I've used him before to check the integrity of various people. He owes me a lot of money, which I'll probably never see, so I let him off something from his debt whenever he helps me like this. I wanted to test you, Blake.'

'Why?'

'Because I have a proposition to make to you, and I had to be really certain before I told you. I gave you a chance to make a lot of money, last year, backing Rainbow Trout. Right? You didn't believe me, and you lost the chance.

'Now a lot more people owe me many more favours, and I'm going to cash them in the same way as I did with the bookies then. Draw my pension, is how I look at it. There's going to be a war, Blake, and all this business could fold up overnight. No chance then to have favours repaid. So I'm cashing in now, while I can. And I'm cutting you in because I need someone I can trust. Better half a loaf, eh?

'Now, the deal. Every now and then I hear on the bugle that this horse or that is going to win a certain race. The fixers ask me to limit what I put on in case it affects the odds, and simple punters get suspicious. But now I've a chance to make a real once-and-for-all killing and I'm taking it. I want you to bet on three different horses on three different courses.'

'In my own name?'

'Of course. And in person. I want you to be seen, so the bookies will know you exist, that you're not just a false name over the 'phone. I'll lend you an imposing car and I'll advance you cash. Ten thousand quid.'

'A hell of a lot of money,' said Blake. It would take him twenty years to earn that on his present salary. 'You are sure you can trust me with that amount?'

'I'll take that risk,' said McMoffatt.

'What's in it for me, then?'

'Double the money – twenty thousand. In notes. In a suitcase, minus the money I staked you with when you came to see me, of course.'

'You're on,' said Blake at once. 'Now, what about that drink you offered me?'

So it came about that on Thursday of the following week, Blake drove a hired Buick Eight saloon west to Exeter and put £2000 in fivers to win on a horse of which he had never previously heard, and whose name did not appear in any tipster's list. The horse came in first at 32 to 1. A steward's objection was disallowed.

The next day, Blake travelled north to Doncaster, splitting £6000 among three bookmakers on a horse to come in second. The horse obliged after another objection was overruled. On Saturday, he motored south to Newbury, and put £2000 on an outsider to finish third. The outsider finished third.

Later that evening, Blake drove on to Marlow. The car park at the Compleat Angler on the edge of the Thames was filling up. He noticed two MG Midgets, a Triumph Dolomite roadster, an Aston Martin, a Cord Sportsman. As Blake walked purposefully through the bar towards the restaurant that overlooked the river, McMoffatt hailed him with well-feigned surprise.

'My dear fellow, fancy seeing you here on a Saturday night. Thought you'd be up west.'

'Rather off my beat, this,' Blake admitted. 'Thought I'd drop in – I'm on my way back to Town.'

McMoffatt ordered two brandies.

'So am I. But by train. Could you by any chance give me a lift instead?'

'Of course. Whenever you're ready.'

They finished their drinks quickly. McMoffatt left a five-shilling tip on the counter, glanced casually around the bar; no-one seemed interested in them. He led the way out of the hotel, said nothing until he climbed into the front seat. Then he asked the question uppermost in his mind.

'Got the money?'

'In the boot. In a suitcase. Locked and chained to the floor. Here are the keys.'

'Good boy. Then let's get the hell out of here in case anyone else knows what's in it, too.'

Blake drove fast all the way to London, parked in Jermyn Street, began to climb out for McMoffatt to take the wheel.

'See you at eight o'clock tomorrow evening,' McMoffatt told him. 'Then you'll have your share in tenners.'

'I can use it,' said Blake. 'I'm down in your books as owing you ten thousand pounds – plus that original nine thousand pounds. A lot to be in hock for when you're earning a tenner a week.'

'Paper entry only,' grinned McMoffatt. 'So that I can charge it against tax as a business loan that never will be repaid. That way I make it on both sides of the street. Can't be bad, eh? Eight o'clock tomorrow night, then, and you'll be in credit.'

As Blake closed the car door, all the lights in Jermyn Street went out.

'What the hell?' cried McMoffatt in amazement. Then he remembered.

'Ah! Black-out trial in case there's a war. It was in the papers. I'd forgotten. They'll come on again in a few minutes.'

In the dimness of an early September evening, people were blowing whistles and calling to each other. A girl giggled. Torches glimmered like glow-worms along the pavements. A man stumbled heavily against the side of the car, and shouted angrily. Blake smelled methylated spirits on his breath. In the glow of the side lights, he looked unshaven, shabby, a down-and-out. He bent down shakily to peer into the driver's window.

'Nearly broke my bloody arm,' he said angrily. 'Got the price of a drink, gov?'

'You've had enough already,' McMoffatt told him. 'Beat it.'

Blake saw another man's face pressed briefly against the rear window of the car; thin, alert, with bright eyes, not a drunk. Then they were both gone.

'Who are they?' asked McMoffatt. 'Couple of drunks? Who cares, anyway? Until tomorrow, then.'

Blake stood watching the Buick's tail-lights diminish down the street, then went up to his rooms, pulled the curtains, sat down in the sagging armchair and turned on the radio. An announcer broke into a variety programme with a brief news bulletin. The Cabinet was going to meet in Downing Street on the following morning, Sunday. They were awaiting a message from the British Ambassador in Berlin. Unless Herr Hitler withdrew his troops from Poland by eleven o'clock that morning, a state of war would exist between Great Britain and Germany. There were reports of troop movements in Germany. Holiday-makers in France were crowding the Channel ports, eager to return to England. Black-out exercises were in operation in London and along the South coast.

War. Blake switched off the radio. He had been so busy thinking about his bets that, unlike McMoffatt, he had totally disregarded infinitely more important events happening in Europe. He felt a sudden almost overwhelming sense of unease and foreboding.

Blake switched off the light because of the black-out, opened the curtains and looked out over the still-dark street. People were singing, laughing and calling to each other. Several young men were kicking a tin can like a football along the middle of the road, passing it expertly from one side to the other. Cars moved past slowly and warily on sidelights.

Blake closed the curtains and turned on the light. He did not feel hungry. He had been travelling too much over the last few days to have any appetite, and yet it seemed too early to go to bed on such a night, possibly the last night of peace.

He poured himself a brandy and soda he really did not want, and sat, looking at the bubbles rising in the glass. The telephone rang, jerking him out of his thoughts. He picked up the receiver, Jerrold was on the line.

'Where have you been?' he asked Blake accusingly.

'Why?'

What the devil was it to do with Jerrold?

'Your boss, McMoffatt. He's dead.'

'Dead? But I saw him only minutes ago.'

'Then I hope you said goodbye, for you'll never have the chance again.'

Blake felt muzzy, as though he had been suddenly awakened from a long drugged sleep.

'I don't understand. Is this a joke, or something? What's happened to him? A car accident? Heart attack?'

'Neither. He drove back to his house in Grosvenor Square, got out of his car, and according to a couple of people who saw him arrive, walked round to the back of it and bent down as though he was looking for something. Then the whole damn car blew up right in his face.'

'Blew up?'

Blake suddenly remembered the drunk reeling against the car, beating on the roof, the sharp disembodied face he had seen pressed against the rear window.

'What was it, a petrol leak?'

'Bomb, more likely.'

'A bomb?' Blake repeated in bewilderment. 'I don't understand you. How could a bomb be in his car?'

'If I knew, I'd have a damn good page one story. All I do know is that the car's a total wreck and still burning, and McMoffatt's dead. We've sent a photographer round there.'

'But why ring me?'

'Because we've had a tip-off,' said Jerrold. 'The buzz is that you're involved. Thought I'd better tell you before anyone else gets to you.'

'Anyone else?'

What did Jerrold mean? How could he imagine he was involved with McMoffatt's death? Again Blake remembered the face at the car window. Could that man have tied some device to the rear bumper? Was that what McMoffatt was looking for when the car exploded? His throat felt dry. He drank the brandy gratefully, and poured himself another.

'The word is you owed McMoffatt thousands,' Jerrold continued. 'It's down in his books, apparently. Then there's been some funny business at the races. You were seen at three courses this week, putting on heavy bets.

'So what? That's my affair.'

'Not if it isn't your money. And not if you're betting on rigged races. Bookies don't like that – not if you're taking a lot of money off them. Our informant says they've made their feelings plain to your late employer in the most convincing and finite way. My feeling is that you could be next on their list. So, as an old friend, if you've got your skates or running shoes handy – get 'em on!'

Blake was fully awake now. Something about Jerrold's sudden concern was wrong, out of character. Why should he suddenly ring him, stressing his friendship – unless he wanted to be certain where he was? Had Jerrold told Gieves that he was the adventurer after his daughter's money? Or was there someone else?

A thumping on the street door two floors below momentarily scattered Blake's thoughts. He switched off the light again, put his head cautiously out of the window. A car had stopped outside the building and a man was leaning with his back against it, arms folded, while another man beat on the front door with his fist. Blake drew the curtains.

'Are you still there?' Jerrold asked urgently. 'I hear a banging noise. What's happening?'

'Someone's at the front door. One of your reporters?'

'Impossible. They're all out covering other stories. This mock black-out is our page one lead. More likely the callers just want a quiet word with you, as I said. But don't open to them, whatever you do.'

'What the hell is this about? I'm absolutely in the clear.'

'You've been set up,' Jerrold replied patiently. 'Can't you understand that?'

I understand perfectly, thought Blake. But by whom – you or someone else? The man in Jermyn Street began to kick the front door.

People were shouting down at him angrily from other rooms.

'Shut up!'

'Get out of it!'

'Cut out that noise.'

'I'll ring the police,' said Blake. 'Tell them what you're telling me.'

'Don't waste your time. They'll be sewn up. How do you think all this illegal gambling's allowed to go on? Graft, that's how. Well, I've done my good deed, warning you. So good night. Sleep well.'

Blake replaced the receiver. Immediately, it began to ring. He put out his hand to pick it up and then paused. Whoever was after him – if Jerrold was right and anyone was – might not be certain he was at home. But the moment he answered the telephone, they would know. And at that hour on a Saturday night, he could not think of any other reason for anyone calling him.

He let it ring, walking around the room, opening drawers, piling clothes into a suitcase. It was time to leave, to disappear. But where could he go? Where could he hide? He had no close friends or relatives here, or indeed anywhere else, on whose doorstep he could arrive unannounced, late and afraid, virtually a refugee. And what about the money due to him from McMoffatt?

He dialled his number. There was no answer – so it seemed he had said goodbye to that windfall. Blake now felt panic begin to surge like a tide within him, and tried to force himself to think calmly, rationally. He heard footsteps run downstairs, and confused shouting in the hall. Someone had come out of another room and was going down to open the front door. More shouting, and then the drum of heavy feet racing up the stairs. It was too late now for Blake to lock his room door, and even if he could have done so, whoever was coming up the steps two at a time could smash its simple lock with a single blow. He placed himself behind the door, and waited.

A man kicked the door open and charged through, head down. Blake tripped him. A second man stumbled over the first and fell. As they lay writhing and cursing on the floor, Blake picked up a vase, and broke it over the first man's head. Then he grabbed his suitcase, and ran down the stairs and out along the darkened street.

He had neither plan nor destination in mind, only the knowledge that he must escape, somehow, somewhere. As he reached St James's, the street lights came on again with a dazzling glare. The all-clear siren was blowing, and people crowded out of a restaurant to cheer and clap. A man in a dinner jacket raised a glass of wine to him on the pavement, as though he was running a race. A taxi, 'For Hire' sign alight, slowed helpfully. Blake jumped in.

'Where to, guv?'

'Grosvenor Square.'

He gave the first name that came into his mind. The taxi accelerated away.

'What number?'

'Just round the Square,' Blake told him. He peered out of the rear window. No-one was behind him.

A police Wolseley and an ambulance were parked outside McMoffatt's house. The Buick Eight was on its side, paint blistered, back blown open. Firemen played hoses on steaming raw metal and policemen held back a small crowd of onlookers. Blake saw a body on the pavement covered by a sheet.

'What number, guv?' the cab driver repeated.

'Back to Piccadilly,' Blake told him.

He was not being followed; he was sure of that. But where

96

could he go? They passed the Ritz, and the Park loomed dark and empty to the left – a sombre contrast to that sunny day he and Jerrold had set off with Corinne. Shops were brightly lit on the right; showrooms for MG, Sunbeam-Talbot, Humber; Green Park underground station. Several young men in sports jackets and flannels and trilby hats had gathered around the brilliantly lit window of a requisitioned shop. In the window was a model destroyer, all grey paint and guns, an aircraft suspended from a string, the poster of a smiling young soldier in shorts, uniform jacket and cap, holding a football under his arm. 'Join the modern army,' he read. 'Work and play the world over.'

That poster make Blake's mind up for him. He would join up, and immediately submerge his identity in the safe anonymity of uniform. If Lawrence of Arabia could do this successfully, so could he. Who would come searching for a private soldier in barracks? He could bide his time, work out a response to his pursuers – and then buy himself out when it suited him. And if war did come, as now seemed likely, then that would help to pay all debts, even his own, for he would have been called up in any case.

'This will do,' Blake told the cabby. 'Stop here.'

He did not wait for his change, but ran into the shop. An over-age sergeant, grey hair short and bristled like steel wool, wearing waxed moustaches and two rows of medal ribbons, sat behind a desk laboriously writing with an Army issue pen. The nib spattered drops of ink on the page. He looked up, frowning, as Blake approached.

'Just closing,' he said. 'Only kept open so long because of the crisis. Lucky to find me here at all on a Saturday.'

'Then it's the only good luck I've had all day,' Blake told him.

'Don't be too sure,' said the sergeant ponderously. 'Only the infantry left. All the rest have waiting lists.'

'Give me the form and the King's shilling,' Blake said. 'I don't care what I join so long as you can get me out of London fast.'

'Like that, is it? Got her in the club, have you?'

'Worse, much worse,' Blake assured him.

'Can't attest you tonight. Got to have your medical first. Earliest they'll do that is Monday – unless war breaks out tomorrow, of course. You could have your medical in Chatham or Dover. I can give you a warrant for either. Catch a train tonight, if that's any help to you. Have to make your own arrangements, bed and breakfast, though.'

'Gladly.'

The sergeant picked up a travel warrant and dipped his pen into an issue bottle of ink.

'Right, then,' he said briskly. 'Let's be having you. Name, age, next of kin.'

4

Darkness fell gently, like an immense and silent shroud, across the empty paddy fields. In the brief Burma dusk, the low mud ledges that divided these fields into huge squares gave the landscape the appearance of a giant patchwork quilt. During the monsoon months, when rain poured down almost ceaselessly, these squares would fill with water, and soldiers marching over them trudged in water up to their knees. Their feet swelled like sponges and the skin on their legs grew soft and sodden. Leeches, sliding slimily under the tongues of their boots, would gorge on their blood and grow to the size of cigars.

Now, as Blake looked over the empty darkening scene, this was weeks away and the air still felt dry and dusty, thick with the chirp and twitter and tick of unseen insects. It was against all orders to smoke openly, but a cigarette kept away mosquitoes, and to conceal the tell-tale glow, he and others had devised a simple shield. In the lid of an empty cigarette tin they punched a hole just large enough to accept a cigarette, and knocked a few smaller holes in the base of the tin to allow the smoke to escape. What no-one saw, no-one cared about.

Earlier that day, he had glanced in his diary and noted with surprise that it was nearly five years since he had joined the Army; five years since McMoffatt had died and he had taken a taxi along Piccadilly to the recruiting office. It might have been fifty years, or even a century, for events had telescoped so closely into each other that in retrospect it seemed that months passed with the speed of days. To Chatham to enlist as a private soldier; to Dover, as a lance corporal; then to India and on to Belgaum, near Bombay, to the Officers' Training School, and now, as a captain, he was second in command of an infantry company in the Arakan.

He had never even heard of the place before, but its long stretches of empty beach and miles of rice fields, with sudden jumbled clusters of elephant grass and bamboo and jungle stretching to the Mayu range of mountains, had been a kind of home to him for the past eighteen months.

In those five lost years, he thought ruefully, he could have established himself in some worthwhile way; qualified as a doctor or a barrister; made a fortune in business, and yet all he had done was to mark time, counting it sufficient that he was still alive, not wounded, maimed, blinded, like the poor devils he had watched being evacuated to some casualty clearing station miles away, tied to bamboo frames on the backs of mules because they were too weak to walk, and no ambulance could traverse the narrow jungle tracks.

On several occasions, Blake had tried to improve his finances in the only way he felt open to him – gambling – but totally without success. He had lost money on racetracks in Cape Town, where the troopship carrying him to India had stopped briefly; and in Bombay and Calcutta, where, too late, he had learned that many of the races were rigged. The only letters he had received in the Arakan were from bookmakers or debt collecting agencies, forwarded from half a dozen intermediate addresses. He returned them all to their senders with the same advice scribbled on the envelopes: 'If you want the money so badly, come and get it.'

Some day, he realized, he would have to settle with them, but he put such unpleasant prospects out of his mind as often as possible. For the moment, it was enough that he was still alive when so many others of his contemporaries had been less fortunate.

All around him he could hear a faint rustle of movement. The company were on the alert, at stand-to for the day's most dangerous time: the last hour before total darkness. He could hear the familiar, muted click of rifles being cocked, of actuator handles on Tommy guns being pulled back. Men with eyes red-rimmed with dust and heat and weariness watched for the slightest movement beyond a rapidly shrinking horizon.

Someone jumped heavily into the slit trench beside him. He smelt gin and he knew that the company commander had arrived. Before the war, the major had worked in a suburban grocer's shop. Blake often pictured him slapping mounds of butter with flat wooden spoons, diligently slicing bacon on the machine, selecting the biggest, brownest eggs for the richest customers.

He was a short, chubby man, who sweated inordinately and resented Blake's looks and background. He also believed that Blake was very rich, which increased his envy and fuelled his dislike.

'A job for you,' he said shortly, without any preamble. 'Something special. Brigade's just been on to the CO. The Japs have a launch coming up the river tonight with supplies. I've got the map reference for a jetty they're supposed to stop at. They're due about midnight. If you leave here at nine, you should be okay.'

'But we've just come back from a three-day patrol,' said Blake.

'So you'd better go out again. Keep your weight down. Come over to company office soon as this is over, and I'll give you the griff.'

Half an hour later, after stand-down, Blake was sitting in a primitive bamboo hut called a *basha*, lit by a single, shaded hurricane lamp. The major was a heavy smoker; he lit a fresh cigarette from the stump of one still in his mouth. Across the bamboo table sat a third officer, a stranger, dark-skinned and quiet; in the dim light, Blake could not make out his features clearly.

'This is Chet Bahadur Rana,' the Major said. 'Captain. Intelligence. Attached to Brigade. He's coming out with you tonight.'

Blake shook hands with Chet. It was not unusual for officers to arrive, to make one patrol and then to leave the day after they returned. Explanations were rarely given or even asked for. They might be medical specialists, making a field study of malaria or sweat rash, or signals wallahs testing radio equipment. They came and they went, quickly and unremarked on. Captain Chet Bahadur Rana must be only one of many such itinerants.

'Been up here before?' Blake asked him. If he was to be stuck with the fellow on this lunatic scheme until dawn, he might as well find out what he could about him. He had neither the time nor the wish for passengers.

'Never,' Chet replied. 'I was only detailed this afternoon to report at once. So I came right over.'

'Just to this battalion, I suppose?'

'No. To this company. They even gave me your name.'

Odd, thought Blake; but then the whole war seemed odd and far too long in the tooth. He no longer asked for explanations.

'So I'll have to be your guide,' he said. 'On the basis that in the country of the blind, the one-eyed man just has to be king.'

'This isn't a bloody mothers' meeting,' said the major crossly. 'All your quotations. Not at Oxford now, you know. And you've not got all night.'

'I thought we had,' Blake retorted. 'You said the launch wasn't due until midnight.'

'But you've got to brief your men, check your weapons,' said the major irritably, lighting another cigarette.

An hour later, they were on their way in single file, twenty men wearing jungle green, sweat-soaked uniforms and gym shoes for silence instead of boots. Bandoliers of ammunition for rifles and magazines of cartridges for the Tommy guns were slung around their bodies. They had rubbed black boot polish mixed with anti-mosquito cream on their faces and the backs of their hands, and they walked from long practice with scarcely a sound, apart from the soft scuffing of rubber-soled shoes in the dust.

The moon had risen. It was not full, but half-hearted and thin – like my enthusiasm, thought Blake. How his ambitions had shrunk virtually to vanishing point! Once, success had been his aim. Now, it was simply survival – and the hope that some day, somehow, he would find money to pay his creditors.

Trees held up a lattice of branches against the feeble moon. Dust rose, thick as flour, as they marched, and coated faces already streaked with sweat. When anyone brushed away a mosquito or a night moth, it was like rubbing sandpaper across his skin.

Blake calculated that they should be able to sink the launch; the difficult part would be to escape afterwards. According to the map he had studied under the hurricane lamp, there was a small village on the edge of the river, where the launch should berth. They reached this shortly before midnight; a little line of black dots on the map were suddenly translated into square bamboo huts. Some, built up on piles, had pigs snorting underneath; other huts crouched on the bank, in dark silhouette against the silvery reflection of moon on water. Outside some of them, fires flared smokily, lit to cook an evening meal and left burning to ward off evil spirits. From the rim of darkness surrounding the village, dogs barked a warning of the approach of strangers, and beyond them, in the jungle, hyenas wailed.

Mosquitoes buzzed and hummed in Blake's ears as he halted

the patrol. From the end of the village a jetty poked its long wooden finger over the river. Several canoes carved from hollowed-out logs were moored to its upright supports. For a moment they reminded Blake of punts moored off the Cherwell boathouse in Oxford, so much a part of the past that they might have belonged to another life. In a sense, he thought grimly, they did. They were part of a faraway scene lit by the kindly lamp of memory. This was reality: the smell of fear and danger, the raw rash on his body where the straps of his pack rubbed his soft sweating skin, the taste of exhaustion on his tongue; and in the back of his mind, gnawing doubts about the value of the whole affair.

The tide was low, and frogs croaked asthmatically on stinking mud. Now and then, he could hear a crocodile slither into the water. The men lay, rifles and Tommy guns cocked, in a semicircle facing outwards, a hundred yards from the nearest hut. The earth felt warm through the thin stuff of their uniforms. Blake hoped that the dust that swirled about them did not irritate anyone's throat; a cough or a sneeze now could be fatal.

He glanced at his watch; its luminous hands showed ten minutes to midnight. They would not fire until the launch had tied up at the jetty because they would have a far better chance of hitting a stationary target. Some would aim at the engine, others below the water-line. One concentrated burst of fire, then they would withdraw hurriedly before any Japanese reinforcements could arrive.

A hand touched his elbow. He turned. Chet was by his side.

'Down to the right,' he whispered. 'A small boat.'

Blake raised himself carefully on his elbows. He felt so tired he wondered whether he had momentarily dozed off. He should have been alert to any movement; after all, he was in charge of the operation. This fellow Chet was proving useful. He strained his eyes and could just see a man paddling slowly away in a wooden canoe. Was he only a fisherman about to start his night's work – or had the man seen the patrol arrive and was now off to intercept the launch and warn the Japanese crew? Either way, there was nothing they could do about it. If they fired on him, they would only give away their own position.

Blake had to let him go, but he felt uneasy, as though unseen eyes were already watching him. How had the movements of the launch been discovered in the first place? Had someone deliberately fed them the information to lure them into a trap? His scalp prickled at the thought. Was this totally absurd, the figment of a tired mind – or was it true? If it was true, they had walked right into a trap they had set for their enemy. That idiot major; Blake should have checked with his sources of information before he had agreed to this. Questions chased answers and never caught them.

The dogs suddenly stopped barking. Was this a good sign or a bad one? The locals, at this hour, should all be in their huts, with bamboo doors closed, smoke filling their tiny rooms to drive out mosquitoes. So why wasn't this man with them? It was useless brooding on the problem.

'Pass the word,' Blake whispered to Chet. 'Five minutes to go. Safety catches off. No one to fire until I fire. Then, a couple of mags and fall back with me.'

He heard the murmur of the message being repeated, man to man, and wondered what sense it would make to the last man who heard it. Would it be any more accurate than words he had heard whispered so often at pre-war parties, and passed on down a line of people, to emerge at the end as a nonsensical paraphrase?

The faint throb of an engine drove these thoughts from his mind. The sound grew louder, like a heavy heart beating, as a launch came into view. She was old-fashioned, sitting high out of the water, like a lifeboat, with a wooden cabin and a mast. A faint haze of exhaust smoke billowed round her stern like steam. The fan-like wash she set up made reeds and rushes nod and tremble at the edge of the river. He could not see any sign of life aboard.

She approached steadily, very slowly drew level with the jetty, and turned. A man came out of the cabin and jumped on to the jetty, carrying a rope. He wore Japanese uniform with puttees. A second soldier followed him, and stood, one hand on the cabin roof to steady himself. The engine stopped. There was no sound now but the dying chuckle and suck of the launch's fading wake against the jetty. Blake raised his Tommy gun and took aim at the first soldier.

His finger tightened steadily on the trigger, and then, before he could take second pressure, a hail of shots poured at his patrol from the nearest hut.

Blades of flame stabbed the darkness. Blake emptied one magazine into the launch cabin, sprayed the edge of the jetty with another. He threw away the empty magazine, snapped on a third, turned towards the huts and raked them with fire. Other members of the patrol were also firing, some into the huts, others into the launch. He heard shouts and cries of pain and anger and then the launch suddenly erupted in a great orange ball of fire as her petrol tank exploded. In the huge blaze of light he saw his men kneeling, lying, desperate to find what cover they could, but all still firing. The sight was like a waxwork military tableau; nothing seemed real except the hail of bullets.

'Get back!' he yelled and waved towards the darkness on the far side of the village. In the diminishing glare of the fire they ran, bodies bent double as though, by drawing in on themselves, they could minimize the area they offered as a target.

Blake waited, firing systematically into the huts, one after the other, until he calculated that all his men would be through the village and out into the comparative safety of the dark beyond.

As suddenly as it had started, the firing stopped. He could hear men calling to each other in unknown voices. Were they Japanese or Burmese sympathizers? There was a loud clucking of hens, and snorts and grunts from hogs, and a frantic mooing from water buffaloes disturbed and terrified by the noise. In the background, the launch was sinking slowly, blazing wood and red-hot metal hissing in the water.

Every door in every hut stayed closed, but were eyes still watching them through holes cut in the walls – peering out through chinks in the bamboo walls? Blake and Chet ran along the river bank, not the way they had come, but out beyond the village, intending to go behind it in a wide circle, to check whether any enemy reinforcements had arrived.

Blake's eyes were still dazzled by the blaze from the launch, so he did not see the thin trip wire that had been stretched across the track, tree to tree, a foot above the dust, with sharpened slivers of bamboo sticking up out of the earth like dagger blades. He fell heavily, and his Tommy gun clattered out of his grip.

For a moment he lay, gasping for breath, momentarily unable to comprehend what had happened, even where he was. He ran his hands automatically over his body. He was still in one piece. He stood up, cursing his stupidity in not moving with greater care. As he moved, pain swept up his right leg like fire, and he collapsed on the ground. He had broken or sprained his ankle.

He felt his right boot grow suddenly and uncomfortably warm, as though water was pouring into it from a hot tap. He put his right hand down and felt the sharp edge of bamboo, rough as a file, sharp as a razor. A bamboo spike had gone through the side of his foot. He was bleeding badly. He wrenched out the spike, gritting his teeth against the agony of tearing it from his flesh. Then he summoned all his strength and began to crawl forward. He had to escape somehow or capture would be certain; capture meant torture and, very likely, death. At that stage of the war in Burma, he could expect nothing else. So far as the Japanese were concerned, any soldier taken prisoner had already experienced such disgrace that he had forfeited his right to live.

Someone knelt down by his side, reached out for his Tommy gun. Blake's grip tightened stubbornly on the stock.

'Give it to me,' he heard Chet whisper. Blake handed it over. Chet slung it round his chest, then bent down, helped Blake to his feet and heaved him up on his back like a sack of coals. He began to walk forward cautiously. Chet had no breath to speak, and Blake kept his teeth clenched because of the pain that engulfed him now like a roaring tide of molten metal.

A voice spoke urgently from the dark: 'You all right, sir?'

They had reached the other members of Blake's patrol. He recognized his sergeant's voice.

'Surely,' Blake replied. 'Let's go. Any casualties?'

'None serious, sir. Few shrapnel cuts, that's all. Sure you'll be okay?'

'Hold him while I tie up his ankle,' said Chet. 'It won't take a minute.'

Blake lay, fists clenched, teeth together, so that he would not cry out as he felt the bandage from Chet's field dressing tighten around the throbbing agony that only minutes before had been his ankle. Why the devil was he tying the knot so tightly? Couldn't he be more gentle?

Finally, they set off through the darkness, in single file, two men out in front as scouts, two behind in case of any attack from the rear. The glow from the launch faded suddenly as the hull submerged. The moon hung like a pale melon in the sky, and there was no sound except for cries from distant jackals and the faint muffled curses of men marching through the dusty humid night.

Sometimes, long afterwards, Blake would awake from a nightmare, and start up in bed, damp with sweat, recalling the agony of that journey on Chet's back. Low hanging branches from trees whipped his face, but he scarcely felt them. His whole body seemed a writhing mass of pain. Gradually, too, he began to feel light-headed, weaker, as though he was no longer personally involved but somehow only an onlooker, seeing something that did not concern him. He had no idea of time or distance, and only realized vaguely that they reached the outer sentry of the company position shortly before dawn. Chet croaked the password. The sentry lowered his Tommy gun, waved them through along a mule track.

Minutes later they were back within the safety of the company's perimeter, within a reassuring rim of barbed wire and booby traps. Chet set down Blake gently on the ground. The dawn was coming up now, pink and streaky and pale. A cookhouse fire was already lit, and a blue spiral of wood smoke rose up in the windless air. Two orderlies carried out mugs of tea, thick with sweetened condensed milk. The men drank greedily. Sweat started out at once on their foreheads, spreading in dark patches on their thin denim battledress blouses.

The major waddled towards them.

'You bad?' he asked Blake.

'Nothing to speak of,' said Blake weakly. His head seemed clearer now. He was acutely aware of the brightness of sunrise and things he had never really noticed before, like the different shades of green leaves, the cobalt colour of an early morning sky.

A medical orderly came out of the nearest bamboo *basha*, carrying a tray of syringes and small bottles. He moved from one man to the next, dabbing antiseptic on cuts and shrapnel grazes, jabbing his needles into arms or legs.

He reached Blake.

'Only a cut in my ankle,' Blake assured him.

'Let's have a look, sir,' said the orderly and knelt down by his side. He busied himself with swabs and a square of gauze. Blake saw a bottle of blood being connected to a rubber tube.

'What's that for?' he asked curiously.

'You, sir. Bit more than a cut. A spike of some sort has entered the main artery. If it hadn't been for that Gurkha officer who bound it up and brought you in, you'd have bled to death.'

Dermott stood well back from the window of his hotel bedroom, in case anyone from any of the houses across the road could see him, or, worse, photograph him, but where he could still command a view of the crowded street.

He wrinkled his nose in distaste at the sights and smells; cowpats piled in pyramids for fuel, the rickshaws, the squeak of truck horns, the cries of sweetmeat sellers. A rather different view from the don's rooms in Oxford, he thought. But that was to be expected, for that was Oxford and this was Benares, the holy city, where faithful Hindus from all over India came to die, believing that if they could only do so by the banks of the holy Ganges river, their souls would be instantly transported to paradise.

Dermott dismissed the whole idea as absurd, of course. It seemed as ridiculous as claiming a holy status for the cows that wandered unhindered through bazaars, flies swarming around the mucus from their mouths, as they stolidly munched vegetables from the stalls; or the role of monkeys in the monkey temple, scurrying about wildly, jumping on bells to ring them, swinging from gutters, attacking visitors; as grotesque as the mutilated beggars with swollen trunks, propelling themselves along through the crowds on trolleys the size of tea-trays.

Dermott glanced at his gold watch; Jerrold was late and Dermott hated unpunctuality. He sat down and examined his fingernails, which were perfectly manicured. He was about to pour a second gin when Jerrold came into the room.

'Sorry I'm late,' said Jerrold. 'The traffic was held up by a procession. Quit India. All that stuff.'

'You should have made allowances,' Dermott replied tartly. 'Anyhow, you know why I called you here? This bloody Nepal business. London's been on to me again. They're desperate for action. Today, if possible.'

'Impossible, today. I've been sending regular cables to the *Globe* about the political situation there, as I agreed.'

'I know. I've seen them in the censor's office,' Dermott told him. 'But nothing's appeared in the paper.'

'That's not my fault,' retorted Jerrold quickly. 'Papers are so small these days, and with the war as it is, you can't expect them to print much about some country no-one's ever been to or heard of. I did my best.'

'Excuses,' said Dermott shortly. 'London needs more than your best – they want results. England expects, and all that.'

'So what's your idea, then?'

'It's theirs, really, and ingenious for a change. Sit down and I'll tell you.'

Through a thick blue mist of cigar and cigarette smoke swirled by the slow turning blades of overhead fans, disembodied faces loomed and shimmered like lost and disturbed ghosts.

Blake recognized the sharp acquisitive face of the Maharani of Bundar. Gold-framed diamonds in her nose glittered like tiny, fiery stars as she looked enviously at the pile of rupee notes in front of the winners' places. She might be one of the richest women in the world, and to her a year's winnings here would only be so much small change: yet it was money, and money meant more to her than anything else; not to spend, just to possess.

The public relations major wearing an overstarched khaki drill bush jacket watched the wheel intently, his head moving almost imperceptibly from left to right with each revolution. Sweat stains beneath his armpits showed the strain of being a loser for the fifth night in succession.

A dark-skinned man sat just beyond the circle of light cast by the shaded lamps above the table. Blake sensed rather than saw a glint of gold-capped teeth, gold rings, a gold wristlet watch. The man snapped his fingers. Instantly, a waiter brought him a bottle of champagne with two glasses on a silver tray. The man toasted the Maharani. Blake could see his eyes now, glittering green as jade.

'Will your excellency wish for another bottle?' asked the bearer in English.

'When I have won some more – a lot more.'

Davichand Rana smiled expansively at the other gamblers around the table. His teeth glowed almost phosphorescently against the dimness. An American colonel with an Italian name stubbed out three inches of cigar in the ivory ashtray at his elbow. Immediately, a bearer whipped it away and replaced it with another already washed and scented. The colonel lit a new cigar, and watched the wheel with the greedy hog-eyes of the compulsive gambler.

There were other faces, dark and pale. Blake wondered as he

watched them whether he appeared as contemptible to them as they seemed to him. The room was silent as a church – or a tomb – for the stakes were high. Thousands of rupees changed hands each time the wheel stopped. Whose hands would next reach out with lacquered or blunt or bitten fingernails to claw in those crisp, neat bundles of freshly issued notes in their new elastic bands?

I'm down seventeen thousand chips, thought Blake. Seventeen thousand at, say, thirteen rupees to the pound. About thirteen hundred pounds; not far short of two years' army pay. What am I doing here among the rich? I can't afford to lose a single rupee, not even one anna, yet I am digging my grave deeper with more debts – for what? The mesmeric attraction of a turning wheel, the absurd belief that one time it must favour me?

I'll bet on twenty-one, he thought, as though this was the answer to his problems. Twenty-one could be his lucky number. Blake had been twenty-one when he left Oxford. Two and one added together made three, the prime number. Perhaps he should bet on three? He had been nine – three times three – when his mother left home. Lucky or unlucky? He tried to disbelieve that any number could be either, for what were good or bad luck, but the results of wise or foolish decisions? There were neither punishments nor rewards in life, only consequences. Who had said that? Shaw? Voltaire? No. Ralph Ingersoll, for what it mattered. Did it matter? In the last analysis, did anything matter very much?

His mouth felt dry, his lips almost cracking. He sipped a *nimbu pani* nervously; the sharp lemon drink brought sweat out on his forehead. His back suddenly felt damp under his light khaki shirt. His wounded ankle began to throb as though it possessed a heart of its own.

Oh, God, *make* the number come up. Ten to one. Fifty thousand chips. He deducted the seventeen thousand he owed. He would be thirty-three thousand up. Then he would call it a night, have a whisky, straight, and leave. Lady Luck could only smile once. The wheel began to slow. The glittering silver ball rattled against raised points. The wheel stopped.

'Twenty-three. Lucky number, twenty-three.'

The croupier's voice, like someone calling from the spirit world, cut through the fog of smoke and disappointment. Blake could smell the scent of fear; men and women were gambling more money than they could afford – probably, like him, more than they possessed. This was a disease, but where could he find the cure?

The croupier pushed piles of Bank of India notes from one end of the table to the other. He looked up to see who had won. A podgy lieutenant, already prematurely bald, his face beaming like a beacon, scraped the money together, crammed it in-elegantly into his bush-jacket pocket and left.

Blake signalled to the waiter, who poured out an enormous measure of gin into a glass, added fresh lime juice. Blake drank it quickly, eager to block out the misery of another loss. The drink tasted bitter on his tongue, sour as the thought of another debt to pay. Why the devil did he gamble? There was no sense in it, no reason, no hope whatever of winning consistently. You were playing against a mathematical equation: your number could only come up once in so many hundred or thousand times. That was the chance you took; luck had nothing to do with it.

At first, the money, the prize, had not really been important, but the challenge was. Now the challenge had gone and only the debts remained. He was suffering from a kind of dichotomy, as though one part of his character must forever fight or bid against another part.

He had been fortunate (he would never say lucky) and he felt he had to keep testing his fortune, just to make sure it had not diminished, or worse still, deserted him. What was an effort to others often seemed effortless to him, and he kept gambling because he wanted to prove to himself he had not lost the knack.

He reasoned, as he had heard so many other gamblers reason, that the pendulum could only swing in one direction for so long. Winning or losing was like watching the tide come in – or go out, although he knew that this analogy was totally false. Gambling had nothing to do with any pendulum or tide. You just poured your money away and hoped, absurdly, but still fervently, that somehow it might come back, doubled, tripled, quadrupled.

As Blake finished his drink, looked around for the waiter to bring another, a voice spoke softly into his left ear.

'Don't you wish sometimes you could swop even all your good looks, my dear fellow, for that fat subaltern's good luck?'

Who the hell?

For a moment, Blake's eyes, strained by staring at the wheel and the shining ball, refused to focus. Then to his amazement he recognized Jerrold, smiling.

111

Jerrold in a starched khaki drill shirt, sleeves folded and neatly pressed, and wearing dark green slides with gold lettering 'War Correspondent' on each epaulette.

They shook hands.

'What are you doing here?' Blake asked him. 'There's no war to write about in Benares surely.'

'Quite true,' Jerrold agreed. 'I've a couple of weeks off. Leave, I suppose you'd call it. And you?'

'The same,' said Blake. 'I was in Burma. Got a nick in my leg. Thought nothing of it, but then a signal came through that a new medical convalescent leave centre had started here in Benares, and quite unexpectedly I was posted here for two weeks.'

'You can't convalesce much in this casino, surely?'

'I'm not really trying to. I am attempting to rebuild my finances.'

'Not a way I'd recommend,' said Jerrold. 'You look as if you could do with another drink, with that empty glass in your hand.'

'So far, I'd agree. The wheel's been against me.'

'It always is,' said Jerrold. 'You should know. Didn't do your friend McMoffatt much good in the end, either.'

'He was a nice guy. Extremely kind to me. Did they ever find out who blew him up?'

'A bookie's ring, so the word went. But who's going to spend too much time trying to find out who's killed one bookmaker, when there are millions of worthy people dying on the Russian front alone?'

They crossed to the bar.

'Two whiskies,' said Jerrold.

'Sorry, sahib, no more whisky,' the barman replied quickly. 'All is just now finished.'

Jerrold folded a five rupee note into four, the size of a postage stamp, flicked it across the bar at him.

'Two whiskies. *Jaldi*.'

'Coming, sahib,' said the barman instantly.

'You know your way around,' said Blake.

'On expenses, it's easy,' Jerrold admitted.

They toasted each other, but the small initial pleasure Blake had felt at seeing Jerrold was evaporating as quickly as his surprise that he should also be here in Benares. They had nothing much in common except three years on the same staircase. Also, there was the matter of the three thousand pounds Corinne's father said he had paid to Jerrold. He must not forget that; he must never forget that, no matter how much he owed, how much he drank.

'I've got a house here,' Jerrold explained. 'Belongs to our local man, actually, but he's in Bombay for two weeks, so I'm using it *pro tem*. Come back and have dinner. Unless you've anything better to do?'

For a moment Blake was tempted to say he had all manner of other, better things to do, but a meal, even with Jerrold, would be better than eating on his own. Also, it would be free. How far had he sunk, if this was an important factor? Soon, he would be grateful for a soup kitchen.

'Glad to,' he said briskly, trying to sound enthusiastic.

They came out of the casino into the hot darkness. Crickets whirred like ratchets, and the strange elusive scent of night-blooming flowers, of spices, sacred dust, thousand-year-old tombs, the smell of an ageless India, engulfed them like a woman's warm arms. A car pulled out from the shadows. Jerrold held open the door.

'On the office, too,' he explained, climbing in the back beside Blake. They drove out of the town, along wide empty roads. Single storey houses with lights burning on white walls lay at the centre of huge dark gardens. *Chowkidars* with staves and lanterns stood guard at whitewashed gateposts. This was the rich man's end of town; Jerrold must be moving up in the world to live here. The car stopped under a high-roofed storm porch. Two lanterns on the ends of chains swayed in the breeze. Blake noticed that the dust on the drive had been hosed. A guard in khaki uniform with polished brass buttons saluted them gravely. Another servant opened the door.

'If you want a wash, it's on the right,' said Jerrold. 'Then come and have another drink before dinner.'

The cloakroom was luxurious; three new towels, two smooth, one rough, on a heated rail; two illuminated mirrors above the wash basin, one with a magnifying glass. Packets of Alka-Seltzer, a bottle of aspirins, a gold inlaid hair brush, three different kinds of soap, were laid in a row. A warm feeling flooded through Blake at the sight of such unaccustomed luxury.

Jerrold was waiting for him in a sitting room, two beakers of gin and lime misty with ice on a side table.

'I feel I owe you something after everything went wrong with

113

that series I was going to write about Corinne and you,' said Jerrold, handing him a drink.

'I could have used the money,' Blake admitted. 'My father had just died, and everything went to pay debts.'

'I had no idea. Always thought of you as being rich. You seemed to have everything I wanted. You were everything I wanted to be.'

'What happened to Corinne?' asked Blake, to change the subject.

'She's still a semi-invalid. Paralysed from the waist down. But she could recover. There's hope.'

'There's always hope.'

'Especially where she's concerned. I married her, you know.'

'Married her?'

Blake did not even try to keep astonishment out of his voice. 'I didn't know.'

'No reason why you should.'

'Ever hear of Glover these days?' Blake asked him to change the subject again, as though they had been discussing nothing more important than a change in the weather.

'He was doing well, last time I heard. Went into property.'

'In the war? Not much chance there, surely?'

'Every damn chance – if you're smart.'

'I'm not,' said Blake thickly. The drink was stronger than he realized – or he had drunk too many. 'Tell me.'

'Delighted. Glover worked out a formula, proved it worked once, and then just kept on repeating it. Say you have a young fellow, just married, say, called up in the Army. He's captured at Dunkirk, or in Norway. His house only cost, say, three hundred pounds before the war. Maybe there is only fifty pounds owing on it, but his wife is hard pressed to keep up the payments. She has no one to advise her and his Army pay as a PoW hardly feeds the budgerigar.

'Bills mount up. Rates. Gas. Coal. Electricity. The fridge is repossessed. Then the radio. She's frantic with worry, doesn't know which way to turn, and it all proves too much for her. She just can't cope any longer. So she does a moonlight flit. Or, more likely, she meets a man in a reserved occupation, making a lot of money in a factory – and clears off with him. Either way, the result's the same. An empty house.'

'So where does Glover come in?' Blake asked him.

'At that moment. The building society want to get it off their back, for they're not equipped to sell houses. After all, probably they're only owed fifty quid. Maybe even less. A tenner, even a fiver. Anyone who can pay them simply what they are owed, gets the house. Glover's been buying property like that ever since the blitz.'

'How did he raise the money?'

'Borrowed it. On the security of the properties he was going to buy. Smart boy, because there's no risk. If we lost the war, everything would go. As we're winning, Glover will be made for life.'

'You haven't done so badly yourself,' said Blake.

'Not on Glover's scale,' said Jerrold enviously.

'You don't miss many chances,' Blake told him. 'I know. I saw Corinne's father.'

Just for a moment a shadow crossed Jerrold's face and as instantly disappeared.

'He said you had taken three thousand pounds off him,' said Blake. 'Said you needed it to buy off some cad who wanted to marry Corinne for her money.'

'Absolute balls,' retorted Jerrold angrily.

'I'm glad to hear it. Just for a moment I thought you might have meant me.'

'Is that likely?' asked Jerrold. 'When I was already helping you out with your scheme to boost that gambling club or whatever it was you were involved in? When I rang to warn you that whoever did for McMoffatt was looking for you? Shouldn't think that you were in too strong a position with old Gieves yourself – if he knew the truth.'

'I saw him and told him how sorry I was.'

'But not about your basic scheme, to pretend you liked his only daughter – just for a bit of publicity – and a thousand pounds?'

'No. Not about that. It didn't seem relevant.'

'Nor does the money he paid me. That was for something else altogether. An investment.'

Blake could see he had needled Jerrold, which might be unwise, for at this moment in his life he needed any friend he could find.

Deliberately changing the subject for the third time, he asked Jerrold: 'How is old Gieves? He's not dead, or anything?'

'Not physically, so far as I know, but financially, he's through. He was a fool. Sold out his firm for shares in what seemed a booming rubber company – and when the Japs invaded Malaya he lost everything.'

Blake wondered whether Jerrold had married Corinne before or after this, but did not like to ask a question to which he felt he already knew the answer.

'Now let me ask you a question, for a change. Any idea how much you owe in gambling debts?'

'Some.'

'Well, let me put you in the picture, as you like to say in the Army. There was nineteen thousand pounds to McMoffatt back in 1939. His executors have been adding interest, of course. Eight per cent, at least. So now you owe them, say, twenty-five thousand pounds. A lot of money.'

'I owe them damn all,' said Blake heatedly. 'McMoffatt gave me some money to bet on his behalf. And advanced some more against family securities which he took over.'

'Nothing about that in his company's books, so I'm told.'

'Then you've not been told the truth.'

'That could be difficult to prove, you know. Creditors can't sue for a gambling debt, but bookmakers sometimes use other less pleasant methods of persuasion. You can't deny that on paper you owe that amount. You've also had a few unfortunate flutters out here. Like tonight, for example.'

'What about that?'

'It could be considered unbecoming in an officer and a gentleman if you went back on your word. Especially, in the present political set-up here, to rich Indians who run casinos.'

'I have never gone back on my word.'

'You haven't paid, either,' Jerrold pointed out.

'I will. When I have the money.'

'That's what everyone says. But you're not really going about raising the money very successfully.'

'What the hell has this to do with you?' asked Blake angrily.

'I like to see who wins and who loses. And, whatever you say, I have tried to help you in the past. And now there's a chance I really can help you solve your present financial problems.'

'How?'

'There was a fellow in that casino tonight who's a very heavy gambler. Name of Davichand Rana. A general in the Nepalese army, no less.'

Blake shrugged. The name and the rank meant nothing to him.

'He was sitting next to the Maharani of Bundar. Shared a bottle of champagne with her.'

Blake nodded without much interest. He vaguely remembered a dark skinned man with green eyes, sitting on the edge of darkness, just beyond the pool of light above the table.

'What about it?'

'I thought you would have known him.'

'Why should I? I've never been to Nepal in my life.'

'It could be useful to you and me – and a lot of important people – if you got to know him.'

'Why?'

Blake looked at Jerrold closely. He was surprised that he had never previously noticed how close together were his eyes, how thin his lips, like the tight metal mouth of a purse – or a trap. He sensed warning signals. This man dislikes me, he thought. But why? What have I done to arouse his enmity? He could understand Glover disliking him, but why Jerrold?

'I'd rather let someone else give you all the details. You are staying to dinner?'

'Well, you invited me.'

'So I did. Then let's have another drink, just to put you in a receptive frame of mind. You'll learn something about history tonight. Maybe about geography, too, and most important of all, about recouping personal finances, when they've taken a tumble.'

Jerrold smiled, but there was no humour, no warmth in his smile; it was simply a muscular contraction of his mouth. A bearer wearing a starched white uniform, with a red and gold belt and a turban, opened the door and bowed.

They walked into the dining room. The meal was splendidly served: iced soup, fillet of *bekti*, a river fish with a pungent sauce, followed by slices of chicken breast with garlic and pilau rice.

'Rather different to the soya links and dehydrated potatoes I've been living on in the Arakan,' said Blake appreciatively.

'I'm disappointed in you,' Jerrold told him, shaking his head sadly. 'I thought you'd be rather smarter than that.'

'I was once,' agreed Blake. 'But the wheel of fortune turns. It's gone up for you and, as I told you, down for me. But only temporarily, of course.'

'The wheel of fortune,' said Jerrold musingly. 'Shows how gambling is always in your thoughts.'

Blake shrugged. He felt glad he had not told Jerrold of a meeting he had had earlier that evening in the leave centre. Another officer, much older, with the florid face and soft marzipan nose of a drinker, was standing in the entrance hall, reading typed orders pinned on a notice board. As Blake passed by, he looked as though he felt he should know him, but could not quite place him.

'You are Richard Blake, aren't you?' he asked him hesitantly.

'Yes.'

'Thought you were. Don't remember me, do you?'

'Sorry to say, I don't.'

'We used to work for the same boss. McMoffatt.'

'In what capacity?' Blake asked him.

'Office work, book-keeping.'

'I remember his office, but I don't think we ever met.'

'Remember the figures do you, then?'

Blake shook his head. What did the fellow mean?

'McMoffatt, you might say, was the last peacetime casualty,' the officer went on. 'He was owed a lot of money when he died. Quite a whack by you.'

'Not really,' said Blake.

'Yes, really,' the other man replied sarcastically. 'I don't like people welshing on their debts. Others in London share my view. They'll come looking for you, soon as you get back. They'll want the debt repaid.

'There is no debt,' Blake replied.

'*I* believe you,' said the officer. He grinned, to expose a row of nicotine-stained teeth. 'But thousands wouldn't. Correction. Millions wouldn't. And among them are the fellows you'll have to convince, Dicky, my boy. Thousands of pounds you owe, and they'll want every penny. It's their right.'

It was curious that this stranger, who to the best of Blake's recollections he had never seen before, should make these accusations about debts that did not exist – and here, only hours later, Jerrold was doing exactly the same thing. Could it be coincidence? It must be – mustn't it? Blake felt suddenly weary, less confident.

Jerrold was talking again, scattering Blake's uneasy thoughts with the urgency of his voice.

'How would you feel,' he asked, 'if I could arrange for all the debts you say you don't owe, and all those I know you do owe, to be paid off? The slate wiped clean?'

'Depends what I have to do for it.'

Jerrold leaned across the table, his face so close that Blake could smell stale cigar smoke on his breath.

'I am not just a newspaper man,' he explained in a hoarse whisper.

Blake showed the polite surprise which he thought the statement required.

'I do the odd job for the Foreign Office. The India Office. In fact, any bloody government office – if they pay.'

'What do you mean, the odd job?' Blake asked him.

Jerrold was making himself sound like a plumber, or a self-employed electrician or decorator who worked from the front room of a terraced house; the sort of man you paid in notes and did not ask for a receipt. In a sense, of course, Blake realized that was how he had pigeon-holed Jerrold in his mind: a rather cheap man on the make. A quick deal here, a swift turnover there, the illicit cigarette shielded by the palm of his hand in a non-smoking area.

'I mean Intelligence stuff. I meet all sorts of people in my job, you see. You are helping the country in your way. I help it in mine.'

'So how do you propose to help me?' asked Blake. 'Let's get down to basics and stop horsing around. What is the proposition you keep hinting at?'

Jerrold glanced at his watch.

'Two friends have promised to drop in for a drink before midnight. They will explain it better than I can.'

'What if I hadn't been here?'

'Ah. That would be a different matter, now, wouldn't it?'

'Who are they, these two?'

'One is Colonel Howard, retired colonel, actually. He is an adviser to the Viceroy. The other is out from London. Mr Dermott. A bit of a pansy, but high-powered.'

'How the hell do they know about me?' asked Blake.

'Questions, questions. Now let's have a couple of ports apiece and a cigar. I can charge it all to expenses for entertaining.'

Colonel Howard looked like an actor playing the part of a colonel. He wore a white tuxedo with a red flower in his button-hole and a red handkerchief in his top pocket to match it. His skin was unusually pink and shiny, as though stretched over the skull of a larger man.

Dermott, Blake did not care for. There seemed something reptilian about him with his cold eyes, his wide nostrils and high-pitched voice. He seemed like a man constructed from the left-overs of other people; a hybrid, or, in racing terms, a rig.

'Spot of leave, eh?' Howard asked Blake cheerfully as they shook hands.

Blake nodded.

'Makes me wish I was in your shoes,' Howard went on unconvincingly, pouring himself a tumbler of brandy. The bearer brought in coffee and cigars on a tray, set them down, bowed and left them alone.

Dermott and the Colonel made talk so small it was barely minuscule, glancing sideways every now and then at Blake as though trying to appraise him without his knowing. Jerrold sat at the back of the room, drinking steadily, saying nothing. At last, impatiently, Howard glanced at his watch.

'I feel I really should be going,' he said. 'I have a report to write for H.E. in Delhi, and must get it to the cypher people tonight.'

He stood up, poured himself another drink, and, glass in hand, stood watching Blake. A little brandy spilled over the edge and trickled down his fingers. He licked them clean.

Jerrold said, as though on cue, 'I was mentioning to my old Oxford chum here you might have something that could interest him.'

'What did he say?' Dermott asked Jerrold, as though Blake was not even in the room.

'He said, he'd like his debts paid,' said Blake. 'But, understandably, he wants to know what he has to do to reach that happy outcome.'

Dermott drew on his cigar.

'Napoleon used to say that one good spy was equal to twenty-five divisions of men,' he said. 'He was right, too.'

'Possibly. But I don't want to be a spy, good or bad,' Blake replied. 'I've enough problems as it is.'

'No-one's suggesting spying,' said Dermott. 'What I am trying to put to you is that you could help your country in a way far beyond anything you could do as an infantry captain.'

'How?'

'I don't know whether you're a political animal or not, but it's pretty clear that India will become independent after the war. Whether that day will mark the beginning or the end of the most stable time in India's history is another matter. What we are concerned with now is that since India has always been referred to as the brightest jewel in the Empire's crown, if we lose that jewel, everything else could begin to break up.

'Other countries may want to leave the Empire – and most probably will. Britain's role in the world will obviously diminish, because to be a world power you either need to have a huge landmass yourself, like the United States or Russia, or control other large areas of land, as we have done for the last two hundred years.

'A rich man can ignore losses that would cripple someone who isn't wealthy. We will then be in that second situation, and all kinds of treaties will become more important to Britain, as we become less powerful.'

'Come to the point, for God's sake,' said Howard irritably. 'I have to get back to do that report.'

'And I must fill in the background for him,' retorted Dermott.

'You have,' said Blake. 'What are you asking me to do?'

'Here are the basic facts,' Dermott replied. 'One treaty especially concerns His Majesty's Government in the event of India's becoming independent. This deals with the agreement we have with Nepal to supply Gurkha soldiers for the Army. We are most anxious to maintain this arrangement. Nepal is also keen, for these excellent soldiers are a very valuable source of revenue to their country. What concerns us is that the treaty could be nullified, with irreparable loss to both countries.'

'Why? If they both want to keep it going?'

'Because treaties are not made by countries, but by politicians. In the case of Nepal, by prime ministers. There is a king, of course, but he is only a totem. Some say he is virtually a prisoner in his own palace. Political power lies in the hands of one family, the Ranas. The post of prime minister is hereditary for them, not always father to son, but perhaps father to nephew to cousin, and so on. Our information is that the next Rana to be prime minister could abrogate the treaty.'

'Why?'

'Because he can see political or financial mileage out of it for

121

himself. He might receive money or other favours from the Americans or the Russians, not because they give a damn for Nepal, but because losing the Gurkhas would weaken Britain, and that is what they both want for different reasons. And after five years of war, largely financed by selling our overseas investments at give-away prices, we need further weakening like a haemophiliac needs to be bled by a barber-surgeon.'

'So how will I get my debts paid?' asked Blake patiently.

'By helping to persuade the Nepalese that the man who is now next in line should *never* become prime minister. We want you to show him up as a poltroon, someone incapable of running a lavatory, never mind a country. We want you to make him look a fool, an idiot, blinded by his own personal greed. Other members of the Rana family will get the message. Like so many people in the East, they cannot stand criticism, and death is almost preferable to public embarrassment. They will pass over this man quickly, and the next in line will become prime minister, a fact that will help his country enormously – and ours – because he fully appreciates the value of this treaty.'

'The fellow who's no good was in the casino tonight,' Jerrold explained. 'I mentioned him to you.'

'I thought you said he was a general?'

'He is. They all are. From birth.'

'So how do I fit in?' Blake asked.

'We have worked out a scheme,' said Howard.

'You mean, I have worked out a scheme,' interrupted Dermott quickly.

'Well, together we have produced something that's simple and effective, two qualities a military man like me admires. This Davichand Rana is damned greedy. He may be nearly as rich as Croesus, but that's still not rich enough for him. We propose to offer him the chance of incalculable wealth in return for what, to him, will seem a relatively small investment. We will give him the offer of buying all the trading rights on the Irrawaddy River in Burma in perpetuity.'

'That is where you come in,' Jerrold told Blake.

'But there aren't any such trading rights,' Blake pointed out. 'How do you expect a man shrewd enough to be in line as the next prime minister of the country to believe there are?'

Dermott leaned towards him so that Blake could see little flecks of matter in the corners of his eyes.

'Because you will persuade him there are, that's why. Not on your own, of course. We are having a proper document drawn up. Vellum, seals, legal phrases. This will be prepared by the finest European lawyers in India. It will be signed by Lord Louis Mountbatten, the Supreme Allied Commander, South East Asia, by Field Marshal Sir William Slim, commanding the Fourteenth Army, by Sir John Baldwin, who commands the Third Tactical Air Force. By Uncle Tom Cobley and all, if need be. Rana can take this document wherever he likes to have it checked. The signatures will all stand up. The document will be absolutely waterproof, copper-bottomed and A1 at Lloyds.'

'The signatures, of course, will be forged,' added Jerrold.

'But he must still know there are no rights to sell,' protested Blake. 'The Irrawaddy Flotilla Company carries goods on the river, and that's about all. I suppose you are not offering that in the deal?'

'Of course not. Trading rights is a wide term. It can include mineral rights. Oil exploration permissions. All kinds of concessions in and along the banks of the greatest river in the East.'

'I think the idea's absurd,' said Blake shortly.

'You are entitled to your view,' Howard allowed magnanimously, pouring himself another brandy. 'But consider what goes on along the banks of the Ganges here. Every Hindu in India believes they must make at least one pilgrimage to the Ganges in their lifetime. When they grow old, or if they fall ill, they believe that if they can only reach Benares, then they are certain to go at once to paradise when they die.

'Hindus revere the river so much, they have a hundred and eight different names for it. "The Destroyer of Poverty". "The Mother of all that Lives and Moves". "A Light amid the Darkness of Ignorance". "The River that flows like a Staircase to Heaven". And so on and so on.'

'Actually,' Dermott interrupted, 'the water does seem to possess what are, shall I say, unusual qualities. If you drank half a glass of water from some other rivers, the Jumna, say, or the Hooghly in Calcutta, you wouldn't stand much chance. But the Ganges *is* different. A scientific analysis might show why – if one hasn't already been made.'

'Whether it has or not,' said Howard, 'millionaires, educated people, as well as the poor – all pray that after death their bodies will be burned in the ghats on the bank and their ashes scattered on the water. Thousands of tons of filth and sewage pour into the Ganges every day. You'll see people defecating and urinating all along its banks, and the bodies of drowned dogs, cats, goats, bloated and putrefying, floating past, and yet every morning, at dawn, thousands of believers are there, too, on those same banks, drinking the water, washing in it, cleaning their teeth in it. And why? Because they believe that this is required of them if they wish to enter into their particular heaven. They have faith. They believe because they want to believe. And Rana will want to believe, simply because there's so much money in it for him.'

'How much money?'

'We are offering him the rights for ten million pounds sterling,' said Dermott. 'An immense bargain.'

'For whom?'

'For him as an individual. And though he doesn't care about this, of course, for Nepal, and Britain, with the Gurkhas.'

'We're not asking him to put ten million pounds on the table as though he were buying a used car, Blake,' explained Dermott. 'We only seek a deposit of one million or its equivalent in rupees as an earnest of his good faith, and then only after he has made every check he wants.'

'What if he took the document and showed the forged signatures to Slim, say, or Mountbatten? The whole scheme would fall apart at once.'

'Certainly, but he won't. For several reasons. First, he has no direct access to any of them. He can only approach them through intermediaries – our own people. Second, he believes, because he is vain and greedy, that he alone has been specially selected to receive this offer – which of course is quite true. Third, Davichand Rana's solicitors will check signatures against public documents carrying those signatures, and will confirm they are exactly the same because they will be absolutely impossible to fault. He and anyone else he nominates can carry out any check they like. We've thought this out thoroughly, you know.'

'When you want something desperately,' said Jerrold, 'wealth or a woman, or whatever, you have a blind spot. You may hear warning bells in your mind that this deal could be troublesome or that woman is not really right for you. But that only makes you all the more determined to secure them, to prove the warnings were all wrong. You deliberately disregard them. You have tunnel vision. You only see what you want to see, straight ahead. And any question he cares to ask can be answered.'

'Who will his lawyers approach first of all, then?' asked Blake.

'For a start, our lawyers,' replied Howard. 'Lawyers like dealing with each other. That way, both sides increase their fees, and they trust each other. They're professional people, with high moral standards. Men of honour, you might say.'

'Unlike us,' said Jerrold and smiled at each man in turn; none of them smiled back.

Dermott, with his pale, blue, unblinking eyes, examined his fingernails. Howard glanced at his watch, wondering whether he had time for another drink, even a small one, a chota peg, before he left; that damned report nagged at him like an aching tooth.

'So where do I come in?' Blake asked Jerrold.

'You sell Rana the basic idea,' Jerrold replied. 'You have the charm, the good looks; you're the archetypal British officer. Public school, Oxford. You look the part of an English gentleman, so he is half ready to believe you as soon as you meet. If you were five feet tall and bald, with bad teeth and a gorblimey accent, you'd have problems, agreed. But you won't have any. Looking the part is more than half the battle.

'Who would you instinctively trust, if you faced a serious operation? A surgeon in a Savile Row suit, with a Rolls outside his Harley Street consulting room – or an unshaven scruff in a turtleneck sweater and plimsolls? He'll trust you.

'He will pay you the equivalent of one million pounds in rupee notes of high denomination. You may be surprised how little room they'll take up – you can pack them all in a small suitcase.'

'No doubt. But how do I persuade someone I've never met to part with a million pounds for something that doesn't exist?'

'We'll brief you fully on that when the time comes,' Howard assured him. 'It won't be anything like so difficult as you think, I can promise you.'

'Now, having taken the money from him,' Jerrold went on, 'you hand it over to me. I put it in the bank. Of course, you will have to admit to me that you tried to set him up and there will obviously be a court of inquiry. You may even be court-martialled.'

'Thank you very much,' said Blake dryly. 'And then?'

'And then Davichand Rana will be publicly ridiculed. Just

think what the newspapers will make of it. "British Army Captain swindles Nepal's potential Premier out of ten million pounds."

'Every important paper in the world will run that story. I know, because I will write it, and the *Globe* will syndicate it. Rana will not have lost anything in cash, because naturally we will pay back to him every anna. But what he will have lost is his most valuable asset, his credibility. And we will have saved – with your help – a treaty beyond price to both our countries.'

'You sound very convinced and convincing,' said Blake. 'If I agree that it's worth having a go, what's in it for me?'

Jerrold smiled.

'We have already worked out what you owe in gambling debts in England. In round figures shall we say it's twenty-five thousand plus. As a British captain in India your pay is roughly eight hundred pounds a year. If you didn't spend a penny on yourself, not a single mess bill, or dhobi, and so on, it would take you thirty years at least to pay that off. Add your debts here, and it would take another five. The proposal is to pay everything you owe, so that you can start with a clean slate.'

Blake shook his head.

'It's not on,' he said. 'At the least I'll be court-martialled with so much money involved. And what sort of sentence will I get? Reduced to the ranks and ten years inside?'

'Nothing like that,' said Dermott, shaking his head. 'We'll have a word with the judge advocate's people. You probably wouldn't even come down below lieutenant. You might be sentenced to a couple of years, agreed, but that would only be on paper, old boy. You'd be out again within the week. What do you say?'

'No.'

'Why the hell not? Damn it, we're paying you enough.'

'Twenty-five or six thousand pounds and the hope of a lenient sentence – not even the promise – against a million? What sort of a deal is that?'

'What do you want, then?'

'A proper fee. The labourer is worthy of his hire. Say five thousand pounds on top of all my debts, and the guarantee that I will only get a reprimand.'

'We cannot give you a firm guarantee,' replied Dermott. 'You will have to go through the motions of being sentenced. But I give you my word we will get you out in double quick time.'

'In writing?' asked Blake.

Dermott looked at the others irritably.

'How can I possibly put it in writing? Be sensible. But I am telling you this in front of these two witnesses, and they agree with me.'

The other two men nodded.

Blake lit a cigarette, examined the glowing end for a moment and made up his mind.

'All right,' he said. 'I'll do it on the absolute understanding there is no physical harm to this Davichand Rana fellow.'

'Absolutely none, my boy,' said Howard at once. 'All academic stuff.'

'You may not even have to deal with him direct,' said Dermott. 'We want to get at him through a close member of his family. His nephew.'

'And who's he?'

'Captain Chet Bahadur Rana.'

5

Up through the terraced fields in the foothills beyond
Kathmandu, over thin and sparkling icy streams, the official
runner came. He carried a long bamboo pole, symbol of his
office, that marked him as a man to whom every help should be
given, on pain of death to refuse, for he bore a private message
to Davichand Rana.

Tiny bells on the messenger's ankles tinkled as he ran, barefooted, his face shining with the sweat of exertion. The bells gave
warning of his approach; his way must be cleared, and if he
needed food or drink, they must be instantly provided. As he
came to the outer limits of the city, he bent low, removed the
bells, stuffed them in his pocket and ran on more swiftly and
silently until he reached the gate of Davichand Rana's palace.
The guards saw his pole and instantly waved him through into
its large courtyard.

White marble walls colonnaded with Italian pillars shone pink
in the afternoon sun, like decorations on a gigantic iced cake.
Their image was reflected in an ornamental lake where water
cascaded over lifesize Lalique mermaids. The runner reached the
marble steps of the palace, paused briefly for breath and then
bounded on up the wide stairway.

Two great doors opened and closed silently behind him. He
was standing in a vast hall, lined with gilded mirrors from tessel-
lated floor to Florentine ceiling. A single fountain sprayed into
a circular pool where gold and silver fish moved lazily beneath
the plate-like leaves of water lilies. Larger than life tigers snarled
silently at him from huge paintings on the walls. The hall had a
strange empty coldness about it that chilled the man's simple
heart. He stood, panting for breath, eager to deliver his message
and be away, back to the humble world he understood, but proud
of his calling, and noting all he saw to confound stay-at-homes
in his village with the splendour in which Davichand Rana lived.

A uniformed orderly approached him.

'I have a special message for Maharajah Davichand Rana,' the messenger told him importantly. 'To be delivered in person.'

'I am here,' said a deep voice behind him.

The man turned and bowed low in the strange fashion dictated by Nepalese protocol, so that from his hips his body was briefly horizontal to the ground. Still in this position, he handed the bamboo pole to Davichand Rana, who opened a small gilded box fixed to one end and removed a sealed envelope.

'Who gave you this?' he asked before he broke the seal.

'A runner, your Excellency. He said it was of the utmost importance and that I was to make my best speed to you. It originated, so he said, from India. The sacred city of Benares.'

He paused, hoping to be commended for the way in which he had run steadily for several hours without a break over the last lap of his journey. But Davichand Rana was not a man to give praise easily.

'Why are you not wearing your bells?' he asked him sharply.

'I removed them, your Excellency, so that I could run the more speedily and directly through the city.'

'So you say. But you know the ancient law. You wear bells so that all can hear you and know you are an official messenger. Only runners with evil intent, who have something to hide, remove their bells. They fear that others may hear them, so they deliver their news in secret. You know the punishment for those who run in silence? Then you must accept it. As a lesson to you, and an example to others.'

Davichand Rana turned to two orderlies who had followed him from the inner room and nodded towards the messenger. Immediately, they seized the man and carried him, crying out in alarm, through the back corridors of the palace to a small courtyard. Here, one orderly slipped a loop of rope around his neck, pulled it tight and punched him hard in the back. As the messenger sank down, gasping for breath, they tied the end of the rope around both his ankles, knotted it and then bound his wrists up into the small of his back. One of them rolled a rag into a ball and pushed this into his mouth. The messenger lay groaning and rolling on his side, choking for breath, like a trussed chicken. Davichand Rana came out and stood watching him.

'Release him in four hours,' he told an orderly.

'He is weary from his journey, your Excellency. He may not live that long.'

'In that case, he will have released himself. You heard my orders.'

Davichand Rana walked back into his palace to his study, and opened the envelope. It contained a small piece of paper with one line written in pencil. An agent was reporting the fact that a British Army captain named Blake was due to arrive in Kathmandu to visit Chet Bahadur.

There must be some special significance in this, thought Rana. No foreigner was allowed to visit Nepal without an important specific reason, and this reason he would have to discover. It must concern him, otherwise the agent would not have thought it necessary to send him the information.

Davichand Rana stood for a moment, looking out of the window at the jets in the fountain, pondering on possible reasons for the unexpected visit of a stranger.

On the other side of Kathmandu, another man was also standing deep in thought at the window of a small house. A few yards away was a palace with a thousand rooms – and all of them empty, a hollow monument to vanished majesty. For this man was the King of Nepal, who lived in such a modest way that it appeared to emphasize his lack of political authority.

The window overlooked a lawn. Swinging hammocks and canvas chairs were dotted about the grass, which was studded with incongruous concrete mushrooms. Stone dwarfs holding fishing rods squatted by tiny ornamental pools. The sight might have been in keeping with a suburban back garden in England, but surely not with the grounds of a king's home in Kathmandu?

The scent of flowers was very strong in the air and the cooing of pigeons in trees outside came clearly through open windows. The King of Nepal, whose name, Tribbhuvana, meant someone who dwelt not in one world but in three – the material, the spiritual and the human – was tall. His height was accentuated by his white Nepali shirt with a tape at its throat, his long tweed sports jacket and his white jodhpurs. His face was grave and pale. Sometimes it seemed more like a stone carving than the face of a living man, and his dark eyes possessed an infinite sadness. A high wall was topped with broken glass embedded in concrete, and strands of barbed wire surrounded the wall. A soldier, rifle slung over one shoulder, patrolled its inner perimeter. The high wall was not only to keep people out, the king thought bitterly – it had a more important purpose: to keep him in.

He was no less a prisoner than the wretches incarcerated in the city jail for trying to organize resistance to the ruthless rule of the Ranas, chained to cell walls by wrists and ankles for five, ten, even fifteen years. They were there, as he was here, not as prisoners who had to be punished for committing a crime, but because if they were free, then they might conspire to overthrow the Ranas.

The King knew that Nepal needed most desperately to be rid of the Ranas, but of course he was king only in name; without power, without prerogative, a subject monarch. He was permitted no formal contact with the outside world, in case he might canvass support for his covert campaign against the Rana dynasty. The only reading material the Ranas allowed him were American and British mail-order catalogues. His sons had been removed from his care at birth, and he was only allowed the companionship of his daughters, because girls were believed to present less threat to the Rana regime than boys, who, under a father's influence, might grow up to resent dictatorship.

It seemed incredible that a king could be reduced to this – especially when his subjects still believed he was a direct descendant of Vishnu, the Blue-Necked One, who had created not only this world, but every other world.

Seventeen hundred years earlier, a farmer ploughing a field outside Kathmandu struck a stone with the fire-hardened blade of his harrow. To his astonishment he saw milk well up from this stone through the earth. With a local priest, he dug frantically and finally uncovered a gigantic stone image of Vishnu. The god lay with his legs crossed at the ankles, his head on a pillow made from several heads of one great serpent. The blue coils of the serpent's body folded beneath him formed a kind of bed on which he lay, awaiting his next creation.

Vishnu, so legend said, had once drunk poisoned water and in an attempt to find pure water he had climbed the peaks of the Himalayas, the Abode of the Gods, and shattered a rock with his trident. This released three streams of the purest water which poured down the mountains to form the lake – or tank – of serpents, now the valley of Kathmandu. The lake turned blue from the poison which had afflicted him. It was essential that the earthly body of every king descended from Vishnu should be free from any poison, and for this reason a special ceremony attended the death of every king.

Throughout the king's life, one priest had lived close to him, eating the same food, totally dependent on the king's generosity. In return, when the king died, this priest agreed to accept any demons and devils released by his death. To mark this acceptance, the priest would pound a bone splinter taken from the king's skull into powder, and eat it. Then he would accept traditional gifts – hundreds of thousands of rupees, a richly caparisoned horse, two royal elephants – as compensation, and leave Nepal to spend the rest of his life in luxurious exile in India.

As the now very rich priest rode out of Kathmandu for the last time, crowds would line the streets to jeer at him, partly from tradition, partly from envy, with the mocking chant, 'He who rides an elephant steals its corn.'

The Rana hierarchy had done much more than simply steal corn: they had stolen a whole country, his country, the King thought bitterly. Their rapaciousness kept the Nepalese poor. For their own private purposes and profit, one family had deliberately kept Nepal isolated from the rest of the world, untouched by progressive change of any kind; political, economic, medical, for nearly a century.

Every attempt to overthrow them – and there had been several – had failed, because the Ranas maintained a remarkably efficient private intelligence system. But one day, so the King believed, an uprising must succeed. If it failed, there might never be another opportunity. For this reason, the King intended to lead the revolt himself. But how – and when?

Unable to foresee such a time, he pressed his hands wearily against his eyes, and stood, immobile as one of the statues in the garden, while evening darkened the grotesque stone gnomes on the palace lawn.

London. April, 1944

Glover paid off his taxi and stood in the shabby South London street, contemplating a scene of almost total desolation. The driver pointedly rattled coins in his palm. When he realized that Glover was not going to add even a threepenny bit as a tip, he touched his cap derisively with two fingers and drove away.

Glover was used to such behaviour; it did not embarrass him. He never tipped, and when he was finally shamed into paying any bill, it was only after lengthy argument as to its exact size and accuracy. That way, his money earned interest for him. If he paid promptly, the same sum would simply earn interest for other men. These matters were important to him. You had to have known poverty before you could give money its true value, and in Glover's estimation, he had been poor.

He walked slowly along the ruined street, tapping the paving stones with his stick. He did not really need a walking stick, of course, but he resented jibes and sneers that he should be in one of the services because he appeared healthy. However, an amenable doctor in a Wimpole Street mews had helpfully given him a medical certificate which declared he had a weak heart and a family predisposition to sugar in his urine.

Part of the street had been roped off, and at the bottom of a huge crater made by a parachute mine, a red double-decker bus lay on its side, like a giant's discarded toy. He passed warning notices, 'Gas Leak', 'Unexploded Bomb'. He was the only person in the street, apart from a man wearing the blue battledress of the National Fire Service, who sat on an upturned box reading an evening paper. He looked up enquiringly at Glover. His orders were to stop any stranger from entering the bombed houses. There had been reports of looting.

'I'm on the insurance side,' Glover told him, before the man could ask any questions. People found something reassuring in the mention of insurance; it seemed at once both harmless and helpful.

'Houses at the far end are the worst hit,' the fireman explained. 'Don't think they're safe. They've all been evacuated.'

'Are they owners or tenants?' asked Glover.

'Rented, far as I know,' said the fireman. 'From an old woman who lives just across the way. Been living on the rents for years, poor old soul. Now she's living on sod-all.'

'I had better see her,' said Glover. 'What is her name?'

'Mrs Simpson. She's at home. I know, for she's just made me a cup of tea. Not the usual landlady type.'

Glover crossed the road, sniffing with his long twitching nose for any telltale whiff of escaping gas. It would never do to be blown up on such an errand; that sort of accident only happened to other, less careful people. He stopped outside the house

133

that the fireman had indicated, and examined it with a sharp professional eye. All the windows had been blown out, and their frames covered with sheets of white paper that crackled like dry skin in the afternoon wind.

He hung a mental price tag on the property, then tapped gently on the front door with his knuckles. Experience had taught him that a peremptory bang on a door knocker or a harsh ring of the bell frequently did not bring any response. Householders on the level at which Glover dealt invariably associated such an urgent summons with bad news, a visit from the rent collector, or some other equally unwelcome caller.

The door opened a few inches. A woman cautiously pushed her head out and looked at Glover enquiringly. She was small, with grey wispy hair. She wore a nondescript grey dress, wrinkled stockings, bedroom slippers.

'I have come about the trouble you have had, Mrs Simpson,' Glover explained, adjusting his explanation to her. Had she appeared more in command, he would have appeared more obsequious, eager, even privileged to help in such a time of stress and fear.

'You from the council, then?' she asked him without much interest.

'Working with them,' replied Glover carefully.

'You'd better come in.'

They introduced themselves in the narrow hall, with its lincrusta wallpaper and a strong smell of cabbage water and cats.

'Well?' she asked him. 'What can I do for you?'

'It is what I hope I can do for you, Mrs Simpson,' Glover corrected her in an avuncular way.

'I'm a solicitor specializing in property work of many kinds. I was very sorry indeed to learn of the damage you have suffered. In how many properties? Ten?'

'Fourteen,' she corrected him proudly. 'When my old man died, I inherited them all.'

'It must be a great blow. I understand these rents were your livelihood?'

'That's right. All gone. Everything. And the council don't know when I'll get compensation. Nor do they care.'

'That is exactly what I came to see you about, Mrs Simpson. You don't want to be bothered with a lot of form-filling, and visits by nosy parker council officials and so on. They make the war an excuse for any kind of delay. Don't you know there's a war on? they ask. You should know. You, of all people, Mrs Simpson.'

'You're right. Well, how can you help me?'

'I think – I can't promise anything, mind – but I think I could find a client who I could persuade to take all these problems, all these difficulties, off your hands.'

'There's nowt in it for him if he does,' said Mrs Simpson shortly. 'There are no rents now.'

'Agreed. But my client has a great civic sense. It is his way of aiding the war effort, helping people like you, saving them from needless bureaucracy. What would you say the houses are worth?'

'Well, they were all freehold. I would have said that before this, they were worth perhaps two hundred pounds each. But now, who knows?'

Glover turned away, nodding sadly as though the thought of so much loss was too great for him to bear, if only by proxy. He stroked his chin, pulling his fleshy nose with thumb and forefinger as he reached his decision.

'Since there are sadly no houses at all now, Mrs Simpson, only piles of brick and rubbish, you have, on your own estimate, lost an investment worth two thousand, eight hundred pounds. A huge sum of money.'

'Every penny I possess,' she said desperately. 'Next thing, if they don't pay compensation, bomb damage or whatever they call it, I'll be on relief.'

Her voice rose; she was very close to tears.

Glover allowed his hand to rest gently on her shoulder.

'I think not, Mrs Simpson. How about a thousand pounds?'

'One thousand pounds?' she repeated in amazement.

For a moment Glover thought she was going to refuse and was already forming the words he used on such occasions 'simply as an initial payment', when Mrs Simpson burst into tears.

'I don't know how to thank you. Do you know I was actually on my knees praying to God to help me when you knocked on the door? And He has. A thousand pounds! Are you sure?'

'I am certain,' said Glover quietly, but wishing he had only offered the stupid woman seven fifty.

He took the letter he had already written to himself about the sale of property from his pocket, filled in the sum of one thousand pounds and the number of houses and their addresses and handed it to Mrs Simpson.

'Just sign here,' he said, 'and you will have no more trouble.'

On the way back through the rubble to the nearest bus stop, Glover did a rapid mental calculation. At the start of the war he had still been living in his father's house in North London. Now he owned 385 properties, including shops, several small garages, a public house; and he had just bought sites of fourteen more, all for a tiny fraction of their real value. Once the war ended – and despite the flying bombs and the parachute mines, this could not now be long delayed – he would never be poor again. Instead, he was on the way to becoming very, very rich.

Kathmandu. April, 1944

Chet Bahadur waited on the edge of the grass airfield and watched a tiny dot, the size of a flying tadpole in the sky, gradually take the shape of a Dakota, coming in to land. It flew down against the distant white-capped outline of the Himalayas.

Nepal, thought Chet, must not only have the highest airfield in the world, but is also surely the only kingdom where, in times past, according to legend, gods and men fought as equals against a common enemy. Such days of glory had long since gone, of course. Now, the descendants of those men who had marched proudly with the gods were reduced to the level of coolies, carrying vast piles of rice straw on their backs around the airfield perimeter, toiling like busy ants with no time to speak, only to work.

The first King of Nepal had described his kingdom as being like a root between two great stones. On one side lay China, huge, brooding and remote, and on the other, India, with its teeming millions. Nepal lay in between, an obstacle in the aspirations of either country towards Tibet and Afghanistan. The tiny kingdom, barely five hundred miles long by as little as fifty-six miles across, was like a mountain fortress. Chet had therefore been as much puzzled as surprised to be told that a junior and totally unimportant captain like Richard Blake should have been allowed access to the forbidden city. Princes and potentates from half a dozen countries had all been tersely refused admission, so clearly Blake possessed some unusual influence. But what could this be?

The British Resident had come to see him early that morning to explain that this young officer (with whom, he carefully pointed out, Chet had served briefly in Burma) was flying on a short visit to Kathmandu, and wished to visit him. Chet felt both pleased and flattered to be sought out in this way, for the last European visitor he had received personally here had been the Scottish Dr Drummond, nearly six years previously.

Chet shook this memory from his mind, and walked forward to greet Blake coming down the aluminium steps from the aircraft.

'Welcome to Nepal,' he told him warmly. 'My palace is at your disposal.'

'How extremely kind of you. But I do not want to impose on you in any way. I understand there is an adequate hotel in Kathmandu?'

'You understand correctly. But since I employ three hundred indoor servants in my palace, you will not inconvenience me by being my guest. On the contrary, it will give me the greatest pleasure to entertain you. And I can promise that you won't be asked to help with the washing up!'

'That is an invitation I must accept,' replied Blake as Chet led the way to his car; the same one, Chet recalled, in which he had collected Dr Drummond at the Indian frontier. He still felt responsible for Drummond's death. Somehow, Davichand Rana must have discovered the real reason for the doctor's visit, and that knowledge had been Drummond's death warrant. Chet hoped Blake had not spoken to anyone about his reasons for coming to Kathmandu, whatever they might be. Silence was more than the safest policy; in Nepal, it was the only policy.

They drove through the sunshine towards the city. Women squatted outside small houses filtering grain through sieves of plaited straw. Their children kept hungry chickens away from the husks by waving fans of peacock feathers at them. Primitive whitewashed buildings perched on terraced slopes. Vividly painted eyes, blue and white and red, kept watch over travellers from their wooden doors. On a monastery, halfway up a hill, a tattered prayer flag flapped in the breeze.

Chet nodded towards it.

'Our priests write requests on these flags,' he explained. 'Then the wind carries them up to heaven.'

'How do they get an answer?' Blake asked him.

'In the only way any prayer is ever answered. By what you ask

137

for happening – or not happening, which may in itself be a blessing. But, as with all religions, an answer is never guaranteed.'

'There is no guarantee for anything in life, except that one day we all are required to leave it,' replied Blake soberly.

'A melancholy statement, but true,' agreed Chet. 'But surely you are here to enjoy yourself, not to pronounce on such sombre matters? We can offer you mountaineering, trekking, shooting – on foot or from the back of an elephant, if you like. Everything, except one thing.'

He paused as though he had said more than he intended.

'Freedom?' asked Blake quizzically.

'This driver does not speak English well,' Chet replied quickly. 'Even so, he knows a few words. And that is an unwise word to use in this country. If our conversation is to touch on that subject, I think it would be prudent to continue it elsewhere.'

He leaned forward and spoke to the driver. The man turned the car into a narrow unmade track above the gorge. Far below, through a deep gash in solid rock, so sheer that it looked as though cut by a giant's knife, a river frothed and foamed over boulders as big as buildings. At the top of the gorge, the car stopped. Chet and Blake walked out of sight of the driver, in a now totally silent world. Even the river was too remote for the roar of the water to carry up to them. Blake looked back over the green plain that rolled on to foothills grey as elephant hide towards distant mountains wreathed in drifting white clouds.

'This is the plain of Nepal,' Chet explained. 'Once it was the bottom of a great lake, so deep that it contained serpents of enormous size. An immense lotus blossom floated on the surface and glowed with a strange blue radiance like a neon sign. From every country in the East, holy men made pilgrimages to see it, and to marvel, because they believed it was a manifestation of the Lord Buddha.

'One of the most holy men in China decided that he must examine the blossom in detail. This was impossible to do, because no local boatman dared approach it too closely, so he drew his fiery sword of wisdom and sliced this gorge where we are standing. The water from the lake poured out, the level dropped, and where the lotus settled on the ground, he built a shrine, our greatest temple, Swayabbunath, and a city, Kathmandu.'

The mention of the lotus brought back to Blake memories of the punt of that name which he and Glover and Corinne had taken on the river at Oxford. That seemed an eternity away; in a sense, it was.

'Do you believe that story?' Blake asked.

'Do you believe in Adam and Eve?' replied Chet. 'In India and Nepal, a great lake is often known as a tank. Because this tank was so deep, Karkota, the king of all the serpents, lived in it, and so many other snakes, that the local name for the lake was the Tank of Serpents.

'We venerate serpents here in Nepal. They must never be harmed because they can control the amount of rain that falls during the monsoon. It is essential for the rainfall to be heavy if we are to have good crops of rice and millet. So, every year we hold *Naga Panchhami*, a special festival for snakes, to seek their good will.'

Chet paused.

'However,' he added, 'some of us feel that this veneration does not apply to people we privately refer to as serpents or reptiles, and never by their real names in public.'

'Do you mean some of the Ranas?'

Ched nodded.

'I am a member of that family, for it is large. Many in the family are good men, but one who seeks power, and indeed who may well soon seize supreme power, is in my view, an evil man. He wants power for himself, just as he wants wealth, not for any worthwhile purpose, or even to enjoy, but simply to possess, so as to exercise control over others, over our whole country.'

Blake remembered the Maharani of Bundar sitting next to Davichand Rana in the casino in Benares, but she was only covetous of cash, not power. There was an important difference.

'So you would be relieved if he did not become prime minister?'

'It would be a tragedy for Nepal if he did. However, it is unlikely that he will not achieve this ambition.'

'Not necessarily.'

Chet looked at him sharply.

'Why do you say that?'

'Because my visit here is not entirely recreational. It has to do with such a situation.'

Chet looked around him nervously; this was most dangerous ground.

'Let us go away, somewhere else, before we discuss it, then.'

'But why? No-one can overhear us here, surely?'

139

'There are lip-readers,' Chet explained. 'People learn what others say by watching their lips through a telescope. It is an art much practised in the hills.'

They walked back to the car and drove into the centre of the city.

'I will show you a place few Europeans have ever visited,' Chet explained. 'We should be secure there from other ears and eyes.'

They reached a square where huge carved dragons guarded the entrance to a temple. Chet ordered the driver to stop. They climbed out and walked through crowded, narrow streets. Beneath a huge screen, a giant bronze bell soared, large as the dome of a small pagoda.

'That was built to call the faithful to prayer,' Chet explained, remembering that the last person to whom he had explained its significance had been Dr Drummond. 'Now it marks the start of curfew every evening. No-one is allowed out on the streets at night under threat of immediate arrest.'

Chet led the way into an open courtyard. Like an Elizabethan inn, this was surrounded by a high wooden gallery. Pigeons fluttered in and out through holes in the walls, cooing gently, but there was a sunlessness about the yard that made Blake shudder. Even in the city's heat, it felt chill.

From an upstairs window, he caught a brief glimpse of a little girl in a red dress, watching him. Her face was so heavily made up, it appeared like a painted mask, totally without expression. Sunken eyes ringed black by kohl looked down on them both impassively. A red dot marked her forehead and he glimpsed a glitter of silver bangles on her wrist. Then an older woman in the room took her arm and drew the girl away from the window. A curtain dropped.

'That is Kumari, the living goddess,' Chet explained. 'You are privileged to see her. It is rare for a foreigner to do so.'

'Who is she, exactly?' Blake asked him.

'To you, probably only a young girl, who can be aged from four to fourteen, but she has a special significance in Nepal, and every year at the end of the monsoon the faithful take her in a chariot around Kathmandu. This is one of only five or six times a year she is ever seen by people outside the temple. On this particular trip, she will bless our King, who stands in need of every blessing he can receive.'

'But how can a little girl be a goddess?'

'There are two explanations. One says that, generations ago, the lovely goddess Taleju, who protected the royal family, was playing dice with the king of those days. He was so fascinated by her beauty that he forgot himself and leaned across to touch her – and, at this, she immediately vanished from his sight. However, she did not wish to leave the kingdom unprotected, so she returned in the form of a virgin girl, to be worshipped as if she were the goddess herself.'

'What is the other story?'

'Rather less romantic,' admitted Chet dryly. 'About two hundred years ago, the last Mala King of Kathmandu had intercourse with a very young girl, who died as a result. In a succession of nightmares he was informed that he should start the institution of the Kumari, the living goddess, and once every year must convey her around Kathmandu as a penance for his sin.

'Kumari is selected by priests and elders, and must possess thirty-two characteristics, what they call "perfections". She must have a neck like a conch shell, for instance. Her hands and feet must be veined like a duck. She must possess well proportioned nails, long toes and so on.

'One by one, candidates are weeded out. The final two or three are then put into a darkened room, surrounded by the severed heads of goats and buffaloes. The girl who shows the most courage and composure in these ghastly surroundings becomes the new Kumari.

'Incidentally, she can only be chosen from the daughters of goldsmiths of the Sakya clan, just as our prime ministers are only chosen from among the Ranas. But they do not need to possess as many perfections as Kumari, of course. In fact, some have almost none.'

'You feel confident in talking here?'

'As confident as I can be anywhere in Kathmandu.'

'Then, to be as brief as possible, I understand that if Davichand Rana becomes prime minister he may abrogate Nepal's agreement with Britain to supply Gurkha soldiers?'

Chet inclined his head in agreement.

'That is a possibility.'

'And that is why I am here. This war will probably be over within a matter of months, and then demands for India to receive independence will increase. Other countries now in the British Empire may also go their own way. If our arrangement with

141

Nepal is annulled, our long links with the Gurkhas could end. We shall not be able to recruit them any more, which will adversely affect our forces and Nepal's economy – in about equal proportions. The British government is anxious to avoid such a state of affairs. I have been asked to try to prevent this.'

Chet looked at him in amazement.

'How can you possibly do that?' he asked.

'I don't know whether I can – or indeed whether anyone can. But I am told that ridicule is one weapon against which Davichand Rana has no defence. If he were made to look a fool publicly – not just before a few but, say, in the eyes of the whole world – then it is thought unlikely that he would succeed to the premier's office.'

'That is so,' agreed Chet. 'But how do you come into this? You've never even met him.'

'I will,' said Blake. 'He'll see me, because I have a proposition to put that will interest him. The prospect of immense wealth – forever. Golden bait indeed.'

'Are you serious?'

'Deadly serious. So are the people who sent me.'

He explained the proposal that had been put to him in Jerrold's flat in Benares. When he finished, Chet was silent for a moment. Then he nodded his head slowly.

'Whoever thought that out was a good psychologist. It is the sort of thing that would interest my uncle, but he'll make every possible check first. He is not a fool. He will want every kind of corroboration, just in case the offer isn't all it seems.'

'Allowances have been made for that,' Blake assured him.

'Then,' said Chet, 'assuming he finds no fault in this extraordinary scheme, what is your personal reason for approaching him? He is bound to ask you. And, as I say, you've never met him. Very few people outside Nepal have ever heard of him. Why choose you for such a purpose, in any case?'

'The most difficult part of my assignment is explaining why I have come here. The plan is to discredit Davichand Rana at one remove. Obviously, I could not approach him out of the blue, as it were. But I know you. So they want me to sell you this idea. Then you can sell it to Rana, so that he lends you the money to take up the option.'

Chet smiled.

'So you've flown up here to the forbidden city, the most difficult capital in all the world to enter, simply to make me help my uncle look a fool?'

'Those are my instructions,' Blake admitted reluctantly. 'And I felt I had to inform you of them personally. And also that I've no intention whatever of carrying them out. You saved my life. I could not begin to repay that debt, so I would hardly wish to increase it by involving you in this political charade.'

'What would you get out of this – if Davichand Rana agreed?'

'Money,' replied Blake simply. 'By your standards, Chet, almost nothing, but by mine, a considerable amount. I was brought up to believe that my father, a widower, was rich. I went to Oxford and lived in a style that maharajahs adopt when they are undergraduates. They can afford it. I couldn't.

'Then I suddenly discovered my father had mortgaged everything he owned just to give me the chance of living like this, which he'd never had – then, when all the bills came due, rather than face what to him seemed total disgrace, he took his own life. I gambled to try and pay my debts – and his. It seemed the only hope I had.'

'And you lost?' said Chet.

'Every time. My debts will all be paid – if I can carry out this plan. Which, of course, I have no intention of doing. And now that I've explained everything, I'd better be on my way back to Benares.'

'Not just yet,' said Chet quietly. 'You have almost sold the scheme to me. Together, we can sell it to Rana.'

'Together? You mean, you want to go on with it?'

'I do. I assume, before I give you my reasons, that you plan to pay him back his deposit – or, if not you, whoever approached you, will do so?'

'Of course. Every anna. This is not a swindle. Only an attempt to make him look foolish.'

'I see. Sort of gentle persuasion, British style? Well, I'll help you all I can – on one condition. That you do not pay back the money you extract from him. I regard that as belonging to my family. He has swindled us out of far more than that in land and property over very many years. Do you agree?'

'I cannot either agree or disagree. I can only carry out my orders. You would have to see the man who got me involved in the first place. Rex Jerrold. He's in Benares right now. He's the go-between.'

'I may approach him, if you give me his address. But fitting though it will be to extract from Davichand Rana money he has stolen from my family in a variety of ways, I have another more important reason for wanting to help. What you propose represents the only opportunity I have ever known – probably the best anyone has ever had for the last hundred and fifty years – to weaken the hold of the Ranas on this country.

'We are still living in the Middle Ages here, Blake. We have no freedom of speech or writing, barely of thought. People are denounced, spied on, arrested on the word of someone who envies them, without any corroboration or proof. I brought you to this temple where no-one can overhear our conversation because I am afraid to talk freely in my own palace, or even out in the countryside. And if life is like that for me, a member of the Rana family, then think what it is like for people without money or influence of any kind. So I want to go ahead with your proposal – and there is another private reason. I want to show you a place where I sometimes go and pray for someone else who tried to help me years ago.'

They walked back to Chet's car and drove out through the city, up neatly terraced slopes, past the great Buddhist shrine, Swayambhunath, built more than two thousand five hundred years earlier. From the four sides of this ancient building, painted eyes of the ever compassionate Buddha watched over the city. Huge and searching, they stared unblinkingly as the car went past. Between them was a third smaller eye, symbolic of wisdom, and instead of a nose, a curious hieroglyphic like a question mark.

Chet nodded towards it.

'That is how we write *ek*, Hindi for the figure one, symbol of total unity – which could come about if your proposal is agreed. And not just as a figure painted on a wall, but as a fact. A wonderful prospect!'

The driver stopped the car near the peak of a small hill. The two men climbed out, walked across springy turf to a mound, the shape and size of a grave. It was covered with freshly cut flowers. Blake bent down to read the inscription carved on the small headstone: 'To the memory of Dr Jamie Drummond, who died June 17, 1938.'

Dr Drummond. Distant bells of memory began to ring faintly in his mind. He remembered sitting in a bar in Jermyn Street, reading the report in the evening paper of his father's suicide and of the death of a Dr Drummond, killed by an elephant in Nepal. Was this the same man?

'Yes,' said Chet. 'But he wasn't just killed. He was murdered.'

'Are you sure?'

'Unfortunately, yes. A friend told me that a Scottish doctor was in Darjeeling, on holiday, and I asked this friend to invite him on my behalf to Kathmandu. I fixed the entry permit and so on, for there was hope then, as I may already have told you, that I would be allowed to study medicine at Dr Drummond's old university. That was my excuse for bringing him here. In fact, I wanted him to examine my father, to diagnose a strange illness from which he was suffering.'

'And did he?'

'Yes. He confirmed my own suspicions that my father was being deliberately poisoned. My father was then the one man who stood in Davichand Rana's path to supreme power. He was the most likely choice as next prime minister.'

'And what happened?'

'The poisoning ceased. Then it started again a few months later. My father died the following year.'

'But surely there were traces of poison in his body?'

'It is our custom to cremate our dead.

'Dr Drummond was killed by an elephant – that deliberately charged him. Yet elephants are very mild animals – unless they are deliberately irritated to madness. Davichand Rana has trained several elephants to kill – a long process, which shows his dedication. First, the *mahouts* mark out a straight narrow path on the ground by driving sharpened stakes into the earth on either side. Then they tie a goat to a post in the centre of this path and drive the elephant towards it. The wretched beast can't go back or escape on either side, so he has to go ahead and trample the goat to death. Make him do this a dozen or so times, and he becomes accustomed to killing. In the end, the elephant doesn't care whether he's trampling an animal or a man.

'The old Mogul emperors, who used elephants to carry cannon, would make them fierce before a battle by mixing cat meat in their food and squirting chilli juice into their eyes. They couldn't see where they were going and so they just raged on blindly, running away from their own pain.

'I examined this particular elephant's eyes afterwards, and the

145

mahout admitted he had done this. On orders, of course. I need not say from whom. I want to avenge Drummond's murder, and the murder, over many painful months, of my own father.

'Some serpents in the great tank were poisonous, and so is the man who now seeks supreme power. If he achieves his ambition he could poison our entire nation.'

For a moment, the two men stood in silence above the lonely grave. In the distance, workers were singing as they tilled the rice paddy fields. The wind took their song so that it sounded thin and distant, like voices from the air.

Chet turned to Blake.

'Now I suggest we return to the palace. You can have a bath, change and we will enjoy an aperitif together. Then I will see my illustrious uncle, and sow the seed of what I pray will one day grow into a tree of freedom.'

Cheltenham. April, 1944

The matron came into Corinne's room and smiled with the false brightness of someone whose working life was spent in the second-hand shadows of other people's deaths.

'A letter for you,' she said cheerfully. 'All the way from India. Do you think I could have the stamp? I've a young nephew who collects them.'

'Of course,' said Corinne at once.

She took the envelope and looked at her husband's writing. Mrs Rex Jerrold. How odd to think she was no longer Miss Gieves. She did not feel any different, yet so much had happened since she last received a letter addressed to Miss Gieves. She put the envelope on one side to open later, for she always felt a faint dismay when she received letters from her husband, although he was only a husband in name.

Why had he married her? She was crippled, and according to her doctor, might always be crippled, and she had not even known him well. Perhaps he had confused pity for her with love? There was, of course, another possible reason: that he had married her because she was rich as well as incapacitated, and if she died early he would inherit a fortune. That was when she still had a fortune to inherit from her father, before he lost his mills. This thought lurked in the dark shadows of Corinne's mind, but it was never far away. It was there when she went to sleep and

146

when pain awoke her in the silence of the night. Now that she no longer had any expectations of wealth, would her husband leave her after the war?

She had read of a new operation, which was being pioneered in a hospital on the west coast of the United States, but what hope had she of ever travelling to the States in the middle of the war, or of paying for such an operation, which would doubtless be ruinously expensive?

Mrs Gieves claimed that she wasn't well enough to look after Corinne at home but she visited Corinne every Sunday and brought flowers and fruit when she could, and they would sit together in the bedroom or out on the lawn, according to the weather, and make small talk. Both were always secretly glad when the visiting hour ended.

The matron said, 'I'll make you a nice cup of tea.'

'Thank you,' said Corinne.

It was always a 'nice' cup of tea. What was nice about it? There was no sugar, only sweetener; no proper milk, only milk powder, because in the fifth year of the war, supplies were short and rationing strict, but she meant well, even if she was inquisitive. She wanted to know about Corinne's husband, where he was, what friends he had. She read his reports in the *Globe* and somehow, she also knew Blake's name – Corinne could not imagine how. She often asked about him. Was he still in India? Did Mr Jerrold ever see him? Perhaps this was only her way of finding something new to talk about, which could not be easy when she had many patients who were so incapacitated as to be virtual prisoners in their rooms.

Corinne watched the matron leave the room and then picked up the envelope. Her husband never had any real news: he was always leaving one town, or arriving somewhere else. She wondered where he was now, and then where Blake was, and David Glover. Each had gone his own way, out of her life. Of them all, she thought most often about Blake.

Her last memory was seeing him at the wheel of the car, when he turned and smiled at her, handsome like a Greek god, as she always remembered him. He would have done his utmost to help her, of that she was certain. But she never had the opportunity to put this faith to the test. Now, she probably never would.

Sitting in her wheelchair, her thin hands holding the letter, which she must soon force herself to open and read, memories of what might have been, and the contrast with what was, overwhelmed her like a great dam bursting. Corinne's shoulders began to heave with sobs. She was still crying when the maid came in to put up the blackout curtains.

6

Davichand Rana looked up from his marble-topped desk as his male secretary entered and bowed.

'Your nephew, Chet Bahadur, wishes to see you, your Excellency. He says it is a personal matter.'

Davichand Rana nodded. He had been expecting this visit ever since he had learned that an English officer was arriving in Kathmandu. Chet came into the room and bowed with his hands pressed spatulate, a mark of respectful greeting.

'It is an inconvenient time,' his uncle told him curtly.

'This matter will only take a few moments,' Chet assured him, 'but it is one on which I feel you are the only person who can advise me.'

'What is it about?'

'Money, Excellency.'

'Indeed? You are in debt?'

'On the contrary, sir. I have just been given the opportunity of acquiring more money than I understand Nepal possesses at the moment in her national treasury.'

'You have? That must indeed be a remarkable proposition,' said Davichand Rana dryly. He had not expected an absurdity like this.

'I have been approached, Excellency, by a British officer, a Captain Blake; with whom I served briefly in Burma, and to whom I rendered a trifling service which he has magnified into saving his life. He has come to Kathmandu to make this offer on behalf of his country's government. I intend to take it, subject of course to your approval and, as the prime minister designate, with your permission.'

'I am not yet prime minister, although the auguries are such that this may well come about. Why do you not seek the permission and advice of the present holder of that office?'

'Because, Excellency, I believe that you will shortly be appointed prime minister, and this is a matter which could affect the country's future, not just for one or two years, but permanently.'

'You intrigue me. Pray proceed.'

'It is generally agreed, Excellency, that, at the conclusion of the present world hostilities, demands by Indian nationalists will result in India becoming independent of British rule. It is then possible – and I think probable – that Burma, Malaya and perhaps other countries within the British Empire, will also seek independence. This will materially increase the importance of Nepal to British interests. And in order to foster friendship between our two countries, it has been proposed that I take advantage of this political situation.

'I think it is also acknowledged, Excellency, that the main waterways of India and Burma are of paramount importance, not only as a source of water but for moving freight over long distances at a fraction of the cost of transporting similar quantities of goods by rail or road – if these other means of transport could even deal with the great amount of traffic involved.

'This is especially true in Burma, where the Irrawaddy River carries far more trading traffic in peacetime than the Mandalay to Rangoon railway and roads combined. What is not generally realized, Excellency, is that the trading rights cf this river, by a private agreement made between King Thibaw of Burma and Queen Victoria of England, as Empress of India – of which country Burma was then a part – are in the gift of the British Government.

'Every company trading on this river, every ship, even every fishing vessel above a certain size, pays direct or indirect dues into a central fund.'

'Are you sure? I have never heard of this custom.'

'Nor have many people, Excellency, but it is a fact. These dues are not listed as such. They may appear as customs duty, or as various other taxes and under all manner of headings to conceal their existence. The total sums involved run into crores of rupees, the equivalent of several million pounds sterling, every year in perpetuity.

'I have been offered these Rights forever for a price equivalent to ten million pounds sterling. Of this, one million pounds would have to be paid on signature of the agreement. The rest would be paid out of revenue accruing over a period of time agreed by both parties.'

'What if Burma becomes independent?'

'That would not affect the issue in any way. The contract would still be binding. The British Government is most desirous of strengthening ties of friendship with Nepal. Britain is a rich country, Nepal is not. What may appear to be a great bargain to us is, by comparison, of relatively little financial value to them. You may give a silver rupee to a beggar and you do not even miss the coin, but to him it can represent a week's food.'

'Where is this officer now?'

'In Kathmandu. At my palace.'

'The proposition seems worthy of investigation, but how can you possibly test its validity? As you explain the matter, it is difficult to believe.'

'I also expressed that opinion, Excellency, and Blake has brought with him a draft document of transaction to be signed by Lord Louis Mountbatten, the Supreme Allied Commander, South East Asia, by Field Marshal Sir William Slim, who commands the British Fourteenth Army in Burma, and by Air Marshal Sir John Baldwin, commanding the Third Tactical Air Force.'

'I would like to see Captain Blake,' said Davichand Rana. 'Is he alone?'

'He is, sir. But in Benares there are two other Englishmen who can vouch for the terms. One is a Colonel Howard, at present on the Viceroy's staff. The other is a Mr Dermott from the Foreign Office in London.'

'How would you raise a million pounds?' asked Rana. 'Assuming, of course, that you satisfied yourself it was a genuine offer which you wished to accept?'

'My father had certain assets, against which I think that a loan of this size could be arranged by the banks. But of course I seek your advice and also your influence, because I realize that such a loan might be forbidden by the prime minister.'

Rana smiled.

'Or by the prime minister designate,' he said softly.

Calcutta. April, 1944

Mr Edwin Lord, the senior partner in Moynihan, Marigold and Lord, the longest established European firm of solicitors in Calcutta, and by many held to be the most prestigious in India, leaned back in his chair and regarded Dermott quizzically.

Mr Lord was in his early sixties. But for the war, he would have retired to the house he had bought in Cornwall years before, where his wife was already living. She had returned to England in 1939, and had been unable to obtain a return passage to India.

He longed now either for retirement or for a return to more leisurely pre-war days, when the office would close at lunch time, and partners could spend their afternoons by the Saturday Club pool, or at the races, instead of dealing with problems like the one which Dermott had presented to him.

He would never have seen Dermott in the first place if he had not brought a personal letter of introduction from a friend in Delhi, but there was no backing out now. Lord cleared his throat and addressed himself to his unwelcome visitor.

'You have informed the Viceroy's office about this?'

'I have, Mr Lord,' Dermott replied. 'All who need to know have been advised of His Majesty's Government's intention to set up an agreement with General Davichand Rana, along the lines of the document I have given you.'

'I have read it closely, Mr Dermott, and I must say I find it an extraordinary proposition. I have been practising in India for some thirty years, and I have also acted for the old Irrawaddy Flotilla Company in Burma, and have had many friends in Rangoon. But never, in all this time, have I heard of trading rights on the Irrawaddy River. If this were April the first I would think your proposition a rather complex and tasteless jape.'

'I wish it were,' said Dermott earnestly. 'But you must appreciate that it is a very important matter.'

'I do. But to whom, exactly? If you are selling these rights, presumably they exist – which I still beg leave to doubt – and Burma becomes independent after the war, as you assume, will the Burmese nationalists honour the deal?'

'What they may or may not do need not concern us in the slightest. All we need from you is a legal document which our Nepalese friend can sign.'

'Why come to me?'

'For the best reason of all, Mr Lord. Because your firm is the most highly regarded in Calcutta, probably in all India. The fact that you are drawing up this agreement will in itself be a virtual guarantee of its authenticity.'

'That is what disturbs me, Mr Dermott. This document concerns rights of which I have never heard, apparently to be sold for a large sum of money to the potential prime minister of a friendly nation. Their validity is apparently vouchsafed by three of the most senior and distinguished officers in the British armed forces, so I presume they have made their own enquiries. What does HMG stand to gain – apart from money? In whose interests has this agreement been prepared?'

'Shall we use the phrase, in the national interest?'

'You mean, it could be a matter involving the Official Secrets Act, Mr Dermott?'

'I do. And I will ask you to sign a letter to show that you accept this, and appreciate the need for total discretion.'

'If I were representing Davichand Rana, could I advise him that it would also be in his best interests to sign?'

'Totally. If he does not, then other means may be used to persuade him.'

'You mean, you will coerce him? Are you saying that he holds views detrimental to the Allied cause, Mr Dermott?'

'No. But if he should become prime minister, HMG is anxious to minimize the risk of his policies being in conflict with HMG's post-war intentions.'

Mr Lord placed the tips of his fingers together, and with his elbows on the blotting pad of his desk, regarded Dermott coldly, his mind still not made up.

'It is in the nature of a bribe then?' Dermott leaned towards him in a conspiratorial way.

'Not a bribe, but a consideration, shall we say?

'I had not intended to tell you this,' he said softly, as though he feared other ears might be listening, 'but this matter is so important to HMG that there could be something very worth-while in it for you. Apart from your firm's fees and necessary expenses and disbursements, of course. Quite apart.'

He paused.

Mr Lord regarded him with small, appraising eyes.

'In what way?' he asked in an equally low voice. They might have been talking in the nave of a great cathedral which could magnify and transmit every word.

'Certain honours and awards, as you know, are in the Viceroy's gift. He acts on advice in these matters, naturally. In this case, he would be acting on my advice.'

Dermott sat back. If this cautious old fool didn't react now, he'd drop the whole thing and consult the next firm of solicitors on his list. But he could see that Mr Lord was wavering.

'We want something legal but short, so that it can be easily understood by laymen,' he continued. 'We do not wish to have lawyers acting for the other side arguing over the exact meaning of this word or that. The matter is simply too important for any delay.'

'Have you any idea of the wording you would find agreeable?' asked Lord, carefully keeping sarcasm out of his voice.

'As a matter of fact, I have. I have a draft of what we think could form the basis of a simple agreement.'

Dermott took an envelope from the pocket of his bush jacket and handed over a folded letter.

Lord read:

It is anticipated by His Majesty's Government that Burma will shortly be reoccupied by His Majesty's Forces and various commercial interests involving Trading Rights upon the Irrawaddy River then become available for disposal. These are in His Majesty's Government's gift and could be utilized to reward suitably deserving parties who may be recommended by the Supreme Allied Commander, South East Asia (hereinafter to be called 'The Commander') who has been empowered to decide which person or persons will be recommended for participation in the said commercial interests.

The aforesaid person or persons, upon such selection, will be entitled to acquire the rights on concessional terms, the sum of £10,000,000 sterling or its equivalent in agreed local currency, at exchange rates prevailing at the date of authorization. And whereas the Commander has, with the approval of His Majesty's Government's representatives, agreed to select a fit and proper person or persons to acquire these rights as above aforesaid, His Excellency General Davichand Bahadur Rana (hereinafter to be called 'H.E.'), being desirous of being selected for this recommendation, has approached the Commander for this purpose;

The parties have agreed as follows:–

1. The Commander has, with the approval of His Majesty's Government, advised H.E. to whom the commercial interests as above outlined will become available on the reoccupation of Burma as aforesaid, that he hereby acknowledges that H.E.

has paid to him (through his representatives) the equivalent sum of £1,000,000 sterling, in local currency, Rupees 13,400,000, being 10% of the total sum as deposit, to be known as 'the deposit'. The Commander covenants that this sum will be held by His Majesty's Government (or their representatives) until the above aforesaid commercial interests are allotted to H.E. as hereinbefore mentioned, when the further sum of £9,000,000 or its equivalent in local currency will become due. This further sum may be paid by H.E. in annual instalments, of an amount and over a period to be mutually agreed, out of revenues received by the aforesaid commercial interests.

2. The aforesaid deposit paid by the said H.E. shall not be withdrawn, but will be kept in safe custody, with a recognized Government Bank such as the Imperial Bank of India or the Reserve Bank of India in the name of Special Purposes Overseas Account (Civil Affairs), South East Asia.

In Witness whereof the parties hereto have set and subscribed their hands above the official seal on the day, month and year first written above and these signatures have been counter-signed by Field Marshal Sir William Slim, Commanding British 14th Army and by Air Marshal Sir John Baldwin, Commanding 3rd Tactical Air Force.

Lord put the paper on his desk. 'You have given this matter some thought, I see,' he said slowly. 'Have you consulted other solicitors about it?'

'No. But London has advised us closely and their legal people have drafted this. It's a very high level thing, Mr Lord. Which is why we came to you. And time is becoming, as you lawyers say, of the essence.'

'Then I will give it my full and immediate attention,' Lord promised him smartly, his mind made up. After so many years as plain Mr Lord, it would be extremely agreeable to be referred to as Sir Edwin.

Kathmandu. April, 1944

Blake stood behind a white silk curtain at an upper window in Chet's palace and watched Davichand Rana arrive. His Phantom II sighed slowly to a halt in the courtyard, and orderlies busied themselves at the doors, bowing obsequiously. Two escorted him

155

up the stairs. Davichand Rana wore a light grey suit, sambur skin shoes and violet tinted spectacles. Blake noted the way in which he compressed his thin lips, how he looked neither to one side or the other: all signs of parsimony, greed and dedication to a central purpose. Could he and Chet use these characteristics to their own advantage?

'There's the target,' said Chet, smiling a little nervously. 'I will make the introduction, then it's over to you. You have everything you want?'

'A large brandy would be acceptable,' said Blake, suddenly realizing what an extraordinary assignment he had undertaken. How could he, an army captain, heavily in debt and without a rupee to his credit, possibly hope to persuade a shrewd and immensely wealthy politician that he was offering him the chance to make millions?

The idea seemed so preposterous that it appeared to defy serious consideration. His greatest ally, of course, would be Davichand Rana himself. Like the pilgrims in Benares and the bathers in the Ganges, he wanted to believe: it was up to Blake to make that belief not only totally plausible, but absolute.

'Brandy will be provided,' Chet answered him. 'Afterwards.'

He led the way downstairs. Davichand Rana awaited them impatiently at one end of the huge entrance hall. Oil paintings of past Ranas, wearing their theatrical uniforms of blue and crimson and gold, with bird of paradise plumes cascading from their hats, stared down at them.

'This is Captain Richard Blake,' said Chet Bahadur. 'My uncle, His Excellency General Davichand Bahadur Rana.'

'It is very rare for us to have a visitor from England,' said Davichand Rana. 'I understand that you are here on business? I welcome you to our country, as, of course, I welcome all expansion of trade and commerce between our two nations.'

He led the way into a dining room. A long polished wood table was heavy with gold plates; lotus blossoms floated in crystal bowls. A faint aroma of sandalwood and crushed rose petals hung in the air.

Behind each chair stood two servants in livery; one to replenish their glasses of wine, the other to offer more food or remove the gold plates as they finished each course. After dinner, over cigars and brandy, when the servants had withdrawn and all beyond the table lay in darkness, Davichand Rana leaned back in his chair and looked questioningly, first at Chet and then at Blake.

Chet cleared his throat nervously.

'Are you ready to hear what our visitor has to say, Excellency?' he asked his uncle.

'It is my pleasure.'

Blake closed his eyes for a moment to marshal his thoughts. Then, putting down his cigar in a silver ashtray, and pushing away his half finished brandy, as though to emphasize that these were both unnecessary distractions, he began to speak.

'I have come, sir, as an emissary on a delicate mission for the Government of India, acting with the authority of His Majesty's Government in London. The matter concerns our two countries.'

He paused.

'You are young to carry such a burden of responsibility,' said Rana.

'That may be so, sir, but I would remind you of the reply of William Pitt, England's Prime Minister at twenty-four in the eighteenth century, when someone made that same comment. Like me, he admitted that he was guilty of the crime of being young. It is a failing that time deals with most effectively.'

'I take your point. Pray continue.'

'You are probably also aware, sir, of the prophecy that astrologers made after what we call the Indian Mutiny of 1857, the year in which the British Crown took responsibility for the Indian sub-continent?

'It was said then by the wisest soothsayers in India that British rule would only last ninety more years. Every other prophecy they made at that time has been proved accurate, so there is no reason to doubt the veracity of this statement. If true – as I am told many in authority firmly believe it to be – British rule will run for only another three years, until 1947. It is my belief, sir, that around that date India will become independent. No doubt Burma, as a neighbouring country, will follow suit.

'The present Governments of India and Britain are therefore most anxious to preserve the closest possible relations with Nepal. Napoleon called the British a nation of shopkeepers, and it has been my country's experience that nothing cements a friendship between countries so much as commerce and trade. For this reason, sir, I have come to Nepal empowered to offer closer commercial ties with your country and mine than have obtained before.

'The link would naturally be predominantly a personal one, because, if I may speak privately, as between guest and host, and within these walls only, I believe that in the event of the present prime minister of Nepal resigning, you, sir, would assume the office in his place.'

Blake paused. His throat felt dry and he was uncomfortably aware of a pulse beating like a metronome in his ears: his ankle pained him as it did in moments of stress. He knew now how William Tell must have felt. Like him, he had only one shot. He must hit the target, for he would not have a second chance.

'That is possible,' Davichand Rana admitted, 'but, of course, I would not wish anything to happen to our present beloved prime minister which could accelerate such a situation.'

'Naturally,' Blake agreed quickly. 'On the other hand, sir, governments are concerned with political realities. Therefore, in the hope that it would help our two countries to draw closer should you assume supreme power, I have come to offer, through your nephew here, an unusual proposition, which I think may interest you I have come, sir, to offer you – through him – the opportunit .o secure in perpetuity all trading rights on the Irrawadd River in Burma.'

'But wl   .actly are the trading rights on that river?' asked Davichan Rana in a puzzled voice. 'I have visited Burma on several occasions, yet I have never heard of them before.'

'Few people have, sir, and that of course can only increase their value, which is already enormous. They have never been fully exploited, and refer to a percentage of fees charged for piloted freight, to the movement of goods by water so many miles north of Rangoon, all mineral and alluvial rights, and various permissions to prospect for oil. The Anglo-Burmese oilfields were, until before the war, one of the most productive and profitable in Asia.'

'What is the price your Government has in mind?'

'I am empowered to ask for ten million pounds sterling, but not to be paid outright, of course. Only a ten per cent deposit would be called for, and the rest could be paid out of revenues as they are received, month by month, over a mutually agreed period of time.'

'So, in your English phrase, I would be in for one million pounds?'

'Yes. Your one and only commitment, sir. All the rest comes out of income.'

'Even so, a very large sum is required of me,' said Davichand Rana slowly, regarding Blake through narrowed eyes. 'I would have to make the most exhaustive enquiries about this proposition before I gave any opinion on the matter.'

'Naturally, sir. We all appreciate that, and to help you, the concession is being handled as a civil matter divorced from all politics, by the European law firm of Moynihan, Marigold and Lord in Calcutta. Mr Lord, the senior partner, has been provided with all relevant facts. He would be honoured to advise you, sir, or any solicitors you care to appoint to act for you.'

'Presumably this is a secret matter?'

'It is indeed a most secret and sensitive matter, sir, and disclosure in whole or in part would naturally nullify all negotiations.'

'What is the estimated income of these trading rights?'

'During the last year for which figures were available – the war has distorted everything, of course – it was in excess of five million pounds. This revenue was dissipated into various other areas, such as customs and excise, taxation, landing fees, mooring dues, expatriate subcontractors and so forth, so that it would not appear as a single sum in the Government of Burma's estimates of expenditure.'

'A fifty per cent return,' said Davichand Rana appreciatively. 'It certainly seems a remarkable proposition. But you will appreciate I cannot come to a decision about it now or even give any indication of my own views. But I will at once instruct my own solicitor in Calcutta, Mr Baird, to enquire further into the matter.'

Blake raised his glass.

'To a happy outcome, sir,' he said.

'For all of us,' added Chet.

Calcutta. May, 1944

Mr Lord sat back in his swivel chair and drummed his fingers on his desk. The punkah, trailing a tasselled cloth fringe suspended from a long pole, swung slowly to and fro above his head in a feeble attempt to dispel the humidity of the Calcutta afternoon.

159

Mr Thomas Baird, senior partner of Jellicoe and Craft, after Moynihan, Marigold and Lord arguably the second most eminent European firm of solicitors in India, regarded him from the shiny leather armchair opposite the desk. Baird was a plump, cheerful man, bald-headed, but with thick tufts of hair sprouting from his nostrils and his ears. They had appeared on opposing sides in several of the more profitable legal cases to be heard in India. Their usual relationship was therefore one of reserve and respect, but now Baird regarded Lord with a scepticism he did not attempt to conceal.

'Totally without prejudice,' he said, 'this is the first time I've ever heard of any trading rights on the Irrawaddy, or any other damn river, come to that. Mineral rights, yes. Fishing rights, agreed. But trading rights?'

He shook his head.

'In general, I would agree with you,' admitted Lord, not too enthusiastically. 'But in this case I am certain these rights do exist.'

'There is no reference to them in any document I can find. Have you any documentary evidence of their existence?'

'As I have explained, you would not expect to find any official written reference to them, for the reasons we have already discussed. There is, if you like, a parallel with the Road Fund in England, into which was originally paid all revenue from car licences. The intention then was to put this money towards the upkeep of roads. But it doesn't simply go towards the roads now. It goes to help balance the budget – along with duty on cigarettes and beer and so forth. These trading rights are lost – or concealed – under other headings.'

'That may be,' said Baird, 'but I can find no record of them ever existing, to be lost or concealed.'

'There are doubtless documents setting them out, of course, but I am informed that all relevant papers are in Rangoon, and so no-one will see them until after the war – if they haven't already been destroyed by the Japs. But you have seen these signatures. Mountbatten, Slim and Baldwin are not the sort of men to put their names to anything which in the slightest degree smacks of chicanery.'

'I have examined the signatures,' Baird agreed, 'and have compared them myself with their signatures on official documents, and they certainly appear genuine. But I still feel I should contact the office of the Supreme Allied Commander, South East Asia, or even Lord Louis himself in Kandy.'

'That is your decision,' Lord replied, 'but, as you can imagine, this is a very sensitive area. I understand that everything must be done on a strictly need to know basis. Any general enquiry would therefore, in my opinion, be unproductive. But, of course, feel free to do as you wish.'

'A million pounds sterling,' said Baird reflectively. 'A great sum of money. I read somewhere that to prosecute this war is costing Britain fifteen million pounds every day. This deal will involve two-thirds of that figure. One million down and nine to follow. It could keep the whole war going from, say eight o'clock one morning to twelve midnight. A very large investment for a private person.'

'And a proportionately large fee for Jellicoe and Craft, if based, as we must assume it will be, on a percentage of the total sum involved,' replied Lord quickly.

Baird said nothing. His fee would clearly be prodigious, and out of all proportion to the amount of work that he or his clerks would be expected to undertake. After all, they were in the middle of a world war. Documents, which in normal circumstances he would have insisted upon seeing, could quite understandably all be in enemy hands, along, most probably, with officials who could have helped him.

He realized that it would probably be pointless to approach any of the distinguished signatories directly on a matter which must have the most serious political undertones, and he had always found Lord honourable, even as an adversary. Lord appeared confident that the document was genuine and that these hitherto unheard-of trading rights actually existed. Also, they were both members of the Bengal Club and the Saturday Club; they had been contemporaries at Cambridge. There was no doubt about it, these things mattered. So Baird made up his mind, and nodded acceptance.

'Right,' he said. 'I still have some personal reservations, but then I am not called Doubting Thomas for nothing. I am not convinced beyond all argument, but I accept your word. In fact, I either have to accept it or reject it. And in that case, I would have to go back to my client and admit failure.'

'Then, I have no doubt he would immediately seek the services of another solicitor. He is an extremely rich man, and I think that all our experience with the very rich reinforces my personal impression that they always want more money. This would seem to present him with an opportunity for making a great deal more for what to him must only be a modest investment.

'I think we both have to accept that these are strange times in which we live, and strange arrangements appear to be the order of the day. Would you not agree?'

Baird nodded.

Relieved, Lord pressed a button beneath his desk.

'My English clerk will give you a copy of the draft contract – only he and I in the office have seen it, for security reasons. You can then peruse it further. I very much hope you will see your way to advising your client to sign it. Time, I am told, is pressing.'

'There is just one thing,' said Baird slowly. 'This document, you tell me, has been drawn up and should be signed under English law. I would suggest therefore that the transaction is not carried out in Nepal, but in India to secure the full protection of English law.'

'A wise decision,' said Lord approvingly. 'Would you like the money to be paid in Calcutta or Delhi?'

'I understand from my client that he intends visiting Benares in the next few days, where he has a residence. Assuming he accepts my advice, I would suggest, if it is convenient, that the money is paid over there, by the intermediary, his nephew Captain Chet Bahadur Rana.'

'An excellent idea. Now, early in the day though it is, I suggest you join me in a whisky and soda to celebrate an agreement which I hope will be satisfactory and profitable to all concerned.'

Benares. May, 1944

Dermott lit a cigarette from one half-smoked. The ashtray in his bedroom was already littered with bent stubs, and the air thick with stale smoke. Jerrold sat on the edge of the bed in his shirt sleeves, watching him.

'Think this Rana fellow will bite?' he asked at last.

Dermott shrugged.

'Don't see why not. I would, if I were in his shoes, and offered the prospect of a fortune for what, to him, is a small outlay. We are dealing with one of the richest families in the world, remember.'

'I wish someone would make me an offer like that,' said Jerrold enviously.

'They might – if you were a maharajah. Anyhow, you'll get something out of it. I'll recommend that they up your retainer. If we pull this off, of course.'

'Generous,' said Jerrold sarcastically.

'Well, it is Government money, you know.'

'So I shall get a few hundred a year more from the tax-payers,' Jerrold said. 'And Blake is going to get over thirty thousand.'

'But not for himself. And he will be court-martialled. Might even go down for it. Would you fancy a spell in an Indian prison? Anyhow, how else could he earn so much so easily?'

'That's another question altogether.'

'Exactly. But come to that, how could you earn an increased retainer so easily?'

'If I knew,' retorted Jerrold, 'I wouldn't be involved in the first place.'

Mr Baird sat in a corner of the back seat of the old Essex taxi and stifled a yawn. It was surprisingly cold, even for five-thirty in the morning, and he felt aggrieved at being up and out at such an hour. But when a client as rich and influential as Davichand Rana demanded his presence, he had to swallow his distaste – and increase his fee.

The Sikh driver trundled the yellow car through the sleeping streets of Benares towards the river. Baird had spent nearly thirty years in India, but despite this still felt unaccustomed to the squalor, the poverty and the fog of inertia that seemed to clog every enterprise. Not for nothing was the Urdu word for yesterday – *kul* – the same as the word for tomorrow. And how absurd that he should have to meet Davichand Rana at this hour, simply because the latter wished to make an act of purification in the sacred river at the most advantageous time of day, sunrise. A comparable situation, he thought, would be to discuss a business proposition entailing millions of pounds with a British industrialist in Birmingham at the only time he wished to see you, just before mass or holy communion at seven o'clock on a Sunday morning.

There was too much belief in the right time of day for making a decision, or in the grouping of the stars. No-one would begin a journey or open negotiations on any serious business matter on a Tuesday, or finish them on a Saturday. Some numbers were good and some bad – especially those ending with a nought. And were the stars friendly or hostile? Such absurd considerations counted for more than the nuts and bolts of any deal.

Shops were still shuttered; unshaded bulbs burned feebly outside the surgery of Dr Gomi, Venerealogist, MB (Dacca), and the Jhansi English School (Matriculates Well Taught Here). Dust swirled around the taxi like a strange and alien fog; through it, on either side of the main road, Baird could see rickshaw wallahs, wrapped in filthy rags, asleep in their rickshaws, shafts on the ground. Outside the All India Cycle Repair Emporium, dismantled bicycles lay among piles of chains and pedals, like the component parts of some complex surrealistic design. Watchmen with staves stood watching yellow-eyed dogs root in the debris of banana stalks at the roadside. Others still slept on string mattress beds, completely cocooned in sheets like corpses. It was difficult to believe that within an hour these empty streets would be crammed with country buses and coaches, packed with passengers inside, even on the roof, among tin trunks and wicker baskets of live chickens.

Baird's taxi passed a funeral procession entering a square: twenty men wearing white dhotis, a few women carrying children, a pariah dog, hopeful for scraps. The corpse was borne on a stretcher, wrapped in white robes, dusted with saffron powder and draped in faded flowers. The chief mourners wore orange turbans; some waved yellow flags and others beat drums. The taxi stopped in the square under strings carrying strips of gold and silver tinsel that stretched from upper storeys on one side of the street to those on the other.

'I will wait for you here,' said the driver. 'It is too narrow for a car. You will be a long time, sahib?'

'Half an hour,' replied Baird shortly.

He walked along the street, wrinkling his nose in distaste at the foul combination of smells from human faeces, diesel oil and rotting vegetation. Perhaps some of his aversion stemmed from uneasiness about his present assignment. He did not think that Lord was deliberately lying to him, but perhaps he was not being entirely truthful. Yet what lawyer was when the interests of an important client were at stake, when his fee would be more than most men earned in a year?

He gripped his briefcase tightly as he entered a narrow alleyway. Concrete walls on either side were dark and smooth with grease, where generations of passers-by had brushed their dirty hands. The alley grew narrower and then became a series of stone steps, slippery with urine. The doors of houses on either side were closed, windows shuttered; night air was held to be unhealthy. Electric wires hung from green glass insulators, and in a tiny courtyard a servant crouched on his haunches cooking gobbets of meat in crackling fat above a charcoal fire. The steps widened suddenly and Baird was at the edge of the river, looking down on dozens of small boats that bobbed in the scummy green water, and at hundreds of people who, even at this hour, swarmed about on the foreshore.

Birds dived above floating yellow blossoms. Worshippers crouched under rattan umbrellas. Washermen were already spreading out white vests and shorts to dry on rocks; others still hammered the dirt out of the previous day's washing by beating the clothes on flat stones. Buildings on either side crowded over the river; windows were open here and naked lights burned in hazy rooms; pictures of the elephant-headed Ganesh, the god of good luck, decorated outer walls; red flags drooped in the windless air. Bushes, even small trees, sprouted in the crumbling tiles of ancient houses. Half a mile across the river the far bank lay, still shrouded in mist, with the spires of distant temples pointing thin fingers through the morning haze. Baird had a sudden thought that this was how he had always imagined Camelot would appear from afar, misty, mystic. But close to, would it be a disappointment? Close to, most things, most people were.

A hand touched his shoulder.

'Rana sahib's house is here,' a servant explained. 'I am just now taking you.'

He led Baird through a courtyard with a dripping tap; a goat stood tethered to the wall. Heavy wooden doors opened on oiled hinges, and suddenly Baird had left the squalor and filth and poverty behind him. He was in a room with high windows overlooking the river, furnished in impeccable and expensive European style. There were leather armchairs, shelves of books, a reading lamp on a desk, a fireplace empty of coals now, but filled with lotus blossoms. Davichand Rana was standing in front of it.

'You are late,' he began accusingly.

Baird looked at his watch.

'Three minutes,' he admitted.

'I have to make my act of purification exactly as the sun appears above the other bank of the river. Before or afterwards is not the same. What have you discovered about this Captain Blake?'

'I have only been able to make a few enquiries in the time,' Baird explained. 'I have no access to his army records, of course.'

'I don't want excuses,' said Davichand Rana shortly. 'What have you found?'

'Well, he was educated at Oxford. Worked for a bookmaker in London and then joined the army at the outbreak of war.'

'A bookmaker!' the other man exclaimed in surprise. 'Is he a gambler?'

'He has been seen in the casino here, yes.'

'Is he short of money?'

'He does not appear to be so. He is well liked by the few people I have managed to speak to at the leave centre. Of course, they don't know him well. He has only been in Benares for a few days.'

'Have you met him?'

'I have spoken to him on the pretext that I thought I knew his father. He seems pleasant, an extremely good-looking young man.'

'I am aware of that. I have also met him. Would you say he is honest and to be trusted?'

Baird shrugged.

'I am reluctant to trust anyone totally, your Excellency. Most people have breaking points or, more tactfully, bending points. My father once told me that an honest man has hair growing in the palm of his hand.'

Davichand Rana allowed himself a smile.

'Have you made enquiries of any headquarters about the authenticity of the document?'

'I have a cousin, a major in South East Asia Command at Kandy. There was no time to write and expect a reply, the post being what it is nowadays, so I sent a confidential clerk to see him. This is an especially sensitive matter, because it could be extremely dangerous ammunition in the hands of Indian or Burmese nationalists, and he was unable to persuade anyone to discuss it.'

'So you have discovered nothing?'

'From that source, no, sir. But I have discussed it at length with Mr Lord, who is acting for the other side. His firm is considered to be – next to my own – one of the most respected in India. He appears absolutely confident that this is genuine.'

'Appears? He does not know? He is not certain?'

'Certainty is a matter of belief,' Baird reminded him. 'One can be certain of so little in life. One can have confidence. One can believe.'

'I accept that,' agreed Davichand Rana. 'But even so, a million pounds sterling, with another nine million pounds sterling in the balance, is a huge sum of money.'

'For an enormous potential profit,' pointed out Baird softly.

He was tired of Davichand Rana's prevarication; at each meeting, they trod the same ground. What do you think? What would you suggest? The man was greedy and mean and lacked the courage to decide one way or the other. He was reminded of his wife's stern admonition to their only son as a baby in the nursery: 'Do it – or get off the pot!'

He turned away from his client, so that Davichand Rana could not read his thoughts in his eyes, and stood looking out at the river. Hundreds, possibly thousands more pilgrims and believers had arrived during the few minutes they had been talking. They had already set aside their outer clothing and walked barefoot into the filthy river. Women stood in their saris, pouring water over their heads and bodies from round aluminium pots.

A leper crouched in the scummy water, one hand and half his face eaten away by disease. Children squatted on the steps, defecating, and a pilgrim pushed away the corpse of a dog to bend down and brush his teeth in the river with a split twig. Crows perched on the bloated body of a dead bullock, pecking at its entrails, as the current carried it past the window.

Barges piled high with branches lashed down by ropes and chains moved slowly on the tide, near the burning ghats. There were 52 ghats, one for each week of the year, some more holy than others. Here, corpses wrapped in sheets, feet protruding at unnatural angles, lay in line, while boys toiled to arrange pyramids of sandalwood, and old men manoeuvred the stiff concealed bodies into place, levering them with long poles. Other men raked piles of hot ash and moved unburned portions of corpses – a leg, a skull, a pelvis – over the still-burning embers that glowed like red angry eyes. Now the funeral procession Baird had seen on the road arrived, and the bearers began to lower the latest arrival to the ground.

Bells began to ring, playing an incongruous French tune, "Frère Jacques". Mourners chanted and wailed as an old man touched the pile of logs with a burning splint. Baird saw a sudden flare, heard a roar of petrol as the wood caught fire. The body started upright as though still alive when the sudden fierce heat tightened dead stomach muscles. Boys beat the corpse down flat with poles. Baird turned away, unwilling to watch any more.

'You find it distasteful?' Davichand Rana asked him, watching the lawyer's face closely.

Baird shrugged.

'Every religion has elements that can offend people of a different faith,' he said carefully. 'I personally think that your custom of burning dead bodies is much more hygienic than burying them, as we do. What I can't understand, however, is how so many people can bathe in this water, which must be thick with germs – cholera, typhoid, dysentery, every known disease – and actually drink it without coming to any harm. Even a few drops would kill a European.'

'Pilgrims believe it will do them good, and so it does,' Davichand Rana replied. 'You believe the water is poison, so to you it might be so. It all depends on your attitude.'

'And what is your attitude about this proposition?' asked Baird. 'What decision have you made?'

Davichand Rana stood for a moment in silence, watching an old man crawl down the steps on all fours, too weak to stand, but still desperate to reach the sacred river and let its tide carry him on to paradise beyond all poverty, all pain. *Belief*. That was the strongest element of all.

As he watched, the river was suddenly transformed from a sluggish stream of dirty mud and oily sewage to a wide channel of liquid gold. The sun climbed slowly above the far bank, melting the mist, driving away all haze, so that what had previously been squalid and filthy was now bathed in a total golden glow. Truly, this was a holy river, with magical properties; that was why it was known as Ramya, the Beautiful; Punya, the Auspicious; Bhagya-janani, the Creator of Happiness.

The sight and the thought seemed somehow symbolic and auspicious. But if he delayed any longer, the sun would be up and he would miss the moment of total purification.

'I will make arrangements for my nephew to receive the money and I will sign the agreement. Leave it here with me,' said Davichand Rana. 'Now I will bid you goodbye.'

Davichand Rana turned, walked out of the room. Baird waited for a few moments at the window, watching more pilgrims go down the slippery steps, submerge themselves and pour the water rapturously over their heads. Then he saw one figure, taller, more commanding than all the rest, wearing a white dhoti with a gold edge.

Davichand Rana overtook other older, slower, poorer pilgrims and walked proudly and confidently into the sacred river. Then, before he immersed himself in the water, he folded his arms across his chest and stood for an instant, bathed in the glow of the risen sun, a figure of solid gold.

Blake was sitting in a broken armchair in the leave centre reading the *Onlooker*, the Indian equivalent of the *Tatler*, when the mess bearer came into the room.

'Sahib just now coming to see you,' he explained.

Blake followed the man out into the entrance hall. Chet was waiting there, smiling.

'I've got it,' he said simply. 'In my hotel.'

They drove in his car to a small private hotel, went upstairs to Chet's room. By a single bed, under an illuminated wall text, 'Thou God seest me', stood a small leather suitcase with two straps and cheap brass buckles and a crude brass lock. Blake had seen dozens of similar cases for sale in the bazaar. Chet opened the suitcase. It was packed with hundreds of thousand-rupee notes, bound with elastic bands in bundles of fifty. For a moment, both men stood in silence, regarding this solid evidence of wealth. Blake was looking at more money than he could ever expect to make in all his life – and still it represented only a fraction of Davichand Rana's wealth.

'I've counted it once,' said Chet. 'At the present rate of exchange, it's one million and three pounds. Couldn't get it closer in rupee notes of that size. Want to check it?'

'No,' said Blake. 'It'll all come back to you in a matter of days, anyhow. I'm not going to spend it. Unfortunately.'

'You do know what you are doing, I suppose?' Chet asked him seriously. 'You're putting yourself out on a limb. You've no guarantee they won't roast you at the court martial. You might get ten years. Can you trust them not to shop you, make an example of you?'

'I have to trust someone,' Blake replied. 'After all, I am acting on their orders. And they have promised to pay my debts.'

'In writing?'

'No. There's nothing in writing.'

'I don't like the sound of it.'

'You will,' Blake assured him, trying to sound supremely confident. 'When Jerrold gives you all the money back. In a sense, I feel I'm also paying a debt I owe you, or at least part of one, for saving my life. Perhaps as a bonus – interest, if you like – this will also help your country.'

Chet turned, held out his hand.

'I didn't quite know what to make of you in the Arakan,' he said. 'You seemed so sure of yourself. I wasn't even sure I liked you. Too good-looking, too much the typical upper-class British officer.'

'That is what your uncle thought, too. Largely why I was selected for this job.'

'Now I think you are something more. A bloody good bloke, as you English would say.'

He punched Blake playfully in the chest. Blake grinned. Chet locked the case.

'Give me the key,' Blake told him. 'I want to be able to open it again.'

He carried the case downstairs. Outside, he hailed a passing taxi.

'Leave centre,' he told the driver, and sat gripping the case, which he placed beside him on the seat. It seemed somehow out of keeping to let the equivalent of a million pounds travel on the floor of a shabby open car.

Blake carried the case to his room, locked the door and checked the time. Five minutes to twelve. He had agreed with Jerrold to hold the money for twenty-four hours, which would mean until noon on the following day, then he would take the suitcase to Jerrold, who would return its contents to Chet. What happened to the money then was beyond his control.

Blake wondered, just for a moment, whether he should first remove the equivalent of the fee he had been promised, in case there was any trouble with Jerrold or Howard, or that odd man with the pale eyes and the high voice, Dermott. Once he had done what he had agreed to do, he would be, as Chet had just pointed out, totally in their hands, relying on their good will. He had only their word that they would pay his debts, and in any dispute there could be three of them against his single testimony. But why should there be any dispute? This wasn't their money; he was working strictly to their plan. Surely it was in their interests at least as much as in his that the scheme worked smoothly?

Blake looked about for a safe place to conceal the suitcase. The leave centre had no place to deposit any articles of value; he knew, because he had already asked. Annoyingly, the suitcase was just too big to fit into the cheap wardrobe in the bedroom and too thick to go under his narrow bed. He had brought his bedding roll with him from Burma, and the bearer had folded this up neatly in a corner of his room. Blake unrolled the bedding roll and draped it over the suitcase by one side of the chest of drawers. It was not very secure, but possibly safer than taking out the money and putting it in one of the drawers under his shirts. There, it only needed a light-fingered bearer to come in looking for a pair of socks or a handkerchief to steal and he'd lose the lot, and that bearer would be richer than a maharajah. Blake smiled at the thought. As he finished re-arranging the roll, there was a knock at the door.

A voice called: 'Sahib. Telephone.'

Blake came out of the room, locked the door, slipped the key in his pocket, followed the bearer down the passage. The telephone was in the hall. He picked it up. An Indian voice spoke softly in his ear.

'Captain Blake sahib?'

'Yes. Who are you?'

'I am just now speaking for Mr Dermott, sahib. He asked me. Would you please come to see him now?'

'What about?'

'He did not say, sahib. Only that it was being very urgent.'

'Where is he?'

'He is just now staying at the Alexis Hotel. It is only five minutes by taxi from you, sahib.'

'Can I speak to him on the telephone?'

'No, sahib. It is a most private matter, and there is no telephone in his room. I am just now ringing from the hallway in most public place.'

171

The man lowered his voice to a hoarse whisper.

'It is most urgent, sahib,' he said. 'I cannot say more in this situation. People may hear.'

The telephone went dead in Blake's hand. He paused for a moment. He did not want to leave such a huge sum of money in his room, yet he was not keen to take it with him. He would ring Jerrold, and ask whether he knew why Dermott wished to see him. He dialled the operator, and gave her Jerrold's number.

'I am not making any connection,' the girl told him after a few moments.

'Please try again.'

'I am just now trying. I am telling you, there is no electrical connection whatever.'

'Is the number engaged?'

'Not engaged. It is not even ringing, I am telling you. No connection.'

Blake put down the receiver. The inefficiency of the Indian telephone service was a constant irritation, but there was nothing he could do about that. A widow, Mrs Keeble, who managed the leave centre, was making out officers' bills at the desk.

'I have a case with a few things in it that mean a lot to me,' he told her. 'Only sentimental value, of course, but impossible to replace. Could I leave it in your care for literally half an hour while I pop out to see a friend over something that's come up?'

'I'm sorry, Captain Blake, but that is not possible. There is a strict rule. We can take no responsibility for any articles of value. There was an unfortunate experience once, so that rule was made. But you have a key to your room?'

'Yes, but there must be another one, or a master key. For cleaning and so on.'

'No-one will go to your room. The cleaning has all been done.'

Blake nodded; there was no point in continuing this conversation. He walked back to his bedroom. The bedding roll seemed an absurd place to conceal a suitcase containing a fortune, so he picked up the case and carried it through to the bathroom. An old-fashioned bath stood on four metal legs about a foot from the wall. He tried to push the case down between the bath and the wall, but the case was too big. He opened the case and packed the money into the soft webbing pack he had carried on his back in Burma. He squeezed this behind the bath. Then he put a spare pair of boots in the case to give it weight, for he had decided to carry this with him.

Mrs Keeble was still adding up bills when he passed her desk.

'I'm going to take it with me,' he told her. She looked up, frowning at being disturbed for the second time.

'That is best, I think,' she replied, without any interest in the matter, and went back to her sums.

Several taxis, open American cars of the early thirties, waited outside the centre. He climbed into the nearest.

'The Alexis,' he told the driver.

A few sad, sallow-faced Anglo-Indians sat in the entrance hall and looked up hopefully as he arrived, then went back to their newspapers; they were obviously waiting for someone else.

There was no-one at the reception desk, so he pressed a bell for service. An Indian clerk came out of a back room, and looked at him enquiringly.

'Mr Dermott,' Blake told him.

'Room number twenty-five, sir. Second floor. He is expecting you?'

'Yes.'

Blake recognized his voice; he was the man who had telephoned. He ran up two flights of stairs and knocked on the door.

'I'm in the bog,' he heard Dermott call. 'Who's that?'

'Blake.'

'Just coming.'

There was a sound of rushing water from the bathroom, and the door opened. Blake pushed his way in. Dermott was in his shirt-sleeves, buttoning his trousers.

'Why the hurry?' he asked in surprise.

'You wanted to see me - urgently.'

'I did?' Dermott frowned. 'About what?'

'How the hell should I know? You telephoned me, or rather that Indian clerk downstairs did, on your instructions.'

Dermott looked at him in amazement.

'I don't know what the devil you're talking about,' he said. 'I asked the front desk to ring for a taxi. I'm checking out. He must have misunderstood me.'

'How would he know my number if you didn't give it to him?' Blake asked.

Dermott shrugged.

'How do I know? Someone's got it all mixed up. Happens all the time in India. 'Phones don't work. Every damn message is bitched up or bowdlerized or given to the wrong person. Sooner I'm out of this place, the better. Apart from that, everything went all right? With the money, I mean?'

'Yes.'

'Good. That's the worst part over,' Dermott told him confidently as he watched Blake run down the stairs.

'This time tomorrow, you'll have paid off all your bills.'

'I hope,' said Blake.

Outside the hotel, he stood for a moment in the harsh sunshine, looking for a taxi. Several rickshaw wallahs passed and slowed, glancing at him hopefully. He shook his head. In disgust, they spat out gobbets of betel nut juice, red as arterial blood, and ran on.

The taxi that had brought him cruised past, flag up. Blake hailed the driver. The car pulled into the side of the road just past the hotel entrance.

Blake put one foot on the running board – and a sudden blow on the back of his head flung him forward.

He fell flat on his face on the rubber-covered floor. Through a haze of pain and breathlessness, he felt rather than saw two men wrench the suitcase from his hand.

'Are you all right, sahib?' the driver asked him anxiously. 'Oh, very bad men. *Budmashes.*'

Blake nodded, sat back thankfully on the imitation leather seat.

'You want to go police station, sahib?'

'No,' Blake told him. What was the point in that? The case only contained his boots – thank God.

'Leave centre,' he said.

The wind, blowing on his face as the taxi sped through the streets, revived him. Was this simply another instance of robbery – or did the thieves know he had received a large sum of money and guess he would keep it in the suitcase? It was impossible to say, and really immaterial. He had heard of several incidents when servicemen had been robbed, usually after someone had lured them into an alley on the pretext of meeting a prostitute. But to be robbed in a public place, in daylight, was rather different. Could the taxi driver be involved? Again, it was impossible to say. Questioning would only produce shrugged shoulders, a great shaking of his head and two words which conveniently blocked all further enquiries: *Nay malum*. I don't know.

Blake paid off the driver, made a note of the car's number, just in case it could prove useful, although when or where he could not say.

He nodded to Mrs Keeble at her desk and walked to his room. Here, he locked the door behind him, and leaned against it for a moment, relieved to be back. Then he went into the bathroom, filled the basin with cold water and dunked his face in it to clear his head. He towelled his face dry and ran one hand between the bath and the wall. Thank goodness – the pack was still there.

Relief flodded over him like a warm reassuring tide. He opened the bottle of whisky – as an officer, he was allowed to buy one cheaply every month – rinsed out a tooth-glass, poured out four fingers of whisky. He sat on the edge of the bath, savouring the spirit and looking at his reflection in the stained mirror above the basin. He wondered who else had rented these squalid rooms, who would follow him when he left, what it would feel like to be court-martialled.

The wind had tousled his hair; he brushed it. When you are the custodian of a million pounds, a millionaire if only for twenty-four hours, you want to look trim, even when the money isn't yours, he thought. Whistling to himself, amused by the irony of his situation as one who is rich and poor simultaneously, Blake bent down behind the bath and slid out the pack.

He balanced it on his knees, undid the two brass buckles, opened the webbing flap. For a moment he sat, staring in horror and disbelief at what he saw.

The money had gone. He was looking at three bricks wrapped in an old newspaper.

Shortly before the banks in Benares closed for business that afternoon, a messenger delivered a sealed, personally addressed envelope to certain individual clerks in five separate banks. This envelope contained an invitation to visit Davichand Rana at six o'clock that evening, and a plain slip of paper on which was typed, without heading or signature, a request for information on one specific financial transaction.

When these clerks arrived at Davichand Rana's house over-looking the Ganges, they were shown into a drawing room and given tea and sweetmeats. They sat, nervously wondering why

175

others had also been invited. Was this to announce good news – or bad?

At a quarter past six, the door opened and Rana's male secretary entered.

'Mr Sen Gupta, please,' he said.

Sen Gupta, a tall thin Hindu in a lightweight blue suit, shabby around the cuffs, stood up, smoothed back his oily hair and followed the man into Davichand Rana's drawing room. The door closed behind him. Davichand Rana shook him warmly by the hand.

'My dear Gupta,' he said, exuding charm as a squeezed mango sweats sweetness, 'how kind of you to come at such short notice. You have details of the matter on which I sought your advice?'

'I have made enquiries, your Excellency,' Sen Gupta replied, 'and no large sum of money has been transferred from our bank to any other within the last twenty-four hours.'

'You are absolutely certain? I must tell you that this is a matter of the gravest national importance.'

'I am certain, sir. I have examined all the relevant documents. No sum above twenty thousand rupees has been transferred anywhere in that time.'

'Thank you. That is exactly what I hoped you would tell me.'

From an inner pocket, Davichand Rana took an envelope with Sen Gupta's name typed on it. He handed it to him.

'You have earned this bonus on your retainer, my friend. Be assured, I value your assistance. I bid you goodbye.'

They shook hands. Gupta bowed nervously, left the room, and the second clerk came in. Much the same conversation took place, and then it was the turn of the third clerk, and the fourth.

'There has been one unusually large movement of funds,' he reported. 'To the Westminster Bank, Strand Branch, London, England.'

'Of how much?'

'A matter of thirteen million, four hundred thousand rupees, your Excellency.'

'Around a million pounds sterling,' said Davichand Rana reflectively. 'To whom was it sent?'

'To the account of Beechwood Nominees.'

'And how did this money arrive at your bank? By cheque? Draft?'

'No, sir. In notes. I did not personally handle the transaction, your Excellency, but the under-manager asked me into his office to help him count them. They were one-thousand-rupee notes, packed into a cardboard box tied with string.'

'Who made the deposit?'

'A woman.'

'Of what nationality?'

'Indian. Moslem. In purdah.'

'Could she have been European in disguise? Perhaps even a man masquerading as a woman?'

'I do not think so, your Excellency. I saw her hands. They were female. She was a small dark person.'

'And the money has been despatched?'

'It went immediately. By telegraph. It is amazing to me, your Excellency, that in the middle of a world war, one can still transfer huge sums of money from one country to another. Provided, of course, one has such huge sums to move.'

'Indeed, yes. We live in a most interesting time,' said Davichand Rana. 'Now, here is a bonus in addition to your usual retainer.'

They shook hands. The man bowed and left Davichand Rana on his own. He saw the fifth bank clerk, but the meeting was perfunctory; simply an exchange of envelopes, and then goodbye. Davichand Rana already had the information he sought.

Chet and he had been swindled, of course – or perhaps Chet was also involved in the duplicity? That bastard, Captain Blake. He would soon deal with him. But who could the woman be? A Moslem. Was she genuinely Moslem, or had a Hindu woman adopted the black veil in an attempt to conceal her identity? He would find out. But first he must officially inform the police of his loss, and let them get to work.

He consulted a small leatherbound book with the names and addresses of officials in receipt of regular retainers. Coloured stars against each name reminded him how much he paid them, and recorded the previous accuracy of their information. Then he picked up the telephone, dialled a number. A sergeant in the CID answered. Like the bank clerks, he received a monthly retainer, but rather larger than theirs, and paid to another name in another city.

'I want to speak to the head of the department on a most urgent matter,' Davichand Rana told him, after giving a code word by which the sergeant would recognize him. Real names could be dangerous.

'One moment, please, sir.'

A click of connections, and a Scots voice said:

'Major Cartwright here. What can I do for you, your Excellency?'

'You can listen,' Davichand Rana told him shortly. 'This is a very secret and important matter, involving not only private persons but governments. I want you to treat what I will tell you with the utmost discretion.'

'Is it wise to speak on an open line, sir?'

'In this instance I have to, because time is our enemy. I want you to find and arrest someone in Benares who has just stolen the equivalent of one million pounds sterling. He is English and his name is Captain Richard Blake.'

7

Davichand Rana stood with his back to the window of his house overlooking the Ganges. The hour of ablution had passed, and most of the pilgrims had departed. The rocks were covered now with washing spread out by the dhobi men to dry; long saris, white shorts, shirts. A beggar crawled painfully across the hot rocks towards the water, his legs twisted together below the knees like the roots of a tree. He had a wooden trolley beneath his trunk, and held wooden blocks in each hand like the pads of an animal, so that he could draw himself along, hoping for a miracle on the bank of the holy river. Davichand Rana turned away in distaste. Doubtless the man had sinned in an earlier life. Maybe in some life yet to come he would be rich, as a compensation for his present infirmities. If he believed that this was likely, no doubt it would be a comfort for him. Belief. Davichand Rana had believed what Blake and Chet and the lawyer Baird had told him, and his faith had failed him. Or, rather, others had failed him grievously.

A servant appeared at the door.

'Your nephew, your Excellency,' he said.

'I have had news of the gravest importance,' Davichand Rana told Chet angrily. 'The British officer for whom I gave you thirteen and a half million rupees only hours ago has disappeared. So, I need hardly say, has the money. What do you know about this?'

Chet stared at him in astonishment.

'Absolutely nothing. Who told you this?'

'I have just been informed by an officer of the Criminal Investigation Department,' Davichand Rana explained, not entirely truthfully. He had already decided how much – or how little – he would reveal about his own involvement.

'I understood that this transaction was being conducted on a high and most secret level. If policemen start enquiring, soon everyone will know. Where is this Captain Blake?'

'He was at the leave centre, Excellency. He had the money in a suitcase that I gave him.'

Davichand Rana crossed the room until he was facing Chet.

'What do you know about this officer?'

'We were together briefly in Burma. But I understood you were making all necessary checks into his background. What did your lawyer say?'

'Lawyers always cover themselves. Blake appeared genuine, so Mr Baird said, as did his proposition.'

'I will go to the leave centre myself, Excellency, and find out where Blake is. He may have left a message. I am sure there is some reasonable explanation.'

'You will stay here,' his uncle told him shortly. 'You might also disappear.'

'But this is absurd.'

'Nothing is absurd when so much money is at stake – and so much else. If this man Blake is only a common swindler, I have lost a fortune. But if he is politically inspired, he could return the money – or part of it – and then use my need for total discretion as a weapon against me.'

'I don't follow.'

'Then I will make it clearer for your apparently limited intelligence. If any word of this transaction should ever become public, it could rebound most unfavourably, not only on my own personal political future, but on the whole concept of Ranas – of whom you are one – as Nepal's hereditary rulers. That could have the most appalling political consequences for our country – and for our family. I intend to take every step necessary to prevent this, and since you involved me in this affair, you will help to minimize all risks.

'You will return to Kathmandu on the next available aircraft. There you will remain under guard until this man and the money are discovered. When we hear why both have disappeared so mysteriously, a decision on your own future will be taken. In the meantime, I am no longer interested in the proposition of buying any trading rights in Burma. I am interested in having my money restored, and in the light of this new and disturbing development, I want Captain Blake to be silenced. Permanently.'

*

180

Blake lifted out the bricks, and weighed them in his hand, as though by some magical metamorphosis or alchemy they would somehow resolve themselves into thousand-rupee notes. They didn't.

He stood up. His face in the mirror was grey with shock and fatigue: he was looking at himself as he might appear in twenty years' time. Blake poured himself another whisky, drank it neat. For all the effect it had on him, the whisky could have been water. Who had robbed him? Some servant, coming in to clean the room? Surely not. Mrs Keeble had told him that the room had already been cleaned. But – had it?

He ran along the corridor to the front hall; Mrs Keeble was hanging a door key on its hook as he approached.

'Anyone ask for me when I was out?' he asked her, without any preamble. 'Or come up to my room?'

'No-one, Captain Blake. Why, what's the matter? You seem very agitated.'

'You're absolutely certain no-one's been in?'

'Of course. I have been here all the time. Why do you ask? Are you expecting someone?'

'No, but someone has been into my room. Something's missing.'

'Missing? What do you refer to, Captain Blake? Those articles of sentimental value? But you took them with you. I saw you.'

'Money,' he said shortly. 'A lot of money.'

'It is always unwise to leave money in a bedroom,' she replied sharply. 'You must realize that. What may seem a small sum to you as an officer can represent a fortune to a bearer or a sweeper who might try the door.'

'I locked the door.'

'Was it broken open?'

'No. Someone either had a key – or got in and out through a window.'

'That's impossible, Captain Blake. All my staff are absolutely honest. They have been with me for years, since the time when this was a private hotel and not a leave centre. And who could have climbed through a window? The bars on them are so close together a child could barely squeeze through. How much money was involved?'

'More than I can afford to lose.'

181

'I can't understand you young officers. You are so casual. It's needless temptation, leaving money around.'

'This was hidden in my pack. And no-one would have seen it unless they came into the room looking for something to steal when I was out. Or else they knew it was there.'

'But that is impossible,' Mrs Keeble repeated.

'I wish it were,' Blake replied bitterly.

He ran out into the street. A taxi pulled out of line.

'The Alexis.'

The Indian clerk was sitting behind the reception desk reading the *Hindustan Times*.

'Mr Dermott?' Blake asked him.

'He has just checked out, sir.'

'Where has he gone?'

'He left no address.'

'Nothing at all?'

'No, sir.'

Blake glanced around the entrance hall. It was empty. He leaned on the desk.

'You telephoned me and told me he wanted to see me. When I arrived, he knew nothing about it, said you must have made a mistake. Did you?'

The clerk backed away from Blake; he could scent trouble and he didn't like the smell.

'I don't know what you mean, sir.'

'I think you do,' Blake told him firmly.

The clerk frowned and put down his newspaper. Blake's right hand shot out. He grabbed him by the tie, pulled him towards him across the top of the desk. He held the clerk so closely that he could see pock marks around his mouth, bristles under his nostrils where his razor had not reached.

'Don't lie to me,' he told him. 'I want to know where Mr Dermott is, and why you rang me. Who told you to ring me?'

'I cannot speak,' gasped the man, choking for air. His fingers clawed at Blake's wrist.

'Who was it?'

Blake clenched his other fist. The clerk's eyes widened in alarm.

'Another gentleman, sir. I have seen him here with Mr Dermott.'

'Was his name Jerrold?'

'Not knowing any names, sir. He asked me to telephone you urgently with that message.'

'Had he been with Mr Dermott before he asked you?'

'I am not knowing, sir. I had been having a cup of tea and came back to find him here, waiting for me.'

Blake released his hold. The clerk sagged back like an empty sack and closed his eyes. As Blake turned away towards the front door, he heard an alarm bell peal in the rear premises. He must really be sinking if he could be taken in by such a simple trick; he was too trusting. Jerrold, Dermott, Colonel Howard – and now this clerk. He had trusted too many too readily. He suddenly recalled Chet's words when he first saw the money in the suitcase: 'Can you trust them?' But what other option did he have then – or now?

A door behind the counter burst open. Two Indian porters wearing khaki uniforms rushed through, each carrying a metal-tipped lathi about five feet long. One brought down his lathi on Blake's head, while the other jabbed the metal end of his stick at Blake's stomach. Blake staggered under the force of the first blow, but managed to dodge the second. In a reflex action, he seized the man's stave, pulled it sharply towards him and then pushed it back, like a lance. The porter fell over, cursing. Blake tore the lathi from his grasp and hit him hard on his shoulder. The man's collar bone snapped like a dry twig. The other porter backed off, and started to blow a whistle. Blake had only seconds to be away; it would be absurd to be detained here on some ridiculous charge of threatening a hotel clerk or assaulting a porter while elsewhere in the city someone was absconding with a fortune entrusted to him. He raced out of the hotel and jumped into a passing taxi.

'Anywhere!' he shouted urgently. 'Quickly!'

'Double fare for fast driving, sahib.'

'Treble, if you like. But *jaldi* – quickly!'

Blake sat hunched in the back of the taxi as it lurched away, scattering cyclists and pedestrians. What did a few rupees matter when you had lost thirteen million? His mind seemed momentarily unable to focus on any course of action. He should find Dermott. But Dermott had left, disappeared. He felt punch-drunk, shattered. Where the hell was he going? Anywhere simply meant anywhere. Or nowhere.

It was pointless to find Chet, simply to tell him he had been robbed. Chet would be as horrified as he was himself. The men he must contact were those who had suggested this scheme in the first place. But where were they?

Had Dermott really left no forwarding address? Whether he had or not, was surely only academic now. Colonel Howard: he had no idea where he would be, either. Howard had mentioned he was with the Viceroy, which presumably meant he would be in New Delhi. But how to reach him in a hurry? He had no address for the man, no telephone number, and to find either in Benares would be impossible in the time.

Blake paused. In what time? Before the thief could get clean away with the money – or before he was supposed to report to Jerrold with it? There was a third reason for haste, and its fearful implication only now became apparent. What if it was thought – no, believed – that he had stolen the money? He drove this thought from his mind; he must think positively.

Jerrold. Of course. He was the go-between, the only person who could help him. Jerrold had persuaded him into this in the first place; he would know who to approach; the police, the security people, or whoever else could help quickly and discreetly.

Blake leaned forward, relieved at having reached this conclusion. He tapped the driver on the shoulder, gave him Jerrold's address. The driver stopped in the middle of the road, reversed to a great and angry honking of horns on country buses just behind him, and turned down a side road. Blake did not recognize it, but then he had only visited the house after dark. The driver turned into the Grand Trunk Road, and passed the station. Now Blake recognized big houses set far back on either side of a quieter road. The taxi drew into Jerrold's front drive and stopped beneath the storm porch. A bearer came down the steps and salaamed politely.

'Mr Jerrold?' Blake asked him.

'Jerrold sahib. He has just now gone.'

'Gone? Where to?'

'He had telegram from London office. He has gone Calcutta way.'

'Calcutta? Are you sure?'

'Not sure, sahib. Just thinking most likely what he said.'

'Have you an address for him in Calcutta?'

'No address. He usually stays in a hotel. The Grand. The Great

Eastern. Many big hotels in Calcutta. House here is just now shut.'

'But he must have left an address, surely? What about the local journalist who usually lives here? Is he back yet?'

'Please, sahib, not understanding. No-one here but me.'

Oh my God, thought Blake, this is a bloody nightmare. How could Jerrold have gone to Calcutta if he was supposed to hand over the money to him on the following day? Obviously, Jerrold had not told the bearer his real destination; Calcutta was at least a day's distance in an express train. He must be somewhere closer. He might even be with Dermott, wherever *he* was. What the devil was he to do now?

Blake nodded his thanks to the bearer. It was absurd to blame the man for not knowing where his master was. He had only himself to blame for not taking better care of the money, but despite the enormity of his loss, Blake still found it impossible to believe that such a fortune could disappear so quickly and so completely.

For one thing, it was difficult to accept that the notes had ever represented so much money. They might have been stage money, Monopoly currency. And even if the notes were genuine, there must surely be some simple reason for removing them – apart from theft, of course?

Perhaps Dermott, or maybe even Jerrold, had taken them for a kind of practical joke – perhaps to warn him to be more careful? They must know that Blake had always been notoriously careless about money; otherwise he would not be in such debt. The reason was not just that he had never been short of money; he was simply not interested in it for its own sake, only in what it could buy: freedom and independence.

Probably, at that very moment, both men were in some bar – maybe even at the leave centre – having a drink together and waiting for him to turn up and enjoy the joke against himself. And even if they weren't, it wasn't his money – or theirs. In some inexplicable way, Blake felt divorced from the whole extraordinary situation. It was as though this was happening to someone else in a play or a film, and he was only an observer, not personally concerned, indeed totally uninvolved. He had no idea how the farce would end, but it must end happily; farces always did.

Blake opened the rear door of the taxi – and the telephone rang inside the house. He looked enquiringly at the bearer.

'Do you think that is Mr Jerrold?' he asked him.

The bearer did not answer. He was already bounding barefoot up the steps into the house. Blake followed him. The bearer picked up the telephone. Whoever was calling must be English, because the bearer was speaking English in reply.

'I am not knowing, sir. He is not here. Another sahib is already asking for him.'

He glanced towards Blake as he spoke.

Blake crossed the room and took the receiver from him.

'Hello,' he said. 'I am a friend of Jerrold's. Can I help you?'

'Major Cartwright, Chief of Benares CID here,' said a Scottish voice, 'I am ringing about an army captain Blake your friend Mr Jerrold knows.'

'What about him?' asked Blake, his throat suddenly tightening.

'You know him?'

'I do.'

'Then where is the bugger? Can you tell me that, eh?'

Blake swallowed; his throat felt tight as though a noose had gripped it. Was he mad? A policeman was asking him where he was.

'What has happened to him?' he asked carefully, answering one question with another.

'It's what's going to happen to him that he should worry about,' said Cartwright angrily. 'He's just swindled a member of the ruling family of Nepal out of a million quid.'

Blake wondered whether he would choke.

'A million pounds,' he managed to say, in a voice he did not recognize. 'But how the devil did he manage to get hold of so much money in the first place?'

'It wasn't his, of course. He was only standing surety or something with it.'

'I don't think that Captain Blake would steal anything,' Blake said. 'He's always struck me as a pretty straight sort of fellow.'

'A million missing says he's bent. But who are you? Who am I speaking to?'

Blake swallowed again. Who could he say he was? His mind felt furred with alarm. His eyes scanned a bookshelf. He saw the spine of a leather-bound copy of Boswell's Life of Johnson.

'I told you. A friend of Rex Jerrold. Boswell's the name. Jimmy Boswell.'

'Well, Mr Boswell, when is Jerrold coming back?' asked Cartwright. 'Where has he gone, anyhow?'

'God knows. I'm trying to find him myself. And Mr Dermott. Do you know where he is?'

'No. Never heard of him,' replied Cartwright irritably. 'I know a MacDermid at the Club, but that's not the same man, I suppose?'

'No. Not the same man.'

'Well, I'll be off. Got to find Blake before he scarpers altogether. A million quid! The bloody nerve of it!'

Cartwright rang off. Blake replaced the receiver with a trembling hand. His knees suddenly seemed weak. He felt like a man in the middle of a nightmare, caught in the vortex of a Kafka plot in which he was being accused of a crime he did not even know he had committed. He must find Jerrold somehow. He turned to the bearer.

'When Mr Jerrold comes back, will you tell him an old Oxford friend was looking for him.'

'Your name, sahib? Captain Boswell, is it?'

'He knows me as Richard,' said Blake and gave him a ten-rupee note. 'The same again if Mr Jerrold finds me within the hour.'

'Where will you be, sahib?'

'In Benares.'

Then Blake paused. Would he still be here? Where could he stay safely, beyond threat of arrest, for even as long as one hour?

'I'll just make a 'phone call before I go,' he told the bearer. 'A local call.'

The bearer nodded. He was not paying the telephone bill, and this sahib had been very generous, which was not true of all Jerrold's friends.

Blake asked the operator for the leave centre. Mrs Keeble answered breathlessly. Blake held his handkerchief over the mouthpiece to muffle his voice and said in an assumed singsong Anglo-Indian accent: 'I am seeking Captain Blake. Can you put me through?'

'I wish I could,' said Mrs Keeble excitedly. '*Everyone* is seeking Captain Blake. There are three officers waiting for him here already.'

'Perhaps one of them is my friend? What are their names?'

Blake heard a whispered consultation at the other end of the line.

'They are police officers,' Mrs Keeble explained more soberly. 'There has been a big robbery.'

'I am very sorry indeed to hear that. A robbery of Captain Blake's belongings?'

'I think so, yes. Actually, he mentioned as much to me before he left. He seemed very agitated. But who are you, please?'

'Captain Boswell,' said Blake and rang off.

So the police were already waiting for him to return. He should go back at once, of course, and explain exactly what had happened. Maybe they already knew, and had arrived to help him? He had nothing whatever to hide and so nothing to fear. He had simply accepted the temporary custody of a large sum of money on the instructions of a Foreign Office official. The fact that someone had removed this money, if only temporarily and for whatever purpose, was nothing to do with him. He had done all he had agreed to do. But how could he prove that this had happened, when Dermott had disappeared and Jerrold was apparently in Calcutta, and without any forwarding address?

If he went back to the leave centre, he might well be arrested for stealing the money, ludicrous as this charge was. Circumstantial evidence was strong, and arrest would mean at the least being confined to his room with two officers to guard him. More likely it would involve incarceration in a local prison, for a million pounds was not exactly a week's float for the local services canteen, and from Blake's experience of military legal procedure, once he was under guard it would be impossible to be released in order to try and find either Jerrold or Dermott. Requests to see them would all go through what were quaintly called 'the usual channels', which, in his experience, seemed permanently silted up.

But so long as Blake remained free, he had at least the hope of locating one or other of the only two men in India who could help him establish his total innocence, and, hopefully, recover the missing money. He owed it to himself to stay free until he could do just this. He walked out to the taxi.

'Where to, sahib?' the driver asked him as they set off.

It was a good question. Blake stroked his chin before he replied. If he stayed in the cantonment, the area where the British lived, he was almost bound to be picked up fairly soon, for he had little money, no change of clothes, not even a razor. He might be able to keep out of sight more successfully in the Indian quarter, in the city, or in the bazaar, down among the ghats on the edge of the Ganges. He would be less noticeable, at least to Europeans, who seldom went there. When they needed any shopping done, they invariably sent a servant to do it. Indians might find his presence surprising, but they were unlikely to report him to the police; they would not regard the police as allies, their paid protectors against the lower orders, but rather as their enemies.

Blake removed the captain's stars from his shoulders and put them in a pocket. People looking for an army captain were unlikely to question a private soldier.

How long would he need to stay under cover? He hoped only for a matter of hours, perhaps for that night at the most. Jerrold must come back soon, because they had agreed to meet at noon on the following day. Blake decided against taking a taxi through Benares, for in an open car he could easily be recognized – and private soldiers could not usually afford taxis; they travelled in rickshaws or horse-drawn gharries. He would stop the taxi near the town and walk the rest of the way.

'How much?' he asked the driver.

'You said treble fare, sahib,' the man reminded him. 'Plus waiting. Eleven rupees.'

He watched Blake nervously: it was a large sum to ask. A bearer was paid thirty rupees for the month's work. Would the sahib keep his word?

Blake felt in his pocket. He had no loose change; the smallest notes were ten rupees each. What the hell, he thought. When you are thinking in terms of millions of rupees what do ten matter either way? He handed two ten-rupee notes to the driver.

'I am sorry, sahib,' the driver replied apologetically. 'Not having any change.' He handed one note back to Blake.

'No,' Blake told him. 'Keep it. People don't always pay you, I'm sure. This will help to even things up.'

'Sahib very generous,' replied the driver warmly. 'God bless you, sahib.'

'I very much hope so,' replied Blake. 'But I've seen no signs of it today.'

'There is always time for good things to happen,' the driver assured him and drove away.

Blake walked down the first alleyway he saw. This was lined with stalls selling silver trinkets and beaten brass pots. Benares was famous for these things – or did they simply come by the shipload from Birmingham to be sold here? Flies buzzed in a humming black cloud around a pile of rotting vegetables; an old man squatted on the pavement to urinate near a holy cow.

Blake was glad that he could see no Europeans. Everyone seemed to be Indian, and hurrying about with unusual speed, as though they all had very important business to do. No-one appeared to notice him, but Blake realized that probably everyone did. What was a British soldier doing in the bazaar? Perhaps coming here had not been such a good idea after all. He must find some place where, like a chameleon, he could merge unobtrusively into the background until he could contact Jerrold. If only he could find a telephone he could keep ringing his house, but Benares did not possess any public telephone boxes.

He reached the end of the alley, and turned into another wider road. Here, several British servicemen on leave were being pulled along in rickshaws, and touts from shops selling watches and cheap cameras ran out as they passed, carrying samples of their wares slung over their arms, eager to make a sale. Blake saw an English woman with a discontented face walking a little girl with the pale, sallow face common to English children who had lived too long in India.

The woman paused outside an open-fronted shop and the proprietor came out and made a gesture of greeting, *nameste*, pressing the palms of his hands together in welcome. She ignored him and stood fingering rolls of cloth. Bearers at once hurried out from the back of the shop with samples of brightly coloured silks, and unfolded them in a flourish of many colours. The woman shook her head. She saw nothing she liked. The shopkeeper bowed; the memsahib was always right. This, Blake judged, was the moment to approach her.

He saluted smartly.

'Excuse me,' he said. 'A strange request, but I wonder if I could possibly use your telephone?'

'Our *telephone*? But it's in our house, oh, three miles away,' she said, surprised. She wondered why this unusually good-looking man was only a private soldier. 'But there is a 'phone in the Alexis hotel, I believe.'

'I know, but that is out of order,' said Blake quickly. 'Couldn't we go to your house? *Please*. It is a very important matter. I cannot say too much about it here.'

Her face showed disbelief. What could be so important to an Army private? This possibility lay far beyond the narrow parameters of her experience.

'I'm sorry, but that's quite impossible. I am waiting for my husband,' she added as though this must explain its impossibility.

The little girl looked up inquiringly at her mother and then across at Blake. She had a squint and a silver brace around her front teeth. A car with a chauffeur in white duck drew up behind them. A plump Englishman, sweating in a too-tight suit, climbed out.

'Some trouble?' he asked belligerently, looking from Blake to the woman and back again.

'My husband, Dennis Browne,' said the woman vaguely.

'What do you want?' asked Browne coldly. He didn't trust these young soldiers. There had been a little trouble already with his wife on two occasions; to be fair, with officers, not privates. The heat; it got to women in a strange way. And this bloke was damned good-looking.

'I was asking your wife if I could possibly use your telephone,' said Blake. 'I have an important call to make, and there are no 'phones available.'

'I am sorry, but that's impossible. Our house is miles away. And we are not going in that direction. Goodbye to you.'

He shepherded his wife and daughter into the car.

Blake walked on.

A jeep cruised along the street with two military police corporals in red caps, looking sharply from side to side. Blake stood, back to the road, peering into a shop filled with *chaplis* and leather sandals.

Were they after him? he wondered. Panic rose in his throat like a bird. How could they be? How couldn't they be? With the equivalent of a million pounds at stake, and the civilian police already seeking him, the military were unlikely to be far behind. The jeep drove past slowly, and Blake walked on. He must not appear to hurry; he must do nothing that could draw attention to himself. A running man always aroused suspicion; no-one remembered a walker. A small boy pattered alongside him with bare feet and tugged at his sleeve.

'You want girl, sahib?' he enquired in a hoarse urgent whisper. 'Pretty girl. All matriculate white girl. Special convent girl.'

'No, no,' said Blake irritably. He shook his head. 'Go away. *Jao.*'

The boy clung on to his sleeve. Long dirty fingernails dug into Blake's arm like an animal's claws.

'I give you good price. Very clean girl. My own sister. First time virgin girl.'

'Please go away,' Blake told him.

The boy tugged his arm, scratching the flesh. Blake shook him off angrily. The boy deliberately fell down on his hands and knees with a great shout and started to scream.

'Sahib, you have hurt me!'

He had given this performance many times before and always successfully. Most soldiers would throw him a rupee note just to shut him up before a hostile crowd could gather.

'Get up and get out of it,' Blake advised him sharply. The boy screamed more loudly.

At the sound, Indians came running from behind their stalls. Many held sticks or staves. Within seconds, Blake was surrounded by a crowd of shouting, angry men.

'You hurt that boy? English bastard! *Jai-hind!* Victory for India!'

They forced Blake back against a stall piled with mangoes. He felt its sharp wooden edge cut into his spine, as men began to belabour his shoulders, his head, his arms with sticks. A hand groped swiftly and expertly in his bush-jacket pocket; he hit out wildly. The stall collapsed and Blake went down under the crowd of flaying arms and staves.

Mangoes cascaded around them like green cannonballs. He jumped up and started to run. The road ahead was now blocked solid by other Indians in *dhotis*, all welcoming any disruption to a dreary life of drudgery. Some held clubs, one a long *dah* used for cutting crops. There was no escape ahead, and no way out behind him. On either side, buildings loomed up. Some had flat roofs built out over the stalls. Goats were tethered on these roofs, and little boys, who had been feeding them bunches of grass, now peered over the edge at the commotion below them.

Then, ahead of Blake, in the sea of dark sweating faces, contorted with rage or glee at the predicament of a solitary British soldier, and the imminent prospect of a lynching – a Rowlandson phantasmagoria of yellow teeth in open mouths, red with betel-nut juice, wild dangerous eyes and shaken fists – Blake saw one man he recognized: the taxi driver to whom he had given an extra ten-rupee note.

This man was also shouting and waving furiously, but only with one hand. No, not waving, pointing. Blake realized that he was trying to direct him towards an opening he had not seen before, barely wide enough to admit a man.

This ran between a medical hall and a shop selling spices spread out on huge flat leaves. He dived into it thankfully. The passage stank of rotting vegetables, and his shoes slipped and slid on stones slippery with urine.

The taxi driver made to follow him and then appeared to stick between the two narrow walls. He turned towards the crowd, shouting and waving both his arms furiously. He could have followed easily enough – but Blake realized that he did not intend to do so. He was deliberately blocking the way of his pursuers.

The alley widened. A goat scuttled out of Blake's way as he raced along it, and he almost tripped over a sleeping white cow. The alley ended in a small courtyard, a well at the base of buildings that towered around it. Washing hung out from verandahs on bamboo poles, and bulging walls carried the scabs of years of neglect. The sun never reached this secret, foetid place. Old women squatted in doorways, shelling nuts. A man, his stomach distended like a grotesque bubble, legs swollen to enormous size, lay groaning on a rope-mattressed bed, too ill to brush away the flies that settled around his mouth and eyes.

Blake paused for a moment and glanced behind him. The alley was curved so that now he could not see the taxi driver or the mob behind him, but he could hear a roar of angry shouting. It must only be moments before the crowd swept past the driver and reached him. He searched desperately for any way out. There was none. He was trapped.

He had heard of cases involving British soldiers on long railway journeys who had unwisely left their train at a station on the route to stretch their legs after days of being cooped up in a compartment, and then had been seized by a mob. Some had petrol poured over them and were set alight; once the crowd scented a kill, he could expect no mercy. How ironic to be on the run from the police – only to be murdered by a mob! Murdered. The word had a frightening ring to it and yet he somehow felt remote from the full horror of his predicament. How could this happen to anyone without cause?

Blake heard a slight cough behind him and turned sharply, clenching his fists in case of attack. A slightly built Indian was standing in a doorway he had not previously noticed. He had the air of a middle-aged student; long hair, high cheekbones, a studious face. He wore a white shirt over linen trousers. His *chaplis*, Blake noted, were polished.

'So you have found us,' the man said in English. His attitude was not particularly friendly, but not antagonistic; wary, cautious, perhaps, ready to go either way if Blake gave the wrong answer. But was was the right one?

'I don't know what you mean,' said Blake flatly. 'Who are you?'

The man stood to one side, and indicated that Blake should follow him through the door. He did so and the man quickly bolted the door behind them. Blake noticed that it was very strong, made of three solid planks of wood, with huge bolts and a chain on a staple. They were in a dark room without a window. It smelled strongly of animals, and he was instantly reminded of boyhood visits to the zoo in Regent's Park: the stench of lions, bears, buffalo, confined for too long in tiny cages. Gradually, Blake's eyes grew accustomed to the gloom.

'Saved, as you English might say, not by the bell, but by these bolts,' the man said.

'Who are you?' Blake repeated. Was this really happening?

'You may not want to know me,' the Indian replied. 'You English hate me.'

'You speak in riddles,' said Blake wearily. Why must he be so obscure?

He followed the man into a second room. The smell here was stronger and the floor was covered with straw. A naked electric bulb throbbed in the ceiling, throwing a weak yellow glow over the sparse furnishings; a bare wooden table, two wooden chairs. Against the far wall, snoring, mouth open, paws folded, leather muzzle removed, a giant bear lay asleep.

'You are in an unusual situation for an Englishman,' the man said, and smiled, as though this did not entirely displease him. 'You are, as you would say, on the run?'

'Yes,' Blake agreed. There was no sense in denying the obvious fact.

'It is a predicament in which I admit I have frequently enough found myself. I know you English, for I have lived in London.

In a bed-sitting room in Earls Court. As a student of politics. My name is Ram Das.'

'Richard Blake.'

They shook hands. This seemed hardly the moment to exchange social pleasantries and biographical details, but at least Blake felt that he was out of reach of the mob, if only temporarily. There was a rustle in the straw as the bear rolled over, snored and flexed its claws. Through the wooden door, they could hear the shouting outside grow louder and closer and more insistent. Women were screaming; whether in fear or anger, Blake did not know. What he did know was that his pursuers must already be in the courtyard. Only the thickness of one door separated him from them.

Another Indian entered the room from the back premises. He stroked the bear's head as he would stroke a favourite cat. He was obviously the animal's handler.

'What is the trouble outside?' the handler asked Blake.

'They are after me,' Blake explained.

'Why?' asked Ram Das. 'Usually, I am in the position of a fugitive. You English say I am a political agitator. Are you?'

'No. It's too involved to explain in detail,' Blake replied. 'But I was entrusted with something of value which I kept in my room at the Army leave centre. It was stolen. The police think I stole it. I didn't, of course. But I can't find the one man who can prove me innocent.'

'Why not?' Ram Das asked him.

'I am told he is in Calcutta. But if I can lie low until tomorrow, there is a good chance he will be back.'

'Who said so?'

Blake shrugged.

'Those aren't policemen outside,' the handler pointed out. 'They want to punish you themselves. Why?'

'A boy in the bazaar was touting for a brothel. He grabbed my arm. I shook him off. He fell down and said I'd hurt him.'

'That is a very common trick,' said Ram Das. 'He probably makes his living at it. But the atmosphere in this place is very volatile. People want independence.'

'Whether they do or they don't,' replied Blake, 'I just want freedom.'

'As with them, my friend. A pity we have not the time to discuss the whole matter. Although I want the British to quit

195

India, I am not against any of them individually. As a race, they have many fine qualities.'

Blake said nothing; he was listening to the noise on the other side of the door. The bear also heard the shouting and stirred uneasily and lumbered to its feet, shook itself, then reared up on its hind legs.

'You see? He knows it is the hour for work,' the handler explained proudly. 'I take him out on his chain. He will dance for one rupee. And I wait until twenty or thirty people pay before he starts! A better living than falling down in the street. But of course I have other expenses. The bear is a hungry animal.'

'You'll not take him through that crowd,' said Ram Das. 'They'd frighten him and he could bolt.'

He turned to Blake.

'And you would never get out beyond the door in one piece,' he said simply.

'Then can I stay here?' Blake asked him. 'At least until the crowd go?'

'They will not all leave, my friend. Some may go, but some will stay behind. They have nothing else to do, or, at least, nothing better to do, which to them is the same thing.

'They know you must still be somewhere in this area and so they will wait for you until you have to come out. Maybe they will knock on every door, or someone will tell them they saw you come in here. It is rather like your English country customs. I understand that you watch when an animal goes to ground, because you know it must come out eventually. You wait. Maybe you even dig it out. Then you kill it. It is sport to you – and to the crowd outside. All men are hunters at heart.'

'They can't wait forever,' Blake said stubbornly.

'But then neither can you. Tell me, how much money have you got?'

'On me? Very little.'

Blake never kept money in his wallet, which was fortunate because it had disappeared when he had been forced back against the stall. He pulled a thin wad of notes, damp with sweat, from his back trouser pocket.

'One hundred rupees,' he said flatly. 'That's everything.'

'Give me fifty,' said Ram Das. 'I would not usually take money for helping anyone on the run, because I know what it's like to be chased and wrongly accused, and unable to trust anybody.

But I have no money at all. Now, at least, with this I can eat.'

'We are living on what the bear provides for us,' the handler explained. 'It is not always a profitable situation, Mr Blake.'

'I understand perfectly,' Blake replied.

He counted out five ten-rupee bills, gave them to Ram Das.

'Now,' said Ram Das briskly, 'you must allow me the benefit of experience as a fugitive, Mr Blake. Let us put ourselves in the position of those who wish to catch you. First, your British police. You have no hat. Your uniform is in disarray, and the British army is very sensitive regarding matters of dress.

'Within ten minutes of reaching the bazaar – if you ever managed to reach it – one of your military policemen would stop you to ask why you were improperly dressed. If you gave him a false name, he would soon check you were lying. Equally, if you put your head out of this door for at least the next twenty-four hours, your fate will be much more unpleasant.'

Ram Das paused.

'What do you propose, then?' Blake asked him desperately.

'You genuinely believe that if you can keep under cover for twenty-four hours more, you should be able to reach someone who can speak for you?'

'I think so. I hope so.'

'Well, my friend, since you cannot leave this place alive in that time, we are left with the only alternative. You must leave it – dead.'

New Delhi. May, 1944

Colonel Howard looked out of the window at the vast pink stone buildings which Lutyens had designed in the Mogul style less than twenty years previously as part of the Imperial Headquarters of British India. The broad avenue, built to impress even the richest maharajah with the pomp and power of Empire, stretched straight as a sword blade to the limit of his sight. On either side lay flat lawns; bullocks pulled mowing machines across them at a steady, unhurried pace. Long canals reflected the burnished sky like enormous mirrors, and the statue of Queen Victoria, first Empress of India, surveyed the whole scene with stony satisfaction. What would she have made of this mess in Benares, he wondered bitterly. And then, more importantly, how could he extract himself personally from it with the minimum of odium?

This shambles could cut into his chance of getting his 'K' when he retired.

Howard poured Dermott three fingers of whisky into a heavy crystal glass, and paused, looking at Dermott with raised eyebrows. Dermott said nothing. Howard poured out another two fingers, more slowly. Dermott nodded.

'I wish we could be drinking to success,' said Howard gloomily. 'I can't think why everything's gone so terribly wrong. Our liaison man with the police here has just had a signal from Benares. This bloody man Blake has buggered off with the money. A million quid.'

'That's not how I read it,' said Dermott sharply. 'Okay, the money's gone, and so has Blake. But that doesn't mean to say he's taken it. They could be two separate incidents.'

'Look,' said Howard thickly, his voice slurred with drink, 'you've got to put two and two together and make them add up. How can they be separate incidents? The money's disappeared, so has he, and the whole bloody scheme's up the spout. We've been conned. It was your idea,' he added pointedly.

Dermott shrugged, took a deep swig of his whisky.

'Someone's got to have them,' he retorted sharply. 'After all, I arranged with Fourteenth Army, saw that they contacted Corps and Brigade and all the rest, to set it up so that Blake would get to know this Chet fellow. That took a bit of doing, getting them together. I never imagined they'd get on. Why should they? They've totally different backgrounds.

'Then we had Blake sent on leave to Benares where he met his old Oxford friend Jerrold. By contrived chance, so to speak. I even arranged for someone at the leave centre to say he'd worked for that bookmaker McMoffatt before the war, and warn Blake that he'd be a marked man when he got home. *That* took a bit of doing, too – and some ready cash – I can tell you. The fact is, Blake was up to his balls in debt – and desperate.'

'All the more reason for him to go off with the money,' Howard retorted. 'You must see that. You overplayed your hand.'

'London didn't give us much time. They just wanted this Davichand Rana fellow out of the running and PDQ, like yesterday. Anyway, it's always easy to be wise too late. But all we have is a garbled report, second-hand, about Blake.'

'But Davichand Rana personally informed the CID that the money's gone, so our man says.'

'Of course it's bloody gone. Davichand Rana gave it to Chet, who handed it on to Blake. Because Blake can't be found immediately, it doesn't mean to say he's scarpered with it. Where the hell could he get to from India in the middle of a war? He's bound to be caught, if caught is the right word. Found, I'd say. He may be ill. Lost his memory. Malaria. Dysentery. Or his wound could be troubling him, and he's in hospital somewhere. He could have been run over in the street. The way these people drive, that's very possible.'

He paused.

'Have you told anyone else about this report?' he asked.

'No,' said Howard. 'I didn't want it to get around.'

'Well, keep mum about it. My bet is that your contact with the Benares CID will be on the blower in an hour or two to say all's well. These buggers imagine half the stuff. Now, what about the other half of that Haig you didn't promise me?'

Benares. May, 1944

The bear stretched itself thankfully, baring yellowed teeth, luxuriating in being even briefly free of the tight, cone-shaped leather muzzle it had to wear for several hours every day.

'What we're going to do,' Ram Das explained, 'is to carry you out of here as a corpse. We will wrap you in a white bandage from head to foot, leaving just enough space around your face to let you breathe and see where you're going, so you don't get disorientated. We will tie you to a bamboo stretcher, so even if you feel giddy, you won't fall. Never do to have a corpse break an arm or a leg and start shouting the odds.'

'We'll take the bear along, too,' the handler explained.

'No-one is likely to interfere with a funeral party, but if they thought of doing so, he would make them think again,' Ram Das continued. 'People are afraid to come too close in case he attacks them. We've used a similar ploy before now to move people the British police wished to apprehend. It may encourage you to know you are not the first – and that it's always worked.'

'Where will you take me to?' Blake asked him.

'To the burning ghats, down by the river. We'll try to arrive at dusk. With smoke from the pyres and in the gathering dark we should be able to smuggle you into a house and take your bandages off. You can wait there till it's totally dark or maybe

199

right through the night, if you want. The rest will be up to you.'

Blake nodded. It was strange and rather humbling to think that, in the space of a few hours, he had been shown more kindness by three people he had never previously met and would probably never see again, than by anyone else in all his life, except his father: a taxi driver, to whom he'd given a larger than usual tip, simply because he had no change, and no time to wait for any, a political agitator, and the owner of a performing bear. Yet men he thought he could trust – Jerrold and Colonel Howard and Dermott – had melted away like snow in sunshine.

And Chet? What had happened to him? Perhaps he should have tried to reach him at his hotel, even though he was very much a secondary figure in events. Could he have taken the money? After all, he had said that he had intended to do so. But surely he would not have left Blake to take the blame? Well, it was too late now to wonder what had happened and why. He was not in command of events – if ever he had been. He would have to go along with the plan of Ram Das. It sounded very dubious, but it was the only one on offer. He lay down on the table.

Ram Das and the bear-handler worked quickly, winding bandages expertly around his shoes, his ankles, his thighs, his body. The bandages they wrapped around his face were loose enough to allow him to breathe, yet tight enough not to slip.

'You must not move a muscle,' Ram Das warned him. 'That would cause a riot of terror. We're going to cover you with saffron dust to show we're carrying a corpse to the holy river, and a garland of flowers, a wreath for the journey. It is the custom.'

'Will I see you again?' Blake asked before the bandages around his mouth muffled his words.

'If not in this world, my friend, then in the next we will meet.'

'I'd rather it was in Benares, and soon,' replied Blake. 'I will owe you rather more than fifty chips if you get me out of this.'

Ram Das patted his shoulder.

'We will have much to talk about then,' he said jocularly. 'Now, we're going to lift you.'

Blake felt a sudden jerk as they picked him up and placed him on a crude bamboo stretcher. The poles creaked with his weight as the bear-handler and Ram Das took the strain. The stretcher swayed slightly for a moment until they steadied it. Usually, four men carried a corpse; only the poorest of the dead had to rely on two.

The smell of the bear grew almost overpowering near Blake's head, and he could sense the beast snuffling and grunting as it stood on its hind legs. He heard a squeal of rusty metal as bolts shot back, the rattle of a chain, and the door opened. Immediately, a great roar of shouts, screams and abuse filled the room. Blake might not understand all that the crowd were saying but their anger and violence were frightening. It only needed one person to look closely at his feet, and see that he was wearing shoes, where perhaps the bandage had not completely covered the soles, and he would be discovered. His flesh crawled with horror at the prospect of being lynched, unable either to run or to fight back.

He lay like a mummy, sweating beneath the bandages, as the two men swung to one side outside the door to carry him down the alleyway. From under the bandage around his face, Blake had a slant-eyed view of the crowds, as they parted to let him go by. Death was a frequent visitor to every house in the yard; there was never any need to ask who had died, who was about to be burned. All that mattered to the crowd was that death had knocked at someone else's door. Their visit would come, of course, but at a later date, and meanwhile time was a river that had no banks.

Blake sensed rather than saw when they came into the main street, and he could vaguely make out shop fronts, stalls, piles of fruit, bales of cloth, sticky sweetmeats spread out on huge plantain leaves. They set off at a jog trot up one street and down another. Now and then, a rickshaw wallah or an empty tonga, driver half asleep, weary horse barely moving, strayed across their path. Ram Das shouted a sharp warning in a high-pitched voice to them: the dead must always have the right of way. Blake heard the constant faint ting-a-ling of tonga bells and all the time, close to his shoulder and his right ear, the heavy, asthmatic breathing of the bear.

Once, they passed another funeral procession, much grander, with paid mourners and men beating drums and playing trumpets. Nearer the river, Blake caught a glimpse of a rickshaw with two passengers. Only one was alive. He sat on the hard Rexine seat. His companion was a corpse wrapped in white and tied to a pole laid horizontally across the floor. The dead man's feet stuck out on one side, his head and shoulders on the other.

Blake wondered whether that person had ever been able to afford to hire a rickshaw during his lifetime. He was reminded of people in Britain who had never travelled in a Daimler or Rolls, until they were conveyed in their coffin in a hearse.

Ram Das slipped on a rotting mango and bumped into the wall of a narrow alleyway leading to the ghats. The blow shook Blake from his reverie. He bit his lip so that he would not cry out, and closed his eyes because he was growing dizzy, bemused, not sure where he was, even who he was. The continual padding of his two bearers, combined with the swinging side-to-side motion of the stretcher as they negotiated tight corners and narrow bends, was making him feel sick. He swallowed hard several times and tried to concentrate his mind on other things, but always his thoughts returned to his present predicament and the missing money, and the nagging worry about what he would do if he could not make contact with Jerrold.

The pace of Blake's bearers gradually slowed from a trot to a reluctant walk and then stopped altogether. Even through his cocoon of bandages, Blake suddenly smelled fear, theirs and his own. He peered out as best he could and saw that half a dozen Indians, all well built and somehow menacing, wearing white shirts and trousers, not the usual dhotis, had stopped their progress.

'Where are you going without any mourners?' one of them asked Ram Das in Urdu.

Ram Das replied in English for Blake's benefit, adopting the sing-song accent of the semi-educated.

'I am telling you, we are just now going to the burning ghats.'

'Who is the dead man?' asked another Indian, also in English.

'My only brother,' said the bear-handler in a grief-stricken voice. 'He has died of plague. I warn you, do not approach too close.'

'Do not delay us, friends,' advised Ram Das. 'The river is in full tide, and we have a place. The wood is piled ready and if we are late, others richer than us may take it.'

'Is it not odd that a poor man, who has not even one mourner to wish him well on his last journey, has English-speaking bearers to carry him?'

'I was educated at the mission school,' explained Ram Das quickly. 'I am matriculate.'

'Not an entirely convincing explanation,' the Indian replied.

Ram Das started to walk forward. The six men moved closer to him.

'Not so fast,' said the man who had spoken first. 'That body is not dead.'

'Not dead?' replied Ram Das in amazement. 'Are you insulting us deliberately? We are poor people, I tell you, but we have feelings.'

'He's breathing,' the man continued. 'Look!'

Blake held his breath until sweat gathered on his forehead and his hands grew damp. Blue, red, yellow lights danced in front of his closed eyes. He hardly dared to swallow. Slowly, he released his breath through clenched teeth. The coloured lights faded, the ringing in his ears subsided.

'He has been dead for a day. It is the gas that makes a little movement. You know what it's like in this weather.'

'I also know a living man when I see one,' the man retorted – and hit Blake in his left kidney. Blake ground his teeth to stop himself crying out, but he could not suppress a muted gasp of pain and shock.

'You see!' the man shouted triumphantly.

'It is the gas, I tell you,' insisted Ram Das.

They crowded more closely around the stretcher.

One of them tapped the soles of Blake's feet.

'He's wearing shoes.'

'Of course, he has shoes. We are not wealthy but we do not go barefoot. If you desecrate the dead in this fashion you will know everlasting torment.'

For a moment, Blake thought that Ram Das and the bear-handler would be allowed on their way. But then another man hit Ram Das sharply in his stomach. He doubled up and let go his end of the stretcher. Blake dropped on to the road.

The shock momentarily stunned him, but he remembered that on no account must he give any evidence of life or pain. All around him now, passers-by began to shout abuse at what they felt was gross interference with a funeral party. He could see feet moving in a complicated ballet of attack and defence, and was conscious of the bear growling, padding around them in a frenzy.

Suddenly the bear gave a roar of anger, and the shouts and screams of the crowd increased. The feet scattered.

Gasping in pain, Ram Das knelt down by Blake.

'Right hand,' he whispered and Blake felt a small metallic object being pushed beneath the bandages. He gripped it, ran his thumb cautiously around the edge of a coin. It had been filed down; he was holding what was virtually a tiny circular blade.

The crowd receded, Ram Das and the bear-handler and the bear disappeared, and he was on his own. The Indians now picked up the stretcher.

With six men to bear Blake's weight instead of two, they proceeded at a far faster pace. Soon they began to bump down steps. Dogs, chickens, goats started up out of sleep, almost beneath their feet. Blake could see red flags flutter from tiled roofs. Sweetmeat sellers were crying their wares, and priests chanted against the boom of beaten gongs and a shrill squealing from thousands of demented birds that flew fluttering from roosts in temple walls.

The breeze changed, and the air grew heavy with the scent of incense. Then he smelled a different, more dangerous odour, an amalgam of hot wood ash and scented wood smoke, overlaid by the crisp unforgettable stench of burning flesh.

His bearers set him down roughly on the ground. He moved his right fingers so that he could grip the sharpened coin between his knuckles. Carefully, and with as little movement as possible, he began to saw away at his bandage. One of the Indians bent down near his head. Blake smelled sweat and hair oil and cigarette smoke. The man unrolled the bandaged part of his face. Blake looked up. Although the sun was three quarters down the sky, it still seemed almost unbearably bright after the darkness of the bandage.

'As I thought, you are Captain Blake,' the Indian said, making a statement, not asking a question.

'Who are you?' Blake asked him. There was now no point in further deception or pretence.

'A friend of someone from whom you have stolen a very large sum of money.'

'Davichand Rana?' asked Blake. The man inclined his head slightly. He did not speak. He and his companions stood looking down at Blake.

'I have not stolen any money,' Blake told them desperately, looking at each man in turn. They regarded him impassively.

'Then you must know who did. And then we will find him, as we have found you,' the leader told him. 'Who has it – and where is it?'

'I have no idea.'

The Indian nodded in the direction of the ghat. Blake followed his gaze. Only feet away, he could see a pile of roughly cut logs, about four feet high, and the same length and shape as a vaulting horse in a gymnasium. He stared at this uncomprehendingly for a few moments before he realized that he was looking at a funeral pyre – his funeral pyre.

The Indian adjusted the bandage about Blake's face so that no-one would be able to see the colour of his skin and then once more they all bent down, picked him up, and carried him towards this pile of logs. His body sagged away from the stretcher as they laid him down on top of it. Even through the bandages around his body, Blake felt sawn-off ends of branches dig into his flesh like sharpened nails.

A Doam, of the lowest untouchable caste, who for generations had provided the fire to burn the dead, approached them. He carried a long staff, its end already ablaze. Only fire from such a source could guarantee salvation; he knew his worth. His ancestors had been doing this necessary work for two and a half centuries.

'He is a beggar,' the Indian explained. 'There is little to spare.'

'It is five rupees for a poor man,' the Doam replied shortly, not too pleased. 'And for that sum he will be consumed by green wood that burns with a low flame and much smoke. Not sandalwood.'

The Indian handed a five-rupee note to the Doam.

'There is still time to tell me,' he said to Blake in English, not looking at him, but out across the sacred river to the far bank as though talking to himself. His voice was cool and cultured; he might be a host at a cocktail party offering a guest a choice of drinks, or one or two cubes of ice.

'I don't know,' Blake replied. 'If I did, I wouldn't be here. You must see that.'

His voice sounded muffled through the bandage that shrouded his mouth, and hoarse with alarm. Within minutes, he would be burned alive. The Indian sighed; the Englishman was being unbelievably foolish.

Blake felt a thin breeze from the river blow beneath the bandages on his face. It felt cool on his sweat-soaked flesh. He tried to keep calm, to force himself to act before the prospect of imminent eternity sapped all willpower, as a serpent's unblinking gaze can mesmerize a bird. And all the while he sawed away with his right hand at the bandage. Gradually, he freed it. Then he passed his hand with the sharpened coin under his body, and began to cut free his left hand at the wrist. This was more difficult to do than he had anticipated. As he sawed desperately, he kept flexing and relaxing his muscles and moving his knees and ankles against each other.

Slowly, Blake felt the bandages loosen. The Doam approached him, hawked in his throat and spat. Blake lay still, holding his breath. The Doam threw some small twigs over him and then touched the flame at the end of his long pole to these slithers of wood. Blake smelled paraffin, but still the new green wood did not catch.

The Doam hawked again in disgust, muttered under his breath and picked up a sheet of newspaper. He rolled this into a ball, pushed it between the twigs, and again applied the pole. The smell of smoke was faint at first and curiously not unpleasant. Maybe the twigs were sandalwood after all, the cast-offs from a richer man's funeral fire. Then the smoke suddenly became acrid and chokingly thick.

Blake had to move now or it would be too late. He bunched his muscles, flexed both hands. His right arm snapped free, but both feet were still trapped. He did not dare to sit up. The attendants would think that any movement was due to the heat tightening dead muscles, and simply beat his body flat. As Blake hacked openly at the bandages around his ankles, he heard a great shout of terror, then screams of fear from across the burning ghats. Shielded by the clouds of thick blue smoke from the cheap damp wood, he rolled slightly to one side.

The bear, leading rope flying loose from its muzzle like a streaming pennant, was racing on hind feet between the funeral pyres. Behind the bear ran the handler, shouting imprecations and orders that the beast neither heard nor heeded. Attendants followed with their long poles. Some hurled burning blocks of charcoal at the animal. Blake guessed that the diversion was for his benefit: he had to go now or stay forever. He sat up, and gasping for breath, ripped away the remaining shreds of bandage from his feet, his face.

The funeral procession that Blake had passed on the way was now arriving. The beat of their drums matched the beat of Blake's thumping heart, and the bray of trumpets sounded above the roar of burning logs, crackling like Gatling guns.

The heat of the fire was already beginning to scorch Blake's body through the bandages. He jumped off the pyre in a desperate leap, but forgot his legs were still tied together, tripped and fell in a great shower of sparks, like a giant firework exploding.

The bear saw this unexpected blaze and reared up, like a giant boxer, beating the air with its front paws. Then the animal changed direction abruptly and fled away from the ghats towards the cooler safety of narrow streets. Doams on their way to meet the procession, with its prospect of princely fees, heard the crackle of burning wood, looked back to see a corpse move, and cried out in horror. Little boys, paid a pittance to gather wood and to separate large logs from smaller ones to start the burning, fled in terror as Blake, half free, half bound, tore frantically at his last remaining bandages. One Doam seized a burning log and flung it at him; he did not realize Blake was alive. He thought that they were all seeing some fearful muscular reaction brought on by the fierce heat.

Blake freed his legs, his arms. All that remained was the bandage bound around the centre of his body. He could feel heat on his flesh through the thin cellular material of his shirt, and smell his hair singeing. He raced, flames pouring from him, between other burning bodies. He had a brief and grotesque vision of charred bones and skulls, of eyeballs the size of blind onions, bulging in their sockets. Then he reached the river.

He did not pause, but took a deep breath and dived into the yellow filthy water. He felt the soft rotting caress of the bloated corpses of dogs and sheep, and his flesh crawled with loathing. Then he was beneath the floating debris. He swam underwater for several strokes before he surfaced, about twenty feet from the shore. He trod water as he unwound the remaining strips of bandage from his body. Then he began to swim strongly and steadily out into mid-stream, taking care not to swallow any water on the way.

When he was well clear of the nearer ghats, he hauled himself up over the far side of a small rowing boat, attached by a painter to a larger craft, and collapsed thankfully on to its duckboards. He lay here for a moment, shaking with revulsion from the foul smell of the river, and reaction from the narrowness of his escape. In the midst of death he was still alive – but only just. And for how long?

He felt too weak and weary to move – and where else could he go, in any case? He had to wait until Jerrold returned and then this nightmare could end. But even as he told himself this, he wondered: would it? And why and how had it ever begun?

Slowly, he relaxed. The day was dying, and the sun dropped steadily down the sky. Blake raised his aching body on one elbow to look over the gunwale. The river banks were still crowded. Patches of red ash glowed like furnace mouths among the burning ghats, and the little birds of evening stretched their wings like tiny parentheses against the darkening sky. Blake made himself as comfortable as he could, loosening his shoes, making a pillow from a pile of fishnets. He would rest until midnight and then swim ashore. It would be safer to move then, when the teeming streets of Benares would be relatively empty. He closed his eyes thankfully.

When Blake awoke, the sun was rising on the far bank of the river and mist drifted silently across the water. For a moment, he had no idea where he was, and then, with rising panic, he remembered. He must have overslept wildly and dangerously, and had awoken at dawn – the hour of greatest risk to him. The owners of the boat might come to collect it, and police would soon be patrolling the city searching for him. He must move at once.

Blake's shirt and trousers had dried on him and his body felt stiff and raw. With every movement he made, he smelled the stink of river water. He felt unclean. He picked up an oar from the bottom of the boat, unwound the painter and steered the little craft out into mid-stream. The swift current carried him along past the ghats, and two round buildings. One was a temple, decorated with images of dancing gods; the other, built in ident-ical style, processed the sewage of Benares city.

Half a mile down river, Blake leaned on his steering oar and turned his boat into the bank. He made it fast to a metal ring on a wooden post and walked thankfully up on dry land. The countryside was flat here, and a road followed the line of the river. He walked along it, past a few poor houses still shuttered against the night air, a rickshaw, shafts on the ground, a hobbled tonga pony asleep on its feet.

Along the road towards him, a garlanded bullock meandered peacefully, chewing the cud. A cluster of vultures, with oily feathers and bloodied beaks, crouched on the carcass of a dead buffalo at the roadside, tearing greedily at its carrion flesh. These extremes represented the gap between failure and success, thought Blake dryly. Which was it going to be for him?

A handful of weak stars faded from the sky, and the crescent moon grew pale against the strengthening sun. A white milkiness of mist still lingered over paddy fields, and between the thin branches of the trees by the roadside, beads of moisture glittered like tears on the cobwebs of the night. He glanced at his Army issue waterproof watch: five minutes past five o'clock in the morning. Early as it was, he must reach Jerrold's house before anyone called attention to his scruffy appearance. They would think he was a deserter, hatless, and with his foul bush shirt and trousers that had dried on his body, his scuffed shoes.

Indians were beginning to appear, from where he did not know. They were already cycling along the road, white dhotis pulled up carefully out of the way of the chain. Where had they come from? Where were they going? They moved with spindly legs on spidery wheels, ignoring him, like silent ghosts of morning. Blake kept on walking.

A goat chewed some millet leaves, and a tiny buffalo, abandoned by its mother, walked desolately towards him, the bell around its neck tinkling. The mist cleared slowly. More cyclists appeared, and then an old truck converted to a bus with a notice 'On Government Duty' painted along one side. Now Blake recognized that he was on the main road, about half a mile from Jerrold's house.

He quickened his pace until he turned off the road into Jerrold's front drive. The house was shuttered and lanterns burned under the storm porch. On the lawn, a peacock fanned its tail of a thousand feathered eyes. The peacock in India is an emblem of good luck, he thought. In England, it means exactly the reverse. Which future is for me?

Blake climbed the front steps, pressed the bell push and heard the bell peal within cool recesses of the house. No sound, no response and yet surely someone must be inside, or the lights would not be burning? Or had they been deliberately left lit to persuade potential thieves that the house was occupied? As he pondered these two possibilities, he heard the faint rattle of a safety chain and the front door opened.

Jerrold stood looking at him, not in pyjamas and dressing gown, as Blake had expected at this early hour, but washed, shaved, wearing a freshly ironed shirt and newly pressed light-weight linen trousers.

'You!' said Jerrold in amazement. 'What the hell are you doing here?'

'Thank God I caught you in,' said Blake, ignoring the question. He pushed his way into the hall, closed the door behind him and leaned wearily and thankfully against it.

'Where have you been?' Jerrold asked him, wrinkling his nose in distaste at Blake's appearance. 'Have you been in a fight or something? You look as if you've been dragged through Benares sewage works. And you smell like it, too.'

'I came to see you yesterday,' Blake told him, again ignoring his remarks. 'Your bearer told me you had gone to Calcutta.'

Jerrold shrugged.

'He got it wrong. I came back twenty minutes after you left, but I'd no address for you.'

'You've heard what has happened, I suppose?' Blake asked him wearily.

'The money's gone?'

'So you know. I had a call from Dermott's hotel saying he wanted to see me urgently. I tried to phone you, but couldn't get through. I hid the money in my pack in the room rather than risk carrying the case – the leave centre wouldn't take any responsibility for valuables – so I only had these two options.

'When I saw Dermott, he said he knew nothing about the call. On my way back, two fellows jumped me as I was getting into the taxi and seized the case. Either it was a chance robbery – or they knew I'd got a lot of cash and thought I'd have it in the case with me.

'But when I got back to my room, the money had gone. I came out here right away to tell you – and then learned that the police were after me. So I've kept out of sight until you'd be back. For goodness sake, tell me what's happening.'

Jerrold did not reply.

'What's the matter?' asked Blake, perplexed. 'Have you taken the money? Is this a joke? What the hell is going on?'

'I think you'd better tell *us* that,' said a Scottish voice behind Blake. He turned. A middle-aged man wearing a starched khaki shirt and trousers, with the black Sam Browne belt and silver badges of a police officer stood in the study doorway.

'Major Cartwright,' he said, introducing himself. 'You are Captain Richard Blake?'

'Of course I am.'

'And yet on the telephone you claimed to be James Boswell?'

'I had a reason for that.'

'And we have reason to believe, Captain Blake, that you have appropriated the sum of approximately thirteen and a half million rupees in notes, the property of a distinguished member of the ruling family in Nepal.'

'You are talking bloody rubbish,' said Blake angrily.

He looked appealingly at Jerrold.

'That's why I came here. For you to sort this out.'

'I'm sorry, but I know nothing about it,' said Jerrold. 'Nothing at all.'

'Do you wish that to be noted as a statement? That I am talking bloody rubbish?' asked Major Cartwright coldly.

He took out a little notebook and a pencil, licked the lead point. He had come up through the ranks, and hated Blake already for what he thought he was.

'You're . . .' began Blake, and then paused. This could be serious. Jerrold and Cartwright were either carrying farce to the point of absurdity – or he was in far greater trouble than he'd ever been in all his life. He remembered the need for secrecy Howard and Dermott had stressed as imperative only days previously. He said: 'I don't know what you are talking about.'

'I have to warn you that anything you say may be taken down and used in evidence,' said Cartwright.

'I can only repeat, I don't know what you are talking about.'

The policeman turned and nodded towards the study. Two other European police officers came into the hall. These must be the men Mrs Keeble at the leave centre had told him were waiting for him.

'You are to be charged with misappropriating the funds as aforesaid, and will be remanded in custody while further investigations are made. For the last time, have you anything to say?'

Blake shrugged. They were idiots, of course. But this would all be cleared up when he could get hold of Dermott or Howard. Then there would be some red faces and apologies.

'Yes,' he said wearily. 'I'd like a bath and a drink.'

The next few weeks passed for Blake in a kind of suspended timelessness. He was never quite sure whether he was being questioned in the morning or at night, for his cell in Benares jail had no window, only a fan in the end of a metal ventilating duct. The cell was lit constantly by a throbbing electric bulb behind a wire mesh protective screen in the ceiling. His shoelaces had been removed, and he was not allowed a razor or even a knife, fork or spoon; nothing but a wooden pallet with a blanket, a mosquito net and a slop bucket.

He received no letters. There was no-one to write to him, and he only wrote two: one to Chet, in Kathmandu, and another to Colonel Howard which he addressed, for want of a better phrase, as care of The Viceroy, Viceregal Lodge, New Delhi. In both letters he appealed for help – a letter, a telegram, even a phone call, anything – to prove his innocence of the ridiculous charge. He did not receive a reply to either letter. Since Blake's watch had also been removed, he was not quite certain of the passage of time, but each morning he scratched a mark on the yellow distempered wall with his thumbnail. At least he would know what day of the week it was.

When Blake was tired, he slept, face turned away from the pulsating light which seemed to penetrate his brain like a drumbeat. When he was awake, he paced up and down his cell or sat on his wooden bed, pondering on his predicament. Finally, a young captain came to see him.

He had a spotty face and wore spectacles, and he brought a folding canvas chair on which he sat while Blake squatted on the edge of his bed, like a guru and his disciple, he thought.

'I am your defending officer,' the captain explained. 'You know you are to be court-martialled?'

'I had no idea,' Blake told him.

'Well, you are. Day after tomorrow. I want to find out if there are any mitigating circumstances.'

'Were you a lawyer in civvy street?'

'No, siree. I was a building society clerk.'

'I'm very grateful to you, but can't I have a qualified lawyer to defend me? Someone who would know all the ropes?'

'Doesn't seem to be one, old boy. I was offered the choice. This job, or escorting a draft of infantry reinforcements to Chittagong. You know what that's like. Bloody awful. They go missing every time the train stops. You're counting heads, they're dodging about. I've done it once. Never again, old boy.'

'Have you ever defended anyone at a court martial?'

The captain shook his head cheerfully.

'Got to be a first time, hasn't there? Now, let's get down to brass tacks. You know what the charges are?'

'Tell me.'

'You're not going to like this, but you are up on three fizzers. First, forgery. Next, embezzlement of an enormous sum of money. Third – in case that doesn't stick – larceny. What do you say to that?'

'I say it's a load of balls.'

'Hardly a defence, old boy.'

'Right, then let's take it charge by charge. What have I forged?'

'Three signatures. And you could hardly have chosen more impressive people. First, Lord Louis Mountbatten, Supreme Allied Commander South East Asia. Then Field Marshal Sir William Slim, and, lastly, Air Marshal Sir John Baldwin. They are not going to like having their names appearing on a document like the one you forged. They deny their signatures are genuine, of course. And they say they've never heard of you – or this so-called contract.'

'I didn't forge anything. I was given that contract already typed and signed.'

'You'll have to prove it. And what about thirteen and a half million rupees? In notes. Take us both a few hundred years to earn that little lot.'

'But I haven't got the money. This is absolute rubbish,' Blake protested.

'So you tell me, old boy. I believe you. But what are you going to tell the court?'

'The truth.'

'Ah,' said the defending officer, tapping the side of his nose with the forefinger of his left hand. ' "What is truth?" asked Pilate. If he didn't know, how the hell will the court?'

'Because I'll produce people who will corroborate what I say.'

'Like what people?'

'Rex Jerrold, for one. The war correspondent out here for the *Globe*.'

'He is back in Burma,' said the captain shortly. 'I've checked. We've sent him a signal, but he hasn't replied.'

'He will,' said Blake confidently.

'Why do you think so?'

'Because I've known him for years. We were at Oxford together.'

'Oxford, eh?' said the defending officer sharply. 'That may not go down too well with the court. It could sort of bias things against you.'

'Thanks. Then there's Mr Dermott of the Foreign Office.'

'Never heard of him. What's his address?'

'I don't know in India. Foreign Office, Whitehall, London, I suppose. And what about Colonel Howard on the Viceroy's staff?'

'He has declined to appear.'

'But can't we make him appear? Can't he be subpoenaed?'

'Difficult, old boy. He's in a very dodgy political position.'

'The hell he is! What about my position? I'm in the *kunji* house, charged with all sorts of rubbish. If there's any justice in the Army, get him here.'

'I say, old boy, no need to take on so. I think our best bet is to try and get this fellow Jerrold. But he is a civvy, you know. And, like Colonel Howard, he doesn't have to appear. We can only make a request – through the usual channels.'

'What the devil is this?' asked Blake furiously. 'I was asked to do something by these people. To help my country, I was told. Something's gone terribly wrong, but that is absolutely nothing to do with me. Now nobody wants to come forward and admit what instructions they gave me.'

He paused.

'What about Captain Chet Bahadur Rana?'

'I've heard the name,' the captain admitted. 'But I don't remember who mentioned it.'

'Well, I'm mentioning it now. He is a member of the Rana family of Nepal. The nephew of this man Davichand Rana who paid the money to him. He passed it on to me. Chet and I were together in the Arakan. I've stayed with him in Nepal and I've

214

seen him here in Benares. He knows about the whole thing, from beginning to end.'

'Damn difficult to get him out of Nepal, old boy.'

'Why should it be difficult? He's in the Army. Can't he be ordered to come?'

'Well, it's a rather odd arrangement with them, I think. Sort of attachment. Honorary commission. That sort of thing. At least, that's what I'm told.'

'Who told you?'

'Well . . . people here. I have been advised, as they say. I don't think it would be a good idea to contact him. A lot of political clout there, you know.'

'That's exactly why I want him. He could get me off any charge immediately. He knows it all.'

'Well, I don't, old boy,' said the captain cheerfully. 'Now, why don't we sit here quietly and you tell me the whole thing? As you see it. In your own words.'

8

From the moment the defending and prosecuting officers entered the room in the barracks in Benares, where the proceedings were being held, saluted, took their places and waited for Blake to be marched in, it was obvious that he was in for a hard time.

All remarked afterwards on the fact that he held himself well. He did not look guilty. Instead, he appeared almost detached from the proceedings, as though this was all happening to someone else and he was not personally involved in any way.

I was not present at the court martial, of course, but afterwards I managed to track down several who were. Among them was a clerk from the Pay Corps who took a verbatim shorthand note which he showed me, so I had a pretty accurate idea of what had happened.

'It's an odd word to use to describe his attitude,' said the defending officer, now back in his old job in a South London branch office, 'but he seemed almost contemptuous of the whole thing. Remember how Gulliver regarded the Lilliputians? They tied him with strings which seemed unbreakable to them – and he just shook them off, because to someone of his stature, they were only threads. I think Blake felt like that about the prosecution claims. He dismissed them all. He was certain that the court would believe his story.'

'And did it?' I asked him.

'Well, no. It was a damn funny defence, let's face it. And I wasn't clued up on all the legal angles. Some bloke in the Foreign Office, who no-one seems to have heard of, whose name doesn't appear on any official list, and who cannot be found, offers Blake to pay all his gambling debts if he'll make a fool of some bloody statesman or general or whoever in Nepal – who he's never even met. I mean, it's ridiculous. At the time I thought it was very thin. But he insisted this was his defence, so I had to go along with him.'

'Who was this fellow in Nepal?' I offered him a third brandy to loosen his memory. We were meeting in the saloon bar of a dingy public house near his office. Men wearing waisted blue overcoats and trilby hats were eating lunchtime sandwiches at the bar. It wasn't the sort of place Blake would have patronized.

'Name of Davichand Rana. He was called as a major prosecution witness. A general or a minister, I think, or both.'

'Both. And how did you react to him? What was your impression?'

'A gentleman, I would think, very used to having his own way. A bit like Blake, really, in that,' said the clerk. 'He said Blake approached him, saying he was acting on the orders of some unnamed superior officer, who urgently needed a very large sum of money towards some secret project in connection with the prosecution of the war.

'Well, Davichand Rana said that his country and Britain had been allies for a hundred-odd years and he had the highest regard for everything British. Gurkhas have served in the British Army for generations, and so on. Naturally, he paid up, so he said, without a second thought. His exact words, actually. A gentleman, like I said.'

'Then why was he complaining?'

'Wouldn't you complain if you'd lost a million pounds? He wanted to get hold of Blake, to see whether the money had gone to whatever purpose it was needed, but he couldn't find him anywhere. Then he heard from a friend that this money had been telegraphed to some bank in London, so he'd lost Blake – and his money. I'd sue if I lost even a fiver. Wouldn't you?'

'I don't know,' I said. 'It's a cliché, but circumstances can alter cases.'

They certainly didn't alter the case against Blake, or perhaps the circumstantial evidence was just too strong.

Jerrold did come back from Burma, and appeared as a character witness for the defence. What came across strongly was not the words he said, but the way he said them. He agreed that he had known the accused for several years; in fact, from the time they were both undergraduates at Oxford. The accused had also been friendly with the girl who was now his wife. This led the prosecution to ask about her. Was it true that she had been severely injured in a motor accident?

'Yes,' Jerrold agreed.

'Who was driving the car?'

Jerrold paused and looked awkwardly at Blake as though he did not wish to incriminate him. Blake looked back at him as though he had nothing whatever to hide.

'The accused,' Jerrold admitted with a show of reluctance.

The prosecution had found a newspaper report of this accident, goodness knows how. They read it out. Blake had admitted drinking champagne less than an hour before the crash in which the girl, Corinne Gieves, was so badly injured that doctors feared she would be paralysed for life. The fact that she was, at that time, heiress to a textile fortune – and that Blake was eloping with her when the crash took place – turned the court slightly in Blake's favour. But when Jerrold, again with much apparent reluctance, admitted that Blake did not marry her after she was crippled, feelings surged strongly against him.

Apart from this behaviour, which in the mess afterwards, the president described as 'caddish', Blake's character suffered two more body blows. The first came through the testimony obtained in England, under oath, from a Mr Marsh, who before the war had managed the branch of a bank in Oxford where Blake had his account.

No-one to whom I spoke seemed absolutely clear about what had happened, but it appeared that Blake had borrowed money in order to buy a used-car business, and then had not bought it. He had paid back the loan, however, and so I could not quite understand where or how he had offended Mr Marsh's code of business ethics.

There seemed something raffish and ungentlemanly about dealing in used cars, at least to the members of the court. It wasn't quite the thing, not done. So another black mark went against Blake's character by association.

Blake had also apprently falsely claimed to Mr Marsh that he had access to trust funds, and this added to the general impression that he was untrustworthy regarding financial matters. He was also said to owe money to a London bookmaker who had died in curious circumstances on the eve of the outbreak of war in 1939.

'How much?' a witness was asked.

'A matter of thousands.'

The witness was a fat, soft-faced officer who, by what seemed to me to be a most curious coincidence, had just happened to be in Benares on leave at the time of the theft. He explained that he had worked for Mr McMoffatt as an accounting clerk before the war. The defence did not question him; as the defending officer readily admitted, he was ill informed as to his rights and duties.

'How much is owing?'

'A very large sum, sir.'

'Can you be more specific?' asked the president of the court, irritably; the room was hot and he had drunk three gins before lunch instead of the two he usually allowed himself.

'As I recall, sir, with interest, it must now be around twenty-five thousand pounds.'

A strange hush greeted his reply, for this was a fortune to the three officers hearing the case, and, indeed, to everyone else involved.

Blake pleaded not guilty to all charges and asked that the Foreign Office official, Mr Dermott, and Colonel Howard should be brought to testify in his defence. Oddly, no-one seemed ever to have heard of Mr Dermott. Blake insisted he had been staying at the Alexis Hotel, where he had personally visited him, but a search of the hotel visitors' book showed that no-one of that name had signed into the hotel at that time.

The reception clerk at the Alexis did admit, however, that Blake had come in very agitated one day, asking for a Mr Dermott, and when he replied that he was not there, Blake had attacked him so severely that he had been off work for three days.

'You remember the date?' asked the prosecuting officer.

'I do, sir. It was the day the money was reported missing.'

Gradually the case against Blake built up like a wall, brick by brick. His story seemed so far-fetched and unsubstantiated that no-one in the courtroom had any doubt that he would be found guilty. In all the circumstances, it was the only possible conclusion.

Blake's company commander in the Arakan gave a grudging testimonial by letter. He said that Blake was brave but 'difficult' – a word he could not amplify, because he was not in court. The description had the effect of making Blake seem somehow wayward and undisciplined.

Jerrold denied introducing Blake, either to Mr Dermott or to Colonel Howard, with any intention of pecuniary advantage to anyone. He said he had not seen Blake for several years, until he ran into him by chance in the casino at Benares – where he pointed out that Blake had lost several thousand rupees. Jerrold invited him to dinner and Colonel Howard, whom he knew slightly, came along for a drink, and brought a friend, a stranger to him, whose name he had forgotten.

Jerrold had not seen either of them again, and certainly when he was in the room with Blake and Howard and this other man, there was no discussion whatever about any sum of money, large or small. The name of His Excellency Davichand Rana of Nepal had not been mentioned.

The president summed up, with some harsh things to say about young men who were brought up in surroundings of wealth and luxury, and so assumed that the world owed them a living. The accused had a long record of gambling, of not paying his debts, of owing large sums of money for many years, without making any attempt to repay his creditors. In fact he even strenuously denied the existence of many of these debts. He had deliberately and constantly lived above his means over many years, mixing with wealthy people, although his own background was one, it would appear, of almost total sham. Nor was extravagance and a total lack of realism in financial matters confined to him; his father had shot himself, owing thousands of pounds.

Blake had held the King's commission, but his conduct was totally unbecoming to what must reasonably be expected of every officer in the British armed services. The sentence of the court was twelve years' hard labour, to be served in a British prison.

'How did he take it?' I asked the clerk.

'He stood bolt upright as if he was on parade, in a position of attention, thumbs in line with the seams of his trousers. He looked around the court in utter contempt.'

'What about Jerrold?'

'He left before sentence was pronounced.'

Bombay. May, 1946

Mr Lord, the senior partner of Moynihan, Marigold and Lord, was reading the *Times of India* in the smoking room of the Bombay Club when he saw Mr Baird come into the room, and waved across to him.

'Thought you were still stuck in Calcutta,' said Baird, as he sat down on a leather armchair by his side.

'I was,' Lord replied. 'But now the war has been over for a year, there are a few more passages. I'd had my name down on the list for months, and suddenly it came up. I'm off home in the *Athlone Castle* tomorrow. What brings you here?'

'Oh, business,' said Baird vaguely. 'I'm acting for a maharajah.'

Lord ordered two whisky and sodas.

'Not name of Davichand Rana, I suppose,' he asked slyly.

'Not this time, thank goodness. Just some ordinary prince who's not sure what life will be like for him when the Gandhi wallahs take over. Wants advice – or comfort. Reassurance, I suppose. Which I can't give him, I'm sorry to say. That world – his world and ours – is ending.'

He raised his glass in a silent toast to his old colleague.

'Damned odd business about Davichand Rana,' he went on, 'and the money that fellow Blake stole.'

'Extraordinary,' Lord agreed. 'Yet what I told you was all quite true. There was a plan to sell those trading rights. All very high level stuff.'

'That may be,' said Baird, 'but there was no plan for Blake to make off with the money, eh? One thing you can never insure against is corruption among your staff.'

'Agreed. And up till now we've never needed to. We've been lucky, I suppose,' said Lord ruminatively. 'Different sort of fellows held commissions in the army in our day.'

'Temptations weren't so great then, either. Even so, the odd quartermaster made a bob or two on the side. But never in all my experience did anyone ask me, or anyone else, to deal with the equivalent of a million pounds in notes. If they had, I might have cleared off with it too.'

'I felt sorry for Blake, poor devil,' said Lord. 'Not that I ever met him, or even heard his name mentioned when the negotiations were going on.

'First I heard was when I read about it in the *Statesman*. Trouble is, if you tangle with these secret service wallahs, they'll drop you right in it if anything goes wrong. Deny everything. Can't even be found sometimes – as when Blake was court-martialled. Like Dermott, apparently. Yet he'd been sitting in my office, close to me as you are now. Makes you think, eh?'

'Makes me feel my age,' said Baird. 'Nothing about what you're telling me now was in the newspaper reports.'

'It wouldn't be. But I've a brother-in-law who was working in the Censor's office. He told me it was all cut out. What appeared just made you think that Blake embezzled the money for his own gain.'

'What he needed was a good lawyer,' said Baird shortly. 'Like we need another drink.'

He pressed a bell for a waiter.

London. June, 1953

I do not know how well Blake was able to keep abreast of happenings in the world outside the prison walls, or indeed whether he made any serious attempt to do so. If he did, he might have read that, in 1951 – six years after he was sentenced – the power of the Ranas in Nepal was suddenly and permanently overthrown. But even if he had read this, he would never have imagined that his actions had played any part whatever in this revolution, let alone a significant part. Nor, I imagine, would he have greatly cared, for so far as Blake was concerned, his assignment had been a total failure.

In fact, it was not, except, of course, so far as he personally was concerned. He had lost the equivalent of £1,000,000 entrusted to him for safe keeping; his debts had not been paid; and then he was committed to twelve years hard labour. And hard labour in the 1940s meant exactly that: breaking stones with an axe from seven o'clock in the morning until it was too dark to see, day after day after day.

Jerrold reported the court martial for the *Globe*, but naturally the real reason for Blake's taking a fortune from Davichand Rana was not mentioned. The case was about an extravagant and improvident British officer who, for his own personal, selfish reasons, had attempted to defraud a member of the ruling family of one of Britain's most valued allies.

Davichand Rana's name appeared in Jerrold's report, and those who knew Nepal well sensed that there must have been rather more to the matter than simply a young and unknown British officer endeavouring to swindle a very rich man. And even if there wasn't, they asked, how did it come about that a man apparently so shrewd and wise as Davichand Rana, a potential prime minister of his country, should fall for such a blatantly obvious confidence trick? The more that Davichand Rana raged in private against the machinations of the British in general, and

Blake in particular, and also against anyone who dared to voice the slightest criticism of his own part in events, the more he diminished his own political stature and credibility.

He would have been better advised to stay silent, but he took advice from no-one – and anyone who had in the past offered him any counsel not totally to his liking, found that at best, they were stripped of their possessions and at worst, incarcerated in jail without prospect of release.

So Davichand Rana did not become prime minister. The man who did was the best alternative, without going outside the Rana family and so causing an unbridgeable rift in that family.

The King took courage and confidence from the discomfiture of his chief adversary. So did many brave Nepalese who had emigrated – fled would be a more accurate word – across the frontier to India, where they worked unceasingly to form a group strong enough to overthrow the Ranas and restore the monarchy. They had, at first, no more success than all the others who had attempted this before them. But they were cheered and heartened by the knowledge that the King was in full sympathy with their aims and he gave them all the encouragement he could; he and they persevered.

The Ranas, who allowed the King to buy anything from the United States or Britain by mail-order catalogue, never queried his purchases, which by the nature of the goods on sale were simple enough. So when it appeared that the King took a fancy to ordering disguises and masks and wigs and strange clothes, claiming a new interest in amateur theatricals, they humoured him. And how could any danger threaten them if he wanted to dress up in odd costumes?

In any case, whenever the King drove out from his palace in his grey Mercury car, an armed Rana officer always sat with him, and other guards followed behind in a second vehicle. When he visited the palaces of his grown-up sons, these escorts would wait in the anteroom, while the King and the princes talked or ate a meal together. This was a long established routine, for what harm could come from allowing the King to meet his family? The Ranas knew where he was and who was with him.

What they did not know was that the King kept several of his new costumes and make-up sets in rooms in his sons' palaces. He would leave his bodyguard on one side of the door, change hurriedly into a disguise – he had longish curly hair which he concealed beneath a wig of another colour – and then slip away through a window to meet emissaries from India. These men brought him news of the growing revolt against the Ranas, and carried back his comments and instructions.

The Indian government was, of course, aware of all this and had its own reasons for being sympathetic to the exiles. When China occupied Tibet, Nepal became the only country lying between China and India. If the Chinese wished to invade India from this direction, they would first have to subdue Nepal. They had already taken steps which could facilitate its occupation and bring them to the Indian frontier. They had offered huge loans and the services of Chinese surveyors and engineers, who planned long straight roads from the Tibetan – now Chinese – border into Kathmandu.

It was therefore in India's own interest for national survival that the government of Nepal should be democratic, and the Nepalese people released from what was virtually a self-perpetuating dictatorship. Otherwise, they might welcome the Chinese, not as conquerors but as liberators.

At about this time the King decided to travel to India himself and lead the fight from across the border. He was friendly with the Indian ambassador in Kathmandu, and a rendezvous was arranged, but this the King could not keep.

A senior member of the Rana family was conducting an illicit affair with a married woman within yards of the proposed meeting place. He sat talking to her in his car – and their presence forced the King to hide for three hours in a ditch only feet away, unable to move in case he was discovered. On such curious and unexpected chances and mischances can dynasties depend and the future of governments and nations lie.

Months passed, discontent in Nepal increased – and then the Ranas gave the King permission to go with his sons on a leopard hunt in the mountains.

The King and his party left his palace in a convoy of five cars. As usual, an armed Rana officer sat in each vehicle. As they approached the entrance to the Indian embassy, the King, driving his own Mercury in the centre of the little convoy, let the leading cars sweep on ahead, and then swung off the road and through the embassy gates. The cars behind, containing his sons, followed him.

The King jumped out. So did his guards, not knowing the

eason for this totally unscheduled visit. They soon discovered. The Indian military attaché, a colonel, invited the King into the embassy building to meet the Indian ambassador. Once inside, the King asked formally for political asylum. This was given, of course, because his arrival had been expected.

The officers raced back to their barracks and returned within half an hour with reinforcements under the command of a general, who demanded that the King return to his palace. This was totally the wrong approach, and the Indian ambassador told him coldly to remove his revolver before any discussions could take place; the King would not speak to him so long as he was armed. The general reluctantly obeyed – he could not very well refuse, because technically and diplomatically he was on foreign soil.

'As your King,' the King informed the angry general, 'I am not satisfied with your treatment of my country, or of me. You will inform His Highness the Maharajah of this.'

The general did so. The Ranas replied by blocking the road to the Indian embassy, so that no vehicle could enter or leave. They also cut off water and electricity to the embassy and prevented food or other supplies being brought in. However, the Indians had expected such a reaction and made sure that the embassy had sufficient water and stores and a portable generator to withstand a long seige. This proved unnecessary, because the King stayed in the compound only long enough for an Indian aircraft to be prepared and arrangements made for him to fly to New Delhi from a country airstrip outside Kathmandu.

The Ranas immediately announced that his grandson, then aged three, would be the new King of Nepal, but foreign governments declined to recognize this hasty move. Meanwhile, news of the King's flight – and the reasons for it – spread across Nepal.

In remote outposts and villages, people rose up against the Ranas. Crowds surged through the streets of every town, demonstrating in favour of the King. Kathmandu was in continuous uproar. Finally, the King was prevailed upon to return.

Fifty thousand people waited at the little airfield where Richard Blake had arrived so many years earlier. They greeted their sovereign's return by shouting the name by which his ancestors had been known: 'The Golden Obelisk'. Now he was back, not just as a regal totem, a titular king, or a kind of living insurance policy for the Ranas, but as a ruling monarch.

One of his first actions was to order a vast red carpet to be taken to the gates of Kathmandu jail. This carpet was unrolled, and the prison gates opened. More than five hundred political prisoners were released, to be garlanded with flowers and walk to freedom ankle-deep in petals.

Thus the rule of the Ranas was broken, never to return. But of all the thousands in Nepal who cheered their political overthrow, how many ever guessed that the British officer who had, if all unknowingly, sown the seed that would later grow into this tree of freedom, was at that moment in jail in England, totally unaware of the importance of his actions?

Blake thought he had failed. But had he been free to return to Nepal, and had the people realized his pivotal part in these great events, they would have garlanded him with golden flowers and carried him in triumph through the streets of the city built on the edge of what had once been a tank of serpents.

I wrote several times to Blake in prison, but I did not receive a reply to my letters. Perhaps he never got them. No-one has many friends when they are down, but it is always prudent to bear in mind the old saying, 'Never hit a man when he's down – he may get up.'

Blake got up, or rather out, in eight years, because in 1953 to mark the coronation of Queen Elizabeth, an amnesty was announced. A number of prisoners were released. Blake was among them.

I had my own ideas about what had happened in Benares in 1944 so far as Blake was concerned, but I wanted to be sure. Lawyers need proof; theories are useless. I had by now built up my own contacts in several local banks in that ancient city, and so it came about that I finally found myself sitting in the private sitting room of a suite in a Benares hotel, with the clerk who had advised Davichand Rana that a large sum of money had been telegraphed to London from his branch on the day Blake received it.

The clerk was nervous, and understandably so. The worst possible outcome, so far as he was concerned, would be that I might inform his manager that he had been accepting bribes over many years.

'I will lose my job, sir, if you inform my superior,' he said miserably.

'Perhaps you deserve to?'

'I have a wife and three children and a widowed mother to support.'

'Your wife has left you,' I corrected him. 'You have no children, and your mother died three years ago. However, there is no imperative need for me to inform your superiors of your venality. So long as I receive an equivalent favour in return.'

'What can I do to help you, sir?' he asked anxiously.

'You can give me the name of the bank to which this money was transferred. And tell me to whose account it was credited.'

'That will be difficult, sir.'

'Life for you without a job will be even more difficult,' I answered him.

'The records may not now be available,' he said wretchedly.

'Make them available,' I told him. 'And bring this information to me here in this hotel tomorrow at three o'clock.'

He was on time, as I knew he would be, perched uneasily on the edge of his chair in the entrance hall. He passed me a single piece of paper, folded over. I opened it. He had typed the name of a bank in London and beneath this the name of a company, Beechwood Nominees, and the date and number of the transaction.

'How do I know that this is accurate?' I asked him.

He looked at me in amazement; he had not imagined that I might doubt his word.

'You lied to me yesterday about your dependants. Why tell the truth today?'

'Because I have to,' he admitted. 'At my age I would find it hard to get another job.'

'You would find it impossible. I would see to that. So if I find that my faith in you has been misplaced, you know the result?'

He nodded. I handed him an envelope with the retainer he had earned. When I left him, he was foolishly counting the notes in a public place.

London. August, 1953

The prison official pushed a piece of paper bearing the prison cypher at its head across the counter. Blake glanced briefly at the list typed on it.

227

'Not a lot of trust here,' he remarked as he picked up the indelible pencil that was chained to the wall.

'What do you expect in choky?' the official asked him.

'Blessed is he who expecteth nothing, for then he is never disappointed.'

Blake signed for the civilian clothes he had been wearing eight years earlier when he had started to serve his sentence.

'There was a comb,' he said.

'Don't see nothing about that here,' the official said sharply.

'It should have been on the list,' said Blake. 'Army comb. Metal. Officer's issue. One. I had it when I came in.'

'Can't help you, mate. Like you said, there's not much trust. If it's not on the list, that's it.'

Blake turned towards the door. His clothes seemed to hang loosely on his body, as though intended for another man – as, in a sense, they had been. He was a different man now: harder, leaner, tougher.

'Fifteen pounds, fifteen and six due to you,' said the official. 'Your earnings. Sign this, too, before you go. If you want the money.'

He laughed, as though he had made a joke. Everyone wanted money – and hadn't this bastard got away with a million quid?

Blake signed again, put the money in the back pocket of his trousers without counting it. A warder slid back two oiled bolts on the wicket gate. Blake stepped through it and the door closed silently behind him, shutting off eight lost years – nearly a ninth of his life, if he accepted the Biblical time span of three score years and ten. And, some would say, his best years at that.

He stood for a moment, breathing the almost forgotten air of freedom. The traffic seemed heavier and noisier than when he had been arrested, but then petrol had still been rationed, and many of the vehicles on the road had still carried white strips painted on their bumpers and mudguards, a relic of the wartime blackout.

Now, the cars were bright as coloured beads. He felt as he had once felt when he was a boy, coming out of the school sanatorium after chickenpox, rather weak at the knees, strangely frail. To cope with the crowds, the rush of a busy world and its incredible noise, would be a challenge he must overcome after years of prison quiet.

He kept at first in the shadow of the high prison walls, then crossed the road to walk in the sunshine. He went into the first café he saw selling pies, beans and chips, and ordered coffee and two eggs and bacon. He stirred in three spoonfuls of sugar, because it was a luxury. Someone had left a newspaper on the plastic-topped table. The pages were greasy with fat and other men's fingers. He read without interest that Drobny and Patty were at Wimbledon; Mau Mau terrorists were being arrested in Kenya; the French were fighting in French Indo-China, and a horse named Darius had beaten Princely Gift by a short head at Newmarket.

The man who served him wore a white apron, stained with tea. He looked at Blake's pale face with total understanding.

'Just got out?' he asked him sympathetically.

Blake nodded.

'Thought so. They all come here. First stop. That'll be four and six, by the way.'

Blake counted out the money, added sixpence for a tip.

'Thank you,' said the man appreciatively. 'Got a job?'

'Well, not yet. But an aim.'

Blake wondered what the café owner would have said if he had explained the scale and complexity of the plan he had worked out meticulously, night after sleepless night, lying on his pallet while the ammoniac smell of his own urine rose from the bucket in the corner of the cell, and he listened to the ceaseless tapping of slow messages from one end of the prison to the other along the water pipes.

Blake took a bus to Piccadilly, changed to another that went down the Cromwell Road. He jumped off at Gloucester Road and walked through squares of once proud houses, now warrens of single rooms for students, unimportant overseas visitors, people travelling light; on the way up – or on the way down. He stopped at the cleanest house with a VACANCIES card in a front window, paid in advance a week's rent on a room. The proprietor was a middle-aged woman with dyed hair and a small, mean mouth, tight as a spring-loaded purse. She watched him suspiciously because he had no luggage.

'Got a telephone here I can use?' he asked her.

'In the corridor. You'll need coins for it.'

'A telephone directory?'

'In my room. Anything more you want, then?'

'No, thanks. Just to be left alone.'

*

I cruised through the unfashionable south-east London suburbs of Abbey Wood and Belvedere until I saw a garage, one of the old-fashioned kind, with a concrete washdown for cars. I parked my Rolls there and told the attendant to wash it and check the oil, while I walked back the five hundred yards or so to the house I was coming to visit. There were not many Rolls-Royces in Belvedere then – although this may not be the case now – and I had no wish to attract attention by appearing at the front door in such an obvious symbol of wealth.

The house was small, one of a row with privet hedges and front bow windows. This was an area, I felt, where Glover would have been at home. He probably owned the street – and the garage.

I knocked at the front door. A faded woman with grey hair and a sallow face, wearing bedroom slippers and wrinkled lisle stockings, opened the door a few cautious inches on its safety chain.

'I don't buy at the door,' she told me.

'I'm not selling anything,' I answered her quickly, before she could close the door in my face. From the description I had been given, she was the person I had come to see.

'I'm in the market to buy something from you.'

Mrs Keeble looked at me sharply, obviously surprised and suspicious. What could she have to sell that a well-dressed stranger would wish to buy?

'You used to live in Benares?' I went on.

She appeared surprised that I knew this.

'That's right,' she admitted. 'With my husband. He worked on the railways. A driver. Twenty-two years, he did. Then a steam pipe burst in the driver's cab. The burn went septic. He was dead within the week.'

I pictured the little Anglo-Indian group of railway workers and their families, carefully keeping themselves to themselves in the phrase of those days, living in small, prim and always neat bungalows near the railway station, not mixing socially with the British because they could never be accepted as equals, and ostracized by the Indians because they were neither of one race or the other, just a sad legacy of a dwindling Empire they had served so loyally.

'May I come in for a moment?' I asked her. 'We don't want to discuss business on the doorstep, do we?'

The word 'business' touched a nerve of memory. She opened the door, and I followed her through the narrow hall into the kitchen. A flypaper hung from the ceiling. The stove was greasy; a cluster of unwashed cups and saucers stood on the wooden draining board. The room had a sad air of defeat about it.

'Who are you, anyway?' she asked me.

'The friend of a former army captain, Richard Blake,' I replied. 'You met him when you ran the leave centre in Benares. Remember?'

'Yes. He was a crook,' she said quickly. 'He's doing time. He stole a fortune.'

'So it was said.'

'Well, what can I do for you?' she asked. 'I'm a busy woman. I don't know anything about him. I only saw him two or three times. You said you wanted to buy something from me?'

I looked around the shabby kitchen, opened my wallet so that she could see ten-pound notes pressed tightly and neatly together, like leaves in a book she would never read.

'I do, Mrs Keeble. Your time, and your help.'

I took out one note, folded it neatly, put it on the table beneath a bottle of tomato sauce. She had probably never seen a ten-pound note before, and she liked what she saw. She ran her tongue around her lips.

'I want to ask whether you can remember anything odd that happened on the day the money went missing and Captain Blake was arrested.'

'I know nothing about that. Who are you, anyway? The police?'

'Heaven forbid! I am a seeker after truth. I believe, Mrs Keeble, that somebody went into the leave centre and stole that money. Not a bearer, or a sweeper, or any other humble servant. And not Captain Blake either. But perhaps someone you might remember, someone you recognized, though no-one asked you about it afterwards. You weren't called to give evidence at the court martial, were you?'

'No. I just signed a statement about Captain Blake. He told me money had been stolen from his room.'

'But you didn't say that anyone else had been into his room?'

'No. I mean, they hadn't.'

She was growing flustered. I took out another ten-pound note and put it on the table, under the sauce bottle. Mrs Keeble looked at it longingly.

I said, gently so as not to alarm her, 'I think someone yo
recognized did go to his room, but you did not think it wort
mentioning.'

'It wasn't that,' she said. 'I was told it was all hush-hush, secre
I'd be in trouble if I let on. So I kept mum. I've thought abou
it often since then, wondering if I did the right thing. But wha
else could I have done? My husband was dead. This Englis
officer said it was my duty to keep my mouth shut, so I did.
was brought up to do my duty. He told me that another office
was trying to blackmail Captain Blake. I don't know why. H
wanted to check that the captain hadn't left some secret paper
in his room. I had the only key.'

'You believed him?'

'Of course. It was wartime. He offered me money, just to le
him have the key. A lot of money then. Enough to pay fo
my passage home to England, which I couldn't possibly affor
otherwise.'

'Wasn't that odd, if it was an official matter?'

'Not really. He knew I shouldn't let him have the key t
someone else's room, and he thought I might get punished i
anyone found out. When you've no money and someone – a
English gentleman – offers you several hundred pounds, yo
don't ask questions.'

'You didn't say anything about this in your statement whe
Captain Blake was court-martialled?'

'I wasn't asked to, and this Englishman advised me mos
strongly to forget the whole thing. Most secret, he called i
Those were his very words.'

'I see. And who was this Englishman?'

Mrs Keeble paused. Her eyes flickered towards the notes unde
the sauce bottle. I took one more out of my wallet, and place
it with the others.

'I found out his name afterwards,' she said. 'He was a wa
correspondent, a Mr Jerrold. Do you know him?'

Mr Dermott lived in more opulent surroundings, in a flat nea
the Albert Memorial. He also took rather longer to locate
because men of his profession do not care for their telephon
numbers to appear in directories.

His flat was in a block built in Queen Victoria's reign, wit
unusually high ceilings and large double doors opening on t

uge rooms. The sun rarely penetrated to the interior of these rooms, so that even in high summer it seemed that a perpetual twilight was somehow preserved within them. This was how Dermott liked to live, out of the sunshine, out of any glare of publicity. For years he had been a creature of the shadows, travelling with many names and appearances, on the passports of half a dozen countries. He stood now, hands behind his back, looking beyond the red buses and the brooding figure of Prince Albert, raised by a mourning Queen, towards the darkening trees beyond.

He employed a housekeeper about whom he would sometimes remark, rather unkindly, and after too many brandies, that not only was she of indeterminate age, but also of indeterminate sex — unaware that this was exactly what others frequently said about him.

His real name was not Dermott, of course, but he had adopted so many aliases and false backgrounds that it was now sometimes difficult for him to separate fact from myth; what had actually happened, from what he wanted to remember as having happened. He was brooding on whether this was important, whether indeed anything in life was genuinely important, except our universal leaving of it, when his housekeeper came into the room to inform him that a gentleman had arrived to see him.

'Tell him I'm not at home,' Dermott replied at once, over his shoulder, not even looking at her.

'I did so. He said he had seen you come in a quarter of an hour ago. He wants to talk to you about something very important. Something that happened in India.'

'I'm not at home,' Dermott repeated stubbornly. 'Say I've just gone out by another entrance.'

'But that's where you're wrong,' I said chidingly, 'for I can see that you haven't.'

I had come into the room behind the housekeeper, and Dermott's carpet was so thick that my feet made no sound. Dermott swung round to face me. He was rather older than I had expected, but of course years had passed since the time of the events I now intended to discuss.

'Who the devil are you?' he asked me angrily.

I told him.

He nodded to his housekeeper to leave.

'I always tell her to say I'm not at home when I am busy,' he

233

explained. 'I have important business to deal with. Please b
good enough to leave.'

'In due course. But first, I understand you used to know
Captain Richard Blake?'

'That fellow who's doing time for a swindle, you mean?
believe I did meet him briefly in India. Why?'

'He was sentenced for a crime of which he was totally innocen
He tried to find you, to ask you to speak on his behalf, for yo
knew he was innocent. But somehow he could not locate you.
have been more fortunate.'

'I have really no idea what you are talking about.'

'Then let me refresh your memory, as the lawyers say.
involved a country, part of which used to be called The Tank (
Serpents. Not all the snakes seem to have been content to sta
in the water, Mr Dermott. Quite a number seem to be out an
about and prospering. Like you.'

He bent over his desk and pressed a switch.

'If this is a threat of some sort, or simply crude and slanderou
abuse, I should warn you that I have just turned on a recordir
machine. It is not in this room, so you will not be able
damage or stop it, should you have a mind to. With this clea
understanding, pray continue. If you so wish.'

'I am glad to do so, because you may care to have a record (
our conversation, Mr Dermott.'

'So what exactly is your reason for coming into my home lik
this, uninvited? I do not think we need prolong a pointle
conversation about a former army officer who was sentenced f(
gross embezzlement.'

'I entirely agree with you. So please tell me just one thin
Who got the money? The million pounds Captain Blake wa
wrongly accused of stealing?'

'I have absolutely no idea. Presumably, an accomplice of his

'I think not. You force me to take a course I am reluctant
pursue,' I told him. 'But unsavoury cases sometimes call f(
unsavoury remedies. You can't treat pox with perfume.'

I took a brown envelope out of my pocket and handed it
him. He slit it open with an ivory paper knife, and shook a
contents on to the desk. All colour instantly drained from h
flesh; his face paled like a wax death mask. He was looking
half a dozen sepia photographs of himself and various youn
boys. Nine-year-old faces looked out of the photographs in

sturbing amalgam of innocence and evil. Dermott leaned across
e desk and switched off the recorder.

'Where did you get these?' he asked me in his high-pitched
ice.

'From someone who has plenty more, and in many different
ses. Your activities may have been suspected in the government
epartment that employs you, but suspicion is one thing, and
oof another. And after the revelations about Burgess and
aclean, the public has a growing interest in the morals of its
ore secret servants. You pay people to procure boys, Mr
ermott. You may not also realize that they sometimes seek a
cond payment – to procure their silence.

'What would it mean to you if these pictures should ever fall
to the hands of the police – with, of course, copies to the
reign Minister – and the newspapers?'

'I could pick up the telephone and have you arrested. Blackmail
a very serious charge.'

'Of course it is. But you will not make that call, because this
not blackmail. This concerns far more serious matters. If
meone like me, without any official status or influence, can
y this sort of damaging evidence so easily, what could someone
th greater resources and evil motives produce? For their
ence, would you not pass on whatever official secrets you know
ust to keep your private secrets from being made public?'

I chose my words carefully, in case the switch he had just
uched was a dummy, and our conversation was still being
corded. But I knew I had him on the run, and running not just
ared, but terrified.

'Now, for the last time of asking. Who got that money?'

'You bastard,' he said thickly, and stood for a moment, irreso-
te. Then he picked up a sheet of plain notepaper from his desk
d wrote two words on it.

'Beechwood Nominees is only the name of the company,' I
ld him. 'I already have that. I need to know the name of the
rson behind it.'

Dermott sighed, as though he was about to burst into tears.
e had aged in the last few minutes. He looked as he would
pear in ten years from now; weary, beaten, bitter. He wrote
econd name under the first and handed the paper to me.

'You can keep these photos,' I told him. 'But remember that
ey are only copies. Should you ever be misguided enough to

imagine that you could recover them all by any act of violenc
please dismiss that idea from your mind.

'If anything happens to me, or if I or certain friends of mi
who will know of our meeting should have the slightest reaso
to believe you might even contemplate such a foolish cours
negatives will be in every newspaper office in Fleet Street with
the hour. I leave that thought with you.'

At the door, I turned and looked back at him. Dermott sto
silently, hands by his side, shoulders slumped in defeat, looki
out over the expanse of Kensington Gardens, the night sudden
dark and hopeless as his heart.

Cheltenham, August, 19.

The matron came into Corinne's room, punched the chin
cushions on the armchair and glanced with a professional eye
the water carafe. She must speak to nurse again about changi
the water more regularly. Really, the sort of people you had
put up with nowadays.

'You have a visitor,' she told Corinne brightly. 'A friend fro
way back, he says.'

Corinne looked up from the novel she was reading.

'Who's that?' she asked, affecting an interest she did not fee

'I had better let him introduce himself, hadn't I?' said t
matron archly.

Blake came into the room, and paused awkwardly in t
doorway. He had bought a bunch of flowers from a stall outsi
the station and he carried them like some kind of trophy. Corin
took a few seconds to recognize him. He had aged since she h
last seen him in a car driving down the Great West Road, yea
and years ago, in another world, another time.

'Richard,' she said in amazement, almost disbelief. 'How ev
did you find me?'

'I was taught in the army,' he explained, 'that time spent
reconnaissance is seldom wasted. About the only thing I did lea
there.'

'Well, what are you doing now? I haven't seen you for .
well, it must be fourteen years. A lifetime.'

'Yes,' agreed Blake feelingly. It would have been even long
but for the amnesty. A nurse came in to change the carafe. I
handed the flowers to her. She went out, leaving them alone.

236

'Do sit down.'

He sat on the edge of the armchair. Awkwardness hung between them like a bead curtain.

'What's been happening to you?' he asked.

Corinne shrugged.

'Not a lot,' she said. 'You know I married Rex?'

'He told me in India.'

'And Daddy lost his money. Luckily, I had a few shares of my own. They bring in just about enough to pay the bills for this place.'

'I'm terribly sorry,' said Blake. 'It was all my fault.'

Corinne shrugged. What had happened, had happened.

'Nothing is ever entirely anyone's fault,' she replied. 'I was probably a fool to come away with you. I was very innocent, you see. But I really did believe we were going to elope.'

'We were,' said Blake, trying to sound convincing.

Corinne said nothing.

Then: 'You heard about Rex, of course?'

'I saw him a number of times in India,' replied Blake carefully, 'but I haven't seen him since.' In Dartmoor you didn't have many opportunities to entertain casual visitors or to keep up with old acquaintances.

'No. What about him?'

'He died, you know. It's the second anniversary of his death next week. He was killed.'

'Killed? Where?'

'In Korea. He was a war correspondent. His jeep went over a mine in the road.'

'I had no idea,' said Blake. 'None at all. I was hoping I could see him.'

He did not say now, because this was not the moment to say cruel things, that he wanted to discover why Jerrold had deliberately abandoned him when a word at the court martial would have saved him. Now, he never would.

'You get a pension?' he asked Corinne.

'Oh, yes. The *Globe* were very good, really. I get a pension. But it's not enough for . . .'

She paused.

'Not enough for what?' asked Blake.

'Well. There is one surgeon in the States who I am told could operate on me with an eighty per cent chance of success. But

237

he's very expensive. If I paid his fee I wouldn't have enough
live on if the operation wasn't a success. So it's a chicken-and-eg
situation. I can exist as I am, or risk the operation. But if it fai
I'll have nothing to fall back on.'

'How much would it cost?' asked Blake.

'Several thousand pounds.'

'I'll get you the money.'

Corinne smiled sadly.

'You? How? Winning at the races? Gambling?'

'No,' said Blake. 'I don't bet nowadays. But I'll find it for you
Somehow.'

'Thanks for the offer,' she said, as though he had remarke
that it was a nice day. She thought Blake had as much chance
turning up with several thousand pounds as she had of bei
cured by a faith healer; probably less.

'Now I've found you,' Blake said, 'I'll come back to see you
And remember what I've said. You will have your operation.
owe you that, at the least.'

He took one of her hands in both of his. It felt very small an
cold, like the hand of a child who had come in from playing wi
snow. He squeezed it slightly. There was no response. He walke
out of the room quietly, almost on tip-toe, his mind made u
He'd find the money. He had a scheme. He'd find money f
Mrs Taylor, too. Years ago he had promised her that he wou
keep in touch. He hadn't, but he'd meant to. Now, he woul
He had meant to do so many things, but somehow promise ha
been substituted for performance. From now on, that sort
sloppy wishful thinking would have no part in his life.

He was so concerned with his own thoughts that he walked o
of the hall without noticing the matron. She was waiting in a
alcove beneath the stairs, near a telephone. As soon as she sa
Blake's back diminish behind the coloured-glass window in t
front door, she took out the visiting card Glover had given
her when he knew where Corinne was a patient. She put tw
pennies in the slot and dialled his number.

Glover had moved his office as soon as the war ended. He wa
out of North London now and in Mayfair, where he had taken
long lease on a large house. Actually, he held long leases o
many large houses in streets that ran down to Park Lane, b
this particular building he had not let off into offices for oth

people, other companies. This one, he had decorated exclusively for his own use. He had scoured auction salerooms and antique shops, engaged the services of the most expensive and talented interior decorators in London, and ordered them to recreate the luxury and grace of a London house two centuries earlier. Enormous curtains reached from the ceiling to the floor in every room. Leather chairs with button upholstery were clustered with deceptive casualness around the Adam fireplace in the hall. Huge carved blackamoors stood on sentry outside the doors of the lift. Once this might have been the house of a nobleman; Glover preferred to think of it now as the palace of a merchant prince.

A receptionist sat in a small recess in the entrance hall where she could see visitors, but not necessarily be seen by them. She looked up from the magazine she was reading as four men came through the heavy, wrought-iron doors backed with thick frosted glass. They began to walk up the stairs at the side of the lift. She stood up as though to question them, but then recognized their leader and sat down again.

He was a frequent visitor. Mr Glover used him for what his private secretary would describe carefully as 'delicate missions'. To further his financial interests it sometimes became expedient to persuade reluctant tenants to forego their statutory rights, and leave premises before their lease was up. This was an underside of the property business to which Glover now gave much of his attention.

She was surprised that her employer had any truck with such people, or concerned himself with seedy properties in run-down suburbs, for he owned streets and squares and crescents of fashionable property, with shops and warehouses and showrooms in prime positions in every major city in southern England. His success had been remarkable, almost unbelievable. Of course, her boyfriend, who had just been demobbed from the Royal Marines, said he was a war dodger. But who cared now? The war was over and Mr Glover was immensely rich, while her boyfriend was still too poor to support a wife. So who had been the wiser of the two? She wrinkled her nose, for she knew the answer, and went back to her magazine.

Glover opened the door of his office to his four visitors, closed carefully behind them. He did not offer them seats.

'I understand you worked for a bookmaker called McMoffatt

before the war,' he said to a plump man, slightly older than the others.

'I did odd jobs for him, yes. Then he got himself killed.'

'I want you to look after a man for me who also worked for him. Name of Blake. I believe he owed McMoffatt a lot of money.'

'That's what I've heard.'

'I never forget a debt,' said Glover, 'and I'm sure, if McMoffatt was still with us, may God rest his soul, he wouldn't forget either. Never forget, never forgive. That's my motto. Now, this man Blake's in London. He's come out of jug, where he's done time for swindling. I think he may want to make life hard for one or two people. I want you to see he doesn't get the chance.'

'Where does he live?'

'In a rooming house. Earls Court.'

Glover handed the man a sheet of paper with Blake's address and telephone number typed on it.

'Don't do anything there,' he warned. 'Too risky. Too many people around. Get him out on some pretext one night. Say you've something important to tell him. Anything. But be discreet and don't get caught.'

'Terminal case?' asked the plump man.

'No,' said Glover hastily. 'Nothing like that. Semi-permanent shall we say. So he will get the message to keep out of things that don't concern him. Forever.'

Glover could not risk four men standing up in court and telling the judge he had ordered them to kill someone, or even to hurt them. They would, of course, if anything went wrong, which made it important to be as careful as he could. He was a rich man now, and the rich must always be cautious; no-one envies the poor sufficiently to wish them harm.

'Just let him know McMoffatt still has friends around who don't take kindly to people who won't pay their debts. Bit of friendly persuasion, so to speak. I make myself clear?'

The leader nodded.

'Perfectly,' he said. 'Usual terms?'

'Of course. In cash. As soon as I read in the papers that this man, who has just been released from jail, has suffered from what the reporters will no doubt call an outbreak of gangland revenge. After all, what did happen to the million pounds he got away with in India?'

'If we find out, we'll tell you,' the plump man promised him, making a joke of it.

Glover did not smile.

The plump man nodded to the others. They went out as silently as they had arrived. The receptionist did not even see them go.

I have heard it said that the poor use time to make money, while the rich use money to make time. And, given sufficient time, Cicero was quite correct when he declared that there is no fortress so strong that money cannot take it.

Thus it came about that, within minutes of the departure of these four visitors from Glover's office, I had their descriptions. A series of informants reported that they drove in a Riley car (the registration number of which they also provided), across London, over Blackfriars Bridge and on into the heavily bombed hinterland between New Cross and Lewisham. Here, whole rows of terraced houses had been totally destroyed by German bombs; many streets existed only in name. Acres of emptiness had been roughly bulldozed flat. Nettles and giant weeds flourished among a litter of old mattresses and car tyres and abandoned perambulators.

This, I recognized, would be an ideal area where dealers with Glover's natural instinct would be buying such bombed sites cheaply in the sure and certain hope, not of salvation, but of one day being able to develop them at immense profit to themselves. In the meantime, they rented out small plots to local traders who dealt in the detritus of those days: army surplus boots, pilots' fur-lined jackets or secondhand cars.

The four men drove to a corner site where rows of shabby cars displayed optimistic if arguable claims ('Good runner'; 'One owner'; 'Perfect condition') in chalk on their discoloured windscreens. Behind these cars stood a wooden hut, which the trader used as an office. Above this a cheap linen banner flapped in the evening wind: 'Aristo Autos: Guaranteed Used Cars'. What was guaranteed, I wondered, except that all cars on display were indisputably used? The men unlocked the hut door and went inside.

My informant asked for my instructions. I told him to write down my orders as I gave them. I could not afford for there to be any misunderstanding between us.

*

241

Blake was in his room off the Cromwell Road when the telephone rang in the hall of the house. The landlady picked it up.

'Mister Who?' she asked. 'Yes. He's here. Hang on, will you?' She called upstairs to Blake.

'You're wanted on the phone.'

'Me?' he asked in surprise. Who could possibly know he was here?

'You're the only Blake in the house, aren't you?' she asked belligerently. He did not bother to reply, but came downstairs, picked up the receiver.

'Blake here,' he said.

A man's voice spoke softly in his ear.

'Captain Blake, as was?'

'Yes.'

'Got a bit of good news for you, then. To do with our mutual friend Rex Jerrold.'

'But he's dead.'

'I know that. But I've been speaking to his widow. She tells me you went to visit her, and she wants you to know there's some money due to you from him. So I thought I'd get in touch, as she can't, the way she's placed. She forgot to mention it when she saw you. Says she was so surprised when you walked into her room, it went clean out of her mind. Apparently, you had some deal going with her husband and he rather thought he'd let you down. Right?'

'In the broadest sense, yes,' Blake agreed.

'Well, he felt bad about it, and since he couldn't help you when you were inside, he intended to do so as soon as you came out. Then his paper sent him to Korea, and he had to make his will. He put you down as a beneficiary, just in case he didn't come back. As he didn't.'

'I had absolutely no idea,' said Blake. Perhaps he had wronged Jerrold? Someone with such a generous instinct could not be all bad.

'Can you tell me how much is involved?'

'Course I can. A lot. Two grand.'

'Two thousand pounds?' said Blake in amazement. 'Are you sure?'

'Certain. That's why I'm ringing you.'

'Who are you exactly?'

'Name of Jones. Used to work with Rex on the *Globe*. I've

the name and address of the lawyer for you to see, and everything. Trouble is, I'm off up to the Manchester office early tomorrow and I'd like to get this sorted out before I go, if I could, for I'll be away a few days. And I'd rather see you face to face than give you all the stuff over the blower.'

'If you're away tomorrow, when can we meet then? When you come back?'

'If you like. But like I say, I'd rather get this out of the way as soon as possible. Now, if we can.'

'Where are you speaking from?'

'South of the river. My brother's office. He sells used cars, and I'm holding the fort for him tonight while he's up in the Midlands at the car auction there. I'll be here till nine tonight, if you can make it.'

'I can make it. What's the address?'

'Aristo Autos. Macrae Road. Just off the Old Kent Road, near the fork to New Cross. There's a bloody great sign. I know it's short notice, and if you can't make it, or you get held up or something, I'll ring you just as soon as I get back.'

'I'll be there,' Blake promised him.

It took him nearly an hour to reach the bombed site; the trolley bus was delayed because of an electrical fault in an overhead power line. It was thus nearly nine o'clock before he arrived and glanced with an interested eye at the cars on sale. In the second row stood an SS 100, like the one he used to own. He examined it, just in case it was his. It wasn't. This car had been tarted up with a huge fishtail on the end of its exhaust pipe and a bonnet strap as thick as a navvy's belt. Blake wondered who was driving his old SS 100 now, whether it had survived the war. But what was the point in living in the past, thinking about what had or had not happened? There was no mileage in retracing memories to the lost land of might-have-been. Life was like a one-way street; you could stop or you could go on. You could never go back.

He knocked on the door of the hut. A young man wearing an ex-Navy duffle coat invited him inside. The room was sparsely furnished with seats taken from old cars, and a wooden table on trestles. A metal filing cabinet stood in one corner near a one-bar electric fire. Framed photographs of exotic cars lined the distempered walls: Delage, Voisin, Hispano-Suiza.

'Mr Blake?' the young man asked him. 'Captain, as was?'

'Yes. But you're not Mr Jones?'

'No. I am,' said a voice behind Blake. A fat man was standing behind the door. He carried a two foot length of rubber pipe.

Blake held out his hand. The man ignored it.

'I came here to get details of Jerrold's lawyer and so on,' Blake told him.

'You'll get what I'm going to give you, matey. And you won't come back for more.'

The man suddenly brought his right knee up into Blake's groin with all the force of a hammer blow. Years in the army, and still more years cracking stones in Dartmoor quarries, had sharpened Blake's reactions, despite his surprise. He leapt to one side, and as the plump man's knee came up, Blake kicked his left shin.

The man screamed at the force of this totally unexpected blow, lost his balance and fell heavily against the wall. A photograph of a Bugatti at Biarritz dropped on his head with a shattering of glass. Blake brought his right hand across the man's throat in a scything motion. He sank face down into a mass of jagged glass splinters.

The younger man in the duffle coat now jumped at Blake, who tipped the table over in front of him.

The edge caught the man in the stomach. He pitched forward like a diver, rolled to one side on the floor, grabbed the electric fire and flung it up towards Blake's face. The wire snapped at the wall plug with a blue flash – and the light fused. Into the suddenly darkened hut, two other men came running.

One hit Blake across the side of his head with a cosh made from a hose pipe. Blake staggered, collapsed across one of the car seats, and managed to somersault out of the door. He landed on the hard, trodden earth and lay, winded, half-conscious. The other new arrival kicked him as he lay. Blake was down, and all but out.

The men I had engaged were crouching as instructed between the rows of old cars, out of sight from the road and the hut. Now, at my signal, they jumped forward. All had served in the Commandos, and I had explained as much as was prudent for them to know about the background to this situation. They were not in any mood to strain the quality of mercy. They came in strongly, wielding pickaxe handles and leather belts with big metal buckles.

I dealt with the plump man who was obviously the leader. It

is a basic axiom of conflict (and human nature) that once the leader surrenders, others swiftly lose their stomach for a fight.

I pinned him against the wall, and one of my men tapped his kneecaps with an axe handle to let him know that we could (and would) willingly and easily break both his kneecaps and possibly his wrists, and then leave him to holler himself hoarse.

Blake lay where he had fallen. I knelt down by his side, rolled him over gently on his back. He did not open his eyes. I felt Blake's pulse, and then looked up at the plump man.

'You've killed him,' I told him. 'You'll swing for this.'

'I don't know what you're talking about,' he replied slowly, as though I was speaking a totally different language. If he spoke slowly, then I must believe him.

The other three men had heard me through the mists of their own pain, and already they were crawling away between the lines of parked cars. They wanted no part of a murder charge; the death penalty was still in force, even for accomplices – and who would admit to striking the fatal blow?

I let them go. My men would follow them home; we could pick them up whenever we wanted. Why bother with monkeys when you can deal with the organ-grinder?

I released my hold on the plump man. For a moment, he did not move – and then he fled as I knew he would. We listened to the drum of his running feet die away on the hard ground. Then the only sound was the flapping of the Aristo Autos banner in the late evening wind.

I motioned to my men, who picked up Blake, and carried him to my car.

'You want any help?' one asked me.

'No,' I told them. 'I will look after him.'

I gave each of them an envelope containing the price we had previously agreed, in new five-pound notes, collected from different banks, to make it more difficult for anyone to trace the serial numbers. The sums were more than they could have earned in six months in their legitimate callings of chuckers-out, all-in wrestlers and night-club bouncers. Even so, they counted the money. Trust is a rare quality in any financial transaction, even on their level.

They drove off in the Riley that had brought Glover's men, but that was their business, not mine. No doubt, with a new colour and different number plates, it would provide them with a useful bonus.

I drove back with Blake to the flat I had rented in Queen's Gate. I carried him carefully upstairs, put him down on the bed in the spare room. Then I removed his shoes and jacket, loosened his collar and looked down at his bruised and bloodied face. He was very pale. I went out of the room to telephone a doctor and an undertaker. Both men owed me favours, and they arrived together; one qualified to deal with the living, and the other to bury any mistakes he might make.

Next morning, I rang the *Globe* with news of Blake's death, and put notices in the personal columns of *The Times* and the *Daily Telegraph*, giving the time and place and date of his cremation. I wanted anyone who had ever known him to have the opportunity of being present. On the day of Blake's funeral, I visited the crematorium, as I have already described, but I could not bring myself to join the so-called mourners at the service. Some, I felt certain, were present to make sure he was dead rather than for any other reason; they were not the type to weep over anything more tragic than a sharp and unexpected fall in share prices.

It was Glover's custom to arrive at his office very early each morning. Usually, he came in at half past seven, not because he had any work to do at that hour, although in newspaper interviews he liked to claim that it was the only time of day his telephone didn't ring, but because he liked to open all letters himself. Some related to private and not infrequently dubious deals about which he was unwilling to let any employee know, on the basis that knowledge was always power – especially if it related to an employer's illegal transactions.

Envelopes addressed in handwriting to Glover's subordinates he would also open, afterwards claiming, if necessary, that he had done so in error. What he really wanted to find out was whether it contained a genuinely private letter (details of which could conceivably be used as a lever against the recipient) or one relating to a deal the employee might be conducting on the side.

Was this paid creature using Glover's time, Glover's stationery, even Glover's stamps, to conduct his or her private business? If so, Glover would instantly provide them with the gift of time to carry on their transactions elsewhere at the expense of some other employer.

On the morning after Blake's cremation, Glover came into the office at about a quarter to eight. He would have arrived earlier, but roadworks in Knightsbridge had delayed his car. He unlocked the two security locks on the front door, and then two more on his office door, and replaced the keys in separate pockets. He was a cautious man. While a thief or a business rival might possibly obtain a copy of one or even two of these personal keys, he thought it unlikely that anyone could obtain four.

He sat down at his desk, took up an eighteenth-century bone-handled letter-knife, began to slit open each envelope and shake out the letters they contained. Sometimes, his poorer tenants wrote him a personal letter, usually on cheap lined paper, because they were not the sort of people who could afford headed stationery. They wanted to ask whether they could buy their house or their shop, and would enclose a stamped, addressed envelope in the hope that this would produce a speedier reply. Glover's reluctance to spend his money, or rather his company's money, even on stamps, was widely known.

Glover would never answer such polite requests. His philosophy was to buy property, not to sell it. Prices were still absurdly low, in his opinion, and were bound to rise astronomically, as time has proved. He always cut around the stamps on such letters, put them in a silver box on his desk – and then threw away the letters with the envelopes.

This morning, Glover picked up the *Globe* and glanced through it until he found a report of Blake's death with a brief résumé of his career. He was described as the archetypal golden boy, who had apparently started with every advantage and ended penniless, a cashiered officer and former convict, dying in a brawl on a bomb site. No-one even knew who or why he had been fighting.

Blake's landlady recalled how he had received an unexpected telephone call, which had pleased and excited him, and he had at once gone out, she did not know where. Yes, he had been a quiet lodger, what little she had seen of him. In the circumstances, she thought, yes, it was lucky that she always insisted on a week's rent in advance. Glover smiled at this last remark; he could admire a woman like that.

A few days previously, he had received a breathless telephone call from the plump man, who reported that Blake had been roughed up, as instructed, and then some other men – strangers – had unexpectedly appeared and joined in the fight. They were led by a well-dressed man who told him that Blake had been killed. Everyone then cleared off as quickly as possible before the police could be called, and this stranger had taken Blake's body away in his car. No, he hadn't been able to get the car's number; the rear light was not working, but no names had been taken, and it would be difficult – he thought impossible – for anyone to be identified. In any case, they could all provide perfect alibis for each other.

So Blake was dead, and Jerrold was dead, and of all the three who had been young on that staircase in Oxford long ago, Glover alone had survived. What had the Abbé of Sieyès said after the French Revolution, when someone asked what he had done during that terrible time of death and retribution? He had replied simply: 'I survived.'

Glover, of course, knew that he had done much more. Not only had he survived so many catastrophes – the war, the possibility of Blake becoming unpleasant, or even highly dangerous, among them – but he had also acquired property all over the country at a time when those of little faith and less capital had been desperate to sell. Indeed, they had often begged him to buy, and accepted his miserly offers with gratitude; on some occasions, even with tears of thankfulness.

Now his property empire stretched like a web from London to Coventry to Birmingham, to Manchester, all areas that had been heavily bombed. He must already be one of the largest landlords in the country, he told himself. And one day he would be the biggest and the richest. The future held no horizons; he might even be knighted, created a peer. All one had to do was to give enough money to charity or a political party, or both – and then appoint a clever advertising agency to ensure that such generosity was widely known.

He pushed the newspaper away from him and leaned back in his heavy leather chair, relishing the prospect. The room seemed elegant as a stage set for an opulent production: Act Two, Scene One – Morning; a gentleman's study in Mayfair. Everything around him was antique or of great value, and most were clearly both. He looked past eighteenth-century buttoned-leather armchairs, past library steps that had come from an earl's house, to the window and rooftops across the road.

One of the heavy maroon velvet curtains moved slightly. Glover frowned. This meant that the window did not fit closely – and he had just paid hundreds of pounds to have all the window frames in the room remade so that they would fit perfectly and keep out traffic sounds and draughts. You couldn't trust anyone now to do a proper job, he thought with sudden anger. No matter what you paid, they still tried to get by with shoddy workmanship. He stalked angrily across the white Aubusson carpet towards the window. As Glover approached it, the curtain suddenly moved swiftly to one side.

Someone stepped out from behind it and faced him.

'Who the hell are you?' Glover asked me, his voice rough with astonishment and fear. He took a step back towards his desk to reach the secret button that I knew would sound an alarm in the nearest police station. Such an action would not further my interests. I took my Smith & Wesson .38 from my jacket pocket and aimed it at Glover's groin. There seemed no point in appealing to the heart of such a man.

Glover stopped in mid-pace, hand still outstretched, wondering whether I was bluffing, but not wishing to put it to the test.

'Come away from that button,' I told him. 'Then stand perfectly still if you want to walk out of your office.'

'You'd never shoot me,' he said, trying to convince himself.

'Try me,' I told him. 'The building's empty for another hour. It would take you that long to die where I'll shoot you.'

'What do you want? Money? I don't keep any money here.'

'I don't want money,' I answered him. 'I wish to collect a debt in some other currency.'

'But I've never even seen you before. How can I owe you anything? Who are you?'

'A friend of Richard Blake,' I said. 'Remember him?'

'Of course. I knew him well. We were at Oxford together. I went to his funeral yesterday. A very sad day.'

He paused.

'I didn't see you there,' he said slowly, almost accusingly.

'You weren't meant to.'

'How the devil could you get in here?'

'Money, Glover, as you must know, is a universal pass key. Enough of it can even open the locks to your office.'

'But why the gun? If you killed me, you would never be able to pursue the claim you say you have against me – whatever it is.'

He was growing bolder now. The initial shock of discovering me had passed; he was trying to winkle a way out for himself. And he could just succeed. His cunning and guile were not attributes I would ever underestimate.

'My charge is very simple,' I told him. 'You have built up a huge property empire by buying from wretched people who had to sell – or starve. You are very rich now as a result, and you hope to be much richer, while many of them are destitute or ruined – like Richard Blake.

'You and Jerrold felt inferior to Blake because you were inferior. And when Jerrold – eager to earn some miserable pittance from a squalid section of the secret service – conspired with the pederast Dermott to manipulate British imperial policy, you both saw how you could turn this to your own financial advantage – and let Blake take the blame.

'When Blake was released, you arranged for him to be brutally beaten up – and then had the gall to go as a mourner to his funeral. An eye for an eye, a tooth for a tooth, a death for a death. Now it's your turn, Glover. The dividend on your despicable investment is due, and I like to pay my debts on time.'

I thumbed the hammer on the revolver. Glover's eyes widened in horror. The flesh on his forehead tightened like a drum-skin. Sweat glistened above his eyes.

'I don't know what you're talking about,' he said hoarsely. 'Blake was one of my oldest friends. I'd never harm him.'

'In that case,' said a quiet voice behind him, 'you'll be pleased to see him here – unharmed.'

Blake stepped out from behind the other curtain.

Glover stared at him with a mixture of horror and total disbelief. How could a man whose coffin only hours earlier he had watched slide forward into flames now be standing in front of him? He wet dry lips with his tongue and coughed as though about to choke. One hand went up nervously to his collar and tore his tie loose.

'There is no need for any violence,' Blake told him reassuringly. 'I don't like violence. I saw enough in the war – and then in prison. I know you don't like it either, Glover, because if you had the slightest inclination towards a fight you would have come down to the used-car site and taken a personal part in the action, instead of simply sending hired men.

'You can pay people to do many things in life, Glover. Now you have your opportunity to do something yourself that no-one else in all the world can do for you. Give me back the million pounds that was sent from Benares to you here in London under your company's name, Beechwood Nominees.'

'It's not yours,' said Glover. 'You stole it.'

I took a step forward.

'There was a poor Anglo-Indian widow, Mrs Keeble, who ran a leave centre for officers in Benares,' I told Glover. 'You probably spent in a week on cigars what she earned in a year. So when your friend Jerrold came along and offered her a large sum of money, by her standards, to let him into Blake's room, she agreed.

'He was so persuasive, she actually thought she was doing something very patriotic. As part of this charade, he then got her to dress up as a Moslem, with her face covered so no-one would recognize her, and hand a parcel of notes to a bank clerk in Benares to telegraph to London.

'It never entered her head to question him. He was English, and in her mind, a gentleman, and that was enough. She was content – honoured, even – that she should be paid what she thought was a lot for doing so little. Now, it's your turn to pay up.'

'I've told you, I don't keep any money here.'

'Possibly, and very wisely, not,' said Blake. 'But you keep deeds here of all your properties, because you don't trust the banks. Jerrold told me once how you used to buy property for a few pounds a time. I want a million pounds worth of your properties at today's valuation to pay back what you stole, plus a similar sum as compensation for serving eight years in jail as an innocent man. A long time, Glover. A ninth of my life.'

'I can't do it,' Glover said desperately, looking from Blake to me, appealing for belief. 'I don't own a single house. They are tied up with companies.'

'Untie them.'

'They would still all have to be conveyed.'

'You are a lawyer. Convey them.'

'No.'

'No?'

I took a step nearer to him. The muzzle of my revolver was now barely a foot from Glover's stomach. He knew I couldn't miss, and so did I. He swallowed once, twice, and his face turned a pale green colour. I thought he was going to be sick, but he was only sick at heart. Then Glover suddenly jumped towards his desk. Blake got there before him, and ripped away a wire that led to the alarm button.

Now Glover seemed to shrink, like a balloon with a leak. He made his decision. In the last analysis it was simply a question of money or pain. To part with any money was to him painful, but not so painful as having a large hole blown through his body.

He walked to a wall safe, spun the combination and pulled out a pile of beige folders bound with pink tape. He stood looking at them on his desk.

'Your staff will be arriving soon,' Blake told him. 'If you want them to find you here unhurt, move yourself.'

Blake and I sifted through the deeds on his desk. We selected prime sites, leaving Glover with the shabby, second-rate, back-street stuff. That was his world, not ours.

'They'll need to be witnessed,' said Glover, playing for time, as we handed our selection to him.

'I'll witness them,' I told him.

He sat down and began to scribble out details on legal forms.

'Put them all on one contract,' I told him. 'It will be quicker.'

Blake read out the address of each property, and Glover wrote them down. There was nothing else he could do now, and he knew it. Finally, he signed two copies of the document and pushed them across his desk towards Blake, who picked one up, read it, signed them both and handed them to me to witness. Blake folded up one copy, put it in his pocket, handed the other one back to Glover.

'I've given my address as care of the bank,' Blake told him. 'I won't be staying in London after this, and I'm not sure of my movements. But don't send any more hard men after me, or we'll come calling on you. And not to have a cosy chat like this. You understand me?'

'I understand you,' Glover told him. 'But how can you still be alive? I was at your funeral yesterday. I actually saw you cremated. Who was in the coffin?'

'No-one,' I told him. 'I found a doctor and an undertaker who could use a few hundred pounds over the odds. One to sign a death certificate, the other to arrange a funeral. He filled the coffin with logs as efficiently as whoever filled Blake's pack in Benares with bricks.'

'Never forgive, never forget,' said Blake. 'I learned that from you.'

'You won't get away with it,' said Glover, trying to convince himself as much as us. He was standing up on his tip-toes now to give himself greater height and authority. He pressed his fingers down on top of his desk like the flattened claws of some predatory bird.

'You'll never get away with it,' he repeated, his voice rising. I was reminded of the old Eastern saying: 'Loss of money is bewailed with louder lamentation than a death.' For Glover, this transaction was like dying by degrees.

'You'll never get away with it,' he said again, as though to convince himself.

'We have,' Blake corrected him. 'Goodbye.'

We walked down the stairs. The receptionist had just arrived, and was hanging her coat carefully on a peg in the alcove off the splendid entrance hall. She had bought the coat in a summer sale and did not want to crease it. She turned away to do this and so did not see our faces, only our backs, as we came out into the fresh Mayfair morning.

The streets were still empty, and after Glover's office the air felt clean and cool. Blake was suddenly reminded of Nepal, of a fresh wind blowing snow from ancient peaks, where once gods had walked with men when the world was young. A florist's stall on the pavement, ablaze with blue bouquets, recalled a magic lotus on a vanished lake. Lotus. The name of the punt in which long ago he and Glover and Corinne had spent an afternoon on the river at Oxford.

Corinne could have her operation now, Blake reflected. Then he would seek out Mrs Taylor, his father's former house-keeper, and all the others who had worked for his father for so long. He would see that they need never lack for money. He might even buy back the old house for himself. And Mr Marsh, in the bank at Oxford: he had not been very straight with him. The least he could do now surely was to bank with him again – and keep the account in credit.

And then there was Ram Das to find in Benares, and the bear-handler, and the taxi-driver. He did not even know their

253

names. But without their aid he would not be alive now, and rich.

They had all helped him without thought or hope of gain. It would be his pleasure to prove that kindness to a stranger can pay unexpected dividends.

Blake turned to me.

'Early though it is, Chet, I think we both deserve a drink,' he said. 'Shall I say, in all the circumstances, a corpse reviver?'

'Message received and understood,' I replied – and slapped him on the back.

New Delhi;
Varanasi (Benares), India;
Kathmandu, Nepal.

Fontana Paperbacks: Fiction

Fontana is a leading paperback publisher of both non-fiction, popular and academic, and fiction. Below are some recent fiction titles.

- ☐ THE ROSE STONE Teresa Crane £2.95
- ☐ THE DANCING MEN Duncan Kyle £2.50
- ☐ AN EXCESS OF LOVE Cathy Cash Spellman £3.50
- ☐ THE ANVIL CHORUS Shane Stevens £2.95
- ☐ A SONG TWICE OVER Brenda Jagger £3.50
- ☐ SHELL GAME Douglas Terman £2.95
- ☐ FAMILY TRUTHS Syrell Leahy £2.95
- ☐ ROUGH JUSTICE Jerry Oster £2.50
- ☐ ANOTHER DOOR OPENS Lee Mackenzie £2.25
- ☐ THE MONEY STONES Ian St James £2.95
- ☐ THE BAD AND THE BEAUTIFUL Vera Cowie £2.95
- ☐ RAMAGE'S CHALLENGE Dudley Pope £2.95
- ☐ THE ROAD TO UNDERFALL Mike Jefferies £2.95

You can buy Fontana paperbacks at your local bookshop or newsagent. Or you can order them from Fontana Paperbacks, Cash Sales Department, Box 29, Douglas, Isle of Man. Please send a cheque, postal or money order (not currency) worth the purchase price plus 22p per book for postage (maximum postage required is £3.00 for orders within the UK).

NAME (Block letters) _____

ADDRESS _____

_____

_____

While every effort is made to keep prices low, it is sometimes necessary to increase them at short notice. Fontana Paperbacks reserve the right to show new retail prices on covers which may differ from those previously advertised in the text or elsewhere.